ArtScroll Series®

Rabbi Nosson Scherman / Rabbi Meir Zlotowitz

General Editors

Echoes of the

by

Rabbi Paysach J. Krohn

author of

The Maggid Speaks, Around the Maggid's Table, In the Footsteps of the Maggid *and* ***Along the Maggid's Journey***

Published by

Mesorah Publications, ltd

Maggid

Heartwarming stories
and parables
of wisdom and inspiration

FIRST EDITION
First Impression ... March 1999

Published and Distributed by
MESORAH PUBLICATIONS, LTD.
4401 Second Avenue / Brooklyn, N.Y 11232

Distributed in Europe by
J. LEHMANN HEBREW BOOKSELLERS
20 Cambridge Terrace
Gateshead, Tyne and Wear
England NE8 1RP

Distributed in Israel by
SIFRIATI / A. GITLER
10 Hashomer Street
Bnei Brak 51361

Distributed in Australia and New Zealand by
GOLDS BOOK & GIFT SHOP
36 William Street
Balaclava 3183, Vic., Australia

Distributed in South Africa by
KOLLEL BOOKSHOP
Shop 8A Norwood Hypermarket
Norwood 2196, Johannesburg, South Africa

THE ARTSCROLL SERIES®
ECHOES OF THE MAGGID

ISBN:
1-57819-260-9 (hard cover)
1-57819-261-7 (paperback)

Typography by CompuScribe at ArtScroll Studios, Ltd.

Printed in the United States of America by Noble Book Press Corp.
Bound by Sefercraft, Quality Bookbinders, Ltd., Brooklyn N.Y. 11232

RABBI
ISRAEL GROSSMAN
BATEI WARSAW
JERUSALEM, ISRAEL

ישראל גרוסמן
רב ור"מ ודומ"ץ
פעיה"ק ירושלים תובב"א

מחבר ספרי שעורי כתובות שעורי גיטין
שעורי קדושין שעור ב"ק שו"ת הליכות ישראל
שו"ת משכנות ישראל שו"ת נצח ישראל
שו"ת אורח ישראל

Tel. 371056 .טל

בתי ורשה ירושלים

בעו"ה ח' שבט תשנ"ט פה עיה"ק ירושלים תובב"א

הגעתי היום בשבחו של ידידי היקר והנכבד המגיד

מוהר"ר פסח קראהן שליט"א

אשר עומד בעזרת ד' יתברך בקרוב להוציא ספר

חמישי בסדרת ספרי המגיד

וכבר אמרתי לברכו ונתתי הסכמה שזכה להפיץ

ברבים את הספרים הנפלאים שלו, שמעוררים

את כל מי שמעיין ויקרא בהם התעוררות גדולה

ורגשי קודש המשלהבים את הנשמה

וזה נוסף על הדרשות הנלהבות שנואם בחסד

עליון בכל העולם, לקרב את אחב"י לאבינו

שבשמים ולהדריכם בדרכי האמונה והחסד

ומשפיע על הקהל להתרחק מן הרע ולהתקרב

לטוב כמו שנאמר סור מרע ועשה טוב

וזכות הרבים תלוי בזה. וזכות אבותיו עומדת

לו כי אביו הרה"ג רבי אברהם זצ"ל שהי' ידיד נפשי

ולהבחל"ח שהסתופף [illegible] בבחינת [illegible]

ואמו [illegible] את כבוד ידידי המחבר שיפוצו מעינותיו

חוצה מתוך נחת ושמחה והרחבת הדעת.

ידידו דו"ש [illegible]

ישראל גרוסמן

הרב ארי׳ ליב פינקעל
9 רחוב אבינדב
ירושלים

בס"ד שבט תשנ"ט פעיה"ק ירושלים תובב"א

לכבוד ידידי הגדול מאוד ומגדול מגדלי הרבנים
בנעם אמריו ושמו הולך לפניו בכל קהלות ישראל
הוא ניהו הגאון רבנו ומורנו הרב המופלג
בתוי"ש מוהר"ר פסח קראוס שליט"א
כשמו יען שמו לעד.

הנני בזה לחוק עלי מגילת ספר את כל תוקף הברכה
הנובעת מעומקא דלבאי למעלת כת"ר הרב המופלא
חכם לב אשר שמו יצא לתהלה ולתפארת בחיבוריו
היקרים המיוחדים והמשובחים לקרב לב ישראל
לאביהם שבשמים.

ברכתי ובקשתי מאת שומע תפלה, יהי רצון
שיפוצו מעינותיך חוצה להשמיע ברמה קול ישראל סבא
ואתה לך בכחך זה והושעת את ישראל
בימיו ובימינו יושע יהודה וישראל ישכון לבטח
ונזכה כולנו לעלות לציון ברנה אכי"ר

ידידו המוקירו כערכו הרם
הק' ארי' ליב פינקל
פה "מיר" ירושת"ו

דוד קאהן

ביהמ"ד גבול יעבץ
ברוקלין, נוא יארק

בס"ד

למחמדי הרב פסח יוסף שליט"א
שמחתי לשמוע שהנך מתכונן להוציא לאור ספר חמישי של סיפורים שמטרתם לעורר לבבות לתורה ולתעודה, ובזה הנך ממשיך בעבודתך בקודש שהתחלת בה זה כמה שנים.

ספר זה מוקדש לזכרו של המגיד הידוע מירושלים הגאון הצדיק רב פעלים רב שלום מרדכי הכהן שוואדראן זצ"ל שהיה נואם בחסד עליון והרעיש העולם בדרשותיו. הנני רואה במה שדבקת אחרי דרכי הגאון הצדיק הנ"ל קיום של כיבוד אב וכיבוד רב גם יחד, שהרי שייכותך להגה"צ באה ע"י אביך זצ"ל ונמצא שכל קשר נוסף על הקשרים שעשית כבר מחזק השפעת האב על הבן במה שנתוסף הרושם של השפעת הרב על התלמיד.

והנני מברך אותך שחוט המשלש לא ינתק וההדרכה שקבלת משני המשפיעים הכבירים האלו לא תמוש ממך עד מאה ועשרים שנה.

אוהבך ומוקירך מאד
דוד קאהן
ז' שבט תשנ"ט

Table of Contents

Author's Preface

As the *Baal Shacharis* begins his repetition of the *Shemoneh Esrei*, on the second day of *Rosh Hashanah*, he exclaims, דָּבָר אֵין בְּפִי וּבִלְשׁוֹנִי מִלָּה, הֵן ה׳ יָדַעְתָּ כֻלָּה, *There is no [adequate] expression in my mouth, nor word on my tongue, behold, Hashem, You know everything.* (See also *Tehillim* 139:4.)

In a sense this is how I feel as I submit the fifth book in what has come to be known as "The Maggid Series." There are no suitable words to express my gratitude and indebtedness to Hashem for this privilege.

When I started to write this book two and a half years ago, I found myself wondering — after having written four books containing close to 400 stories — were there still enough good stories to be written? Where would I find them? Who would be willing to tell them?

The answer came from kind and considerate people both near and far. From places like my native Kew Gardens, from such American communities as Pittsburgh, Dallas, and Los Angeles, from cities abroad such as Jerusalem, Antwerp, Amsterdam, and Manchester, and many, many points in between. Stories unfolded at conventions, on airplanes, at Shabbos tables, on street corners, in *succahs*, and so on — because every person has a story and every community has a story.

Much of the essence of *Yahadus* is related through narratives.

The Torah begins with the majestic narrative of Creation and ends with the sorrowful narrative of Moshe *Rabbeinu's* demise. The Talmud and Midrash are replete with stories that engender inspiration, impart *hashkafah,* and depict the deeds and sentiments of extraordinary Jews.

A story seals the attachment between generations. It is the bond that connects us to our people of the past and will hopefully join us to those in the future. It is my hope and prayer that the stories and parables in this book will indeed inspire, inform, and enhance our identity as *bnei Yisrael.*

The Hebrew word for five, חֲמִשָּׁה, contains the letters of the word שִׂמְחָה, *happiness.* The *Malbim* writes (*Yeshaya* 35:1,10) that שִׂמְחָה is markedly different from other words that connote joy or happiness. For example, שָׂשׂוֹן is the outer expression of joy, such as singing, dancing, and the wearing of festive clothes. On the other hand, שִׂמְחָה is inner contentment, serenity, and heartfelt satisfaction. Upon the completion of this fifth book (חֲמִשָּׁה) in this month of Adar, the month of שִׂמְחָה, it is the sense of שִׂמְחָה explained by the *Malbim* for which I am exceedingly grateful.

And if indeed the stories in this book bring people closer to Hashem or to greater diligence in their Torah study and *mitzvah* observance, then the time and effort expended on this project are my שַׁלְמֵי שִׂמְחָה, *peace offerings of happiness,* presented on the Altar of *Kiddush Shem Shamayim.*

ACKNOWLEDGMENTS

I am grateful to the *Ribono Shel Olam* for allowing me to have come in contact with so many extraordinary people who took a personal interest in this project by giving me of their time and knowledge and opening their homes and their hearts during my travels.

Among them are Rabbi Mottel Aronson (Amsterdam), Rabbi Nachum Aronson (Manchester), Rabbi Asher Arieli (Jerusalem), Rabbi and Mrs. Simcha Bamberger (Manchester), Rabbi and Mrs. Ezra Berkowitz (Zurich), Mr. and Mrs. Leopold Bermann (Zurich), Mr. and Mrs. Shlomo Zalman Braun (Antwerp), Rabbi Lipa Brenner (Brooklyn), R' Ami Cohen (Kew Gardens), Rabbi David Cohen (Brooklyn), Rabbi Shimshon Epstein (Jerusalem), the Rosh Yeshivah Rabbi Boruch Ezrachi (Jerusalem), Rabbi Mordechai Yitzchok Ezrachi (Jerusalem), the Rosh Yeshivah Rabbi Nosson Tzvi Finkel (Jerusalem), Rabbi Elya Boruch Finkel (Jerusalem), Rabbi Binyamin Finkel (Jerusalem), Rabbi Aryeh Finkel (Jerusalem), Rabbi Yisroel Grossman (Jerusalem), Rabbi Yaakov Gutman (Bnei Brak), Rabbi Nachum Mordechai Halpern (Manchester), Mr. and Mrs. Shmuel Tzvi Heimann (Stamford Hill), Rabbi Shimon Hirschler (Stamford Hill), Mr. and Mrs. Alfred Homberger (London), Rabbi Chaim Honig (Antwerp), Rabbi and Mrs. Shmuel Katz (Amsterdam), Rabbi Mendel Kaufman (Gateshead), Rabbi Nachman Klein (Baltimore), Rabbi Pinchus Kornfeld (Antwerp), Dr. David Kranzler (Brooklyn),

Rabbi Chaim Kreiswerth (Antwerp), Rabbi Yaakov (Jackie) Levison (London), Rabbi and Mrs. Yehuda Leib Lewis (Amsterdam), Rabbi and Mrs. Nesanel Lieberman (Gateshead), Mrs. Martha Munk ע״ה (Brooklyn), Rabbi Mordechai Neugroschel (Jerusalem), Rabbi Avigdor Nebenzahl (Jerusalem), Rabbi and Mrs. Michael Orolowitz (Cleveland), Rabbi Rafael Persovitz (Jerusalem), Rabbi Gamliel Rabinowitz (Jerusalem), Dr. and Mrs. Moshe Rosenfeld (London), Rebbitzen Ayala Rotenberg (Antwerp), Rabbi Yeruchem Shapiro (Brooklyn), the Rosh Yeshivah Rabbi Rafael Shmulevitz (Jerusalem), Rabbi and Mrs. Dovid Silverman (Atlanta), Rav Shlomo Zalman Sonnenfeld (Jerusalem), Dr. and Mrs. Yossi Spitzer (London), Rabbi Michel Stern (Jerusalem), my brother-in-law Rabbi Mishel Teitz (Montreal), Rabbi Yehudah Traeger (Antwerp), Rabbi Zev Van Dyk (Amsterdam), Rabbi Shmuel Vitsick (Bayit Vegan/Baltimore), Mr. and Mrs. Menachem Vogel (Manchester), Rabbi and Mrs. Boruch Wasyng (Antwerp), Rabbi Yaakov Yosef Weiss (Manchester), Rabbi Nisson Wolpin (Brooklyn), Rabbi Binyamin Zeilberger (Brooklyn), Mr. Meshulem Zilberman (Antwerp), and Rabbi Moshe Zupnick (Brooklyn).

I thank as well a twelve-year-old boy, Dovid Juravel of Brooklyn, who suggested the title of this book; Mr. Byrech Lehrer and Mr. Betzalel Fixler of Kew Gardens for their invaluable research; and my nephew Avrohom Abraham for compiling the list of sources.

By profession, my *mechutan* Mr. Mordechai Dovid (Max) Perlstein is an accountant (and outstanding in Lakewood's annual *Yarchei Kallah*). However he is an exceptional editor as well. He enhanced many stories in this book with his comments and adroit rewording. I thank him for his caring efforts.

I express thanks to all who were kind enough to give me comments, encouragement, and constructive criticism, be it by letter, fax, phone or personal encounter. Your words enhanced the focus and selections for this work.

❁ ❁ ❁

I acknowledge with awe and everlasting gratitude the work that Rabbi Nosson Scherman did for this book. I would fax a story to him, and usually within hours he had deftly edited it and sent it on its way back. At any given time Reb Nosson is involved with books and articles, skillfully honing and refining the many projects that come across his desk. I take this opportunity to thank him for the work he did, and continues to do with my daughter Chaviva, on her continuing series of *Maggid Stories for Children*.

I will always be grateful to Rabbi Meir Zlotowitz for the opportunities he has afforded me. He is the genius behind Mesorah Publications. Its worldwide acceptance and success is largely due to his creative and attentive mind.

I am grateful to the typists who worked on this book: Rabbi Yaakov Hersh Horowitz, R' Shaye Sonnenschein, Rifky Bruck, and Chumi Zaidman. Mrs. Mindy Schwartz, Toby Vegh, and Hindy Goldner skillfully typset the book and Mrs Mrs. Faigie Weinbaum proofread diligently. Avrohom Biderman supervised the entire process as the book progressed from manuscript to publication. I thank Eli Kroen for creating the beautiful cover of this book. The remainder of the Mesorah staff each has his or her own share in every work that is brought to the public, and I know that I speak for thousands who are grateful for their dedication to perfection, Rabbi Sheah Brander, Rabbi Avie Gold, Mr. Yossi Timinsky, Rabbi Gedaliah Zlotowitz, Mr. Ephraim Perlowitz, Mr. Yitzi Gruen, Mr. Yochi Blatt, Mr. Yossi Hadad, and all the others.

❁ ❁ ❁

In high school I admired a wonderful English teacher. One night at a parents-teachers conference, he said to my mother, "Mrs. Krohn, your son is a good writer, but he will never write a book."

My mother, Mrs. Hindy Krohn, a very talented writer who imbued me with my love for phraseology and writing, was taken aback. "Why do you say that?" she asked.

"Oh, he's too religious," the teacher said self-assuredly. "No one will ever read what he writes." History proved differently. So I thank my mother for her example, inspiration, and constant encouragement.

❁ ❁ ❁

Words are inadequate to express my gratitude to my wife Miriam. Selflessly, she undertook many of the responsibilities of our lives so that I could research the stories that appear in this book. She encouraged me to write this book so that the *tzaddikim* and *tzidkaniyos* we have become acquainted with, both in this generation and in previous generations, may be an influence on us, our family, and hopefully many in *Klal Yisrael*. May we merit to see *nachas* from our children and grandchildren, and they from us.

יִמָּלֵא **פִי** תְּהִלָּתֶךָ כָּל הַיּוֹם תִּפְאַרְתֶּךָ

Paysach J. Krohn
Kew Gardens, New York
March 2, 1999

פסח יוסף קראהן
שושן פורים תשנ"ט

The Maggid of His Era — Rabbi Sholom Schwadron זצ״ל (1912-1997)

An Appreciation

Much that has transpired in my life in the recent past — the books, the lectures, the tapes, and the traveling throughout the Jewish world — has been an outgrowth and direct result of the association my family, especially my father Rabbi Avrohom Zelig Krohn ז״ל and my mother יבל״ח Mrs. Hindy Krohn, had with Rabbi Sholom Mordechai HaKohen Schwadron, the Maggid of Jerusalem. The relationship began when they hosted him on his first trip to America in 1965. (For the exact sequence of events, see the introduction to *The Maggid Speaks*.)

A little more than a year ago, on 22 Kislev 5758 (December 21, 1997), Reb Sholom's soul ascended to heaven. The following Shabbos, *Parashas Mikeitz*, as I reviewed the *sedrah*, three words were so startling, as they seemed painfully pertinent to the tragic loss. In the *parashah*, Pharaoh has two dreams and is frustrated that his necromancers have failed to interpret them to his satisfaction. He relates the dreams and his agitation to Yosef and exclaims, וְאֵין מַגִּיד לִי, *lit., No one can explain it to me* (*Bereishis* 41:24).

I took those words as a personal, painful message. Indeed וְאֵין מַגִּיד לִי, there was no longer a *maggid* for me. For more than 32 years, Reb Sholom, the *maggid* of his era, had been a powerful influence on my life. After the passing of my father, who was his close friend, on *Shemini Atzeres* 5727 (October 6, 1966), there were times when Reb Sholom was like a father and grandfather to my siblings and me. Over the years he was our mentor, role model, and advisor, and eventually he was my collaborator on the first *Maggid* book. The many times that he returned to live in our home, often for months, and in later years to the home of my brother and sister-in-law, Rabbi Arye and Adel Krohn in Brooklyn, cemented a bond that gave us pride and courage in life's darkest moments. We are forever indebted to him.

Literally, the word Maggid means one who narrates a story, parable or event. In the last few hundred years the term Maggid has come to refer to an electrifying orator, a marvelous speaker who enraptures his audience with stories and parables used as vehicles to bring across his powerful message. Men, women and children flock to hear the Maggid because his words are moving, meaningful, entertaining, and inspirational. In our generation, Rav Sholom Schwadron was the Maggid par excellence.

Reb Sholom, however, was a multifaceted personality from whom there was much to learn. It is my hope and prayer that the qualities and mannerisms I have chosen to portray and the episodes I have chosen to detail will be a merit to his soul.

Reb Sholom was a deeply sensitive man who understood the pain and the anguish of an orphan or widow. He became an orphan when he was only 7 years old, as his father Reb Yitzchok died in 1920, and he never forgot his loneliness or the isolation of his mother, Freida Leah.

When he was 60 he gave his orphaned nephew a *sefer* as a *bar mitzvah* gift. He concluded his inscription כָּמוֹנִי כָּמוֹךָ, *I am as you are* [*an orphan*]. This was 53 years after he had lost his father.

I recall one particular *Pesach Seder* we had with Reb Sholom, a few years after my father passed away. That year the first *Seder* was on *Motza'ei Shabbos*. Since it is forbidden to prepare on Shabbos for the following evening, the *Seder* started very late, since all the preparations began only after nightfall.

As an Israeli, Reb Sholom celebrated only one *Seder*. That night would be his only opportunity to fulfill the *Seder mitzvos*. Since Reb Sholom was very punctilious in his *mitzvah* observance, he was extremely careful every year to eat the *afikoman* before *chatzos* (midnight).

At the *Seder*, it is common, and praiseworthy, for participants to discuss *divrei Torah* (Torah thoughts) on the *Haggadah*. Children look forward to repeating that which they have learned in school — and rightfully so, as much of the *Seder* is primarily geared for them. The younger children recite the *Mah Nishtanah*, there are songs to be sung, customs to be followed, recitations to be said, and food to be eaten. It is a time when parents and grandparents reap the rewards of the investment they have made into their children's education.

This all takes time, and I knew that if we were to continue at the pace we were keeping, we would eat the *afikoman* well after *chatzos*. I therefore tried to rush things along. Reb Sholom realized what I was doing and said to me softly but sternly, "אַייל זִיך נִיט, *Don't rush*!" I tried to explain my intention to him, but he wouldn't let me talk. He just motioned with his finger that I continue with everything — no changes.

I tried a second time to move things along quickly, and once again he rebuked me. By the time we ate the *afikoman*, it was after *chatzos* and I felt terrible. I knew he had never violated this precept before, and I blamed myself.

After the *Seder*, when he and I were alone in the dining room, I apologized for having caused him to eat the *afikoman* so late. He looked at me and said, "Your mother waits all year for all her children to gather together for the *Seder*. Her biggest *nachas* is to hear them exchange *divrei* Torah and to see her grandchildren participate in the *Seder*. What right would I have to rush her *Seder*? Causing pain to a widow is a *d'oraisa* (Biblical violation);

eating the *afikoman* after *chatzos* is a *d'Rabbanan*!" (a Rabbinic, and thus lesser, violation).

He often cited and lived by the credo of the verse: וְלֵב אַלְמָנָה אַרְנִן, *I brought gladness to the widow's heart* (*Iyov* 29:13).

❁ ❁ ❁

Reb Sholom acquainted us with a world we would never have known. He introduced us to *tzaddikim* whose names were as colorful as their stories, Rabbi Mordechele Ushminer, Rabbi Chaykil Meletzky, Rabbi Yudel Holtzman, Rabbi Nachum Shadiker, Rabbi Zalman Rav Nachum's, Rabbi Zorach Braverman, Rabbi Yosef Shasil, Rabbi Chaim Tudris, and Rabbi Dovid Baharan, to name a few.

He regaled us with anecdotes of the aforementioned people by demonstrating their high standards of *ahavas Hashem, ahavas haTorah* and *ahavas Yisrael*. For example, Rabbi Nachum Shadiker would fast every day of the week, except Shabbos. However when a guest once came to his home and refused to eat unless Reb Nachum ate as well (the guest was unaware of Reb Nachum's weekday fasting), Reb Nachum did not say a word; he ate with the guest. How else could he fulfill the *mitzvah* of הַכְנָסַת אוֹרְחִים, *hospitality to guests?*

Rabbi Dovid Baharan was responsible for the *kashrus* of the *mikveh* (ritual bath) in Shaarei Chessed. One day he came to Reb Sholom's house in a frenzy and asked, "What is the price they usually charge for use of the *mikveh*?"

When Reb Sholom told him that it was two and half *piasters*, Reb Nachum said worriedly, "They charge me only two *piasters*. I know they are giving me a discount because I am responsible for the *kashrus* of the *mikveh*. However the Gemara says הַנּוֹטֵל שְׂכַר לָדוּן, דִּינָיו בְּטֵלִין, *If one takes money for issuing judgments, his judgments are null and void* (*Kesubos* 105a), so I must go and pay the *mikveh* the additional amount that is coming to them."

Reb Sholom related how one of the most famous Jewish neighborhoods in the world, Meah Shearim, got its name. The area was founded by Rabbi Zalman Rav Nachum's. (Rabbi Nachum Baharan's son was Reb Zalman, and Jerusalemites referred to Reb Zalman by his name and his father's name.) The *parashah* of the week during which the area was formally opened contained the verse, וַיִּזְרַע יִצְחָק בָּאָרֶץ הַהִוא וַיִּמְצָא בַּשָּׁנָה הַהִוא מֵאָה שְׁעָרִים וַיְבָרְכֵהוּ ה׳, *Yitzchak sowed in that land, and in that year he reaped* מֵאָה שְׁעָרִים, *a hundredfold; thus Hashem had blessed him* (*Bereishis* 26:12). With the prayer that the neighborhood would enjoy similar success, they named it Meah Shearim.

Rabbeinu Yonah explains the verse וְאִישׁ לְפִי מַהֲלָלוֹ, *and a man according to his praises* (*Mishlei* 27:21), to mean that a person's character is revealed through the things he considers praiseworthy. Reb Sholom revered the old *tzadikkim* of Yerushalayim, because in a sense that was his own essence. How fortunate we were to be so close to the genuine thing!

He demanded that we be on constant vigilance regarding our level of *ruchnius*, spirituality, just as he constantly reevaluated his own worthiness. He would minimize his accomplishments and downplay his *davening* and learning. Rabbi Yisroel Grossman recounted that when he and Rav Sholom came to America for the first time, Reb Sholom was listening on the plane to tape recordings he had made of *Mesillas Yesharim* and other *mussar* works. He was so frightened of the "impurities" that might confront him in America that he wished to strengthen himself before he stepped on these shores. Tears ran down his cheeks as he listened to his own *mussar* fortifying him for "*treifah*" America.

Reb Sholom related that he once decried his level of *ruchnius* to one of his mentors, Rabbi Elyah Lopian (1872-1970). Reb Elyah listened quietly, letting Reb Sholom complete his entire litany of spiritual woes. "Are you finished?" asked Reb Elyah not wanting to interrupt and perhaps waiting to deliver dramatically one piercing sentence that Reb Sholom would always remember. When Reb Sholom said he was, Reb Elyah sighed and said, "If only I still had your black beard — if only I still had your black beard — " and his voice trailed off. The implication was that Reb Sholom had time to change and improve.

When Reb Sholom would retell this episode he would sigh and say, "Reb Itzeleh (Blazer) Peterburger (1837-1907) once said, 'When one is young he can [change] but doesn't want to, and when he's old he'd like to [change] but he no longer can.' "

❁ ❁ ❁

Reb Sholom was a very methodical man, a carefully thought-out person who did not rush to make decisions. He would rebuke those who did things impetuously. He always used the same expression and would gently admonish me with a mimicked Sefardic dialect as he emphatically said, פְּרִי הַמְּהִירוּת הַחֲרָטָה, *The fruit of rushing is regret*. [This was one of the popular proverbs of a collection entitled *Mivchar HaPeninim*, sometimes attributed to the *paytan* (liturgical poet) R' Shlomo Ibn Gabirol (1021-1058).]

Sometimes before meals he would say to my brothers R' Kolman and R' Arye and me (or to any three males in his presence) "I need you to tell me מוּתָּר לָךְ, *it is permitted to you*." (When repeated three times, this declaration releases, under certain conditions, someone from a promise.) At first he was hesitant to tell us what promise he had made, but eventually it became known. He studied 18 chapters of *mishnayos* every day, six chapters before every meal. If something had transpired which did not allow him to study the *mishnayos* and he had to eat, he would not begin until three people had released him from the vow.

In his youth (1931) Rav Sholom learned a prodigious amount of *Gemara*. In a three-and-a-half month period from *Teves* to *Pesach*, he and his *chavrusa* (study partner) Rabbi Ezra Brizel reviewed *Mesechta Bava Basra* (the largest tractate in *Shas*, with 175 *blatt*) four times! After he was married, he joined the Kollel Ohel Moshe in Jerusalem, where such luminaries as Rabbi Yosef

Sholom Eliyashiv and Rabbi Shmuel Wosner studied. The goal of the *kollel* was to finish all of *Talmud Bavli* and *Talmud Yerushalmi* in five years.

Reb Sholom was inspired to this type of learning because of the influence of Rabbi Meir Chodosh in Yeshivas Chevron and the stories he heard about his eminent grandfather, the Berzhaner Rav, known as the *Maharsham,* for whom Reb Sholom was named.

The grandmother of the renowned Rabbi Meir Shapiro (1887-1933) (founder of the Daf-Yomi movement) was the second wife of the *Maharsham,* Rabbi Sholom Mordechai HaKohen Schwadron (1835-1911). Rabbi Meir Shapiro would often visit his grandmother, and wherever he was there he made it a point to talk to his stepgrandfather in learning.

On one of those visits, Rabbi Shapiro noticed a small group of *talmidei chachamim* waiting for the *Maharsham*. The *Maharsham* had been ill and was trying to get some rest, but he was awakened by the clamor of the people arguing about a halachic point concerning the priestly tithes, which is found in *Shulchan Aruch Even HaEzer*.

The *Maharsham* emerged from his room and asked, "What is the discussion here?" When told the subject of the dispute, he said, "This is explicitly dealt with by the *Darchei Moshe* in *Tur Yoreh Deah, Hilchos Mezuzah* (286 note 4)."

The assembled scholars were amazed. How could the *Maharsham* remember an isolated 12-word comment on *Yoreh Deah* and associate it with *Even HaEzer*?

When everyone had left except for Rabbi Shapiro, the *Maharsham* showed him a notation he had written on the last page of his *Tur Shulchan Aruch*: "Today with the help of *HaKadosh Baruch Hu,* I completed the *Tur* for the 101st time." Then turning to his wife's grandson he said, "What is there to wonder about? If you learn the *Tur* 101 times, you can remember a *Darchei Moshe*!"

Indeed, Reb Sholom often bemoaned the fact that many teenaged *talmidim* in yeshivos learned only seven blatt a year! When he was 19, he learned 700 *blatt* that year!

His brother-in-law, Rabbi Shlomo Zalman Auerbach, once said, "People know Reb Sholom as an extraordinary *maggid*; I know him as an extraordinary *talmid chacham*." The two Torah luminaries were very close and had great admiration for each other. Reb Sholom once bemoaned his eventual fate saying, "What will be with me in the *Olam HaEmes* (World of Truth)?" "Don't worry." Reb Shlomo Zalman said "When you get there, your grandfather the *Maharsham* will escort you on one side, and your *rebbi*, Reb Leib [Chasman] (1869-1935), will escort you on the other side."

Wherever he traveled, he brought along cartons of *sefarim* and manuscripts he was working on. He was a prolific writer and editor, having written and published three volumes of *Ohr Yahel*, the *shmuessen* of his *rebbi*, Rabbi Leib Chasman. He wrote and published three volumes of *Lev Eliyahu*, the thoughts and insights of Rav Elyah Lopian, and he annotated and published more than 40(!) works from his father Reb Yitzchok and grandfather the *Maharsham*, including *Daas Torah* on the entire *Shulchan Aruch, Orach Chaim*.

A friend of mine was involved in a dispute with two business partners. Upset and at his wit's end as to how to solve his problem, he approached Reb Sholom, who was in America at the time. Reb Sholom told him that years earlier he, too, had become involved in organizational politics and rancorous division. "I saw that the best solution was to walk away from the whole thing," said Reb Sholom.

Reb Sholom then did a remarkable thing, one which has remained with my friend until this very day. "I would like to show you something that I carry with me in my wallet," said the venerable *maggid*. And from his wallet he took a worn index card on which he had written a quotation from a letter written by one of the *Rishonim* to his son.

"Do not defile your souls with arguments that destroy the body, the soul, and your finances — for then what else is left? I have seen light-complexioned people become dark, families become afflicted, princes removed from their prominence, large cities desolated, groups split asunder, respected people embarrassed and humiliated because of arguments."

Aaron, the first *Kohen Gadol*, was depicted as one who was אוֹהֵב שָׁלוֹם וְרוֹדֵף שָׁלוֹם, *One who loved peace and pursued peace* (see *Avos* 1:12). Keeping that card with him at all times reminded a great *Kohen* of our generation to emulate his ancestor's demeanor.

❁ ❁ ❁

His joy in life was boundless. Everyone around him was usually laughing or at least smiling. At weddings, he would dance in front of the *chassan* and *kallah* waving his cane to and fro, moving his body in gyrations that didn't seem possible for a man his age or size. Often afterwards his feet would ache, but he felt it was a small price to pay for being able to fulfill the *mitzvah* of being חָתָן וְכַלָּה מְשַׂמֵּחַ , making a *chassan* and *kallah* joyous.

❁ ❁ ❁

To visit Reb Sholom in his home or to be in his presence at any type of gathering was always an energizing experience. By nature he was a happy person, who laughed easily and refused to be broken by the adversities and challenges of life. We knew that he had suffered abject poverty, was plagued over the years with diabetes (he called it sugar), and had severe pain in his legs. Yet he always had an uplifting story, an inspiring thought from a *gadol*, a new interpretation of a *pasuk*, and a notebook ready to write down a good story he heard from others.

But perhaps the two things that etched his personality indelibly on three generations of Yerushalmis were his two distinct legendary voices. The first voice could be heard every Friday night, starting in 1952 and for decades afterwards, in the Zichron Moshe *shul* in the Achvah section of Jerusalem. There he delivered a weekly *drashah* to overflowing crowds of men, women, and children, keeping everyone spellbound for hours! His stories would inspire, his humor would induce convulsive laughter, and his roaring *mussar* — reflecting what he heard from his *rebbis*, particularly Rabbi Leib Chasman, Rabbi Elyah Lopian, and Rabbi Elyah Dushnitzer (1876-1949) — would reverberate off the walls of the old *shul* and encourage people to become better. His grandfatherly personality warmly engulfed all who were present.

His patented exclamations of *pil'ei p'la'im* (wonder of wonders), *noyro noyra'os* (awesome of awesome), and *haflei vafela* (wonder of wonders) became his trademarks that identified him immediately in the minds of tens of thousands of Jews, who heard him throughout the Jewish world. One could homiletically apply David *HaMelech's* phrase, וְהִתְעַנְּגוּ עַל רֹב שָׁלוֹם (*Tehillim* 37:11), *and they delighted with Reb Sholom*. Indeed Reb Sholom lived until he was 85, which is the numeric equivalent of פֶּה, *mouth*, as he was a פֶּה מַפִּיק מַרְגָּלִיּוֹת, *a mouth that spewed pearls*.

His second voice that remains unforgettable was the one he employed in his *davening* before the *amud* on the *Yamim Noraim*, in the Chevron Yeshivah. The words of the *Yom Kippur* sevice itself depict the scene perfectly: וּבְכֵן מַה נֶּהְדָּר הָיָה כֹּהֵן גָּדוֹל, *And so how majestic was the Kohen Gadol*. His piercing cries, his lilting tunes, his *nusach* which reflected the meaning of each word in the service were mesmerizing. The Bais Yisrael of Gur once said, "If you want to do *teshuvah*, listen to Reb Sholom say וּמִפְּנֵי חֲטָאֵנוּ (*because of our sins*)." Throngs of roshei yeshivah, yeshivah students, and laymen would sing and cry with him, knowing from year to year what *niggun* he would sing and just exactly how he would sing it, yet somehow being inspired each year as though it were the first time. Knowing that this great *Kohen* was just over a mile from the *Kodshei Kodashim* (Holy of Holies), where the *Kohen Gadol* in the *Beis HaMikdash* prayed on *Yom Kippur*, one could easily imagine this man at the *amud* of the Chevron Yeshivah, leading all of *Klal Yisrael*.

And although we Americans never heard Reb Sholom on *Rosh Hashanah* or *Yom Kippur*, our family was uplifted to hear his *Nishmas* at the *Seder*, which brought tears to all of us. Who can forget his rousing recitation of Psalm 142, *Maskil L'David*, at huge public gatherings, his heartrending *Lechah Dodi, Keil Adon* or *Chasal Siddur Pesach*? His emotion and connection to the *Ribbono Shel Olam* manifested itself in his *davening* and *zemiros*.

Now, with Reb Sholom's passing, his various voices are stilled until *Mashiach* comes. His teachings and directives can be heard only through others, who will transmit his ideas and ideals. Thus, anywhere in the world where people relate either his stories or his type of inspirational stories, his thoughts or his type of uplifting and introspective thoughts, they will be perpetuating and reliving his personality and teachings. Until the coming of *Mashiach*, we will continue to listen and hopefully be inspired by words that are ECHOES OF THE MAGGID.

תּוֹרַת אֱמֶת הָיְתָה בְּפִיהוּ וְעַוְלָה לֹא נִמְצָא בִשְׂפָתָיו **בְּשָׁלוֹם** וּבְמִישׁוֹר הָלַךְ
אִתִּי וְרַבִּים הֵשִׁיב מֵעָוֹן (מלאכי ב:ו)

Part A:

Fellowship

Renewal in the Garden

The crowd was overwhelming. No one there could ever remember seeing 20,000 observant Jews gathered inside one building. Electricity and excitement were almost tangible, as every person felt part of the story yet at the same time realized he was only a fragment of the story. It was May 1990 and Orthodox Jews from across the continent gathered in Madison Square Garden in Manhattan, to celebrate the Ninth Siyum HaShas of Daf Yomi.

The exhilarated crowd had been energized by months of sustained publicity about the event. It was the place to be if you cared about Torah in America. Tickets were at a premium, as men, women, and children of all ages from every walk of observant life converged on a site heretofore known for its worship of athletic prowess. That night though, it would be those who studied Torah who would be glorified, and those who lived by its instruction who would be lionized. Anything less would be out of bounds and offside.

In the third row of seats, directly facing the huge layered podium, sat a dignified elderly man from Los Angeles, Hersch Leib Mandel, who had come with his son Frank from Manhattan's West Side. The program moved from speaker to speaker, flashbulbs sparkling throughout the stands as people constantly took pictures. The public-address systems blared the voices of the speakers who looked minuscule compared to their exaggerated dimensions on the huge screens around the arena.

Suddenly the elder Mr. Mandel sat upright in his seat. The speaker had a pronounced Oberlander Hungarian accent. Mr. Mandel was sure he had heard him before. That voice — he knew that voice. It was so distinctive, so unique. He turned to his son and asked urgently, "Who is that? I know that voice from someplace."

Frank looked up at the digital scoreboard, which indicated that Rabbi Moshe Neuschloss (1911-1997), the Rav of New Square, was the speaker. Frank turned to his father and said, "It's says on the screen that the speaker is Rabbi Neuschloss of Skver."

Hersch Leib Mandel turned pale and began to tremble. Frank became frightened as he noticed the sudden change in his father's demeanor. Frank took his father's hand in his own and felt his cold, sweaty palm.

"Pa, is everything all right?" asked Frank.

"I need a pen and a paper," said Hersch Leib. "I have to write a note and get it to Rabbi Neuschloss."

"Why, what's the matter?" Frank asked with concern.

"It's a long story, Frank, and it goes back many years. But if he is the person I think he is, he may very well remember it. I know it will stay with me forever."

Hersch Leib Mandel's mind was now somewhere else. A different era, a different country, and very different circumstances.

In the early 1940s Hersch Leib was a yeshivah student in the town of Nyiregyhaza (pronounced Nir-het-haz). The Rav of the city, Rabbi Shia Herschel Landau — known as the Vitker Rav — was also the Rosh Yeshivah. The yeshivah had more than two hundred *bachurim* from many cities throughout Hungary, but Hersch Leib from Opaly was chosen to be Rabbi Landau's *hoiz bachur* (house attendant).

During that era, even before the Nazis occupied Hungary, anti-Semitic Hungarian police, derogatorily known as the Csendorseg (pronounced Zhon-dars), were beating and brutalizing Jews. One Friday night a rumor spread throughout Hersch Leib's *shul* that a Jew had been badly beaten and dragged off to jail.

Rabbi Landau's family had a gentile maid, Mariska,* who was familiar with the customs, language, and rituals of Jewish families. No one of the Rabbi's family would be allowed to enter the jail to see which Jew was being held, but perhaps Mariska would be allowed in.

Hersch Leib gave Mariska some food and told her to find out the identity of the prisoner and to inquire if he had any special needs. When she came to the jail, the guards let her in without any problem. She became frightened when she saw how badly the man had been beaten.

When she was sure that no one was listening, she said, "I come to you from the Jewish community. Here is some kosher food. Who are you?"

The prisoner was not sure if this was a trap or a setup. Yet if she was an authentic messenger he could not bypass the opportunity to get an urgent message to the Jews of the town. "Tell them Uj Lakat (pronounced Ooyei Lokot) is stuck here."

The woman looked at the prisoner strangely. Was that his name? Was he giving over a secret code? She repeated the words *Ooyei Lokot* as she wanted to be sure she had it right.

When she returned home she told everyone how terribly bruised the prisoner was and the strange name he gave. Everyone around the table began trying to decipher the message. They knew that *Ooyei Lokot* meant 'new lock.' Was there a new lock on the jail? Were new guards watching his cell? Did the cell itself have a new lock? Was it a code word?

Suddenly someone called out, "It's Rabbi Neuschloss. The word Neuschloss means 'new lock'!"

Everyone stood up in startled shock at the realization that such a prestigious man had been beaten and imprisoned. Rabbi Neuschloss, an eminent *talmid chacham,* earned a livelihood doing business in various cities throughout Hungary. Almost every *Rosh Chodesh* he would come to Nyiregyhaza, spend time with Rabbi Shia Herschel Landau, *daven* in the yeshivah and talk to the *bachurim* in learning.

---

* Name has been changed.

When Hersch Leib described Rav Neuschloss' physical features to Mariska, and she confirmed that he was indeed the prisoner, everyone began to talk at once about the importance of getting him released. Hersch Leib went immediately to the president of the Jewish community, Mr. Shimon Nemeti, and asked him to approach the mayor of the town to plead for the prisoner's release.

Mr. Nemeti heeded Hersch Leib's pleas and approached the mayor. He explained what kind of personality Rabbi Neuschloss was and that his integrity was impeccable. Nemeti assured the mayor that the Jews in town would vote for him in the next election if he acted magnanimously by freeing Rabbi Neuschloss.

The mayor went to the county jail and, with numerous Jews waiting outside, he convinced the police chief that it was a case of mistaken identity and that the prisoner they were holding was actually a man of great integrity. Within minutes Rabbi Neuschloss emerged.

Hersch Leib was there to greet Rabbi Neuschloss and insisted on taking him to Rabbi Landau's home. It had been a terrible ordeal, and the rabbi was visibly shaken by the incident. When they came home, Hersch Leib asked Rabbi Neuschloss if he wanted him to bring a doctor.

"No, but come with me," said Rabbi Neuschloss. "I need to be in a room with you alone."

They went into a side room and Rabbi Neuschloss said, "Please lock the door."

Hersch Leib was surprised, "Don't you want to lie down first?" he asked.

"Not just yet," came the reply. And with that Rabbi Neuschloss began struggling to take off his jacket and shirt. Hersch Leib could see bloodstains on the back of the shirt. The rabbi then took off his *tallis kattan.* Hersch Leib was startled. "What is the Rabbi doing and why is he doing this in front of me?" Hersch Leib wondered.

Finally after he removed his undershirt and Hersch Leib could see the effects of the lashes and bruises he received, Rabbi Neuschloss said in his distinct Oberlander Hungarian dialect, "Count the lashes and welts that I have all over me, and please be sure to count every one."

Hersch Leib was taken aback. Rabbi Neuschloss saw Hersch Leib's bewildered look and, explained, "As I was being beaten I made a *neder* that I would donate ten *Pengo* (the Hungarian currency) to *tzedakah* for each lash and bruise."

Hersch Leib stood speechless and motionless as he realized he was in the presence of greatness and holiness. Rabbi Neuschloss broke the silence, "Go ahead," he said softly, "count each one and let me know exactly how many there are. I must know what I owe to *tzedakah."*

With tears in his eyes, Hersch Leib counted close to forty welts, cuts, and gashes on the rabbi's face, torso, and legs. When the count was complete, Rabbi Neuschloss calculated the amount he owed to *tzedakah* and said he would pay it after Shabbos. He then washed up and changed into fresh clothes that Hersch Leib provided.

After a few days of rest and recuperation from his ordeal, he was on his way back home. His traveling was curtailed after the incident, and with the Nazi takeover of Hungary in 1944 and the dispersion of Hungarian Jewry to death and slave labor camps, Rabbi Neuschloss and Hersch Leib never saw each other again.

Hersch Leib Mandel's hand was trembling as he wrote in Yiddish, "Dear Rav Neuschloss, If you remember fifty years ago my counting the lashes on your back when you came out of the jail in Nyiregyhaza, I would like to meet you. I am sitting directly in front of you in the third row of seats."

"Frank," Hersch Leib said softly, "make sure this gets to Rabbi Neuschloss. Give it to one of the ushers to give to him."

Frank got out of his seat and went up to one of the walkie-talkie, badge-laden ushers swarming the Garden and asked if he could deliver a message to one of the speakers. "To whom do you have to get this?" the guard asked.

"The one who just finished speaking," replied Frank. "Rabbi Neuschloss of Skver."

"I am his *gabbai* (attendant). What is this in reference to?"

"I can't say," said Frank, "but trust me it's very important."

"I'll go right now, because the rabbi is leaving soon."

Frank and his father watched as the usher walked around the barriers and inched along the back of the dais and handed the note to Rabbi Neuschloss. The *gabbai,* peering over the Rav's shoulder, read the note together with the Rav.

Hersch Leib and Frank watched carefully as Rav Neuschloss read the short note. Suddenly his eyes widened in astonishment and he began shaking his head to and fro as he recalled and relived that painful experience of decades ago.

He looked out into the audience and slowly scanned the third row of seats. Hersch Leib raised his hand and waved it slightly. Rav Neuschloss nodded his head in acknowledgment. He whispered something to his *gabbai,* who immediately left the dais and came down to the Mandels.

"The rabbi would like to see you. Please come with me," said the *gabbai.*

He led the Mandels off to the side of the dais, on the floor of the arena where Rabbi Neuschloss was waiting. As Hersch Leib approached the rabbi, they fell into each other's arms and wept. Oblivious to the thousands around them, two men linked by an encounter of raw anguish and sacred commitment renewed their acquaintance at an event whose purpose was unity.

"You saved my life," Rabbi Neuschloss said as he held onto Hersch Leib.

"It was an honor to serve you," said Hersch Leib humbled and overwhelmed to be in the presence of greatness.

The two men spoke for a few minutes and agreed, "We must remain in contact."

And from that night until Rabbi Neuschloss passed away, the families bridged the 3,000 mile distance from New Square to Los Angeles with visits, letters, and phone calls.

Madison Square Garden had brought many people together for many different reasons. Perhaps, few were as meaningful as this one.

A Matter of Judgment

Rabbi Yitzchok Isbee (1953-1997) was the beloved rav of the Agudath Israel of Avenue L in Flatbush. Aside from being a noted *talmid chacham* and revered Rosh Yeshivah at Yeshiva Tiferes Torah on Staten Island, Rabbi Isbee was a caring person whose concern for everyone, young or old, was extraordinary. At his untimely passing at the age of forty-four, he was mourned by thousands who would miss his humility, charm, and example of *hasmadah* (diligence in learning).

In a moving *Shabbos Shuvah drashah,* Rav Isbee told the following story, which exemplified extraordinary selflessness.

Avigdor Ribicoff,* a kollel fellow in Tiberias, Israel, and his wife Avigail* had been married many years and had not been blessed with children. They sought medical help in Israel and abroad and had undergone various tests and procedures, but sadly, to no avail. Despondency and desperation were beginning to gnaw at the young couple.

Both came from "Litvishe" families and had no connection to chassidic rebbes. Friends urged Avigdor to go for *berachos* (blessings) to various rebbes and on occasion he did so reluctantly. During the summer vacation, when he saw his colleagues taking their children on outings, the pain of emptiness was worse than ever. He had to do something.

Avigdor decided that he would go to the Nadvorner Rebbe, Rav Chaim Mordechai Rosenbloom (1904-1978), a rebbe in Bnei Brak. During his audience with the rebbe he broke down and cried.

The Nadvorner Rebbe listened sympathetically and asked Avigdor where he would be *davening* on *Rosh Hashanah.* Avigdor said he planned to *daven* at a yeshivah near his home in Tiberias, where he enjoyed the *baalei tefillah* and felt comfortable with the pace of the *davening.*

---

* Name has been changed.

"Come *daven* with us," said the rebbe warmly. "The first day of *Yom Tov,* the Torah reading is, וַה׳ פָּקַד אֶת שָׂרָה *And Hashem remembered Sarah* [and blessed her with a child] (*Bereishis* 21:1), and the *haftarah* is about Chanah [who finally had her long-awaited child, Shmuel] (*I Shmuel* 1:1). It's a *segulah* (omen) to have that *maftir*. Come here for *Rosh Hashanah,* and with the *Ribono Shel Olam's* help, things can happen."

Avigdor had never heard that it was a *segulah* to be called for that *maftir,* but he knew that in many *shuls* the *aliyos* were usually sold for substantial sums of money on *Rosh Hashanah*. Did the rebbe mean that he should buy that *aliyah,* or that he would receive the *aliyah* free of charge? He didn't have the courage to ask; he decided he would cross that bridge when he got there. Besides, if it meant having a child, he would pay anything, even if he had to borrow.

Avigdor and Avigail made plans to be in Bnei Brak that *Rosh Hashanah*. On the first night of *Yom Tov,* the rebbe's *shul* was overflowing with people and as Avigdor scanned the crowd, he wondered if the rebbe would even remember him or his problem.

After *davening,* the warm ambiance in the *shul* was practically tangible. With radiant smiles everyone seemed to be wishing each other לְשָׁנָה טוֹבָה תִּכָּתֵב וְתֵחָתֵם לְאַלְתַּר, לְחַיִּים טוֹבִים וּלְשָׁלוֹם *May you be inscribed and sealed immediately, for a good year, good life, and for peace.* People stood on line, gradually making their way towards the rebbe to receive his blessing.

Avigdor stood back, allowing the "regulars" their chance to greet the rebbe first. As he stood off to a side, he noticed another fellow his age, who also seemed to be a visitor. It appeared that the other fellow also knew no one, and he too was waiting for the "regulars" to clear the *shul* before greeting the rebbe.

Avigdor approached the fellow and extended his hand in greeting. *"Shalom Aleichem,"* he said. "My name is Avigdor Ribicoff. Are you from around here?"

"Aleichem Shalom," came the reply. "I'm Yeruchem Lazar* and I'm from Jerusalem. I am here to be with the rebbe for *Yom Tov."*

* Name has been changed.

"Oh?" said Avigdor.

"To tell you the truth," Yeruchem said, "I don't know how it's going to happen tomorrow, but I heard that the rebbe said that if one gets *maftir*, it's a *segulah* for children. Look at this crowd..." He let his words trail off.

Avigdor was crestfallen. He could not believe what he just heard. Hadn't the rebbe told *him* to come get *maftir* tomorrow? That was the only reason he and his wife had come to Bnei Brak for *Yom Tov*. How could both of them get *maftir* at the same *minyan*? For the last month and half he was waiting for tomorrow's *leining* — and now this?

Avigdor did not allow his disappointment to surface. He continued to make small talk with Yeruchem and wished him well. That night Avigdor was in turmoil deciding what to do the next day.

The next morning Avigdor, in deference to Yeruchem, *davened* in another *shul*. And sure enough Yeruchem had *maftir.*

And within a year Avigdor and his wife Avigail had a baby girl.

The rebbe had said that "things could happen." And they did — and all because of Avigdor's extraordinary character in his willingness to relinquish a potential blessing.

When Chanah gave praise to Hashem for having her son, she said וְאֵין צוּר כֵּאלֹקֵינוּ, *And there is no Rock like our God (I Shmuel* 2:2). *Chazal* interpret her words homiletically — "There is no צַיָּיר, *artist,* like Hashem" [Who can fashion one human being in the womb of another] *(Berachos* 10a, see *Rashi).*

In Bnei Brak, the *Ribono Shel Olam* designed events so that Avigdor's compassion and benevolence were tested. And when Avigdor acted extraordinarily, his reward was crafted by the Master Artist of the universe.

The rebbe was right. With the *Ribono Shel Olam's* help, anything could happen. And it did.

Lein Change

The creative *chessed* in this story is brilliant and the sensitivity displayed heartwarming. One can't help but be awed and inspired.

In the Agudas Yisroel *shul* of Baltimore, there are two *baalei korei* (readers of the Torah), Rabbi Moshe Juravel and Mr. Izzy Strauss. Both are outstanding at their craft; their enunciation is clear, they are grammatically precise, and they are always thoroughly prepared. Rabbi Juravel and Mr. Strauss *lein* on alternate weeks.

One Friday night Rabbi Juravel developed a severe sore throat. He was sure he would not be able to read the Torah loudly enough the next morning, and that he might even damage his vocal chords by straining his voice. He tried drinking tea with honey, but nothing helped. All he could do was hope that by the next morning his voice would improve. It didn't.

When he came to *shul* Shabbos morning, Mr. Strauss was already there. "Izzy," said Rabbi Juravel hoarsely, "Do you think you could pinch-hit for me today and *lein*? My voice is not up to it."

"Why, of course," replied Izzy. "I'll begin looking it over right now. And I hope you have a *refuah shelaimah* (*complete recovery*)."

After *Shacharis* Rabbi Juravel went to the *bimah* and began *leining* the sidrah. He struggled to make his voice heard and had to stop numerous times to clear his throat. After the first *aliyah*, he sat down and let Mr. Strauss take over.

After davening, as everyone was leaving *shul*, the *gabbai* approached Rabbi Juravel and asked, "Why did you even begin *leining*? You knew you wouldn't be able to do it."

Rabbi Juravel cleared his throat and replied, "Most people in the *shul* don't know whose turn it is to *lein* any particular week. Had Izzy begun *leining* from the beginning of the sidrah and made any mistakes, people would think he hadn't prepared properly. This way, by my *leining* until *Sheini*, everyone realized that really it was my turn to *lein* — except because of my voice I could not go on, so if Izzy made any mistakes when he took over, people would understand that it was because he was asked to *lein* at the last minute!"

United in Parcel Service

The Sages (*Nedarim* 81a) teach, הִזָּהֲרוּ בִּבְנֵי עֲנִיִּים שֶׁמֵּהֶן תֵּצֵא תוֹרָה, *Be attentive to the children of the poor, because from them Torah will flourish* [because they are not encumbered by other involvements (*Ran*)].

The word Torah literally means *teaching,* hence the Talmudic phrase can be understood to mean that we should be attentive to the children of the poor, for there is much we can learn from them. In this touching story told to me by my son-in-law, Rabbi Shlomo Dovid Pfeiffer, we learn sensitivity from a poverty-stricken family.

Chezky Silverman* of Chicago was learning in a yeshivah in Jerusalem and loving every minute of it. His *chavrusas* were all Americans except for his afternoon *chavrusa,* Yankel Bernstein,* an ebullient young married Yerushalmi.

Yankel and his wife had five children and although the family was poor, his enthusiasm for life and Torah was contagious.

One Thursday afternoon Yankel invited Chezky for the Friday-night meal. Chezky delightedly accepted the invitation as he looked forward to meeting Yankel's family. The Bernsteins lived in an apartment complex on Rechov Shmuel Hanavi. Chezky had been told that the Bernsteins were poor, but he was not prepared for what he saw in their apartment. After *Kiddush,* when he made *Hamotzi,* Yankel was cutting the challah into very thin slices. Could the family be relying on this challah to last for all the Shabbos meals? Chezky, who came from a well-to-do home, could not bear the thought.

* Name has been changed.

The meal soon became an anguished ordeal for Chezky as he saw the minuscule portions of fish, soup, and chicken Mrs. Bernstein served the children. Chezky's own portion was larger than anyone else's, and he felt guilty, for he understood that he was getting more at the expense of the Bernsteins. Although the *divrei Torah* and *zemiros* were lively and the children certainly seemed happy, Chezky vowed he would never come there again for a meal. It just wasn't fair to Yankel's family.

A few weeks later Yankel again invited Chezky for a Shabbos meal but Chezky said he already had other plans. Again and again Yankel invited his younger *chavrusa*, and each time Chezky had another excuse for not coming. Finally Yankel understood that Chezky's excuses were just that — excuses.

One afternoon Yankel said directly, "I've invited you numerous times since you came that Friday night months ago, and each time you refuse me. Did we not treat you right that first time? Were our standards of *kashrus* not up to yours? Did any of my children say something that upset you?"

Chezky was surprised at how sensitive Yankel was to his refusals. He couldn't hide the truth any longer. "I'll tell you honestly, Reb Yankel," he said. "I had no idea how you and your family lived. That Friday night I couldn't help but notice there was not much food to go around the table and frankly I felt guilty eating anything because I knew it was at the expense of your wonderful children." Chezky had to hold back his urge to cry.

Yankel put his hands on Chezky's shoulders and said, "You really are considerate, but let me explain and I think you'll understand.

"My wife and I come from poor families. When we were married, we discussed the likelihood that we would live the rest of our lives below the standards of many of our friends. We decided from the start that if we were to be blessed with children, we would invite guests once in a while to teach the children the *middah* (trait) of *hachnasas orchim* (hospitality to guests).

"We don't have guests very often, but when we do, it is to show the children that we share the *Ribono Shel Olam's* blessings with others."

Chezky understood Reb Yankel's explanation but still couldn't allow himself to eat again at Reb Yankel's home. Maybe sometime in the future he would reconsider, but not now.

As *Lag B'Omer* approached, Chezky planned a trip north to Miron, where thousands gather every year at the tomb of Rabbi Shimon bar Yochai. He mentioned it to Reb Yankel, who assured him that the trip was worthwhile. Reb Yankel said he would go along and bring his two eldest sons.

They planned to meet on Rechov Malchei Yisrael where the buses to Miron were gathering. In a festive mood, Chezky got up early and decided to surprise Yankel's children. He went to a nearby *makolet* (grocery store), bought a few ice-cream sandwiches, and brought them to Yankel's apartment. As he entered the home he called out to the children, "Here, look what I bought for you *lich'vod* (in honor of) *Lag B'Omer*.

The children took the ice-cream sandwiches, dutifully said their quick thank-you's, and scampered out of the apartment.

Chezky was surprised. The Bernstein children could not have been accustomed to eating ice-cream sandwiches too often, and surely it was something special to them. Why hadn't they reacted with greater enthusiastic thanks, instead of just muttering a few words and running off?

A few minutes later, Chezky could hear rumbling up the steps. Before he could turn around there were 15 neighborhood children in the Bernstein dining room around the table. They were each excited as they waited for the two oldest Bernstein children to come into the room.

In a moment the two Bernstein boys came to the table with the ice-cream sandwiches and knives in their hands. With meticulous care they cut the ice-cream sandwiches into small portions and with beaming smiles handed a section to each of the children who were present. Then, in unison, the Yerushalmi children theatrically licked the white lining of ice cream frozen between the brown top-and-bottom crackers, smiling and joking as they devoured their special morning treat.

Chezky observed the scene and turned to Reb Yankel who stood beaming at the dining room entrance. Their eyes met. There was no need for words — they both understood. Indeed the children had absorbed the message.

Perfection at the Plate

Sports in America is not only a multibillion dollar industry, but rare is the child growing up in the United States who has never been involved in some type of sports competition, be it baseball, basketball, punchball, handball, football or hockey. For this reason, people who have grown up in America, both young and old, are swept up and moved as their mind's eye visualizes the unfolding of these incredible events.

However, it is not only an American that can fully appreciate the intensity of this marvelous "sports" story. This tender story also has universal appeal, because it deals with the universal values of sensitivity, self-esteem, and acceptance.

In Brooklyn, New York, Chush is a school that caters to learning-disabled children. Some children remain in Chush for their entire school careers, while others can be mainstreamed into conventional yeshivos and Bais Yaakovs. There are a few children who attend Chush for most of the week and go to a regular school on Sundays.

At a Chush fund-raising dinner, the father of a Chush child delivered a speech that would never be forgotten by all who attended. After extolling the school and its dedicated staff, he cried out, "Where is the perfection in my son Shaya? Everything that Hashem does is done with perfection. But my child cannot understand things as other children do. My child cannot remember facts and figures as other children do. Where is Hashem's perfection?" The audience was shocked by the question, pained by the father's anguish and stilled by his piercing query.

"I believe," the father answered, "that when Hashem brings a child like this into the world, the perfection that He seeks is in the way people react to this child."

He then told the following story about his son Shaya.

Shaya attends Chush throughout the week and Yeshivah Darchei Torah in Far Rockaway on Sundays. One Sunday afternoon, Shaya and his father came to Darchei Torah as his classmates were playing baseball. The game was in progress and as Shaya and his father made their way towards the ballfield, Shaya said, "Do you think you could get me into the game?"

Shaya's father knew his son was not at all athletic, and that most boys would not want him on their team. But Shaya's father understood that if his son was chosen in, it would give him a comfortable sense of belonging.

Shaya's father approached one of the boys in the field and asked, "Do you think my Shaya could get into the game?"

The boy looked around for guidance from his teammates. Getting none, he took matters into his own hands and said, "We are losing by six runs and the game is already in the eighth inning. I guess he can be on our team and we'll try to put him up to bat in the ninth inning."

Shaya's father was ecstatic as Shaya smiled broadly. Shaya was told to put on a glove and go out to play short center field, a position that exists only in softball. There were no protests from the opposing team, which would now be hitting with an extra man in the outfield.

In the bottom of the eighth inning, Shaya's team scored a few runs but was still behind by three. In the bottom of the ninth inning, Shaya's team scored again and now with two outs and the bases loaded and the potential winning runs on base, Shaya was scheduled to be up. Would the team actually let Shaya bat at this juncture and give away their chance to win the game?

Surprisingly, Shaya was told to take a bat and try to get a hit. Everyone knew that it was all but impossible, for Shaya didn't even know how to hold the bat properly, let alone hit with it. However as Shaya stepped up to the plate, the pitcher moved in a few steps to lob the ball in softly so that Shaya should at least be able to make contact.

The first pitch came in and Shaya swung clumsily and missed. One of Shaya's teammates came up to Shaya and together they held the bat and faced the pitcher waiting for the next pitch. The pitcher again took a few steps forward to toss the ball softly towards Shaya.

As the next pitch came in, Shaya and his teammate swung the bat and together they hit a slow ground ball to the pitcher. The pitcher picked up the soft grounder and could easily have thrown the ball to the first baseman. Shaya would have been out and that would have ended the game.

Instead, the pitcher took the ball and threw it on a high arc to right field, far and wide beyond the first baseman's reach. Everyone started yelling, "Shaya, run to first! Shaya, run to first!" Never in his life had Shaya run to first.

He scampered down the baseline wide eyed and startled. By the time he reached first base, the right fielder had the ball. He could have thrown the ball to the second baseman who would tag out Shaya, who was still running. But the rightfielder understood what the pitcher's intentions were, so he threw the ball high and far over the third baseman's head, as everyone yelled, "Shaya, run to second! Shaya, run to second."

Shaya ran towards second base as the runners ahead of him deliriously circled the bases towards home. As Shaya reached second base, the opposing shortstop ran towards him, turned him towards the direction of third base and shouted "Shaya run to third!"

As Shaya rounded third, the boys from both teams ran behind him screaming, "Shaya, run home! Shaya, run home!"

Shaya ran home, stepped on home plate and all 18 boys lifted him on their shoulders and made him the hero, as he had just hit the "grand slam" and won the game for his team.

"That day," said the father who now had tears rolling down his face, "those 18 boys reached their level of perfection. They showed that it is not only those who are talented that should be recognized, but also those who have less talent. They too are human beings, they too have feelings and emotions, they too are people, they too want to feel important."

That is the exceptional lesson of this episode. Too often we seek to find favor and give honor to those who have more than us. But there are people who have fewer friends than we, less money, and less prestige. Those people especially need attention and recognition. We should try to achieve the level of perfection in human relationships which the boys on the ballfield at Yeshiva Darchei Torah achieved.

Because if children can do it, we adults should certainly be able to accomplish it as well.

The Rebbe's Matzohs

In an introduction to the classic *sefer, Nefesh Hachaim* by Rabbi Chaim of Volozhin (1749-1821), the author's son Reb Yitzchak writes, "[my father] would continuously rebuke me when he saw that I didn't get involved in alleviating someone else's pain. He constantly said to me, שֶׁזֶּה כָּל הָאָדָם, לֹא לְעַצְמוֹ נִבְרָא, *This is the essence of man, [he must realize] that he was not created merely for his own benefit."*

It is a credo that we should apply to our daily lives. Hashem has blessed each of us with different talents and resources and it is our obligation to use these gifts not merely for our own gain or glory, but for the benefit of others in *Klal Yisrael.*

Perhaps it is indicative that *Shemoneh Esrei,* in which we beseech Hashem for all our needs, is worded in the plural, הֲשִׁיבֵנוּ ... סְלַח לָנוּ ... רְפָאֵנוּ ... בָּרֵךְ עָלֵינוּ ... שְׁמַע קוֹלֵנוּ ..., *Bring us back ... Forgive us ... Heal us ... Bless us ... Hear our voice ...* Even in his own time of need, a Jew must always be sensitive to the needs of others.

In this light the following story is one of the most remarkable I have ever heard. The goodness and genuine concern it displays are classic. Furthermore, one is left marveling at the insight and foresight of great leaders in *Klal Yisrael.*

In April of 1945, shortly after the Second World War, the Skulener Rebbe, Rabbi Eliezer Zusia Portugal (1896-1982) was in Czernovitz, Bukovina (formerly Romania, but then governed by Russia). Jews who had survived the labor camps and ghettos of the Ukraine found themselves in Czernovitz, and almost all of them were weary, poverty stricken, and brokenhearted.

Pesach would begin in a few weeks and the Skulener Rebbe was concerned how anyone would have matzos for the upcoming *sedarim.* He asked one of his followers, Reb Fishel Kerpel, to go to a local farm and buy wheat, so that it could be milled into flour for matzos.

Painstakingly, Reb Fishel was able to get wheat and a millstone, and the Rebbe's *chassidim* began working feverishly to produce as many matzos as possible. Knowing that there were other chassidic Rebbeim in Czernovitz, he instructed his *chassidim* to seek them out and give them each three matzos for their *sedarim.*

Skulener *chassidim* dutifully followed their Rebbe's instructions and soon it became known that he was giving matzos free of charge to prominent Jews in the area. A week before *Pesach,* Reb Moshe Hager, the son of the Seret-Vizhnitzer Rebbe, Rabbi Baruch Hager (1895-1963), came to the Skulener. "My father sent me," said Reb Moshe. "He needs matzos for *Yom Tov.*"

"Why, of course," replied the Skulener Rebbe. "I am honored to give him matzos for the *seder.*"

The Rebbe took out three matzos and handed them to Reb Moshe.

Reb Moshe thanked the Rebbe profusely, but then added sheepishly, "My father said that he needs six matzos."

"How can I give you six matzos?" asked the Skulener Rebbe incredulously. "It is so difficult to bake matzah, there are so many people who need them and we simply don't have enough to give anyone six matzos."

"What can I say?" said Reb Moshe. "My father insisted that I can't leave the Rebbe's house until I get six matzos. It is matter of *kibbud av* (honoring a father)."

The Skulener Rebbe thought for a few moments and then said, "Then we have no choice. We will give you the six matzos, and please wish your father in my name a *chag kosher v'samei'ach*."

Reb Moshe was ecstatic as he brought the matzos home to his father Rav Baruch.

On *erev Pesach,* Reb Moshe came back to the Skulener Rebbe carrying three matzos. He presented the matzos to the Skulener Rebbe and said, "My father, the Seret-Vizhnitzer Rebbe, said that I should give these three matzos back to the Rebbe."

The Skulener Rebbe was startled. "Now you bring back the matzos? I wanted to give you only three matzos to begin with. Why did your father insist on having six? What is the point of bringing the matzos back now?"

Reb Moshe's reply was classic.

"My father said, the Skulener Rebbe is so kind and considerate that he will probably give out every last matzah and not even have any for himself. Therefore my father took an extra three matzos so that he should be able to give them back to you right before *Yom Tov,* so that you will have matzos for your own *seder*."

And those indeed were the matzos the Skulener Rebbe used at his *seder*!

While the Skulener Rebbe was thinking of everyone else, the Seret-Vizhnitzer Rebbe was thinking of him.

Two great hearts. Two great minds. מִי כְּעַמְּךָ יִשְׂרָאֵל, *Who is like Your people Israel!*

Pardoned

The following poignant story was dramatically told by Rabbi Chanoch Ehrentrau of London, at a gathering of thousands who came to the Binyanei Ha'umah convention center in

Jerusalem to hear lectures on *shemiras halashon* and interpersonal relationships.

The sad but illuminating story sheds light on a basic principle. We are not always aware of the aftermath of our words and deeds. At times words innocently spoken or deeds innocently done cause others pain and anguish. Thus, in dealing with others it behooves us to proceed with the utmost caution and consideration.

In the late 1800s, the town of Telshe, Lithuania, was looking for a rav to succeed Rabbi Yehoshua Heller (1814-1880), a disciple of Rav Yisrael Salanter, who was leaving to accept a position in Vilna. Among the many applicants for this prestigious post was the *av beis din* (head of the rabbinical court) of Telshe, Rabbi Abba Werner.

Reb Abba was convinced he would be chosen as rav in recognition of his service as *av beis din* for many years. To his consternation and chagrin, the community chose an "outsider," a noted *talmid chacham* who had never lived in Telshe, Rabbi Eliezer Gordon (1840-1910).

Rabbi Werner believed he could not remain in Telshe. Shortly after Rabbi Gordon was inaugurated, Reb Abba quietly left the community. He assumed a rabbinical position in Helsinki, Finland, and shortly afterward accepted a position as rabbi of the large Machzikei Hadas community in London.

❁ ❁ ❁

As part of his responsibilities, Rabbi Lazer Gordon oversaw the *shechitah* (kosher slaughter) in the city. Rabbi Mendel Rappaport, a veteran *shochet*, was taken aback when the new rabbbi interrogated him about his knowledge of the relevant laws. He felt that his integrity was being questioned, and after his interview he decided that he would never *shecht* again. Reb Mendel moved to London, where he became a very prosperous businessman.

The city of Telshe flourished and soon Rabbi Gordon became rosh yeshivah in Telshe. The yeshivah became a spiritual center of Lithuanian Jewry, as the yeshivah and its head gained worldwide recognition. (The Telshe Yeshivah in Cleveland, established in 1941, with its subsequent branches in Chicago and Riverdale, New York are extensions of the yeshivah in Europe.)

In 1910 there was a fire that destroyed the yeshivah building. There was anxiety and apprehension as the task of rebuilding the yeshivah seemed insurmountable. Rabbi Gordon undertook to travel to raise funds on behalf of the yeshivah, but his choice of destination surprised everyone. The yeshivah had always been supported by people in Russia, Poland, and the Ukraine, but the rosh yeshivah decided to break new ground and travel to England. Rabbi Gordon arrived in London and went to *daven* at the Machzikei Hadas Shul. As he walked in, he was immediately recognized by Rav Mendel Rappaport, now one of the most affluent *balabatim* in the synagogue. Reb Mendel greeted the renowned rabbi and after *Maariv* invited him to his home.

At his palatial home, Reb Mendel reminded Rabbi Gordon that he had been a *shochet* in Telshe, more than 20 years earlier. He recalled the questions the rabbi had asked when he first met with the *shochtim.* Suddenly Rabbi Gordon realized that Reb Mendel had harbored ill feelings towards him, for he had been offended at the time. "Reb Mendel," exclaimed the Telsher Rav, "I had no idea that you felt slighted. It was certainly not my intention to question your competence as a *shochet.* Please forgive me if I hurt you in any way. I am truly sorry."

"Of course, I forgive you," said Reb Mendel. "I had long forgotten about the matter. Truthfully, you see how it was destined that I come to England. I have *baruch Hashem* prospered here, and things have gone well for me. You can forget the matter and be assured that it is truly an honor to have you in my home."

Reb Mendel then suggested they visit the rav of Machzikei Hadas, Rabbi Abba Werner, to see how they could best raise funds for the Telshe Yeshivah.

When the two rabbis — each an outstanding *talmid chacham* in his own right — met, they immediately began an in-depth Torah conversation. Their breadth of sources was staggering. Rabbis Gordon and Werner reveled in each other's company.

After a while, they began to reminisce about their early days in Telshe. Soon it dawned on Rabbi Gordon that Rabbi Werner, too, had felt hurt years ago. "I thought you would come to ask if you should accept the position." said Reb Abba. "I had been the *av beis din* for many years and I thought they should offer me the position."

"I feel terrible," said Rabbi Gordon. "It was never my intention to hurt you. Reb Abba, I apologize for not coming to you before accepting the position. Please forgive me."

"Of course, I forgive you," said Rabbi Abba Werner. "I realized a while ago that it was the best thing that happened to me. I am very happy here in England, and I would never have left Telshe if that had not happened."

The two rabbis decided they would begin raising funds for the yeshivah right after Shabbos. However, on *Motzaei Shabbos,* after giving a passionate anguished speech about the dire financial straits of the yeshivah, Rav Lazer Gordon fell ill and tragically passed away.

Because of political disputes and tensions between countries, his body could not be returned to Telshe, and he was buried in England.

❁ ❁ ❁

"A while later," said Rabbi Ehrentrau to the huge gathering in Jerusalem, "someone in Telshe, speaking about their beloved rav, cited the verse, מֵה' מִצְעֲדֵי גָבֶר, וְאָדָם מַה יָּבִין דַּרְכּוֹ *A man's steps are from Heaven, but what does a man understand of his way? (Mishlei* 20:24).

Rabbi Lazer Gordon, they explained, was destined to go straight to *Gan Eden* after his death, but there was an impediment in the way. There were two people in the world who felt he had offended them. Hashem wished to remove this obstacle, so He planted the idea in the rav's mind to travel to England. There he met with those two men who felt offended. Once he was forgiven, the path was clear. He passed away with a clean slate

Confidentially Speaking

For many people, information is power and prestige. Frequently when a person has exclusive knowledge about an event or an individual, he is delighted to share this knowledge with others to parade his ability to get "inside information."

However *Chazal* (*Yoma* 4b) teach us restraint. Citing the first verse in *Vayikra,* where Hashem tells Moshe Rabbeinu to transmit to *Klal Yisrael* what He is about to tell him, וַיְדַבֵּר ה׳ אֵלָיו מֵאֹהֶל מוֹעֵד לֵאמֹר, *And Hashem spoke to him [Moshe] from the Tent of Meeting, saying* (*Vayikra* 1:1), *Chazal* deduce that people may not repeat anything they have been told unless they have specific permission to do so! Secret or no secret, we are forbidden to repeat it without authorization.

The following story illustrates restraint, respect, and revelation.

Among the most gentle and caring charities in Jewish neighborhoods today are the Tomchei Shabbos-type of organizations, which provide needy families with food every Shabbos.

Every week, with remarkable efficiency, a group of volunteers picks up Shabbos staples, such as grape juice, challah, fish, chicken, and cake from wholesalers who provide their food free or at cost. Another group of volunteers converges on the building where the provisions are stored. They package the food in cartons, depending on the size of the families. On Wednesday or Thursday, a third set of volunteers delivers the packages to the needy families.

Rarely do any of the volunteers know the identity of the recipients of these Tomchei Shabbos packages. Sometimes, the cartons are left at the front door of the recipient so that there is no face-to-face contact between the volunteer and a family member. In some cities, volunteers are permitted to deliver only to a part of town where they do not reside, so they will not recognize the address or the dweller. Maintaining the dignity of the needy is uppermost in any Tomchei Shabbos volunteer's mind.

In London, R' Yoel Becker* was in charge of fundraising for his local Tomchei Shabbos operation. Two nights a week he visited potential donors. One night he was at the home of R' Zev Kringold* who was known in the past for his charitable donations.

After some small talk, R' Yoel came to the point. "I am sure you know about Tomchei Shabbos," he said to R' Zev. "We are in desperate need of funds and we need your help."

R' Zev didn't question R' Yoel as many others did about the budget, the deficit, and how efficiently the money was spent. "I will give you 100 pounds (the equivalent, at the time, to $180) on the condition that you tell me who receives the food packages."

R' Yoel was surprised. "R' Zev, you know I can't do that," he said. "We never reveal the names of people getting packages. It is strictly confidential."

"Look," said R' Zev, "it is important to me to know that I am helping a specific individual. It makes me feel that I am truly relieving the burden of a fellow Jew." Seeing that R' Yoel was not moved by his plea, R' Zev said, "I will double my donation. I'll even give you 400 pounds!"

"I'm sorry," said R' Yoel. "I won't do it. I have never revealed a name and I won't do it now."

"Look," said R' Zev, getting exasperated. "Make this one time an exception and I'll give you 1,000 pounds! I want to feel connected with the poor family and this way I will."

R' Yoel realized it was hopeless. "R' Zev," he said, "if you gave me 5,000 pounds, I wouldn't reveal who is getting your package or any other package. It's our policy and we will never change it as long as I am in charge."

Suddenly, R' Zev put his hands to his face and wept. "R' Yoel, please put me on your list," he sobbed. "People don't realize that I no longer have the money I once had. My family and I are destitute. I am out of work and struggling every day. I was only testing you. I was ashamed to call you to be put on the Tomchei

---

* Name has been changed.

Shabbos list because I feared that others would find out I was getting packages. I was trying to see if there was any way under any circumstances that you would reveal your recipients — but now that I see that you wouldn't. Please make sure that I am on your list."

> Maintaining another person's dignity is of paramount importance; and it's not always what you do say, sometimes it's what you don't say.

Challenged

It was a freezing night in Spring Valley, New York and a crowd had gathered in a large auditorium to hear a talk I was to give on the topic, "The Carousel of Life — Our Ups and Downs in Daily Living."

As I walked down the aisle toward the podium, I saw a girl in a wheelchair, near the front of the hall. From a distance it appeared she was in her early teens. It occurred to me it must have been diffcult for her to come to the auditorium that night, as she had to brave the cold weather, be brought in a special van, and be wheeled through a crowd of a few hundred people. As I reached her, I stopped for a moment, bent over and said, "Thank you for coming tonight, I hope you enjoy the talk."

She turned to look at me and my heart fell. I was totally unprepared for what I saw. The girl had cerebral palsy and had no control of her body movements. She was constantly swaying, her head moving from right to left, but she was smiling buoyantly. She was saying something to me, but it was impossible for me to understand her in her high-pitched excitable voice. I felt helpless and humbled. A girl sitting next to her said, "I am her sister, she is saying 'thank you'. She's telling you 'thank you' for coming over to her."

"No," I replied, "it is I who should be saying 'thank you' to her for coming on this very cold night."

I was rattled from this short unexpected encounter. I resumed walking to the dais where I would be introduced as the evening's speaker. As I sat listening to the master of ceremonies setting the tone for the evening, someone handed me a sealed envelope. She indicated that it came from the girl in the wheelchair.

The letter was startling and unforgettable.

I was told later that the girl in the wheelchair had dictated the letter to her sister. I share the letter with you, for there is much to be learned from her words.

> Dear Rabbi Krohn,
>
> Let me introduce myself. My name is Rivka Baila. I'm twenty years old. Unfortunately I'm confined to a wheelchair. Until just about a year ago, everyone but my close family thought I was a 'dummy.' Finally after nineteen years of misery, a psychologist named Dr. Sheenan let it be known (through a report of course) that I am "an intelligent lady!"
>
> I'm deeply grateful to you, Rabbi Krohn, for providing me with stimulating and inspiring listening material. I enjoy all your tapes and listen to them many times over. My favorite story is about the bus driver with the handicapped mind. (This story dealt with a bus driver who at first tried to refuse a mother and her son who was in a wheelchair, to board his bus because it did not have an automated lift. Passengers humiliated the driver until he relented. See "Patience and Patients," *Along the Maggid's Journey* p. 79.)
>
> Perhaps you can strengthen this most important point with my letter. People in wheelchairs are still people and should be treated that way. *Those of us who cannot speak know so much more because we spend our time listening.* If you have nothing nice to say, go elsewhere. DON'T STARE! Just smile and say hello — nothing more. That shouldn't pose much of a problem. Then leave if you must.

In closing, do to others as you'd like them to do to you. Treat *everyone* well like a human being. We were also created with a *tzellem Elokim.*

Thank you for listening to me.

Sincerely,
Rivka Baila

Rivka Baila also sent a copy of a letter she had sent to her classmates. This is part of it:

> Dearest eleventh graders,
>
> Hi, my name is Rivka Baila. Most of you smile at me when you see me. Some of you ignore me and stare when you think I don't see you. Don't think I don't see you staring at me like I'm nuts.
>
> Hashem didn't give me the ability to do all the things you can, but is that a valid reason for you to stare? Why don't you thank Hashem for being able to do all the things you do instead of pitying me? I saw you all perform in the play. How I would love to sing like you. I'm not trying to complain, I just want you to understand me.

When we hear or see a girl like Rivka Baila our hearts go out to her. We visualize her challenge, so we feel her pain.

We should however know, that there are many people in "emotional wheelchairs." They feel impeded, restrained, and hampered because they don't have the friends, the funds, the family or the talents that others have. Some of those people are embarrassed by their situation, which is beyond their control.

Those who are blessed with either family, or funds, or friends or talent have an obligation to pay attention, and give time and encouragement to those that have less than they do. It is more important to attend *their simchas* and to invite *them* for Shabbos than the people who have been blessed with more resources.

Everyone wants to be friendly with the "haves" — but our challenge is to be friendly with the "have-nots."

A Jerusalem Triangle

Chazal depict the essence of Jewish character with three radiant attributes. We are רַחֲמָנִים בַּיְישָׁנִין וְגוֹמְלֵי חֲסָדִים, *merciful, modest, and benevolent* (see *Yevamos* 69a). When Jews conduct themselves with these noble traits, their actions are truly inspirational. The following story is a case in point.

Rav Chaim Goldberg of Jerusalem is one of the most trusted men in Israel. Over the last 20 years, Jews around the world have given him many millions of charity dollars to distribute at his discretion to needy families in Israel. Depending on the case, he will provide furniture and household supplies, hire household help, deliver food, pay grocers and butchers, or give cash.

Together with his partner in good deeds, R' Dovid Leib Cohen, R' Chaim investigates requests for help that are brought to his attention, and evaluates their veracity and degree of need. Not until he is confident that the claimed dire situation is indeed authetic will he provide help. Among Jerusalem's many custodians of charity funds, R' Chaim has achieved an awesome reputation as a judge of character and evaluation of the genuineness of claims for help. He receives calls every day from rabbis and social workers beseeching him to help families or indivuals.

One Friday morning I accompanied R' Chaim and R' Dovid Leib to the homes of some of the people he was helping. In order not to embarrass anyone, I helped deliver items to the families, rather than appear as an observer of their sorry state. Their reverence and gratitude to the two benefactors was extraordinary. For one family, he provided new beds for the children, for another he had new closets built, for a third he supplied a refrigerator and clothes for their new infant, and for a fourth family, living in a two-room apartment that had been converted from a bomb shelter, he provided money for a new ceiling and floor. It was startling and frightening to witness such squalor and destitution in the center of Jerusalem.

R′ Chaim dispenses more than money and things. He counsels and advises the families as well. To a very responsible 15-year-old orphaned girl, he suggested a particular yeshivah for her younger brother and worked out an affordable schedule of tuition payments. To a divorced woman, he recommended a strategy of how to find an apartment in a more suitable neighborhood. To a troubled young man, he proposed professional help for marital problems. With a girls dormitory supervisor, he discussed an approach to a despondent 16-year-old who had been abandoned by her mentally ill parents. He assured each one of these people that he would return.

One of the most heartening episodes R′ Chaim was ever involved in took place in the winter of 1992. Moshe and Miriam Gutstein,* both from poverty-stricken families, had been married a few years, but had not yet been blessed with children. Moshe was learning in a Jerusalem kollel which provided a small income and Miriam, who had no professional skills, was unemployed. R′ Chaim was told about their financial plight and tried to give them money, but they refused it, so he devised a plan to help them.

In the Bucharian section of Jerusalem, there was another couple, Binyamin and Brachah Kamchi,* who lived in very cramped quarters with their seven children. Brachah had been sick and found it difficult to go to work, and Binyamin's menial job could not provide adequate funds for his family. R′ Chaim knew the Kamchis needed money to pay for household help, but he knew that they, like the Gutsteins, would refuse to take it.

One day, R′ Chaim visited the Kamchis and told them about the young Gutsteins and their financial hardship. "I have a way we can help them," R′ Chaim said. "I will give you money every

* Name has been changed

week to hire Mrs. Gutstein as an *ozeret* (domestic). If she is employed she won't feel bad about taking money that she rightfully earned." In this way, R' Chaim would be helping both families, while safeguarding their self-respect.

Mrs. Gutstein accept the "job" and soon became very attached to the Kamchi children. She was paid every Friday, for R' Chaim would come to the Kamchi home during the week and provide the money for the *ozeret*.

After eight months, the Gutsteins called R' Chaim and asked if he could come to their home. When he arrived and sat in their small kitchen, Moshe Gutstein began. "I am very grateful to you for finding a job for my wife. The money has been helpful and the Kamchis are wonderful to her. They are very respectful, never demanding, and always pay on time."

"However," continued Mrs. Gutstein, "as one who comes in to their home a few times a week, I couldn't help but notice their tremendous poverty. Their wonderful children don't always have enough food to eat. We have not yet been blessed with children, so we don't have their expenses. I have saved some of my earnings and would like to give it to them, but I know that Mrs. Kamchi will not take it from me. Rabbi Goldberg, maybe you can find a way to give her this money. I think she would take it from you."

R' Chaim was astounded. The Kamchis had been only too happy to help the Gutsteins and now the Gutsteins were in turn anxious to help the Kamchis. And of course, R' Chaim who had orchestrated the whole scheme had helped both of them.

Indeed, מִי כְּעַמְּךָ יִשְׂרָאֵל, *Who is like Your people Israel!*

A Savings Account

In April 1944, 17-year-old Beru (Yissachar Dov) Stern and his family were forcibly seized by the invading Nazis from their affluent home in Ungvar, Hungary and taken to Auschwitz-Birkenau. There, the family suffered terrible ordeals of slave labor and persecution, and eventually Beru's parents and three of his brothers were sent to the gas chambers. Beru, his younger brother Chaim Asher, and their sister Ahuvah managed to survive. The Stern family had been very wealthy before the war, but after the liberation, the children were penniless.

Beru wanted to go to Palestine after the war, but he was ill with tuberculosis and was sent to a hospital in Davos, Switzerland for treatment. Not having proper travel documents, he had no choice but to remain in Switzerland, where he painstakingly began to rebuild his life. Ultimately he moved to London and then to New York. Finally in 1953, he was able to make his long-awaited first trip to Israel.

When Beru arrived in Jerusalem, he made his way to the old Battei Ungarin neighborhood, in the Meah Shearim section of Jerusalem. He went directly to the home of the impoverished Reb Chaztkel Leifer* and his family, to whom his father, Reb Moshe Stern, had sent money for many years. He knocked on the door and introduced himself. "I am Beru Stern, the son of Moshe Stern from Ungvar."

The door flew open and Reb Chatzkel came out and embraced Beru. "I am so glad to meet you," said the elderly Reb Chatzkel. "I thank the *Ribono Shel Olam* that my family and I have finally merited to have a member of Reb Moshe Stern's family in our home."

Beru was offered cake and tea, but he was uncomfortable eating in this poor and unadorned apartment. He felt that any morsel of food he ate would come off the plates of the Leifer family.

"Your father was such a special person," said Reb Chatzkel, in sadness and reverence. "Every *Rosh Hashanah* he would send us enough money to last us until *Pesach* and every *Pesach* he would send us enough money to cover us until *Rosh Hashanah*. But that alone was not the only thing that made him so exceptional. He used to write us the most beautiful letters, in a magnificent handwriting. He would quote verses of the Torah and teachings of our Sages to encourage and inspire us. By the time we would finish

---

* Name has been changed

reading his letter, we felt that *we* were doing *him* a great favor by accepting the money, when really *he* was doing *us* the favor."

Beru was in awe. He hadn't known about the letters, and he was deeply moved to hear these accolades about his father. "Is it possible that you still have some of those letters?" asked Beru slowly. "I would love to see my father's handwriting again. We have nothing from him. No correspondence, no possessions, no *sefarim*. Nothing."

Beru's voice trailed off. He cried as he remembered his parents. His family and their belongings had been totally annihilated, but maybe there was something here that he could recover and show his brother and sister.

"I am sure we still have some of those letters," said Reb Chatzkel. "Come back in a few days and meanwhile I'll try to find them."

Three days later, Beru came back and Reb Chatzkel gave him three letters. Overwhelmed with joy, Beru was speechless. He fingered the letters and read and studied each exquisite line. Indeed, his father had offered deeply sensitive encouragement and the words, a combination of Torah and Talmud, were masterpieces.

"You can have them," said Reb Chatzkel. "We are happy and honored to give them to you."

Suddenly it occurred to Beru that his father had written these letters not on personal stationery but on his business letterhead! This could be the proof he needed that his father had owned this former lucrative liquor distilling and distribution company. Beru had been trying to get reparations money from the Germans after the war, but they had denied him any funds. These letters could be the proof he needed that his father had owned a business before the war.

After a while, Beru noticed another incredible thing. For reasons that he could not understand, the business stationery contained the account number of the bank accounts his father's business held in various Hungarian banks.

With the help of lawyers and the proper authorities, Beru, by virtue of these letters and the information they contained, was able to procure tens of thousands of dollars for himself and his family. Eventually he used part of the money to build a *shul* in Jerusalem.

The prophet Hoshea exclaimed: זִרְעוּ לָכֶם לִצְדָקָה, קִצְרוּ לְפִי חֶסֶד, *Sow for yourselves charity, so that you will reap according to your kindness (Hoshea* 10:12). It is man who sows but it is Hashem who delivers the harvest. The harvest of Rav Moshe Stern's benevolence, in words and in deeds, was delayed so that it appeared in a different country, for a different generation. But it was a harvest that has caused his children and grandchildren to blossom and thrive until this very day.

Content or Contentious

Zalman and Rivkah Rothberg* were married for more than 15 years. They had eight children and Rivkah was expecting their ninth. The two of them got along quite well, but there was one difference between them that often strained their relationship.

Zalman was a meticulous type of person and Rivkah was more indifferent to order, and at times lackadaisical. When Zalman was upset that things were not put away tidily, Rivkah would smile and say gently in Hebrew, זֶה לֹא חָשׁוּב, *"Zeh lo chashuv* (It's not that important)."

It was her favorite expression and she used it often. If Zalman was ready on time and she was late, she would smile and say softly, זֶה לֹא חָשׁוּב, *"Zeh lo chashuv."* Indeed, her relaxed attitude to life resolved many problems and defused many tense moments. Still, there were times when Zalman felt exasperated.

One summer Thursday afternoon, when Rivkah and the children were in their bungalow colony in the Catskills, she called Zalman in the city and asked him to bring up a new checkbook,

* Name has been changed

because she had run out of checks. When they spoke on Friday, she reminded him not to forget the checkbook.

He immediately put a new checkbook into one of the bright orange shopping bags he was going to bring to the family. On Friday afternoon, as soon as he arrived in the bungalow, he gave her the bag with the checkbook in it.

On Shabbos morning, he noticed that Rivka had hung the shopping bag on the post of a crib in their bedroom — and the checkbook was still in it!

Zalman was upset. Rivkah had called him twice about the checkbook. He did exactly as she asked, but she hadn't even taken it out of the bag. Even worse, she just hung it in a place where it did not belong, certainly not over Shabbos!

He didn't say anything, because he didn't want to spoil the tranquility of Shabbos with a complaint. Besides, she would probably ignore his criticism and gently say, "*Zeh lo chashuv* (It's not that important)."

After Shabbos he returned to the city for a week of work and the next Friday he came back again to the bungalow. To his utter dismay the bag was still hanging from the post on the crib in their room and the checkbook was still in it, untouched!

"It obviously could not have been such an emergency," he thought to himself, "so why was she in such a rush that I bring her the checks in the first place?"

Once again he did not say anything. Inwardly, though, he was angry. Sunday afternoon he returned to the city and began his regular weekday routine. Two days later he received a frantic call from Rivkah's friend and neighbor in the bungalow colony. Rivkah had been rushed to the hospital. There were severe complications in her pregnancy, and the best doctors available were attending her.

Frantically, Zalman left his office and drove up to the Catskills, but by the time he arrived at the hospital, it was too late. Rivkah had died in childbirth.

Zalman was crushed.

Shocked friends and family who had gathered at the hospital accompanied him back to the bungalow. When he came into his room, the first thing he saw was the orange shopping bag hanging on the crib post with the checkbook still in it. As tears rolled down his cheeks he removed the checkbook from the bag and put it in his pocket.

That night he wrote the first check from that book. It was for the *Chevra Kadisha* (Burial society). The next day he wrote the second check. It was for the funeral.

After the *shivah,* Zalman took the empty shopping bag and hung it in his closet. And on the outside of the bag he wrote three words — זֶה לֹא חָשׁוּב (*Zeh lo chashuv).*

He kept it there for months.

Every time he saw it, he thought, "Wasn't she right? Weren't those trivialities really insignificant? Were they really worth quarreling about?"

The lesson that he learned in death, we should learn in life. Before it's too late.

Most of the arguments we are involved in — be it in the home, the office, in school, in *shul* or at the workplace — begin with petty things that are truly not worth arguing about.

One biting comment leads to another and soon a small flicker of contention grows into a conflagration of rancor and bitter discords. At times the fire can be extinguished — but sadly, at times hatred rages until it is totally out of control.

The next time we feel an argument brewing we should ask ourselves: Is this a matter for which one could rightfully say, *"Zeh lo chashuv"?*

An Award-Winning Performance

Rabbi Zevi Trenk, *menahel* of Mesivta Chaim Shlomo in Far Rockaway, is an effervescent, magnanimous person whose love for fellow Jews knows no bounds. Reb Zevi does not come home directly from *davening* on Shabbos morning. Instead he makes the rounds of *shuls* in Flatbush, where he lives, gathering people who need a Shabbos meal. It is not unusual for 20 guests to be seated at his table. His *hachnasas orchim* (hospitality) is legendary, as Jews of all ages are welcome in his home.

I once heard that he went to a clothing store to buy a raincoat. When the proprietor asked him what size he needed, he replied, "I need all sizes."

"All sizes?" the proprietor asked in surprise.

"Yes," Reb Zevi said, "My Shabbos guests are all sizes. Some are tall, some are short, some are heavy, some are thin. If they get stuck at my house because of a sudden downpour, how will they get home? That's why I need all sizes of raincoats."

I could not believe this story, so I called his wife, Mrs. Esther Trenk and asked if the story was true. She replied, "I don't know if it's true, but I can tell you we are out of size 42!"

The following story could happen only with Reb Zevi, but there is much we can learn from it.

One night at a wedding, his wife offered an elderly lady a ride home. In the car, the lady sighed, "My granddaughter had such a difficult day in school today and it's a real shame."

"What happened?" the Trenks asked.

"Her first-grade class had a *Siddur* party. Every girl was given a new *Siddur*, and a number of children who had been asked to bring in candies were told to give them out to the class. The teacher had given those children a letter to take home which stated the specific *hashgachos* (kosher certifications) that are accepted by the school.

"Now, either my granddaughter didn't give the letter to her mother or maybe her mother didn't read the letter carefully, but be it as it may, my granddaughter brought in candies that were not acceptable to the teacher. So instead of giving candies to all the children in the class as the other children did, my granddaughter had to remain in her seat where she sat and cried.

"I feel so bad for her," the grandmother continued. "The day a girl gets her first *Siddur* should be a happy, memorable day and now she will always associate her new *Siddur* with being sad and unhappy."

As a rebbi and principal, Rabbi Trenk understood that the teacher could not have allowed the child to give out her candies. A teacher cannot act against school policy. Besides, the girl wasn't the only child sitting in her seat; only a few children were giving out candies, while the rest of the class remained seated. Still, Rabbi Trenk felt bad for the grandmother and the little girl.

Rabbi Trenk asked the grandmother about the girl, her family, and her school.

The next evening Rabbi Trenk called the family and asked to speak to the little girl. When the surprised mother put her child on the phone, Rabbi Trenk in his inimitable excited voice asked, "Is this Adina Kramer* from the first grade of the Bais Faige school*?"

When the little girl replied shyly that indeed she was Adina Kramer, Rabbi Trenk said, "Hello, my name is Rabbi Trenk and I am from Torah Umesorah, the organization that helps yeshivos, Bais Yaakovs, and day schools across America.

"I'm calling to tell you that a raffle was held where the names of all the children who had *Siddur* parties this year were placed in a huge bowl to see who would win a very special *Siddur* with their name printed on it. And believe it or not, you won! So watch the mail in a few days, because you will be getting a special package."

The little girl could hardly utter the words, "Thank you," because she was so overwhelmed. A few days later she received a beautiful leather-bound *Siddur* with her name embossed in gold from Rabbi Trenk, who inscribed it with a moving message.

Two weeks later, Rabbi Trenk received a heartwarming letter in the mail from the family accompanied with a beautiful picture of Adina Kramer proudly holding her new *Siddur* with a bright smile on her face.

---

* Name has been changed

How would we have reacted if we heard the story from the grandmother? At most we might have felt bad for a moment and then forgotten about the incident.

Reb Zevi's action teaches that the dictum נוֹשֵׂא בְעֹל עִם חֲבֵרוֹ, *sharing the burden of a fellow Jew (Avos* 6:6), and feeling their pain, refers to the pain of all Jews, even little children.

Of Noble Character

Rabbi Meir Chodosh (1898-1989) served as the *Mashgiach* in Yeshivas Chevron for more than 50 years, and then in Yeshivas Ohr Elchonon in Jerusalem, where his son Rabbi Moshe is Rosh Yeshivah. Based on the Slabodka style of *mussar,* which accentuated *gadlus ha'adam* (the greatness of man), Rabbi Chodosh's *shmuessen* (ethical discourses) were always uplifting, as he would speak of an individual's infinite potential. He would exhort his students to strive for heights in Torah and *middos* (good character traits), for he believed that with concerted effort every person could achieve greatness.

In 1981, to usher in the *Aseres Yemei Teshuvah* (Ten Days of Repentance, from *Rosh Hashanah* to *Yom Kippur*), Rabbi Chodosh delivered a *shmuess* on the subject of *bein adam lachaveiro,* the relationship of man to his fellow man, and told the following story. I thank Rabbi Moshe Chodosh for sharing it with me.

In the early 1900s, Feivel Wainholtz* was a student of Rabbi Isser Zalman Meltzer's (1870-1953) yeshivah in Slutzk, Russia. Feivel was an exceptional young man and considered a "prize" for marriage. When a prominent gentleman from Charkov, in Ukraine, came to Reb Isser Zalman to seek a partner in marriage for his very special daughter, the Rosh Yeshivah suggested Feivel.

* Name has been changed.

Shortly afterwards, Feivel and the young lady were engaged. However there was a young man in the yeshivah who was jealous of Feivel's capabilities and reputation. When this *shidduch* was announced, he raged with envy. Smitten with resentment, he spread sinister rumors about Feivel. None of them were ever substantiated, but the harm was done: the esteemed family from Charkov broke the engagement, and Feivel was devastated.

Soon afterwards, World War I erupted and the yeshivah in Slutzk had to relocate. The yeshivah was in turmoil as young men tried desperately not to be drafted. Feivel could not avoid the draft and was inducted in the army. One thing after another went wrong, and he became increasingly discouraged and depressed with each passing day.

After the war, he joined the Yeshivas Knesses Yisrael, the famous yeshivah of Slabodka, which had temporarily relocated to White Russia, first to Minsk and then, in 1916, to Kremenchug. By that time, Feivel was an "older *bachur*" and the possibility of marriage was becoming more remote.

The *Mashgiach* at the time in the Slabodka yeshivah was Rabbi Nosson Tzvi Finkel (1849-1927), who was known as the *Alter* (Elder) of Slabodka. The term *Alter* had nothing to do with age; rather, it was used as a term of respect and awe of one who gave spiritual guidance. Rabbi Finkel was known as the *Alter* from his early 30s.

One day in 1919, the *Alter* received a startling letter. The writer introduced himself and then wrote, "A young man Feivel Wainholtz is now in your yeshivah. Many years ago when we were both learning in Slutzk, I did terrible things that caused his engagement to be broken. The rumors that I spread about him were untrue and regrettably caused great harm. I feel terribly guilty for what I did. I know that the *Rambam (Hilchos Teshuvah* 2:9) writes that one cannot get atonement for transgressions committed against a fellow man until he has asked for forgiveness and received it. I want to ask Feivel for forgiveness but I am too embarrassed to approach him personally."

The writer appealed to the *Alter* to approach Feivel in his name and explain how sorry he was and to ask for forgiveness.

The *Alter*, who was extremely perceptive and an exceptional judge of character, felt sure that the writer was sincerely remorseful. That evening the *Alter* took Feivel aside and said, "I understand that years ago, you were engaged to be married."

"Yes," said Feivel, surprised that the subject was being brought up after so many years, "but shortly afterwards everything fell apart."

The *Alter* told Feivel about the letter he received and how sorry the rumormonger was. "He realizes that your *shidduch* was broken because of him, so he is embarrassed to speak to you in person. He requested that I ask you in his name for forgiveness."

Feivel thought for a moment and said, "I realize that the *shidduch* was not destined for me, anyway. Hashem has His ways and I am convinced that if the *shidduch* had not been broken because of the rumors, then it would have been broken some other way. Yes, you can tell the fellow that I forgive him."

The *Alter* wanted to be sure that Feivel was sincere. "But how can you forgive that person, when he did something so terrible to you?" asked the *Alter.*

"It is so many years later," said Feivel. "I have forgotten about the incident and I have gone on with my life. Everything is *b'hashgachah* (by Divine Providence)."

The *Alter* kissed Feivel on his forehead and then bowed his head towards Feivel and said, "Please bless me."

Feivel was startled. Was the *Alter* serious or was this some kind of joke?

The *Alter* repeated himself. "Feivel, please bless me."

When Feivel did not respond, the *Alter* said, "*Chazal* teach, כָּל הַמַּעֲבִיר עַל מִדּוֹתָיו מַעֲבִירִין לוֹ עַל כָּל פְּשָׁעָיו, *Anyone who disregards [his right to] retribution, [Hashem] disregards his transgressions* (*Rosh Hashanah* 17a). You could rightfully have hated that fellow, but instead you forgave him. Hashem has thus forgiven your sins and you are now a genuine *tzaddik*. I would like to have a blessing from a genuine *tzaddik*."

Feivel had no choice but to bless the *Alter.*

❁ ❁ ❁

"Imagine the level one reaches when he becomes a מַעֲבִיר עַל מִדּוֹתָיו, willing to overlook the wrong done to him," said Rabbi Meir Chodosh. "The *Alter* took *Chazal's* words literally and considered Feivel a *tzaddik.* Hence as we begin to work on our *middos* during the *Aseres Yemei Teshuvah,* we must strive towards that goal of becoming a מַעֲבִיר עַל מִדּוֹתָיו.

> Consider, though, the pedagogical genius of the *Alter*. Could there have possibly been a better way to build the self-esteem and the self-confidence of Feivel than by making him feel so genuinely important that only he could rightfully bless the *Alter*? Noble indeed.

In Perfect Harmony

In 1933, Isser Rockove was one of the first *talmidim* of Yeshivah Rabbeinu Yisroel Meir HaKohen (Chofetz Chaim), which opened on Bedford Avenue in Williamsburgh, Brooklyn. The Rosh Yeshivah, Rabbi Dovid Leibowitz (1890-1941), a renowned *talmid chacham* and grandson of the Chofetz Chaim's brother, R' Aaron, was a close *talmid* of his great-uncle and had assisted in the preparation of *Hilchos Succah* in the *Mishnah Berurah.*

Reb Dovid was highly regarded by European *talmidei chachamim,* who remembered him from his youthful days in the Chofetz Chaim's yeshivah in Radin, where he studied from the age of 13 to 18, and from the impression he made as one of the outstanding scholars in the great Slabodka Yeshivah. Thus, when they came to America, many of them would visit him.

In October 1937, Rabbi Elchonon Wasserman (1875-1941), the Rosh Yeshivah of Baranovich, came to America to raise funds for his yeshivah, which was in terrible financial straits. He stayed in the United States until March 1939 and during that period published his pamphlet, *Ikvesa Dimeshicha* (*Epoch of the Messiah*). Reb Elchonon spent *Rosh Hashanah* 1938, in Williamsburgh, *davening* in the Chofetz Chaim Yeshivah with his younger colleague, Rabbi Dovid Leibowitz.

On the first day of *Rosh Hashanah,* after *davening,* as the *talmidim* were saying, "Good *Yom Tov,*" to their Rosh Yeshivah, Isser Rockove heard Reb Elchonon say to Reb Dovid, who was a *Kohain,* "Good *Yom Tov,* Reb Dovid. I think that your singing during *Bircas Kohanim* (Priestly Blessing) was a bit too lengthy. It may have been a *hefsek* (an interruption). (*Kohanim* usually sing a tune before pronouncing the third (וְיִשְׁמְרֶךָ), eighth (וִיחֻנֶּךָּ), and fifteenth (שָׁלוֹם) words of *Bircas Kohanim.)*

"No," replied Reb Dovid. "I consider all of the singing to be part of *Bircas Kohanim,* so it was all one continuous unit."

That afternoon, Isser Rockove went to visit Reb Dovid where a discussion ensued regarding Reb Elchonon's comment. Rav Dovid took out a *Mishnah Berurah* and showed his *talmidim* the *Ramah* in *Orach Chaim* (128:26) which states: *Now that the custom is for Kohanim to extend their singing* ... and the *Ramah* (ibid. 128:45) which states: וְנוֹהֲגִין שֶׁמַּאֲרִיכִין בְּנִיגּוּן (*it is customary to prolong the singing) (see also Mishnah Berurah* note 172).

Obviously Reb Dovid had been correct. Yet, the next morning, Reb Dovid and all the *Kohanim,* per his instruction, sang briefly.[1]

After the *davening,* when Isser Rockove went to greet Reb Dovid he asked him, "I thought you showed us yesterday that the Kohanim may sing at length."

"I shortened the singing for the *kovod* (honor) of Reb Elchonon," replied Reb Dovid.

A moment later Reb Elchonon approached Reb Dovid and said, "Good Yom-Tov Reb Dovid, I checked the halachah and saw that you were correct."

Honesty and integrity in Torah compelled Reb Elchonon to concede the truth. And yet, Rav Dovid, though he knew he was right, felt it appropriate to act in accordance with Rav Elchonon's wishes.

> Two *gedolim* — one goal. Correctness and consideration — in consonance with Torah and *mussar.*

1. Rav Dovid's abbreviated singing was not against Halachah for as long as the assembled had time to recite the intermediate supplication prayers, it was sufficient.

Melody Match

The Sages (*Sotah* 47a) refer to Yosi ben Yoezer and Yosi Ben Yehudah as אֶשְׁכּוֹלוֹת, *grape clusters,* an acronym for אִישׁ שֶׁהַכֹּל בּוֹ, *a man with many skills,* an accolade for a multitalented and multifaceted individual. Rabbi Aaron Yeshayah Shapiro (1904-1981), a rosh yeshivah in Yeshivah Torah Vodaath for more than 40 years, could rightfully be referred to as a man who possessed a cluster of talents.

In the 1920s, Rabbi Shimon Shkop (1860-1939), the Rosh Yeshivah in Grodno, wanted to publish his *Shaarei Yosher,* the classic collection of his *chiddushim* (innovative Torah thoughts), and he wanted a young *talmid chacham* who could understand them and write them with clarity and lucidity. Aaron Yeshayah, learning in the Mirrer Yeshivah, under Rabbi Lazer Yudel Finkel, was selected for the task. He spent two years "on loan" in Grodno with Reb Shimon, working diligently and meticulously. When *Shaarei Yosher* was published, Reb Shimon, in the introduction, was effusive in praise for Aaron Yeshayah's editorial work. The *sefer* is still studied in yeshivos around the world.

Rabbi Yerucham Levovitz (1874-1936), the famed *mashgiach* of Mir, always had his beloved Aaron Yeshayah standing directly in front of him when he delivered his renowned *mussar* discourses. If a doubt arose as to the exact wording or the location of a verse in the Torah, Rav Yerucham would say, "Let anyone here give us the *trup* (the cantillation notes) for the words and Aaron Yeshayah will tell us where it is." He was a master *baal korei* and he knew the entire Torah virtually by heart. Reb Yerucham once said, "When I read my *shmuessen* as Aaron Yeshayah wrote them, I can even visualize my *knaitch* (the swoop for emphasis) with the finger!"

As a *baal tefillah,* Reb Aaron Yeshayah was legendary. Often, *talmidim* who had long since left Torah Vodaath would come back to the *beis midrash* on *Asarah b'Teves,* when he had *yahrtzeit,* to hear him read the Torah and *Haftarah.*

His ancestors were Stoliner *chassidim,* and when Reb Aaron Yeshayah lived in Williamsburgh, Brooklyn, he enjoyed a special relationship to the Stoliner Rebbe, Rabbi Yochanan Perlow (1900-1956). Rabbi Shapiro thus felt at home with those who embodied Torah study, *mussar,* and chassidism.

At a wedding in the town of Mir, Aaron Yeshayah was asked to sing a *niggun* at the *chassan's tisch* (groom's reception) before the *chupah.*

His fine baritone was so stirring that everyone was entranced by his musicality and sensitivity to the meaning of the words in the song עַל זאת. After the *chupah,* as he was on line to wash for the meal, he felt a tug at his sleeve. When he turned around, he was startled that it was the great Rosh Yeshivah of Kaminetz, Rabbi Boruch Ber Leibowitz (1870-1941).

"Are you the *bachur* who sang that beautiful *niggun* at the *chassan's tisch*?" asked Reb Boruch Ber.

"Yes," replied Aaron Yeshayah, a bit embarrassed.

"Can I ask you a favor?" Reb Boruch Ber said.

"Yes, of course," replied the surprised Aaron Yeshayah.

"Please come to one of the side rooms and teach me that *niggun,*" Reb Boruch Ber requested.

Reb Boruch Ber himself had a beautiful voice and had composed numerous *niggunim,* and his appreciation for *neginah* was well known. A *bachur* had once come to Kaminetz to enroll in the yeshivah, but the *mashgiach* told him there was no room, and he would have to look elsewhere. His friends knew that he had a beautiful voice, so they advised him to sit in the back of the *beis midrash* where Rav Boruch Ber would pace back and forth as he prepared his *shiur.* "Sing as you are learning," they advised, "and the Rosh Yeshivah will surely notice you."

The *bachur* did as he was advised, and shortly afterwards he felt a tap on his shoulder. He turned to see that it was Rav Boruch Ber who smiled at him and said, "*Bleibt in der yeshivah* (remain in the yeshivah.)"

Aaron Yeshayah followed Reb Boruch Ber to a small room. They both sat down and Aaron Yeshayah tried to overcome his embarrassment and sang עַל זֹאת as best as he could, to Reb Boruch Ber's delight.

When he finished, Reb Boruch Ber said, "Would you mind listening to me sing it? I would like to see if I learned it properly."

Aaron Yeshayah was incredulous. How could Reb Boruch Ber even attempt to sing it back to him? It was a long, complex song, and he had heard it only twice. Aaron Yeshayah said, "Whatever the Rosh Yeshiva wants."

Reb Boruch Ber sang the *niggun* exactly as Aaron Yeshayah had, and perhaps with even more feeling. Aaron Yeshayah was amazed at how a person could retain a melody so quickly and so flawlessly. When the Rosh Yeshivah finished, Aaron Yeshayah smiled his approval and told the Rosh Yeshivah that he had sung it exactly as it was meant to be sung.

Aaron Yeshayah began to get up. "No, you cannot leave now," protested Reb Boruch Ber. *"Ich vill nisht bleiben a baal chov* (I don't wish to remain obligated). You taught me a *niggun,* now I will teach you a *niggun."*

With that, the world-renowned Rosh Yeshivah of Kaminetz, the author of *Bircas Shmuel,* the *talmid* of Rabbi Chaim Soloveitchik (1853-1918), taught a young man the beautiful *niggun* שֶׁיִּבָּנֶה בֵּית הַמִּקְדָּשׁ, (May the Beis HaMikdash be rebuilt), with its inherent yearning and wistful emotion.

Aaron Yeshayah heard the song once and never forgot it for the rest of his life.

Today, his son Reb Yerucham, named after the Mirrer *mashgiach,* sings it as his father taught it to him, and it is he whom I thank for this wonderful story.

Homeward Bound

It was *Purim,* and her husband had left about an hour ago after having read the *Megillah* for her. The phone was quiet, everything around her was neat and tidy, and in her mind's eye all she could picture were children being driven to the homes of their friends to deliver *shalach manos.*

Tears welled in her eyes as she lay motionless in her hospital room, a tube dangling from an intravenous bottle dripping medication into her left arm. Her three little children were at home, too young to appreciate the frolic with which Jews had celebrated *Purim* over the millennia nor mature enough to comprehend the severity of their mother's illness. Her *shaitel* hid the fact that she had lost most of her hair from chemotherapy treatments. No, the kids couldn't understand.

She had grown up in Borough Park, where *Purim* was celebrated deliriously. She had worn her share of costumes, participated in dozens of *Purim* skits and plays, and prepared *Purim chagigos* for schoolmates and co-workers numerous times. But today, she thought somberly, her room was deathly silent. That's the right word, she thought — death. Who could know the future? They caught "it" in time, she had been told, and she hoped they were right.

No sense getting more depressed, she thought. This is supposed to be a happy day. She tried to think happy thoughts and one came to mind. "Next year this time, if I am alive, with Hashem's help, I will not allow people in my condition to be so miserable on *Purim*. I'll visit them, I'll bring them *shalach manos*, I'll drive their relatives to the hospital. If I can help it," she promised herself, "no Jew who knows what *Purim* can be, will suffer in loneliness as I am today. For that alone, I'll fight to live," she resolved to herself.

The rest of the day was uneventful and quiet, except for doctors and nurses who came in and dutifully asked their questions, received their answers, and recorded information in charts. In their own neighborhoods, people were busy preparing their *Purim seudah,* chauffeuring their children, dressing up, laughing, singing, and collecting *tzedakah*. Maybe we should have two days *Purim* in *galus,* she thought to herself, smiling for the first time.

Within a week she was out of the hospital and within two months she was back to work. The summer came and went, and with it went *Tishah B'av,* summer bungalows, and preparation for another school year. Every once in a while she remembered her vow about bringing good cheer to unfortunate people in the hospital on *Purim*.

She would not forget the horror of the empty stillness of that day.

As winter marched on and spring began to peek through the trees, bushes, and flowers, she began thinking about *Purim*. She called hospital chaplains and Bikur Cholim organizations to get lists of Jewish patients. She reached some of them and offered to visit on *Purim*, but they said they had enough visitors. She offered to bring *shalach manos* to others, but they said family members had already offered to bring "healthy" *shalach monos* this year. She offered to drive relatives of the sick to the hospital but they all had cars, thank you. There weren't any more hospitals within the vicinity of her home to call, and soon her ideas and good intentions were depleted.

She was frustrated and dejected at not being able to accomplish what she knew was important. As she sat in her kitchen, the phone rang. It was her mother. After the routine pleasantries, the conversation turned to *Purim*. "*Purim* is such a difficult time," her mother said. "It's so lonely, everyone is running around and people like me who don't drive, sit home a whole day and wait for some good cheer."

And as her mother spoke, it occurred to her, "My mother is also a person. You don't have to be in a hospital to be a recipient of *chessed*. And being related is no reason to be excluded from those who deserve to feel *simchas Yom Tov*. I was ready to spend two hours on *Purim* bringing cheer to others. Aren't parents and family members entitled to be included among those 'others'?"

And so that *Purim*, she, her husband and three children spent two delightful hours at her parents' home.

"Sometimes we forget," she told me months later, "that charity begins at home."

Guiding The Misguided

One *Elul*, the month of introspection and retrospection before the awesome and solemn days of *Rosh Hashanah* and *Yom Kippur*, Rav Yisrael Salanter traveled to a town where he was to deliver some of his classical *mussar shmuessen* (discourses on ethical behavior).

The Torah reading for the week was *Parashas Ki Savo,* which contains the *Tochachah* (Admonition), a litany of frightful curses and suffering that will befall the nation when it strays from the Torah. The *Tochachah* is always read the second Shabbos before *Rosh Hashanah* as a call to *teshuvah.*

Since it could be considered a personal insult to single out someone to be called to the Torah for the reading of the *Tochachah* — as if to proclaim to the entire congregation that he is deserving of such curses — it is the general custom to call the *baal korei, gabbai* or *shammas* for that *aliyah* (see *Mishneh Berurah* O.C. 428:6 note 17).

In his *Biur Halachah,* (Ibid) (ד"ה בפסקים שלפניהם), the Chofetz Chaim sharply criticizes those communities who do not read the Torah at all on the weeks of *Bechukosai* and *Ki Savo* that contain the *Tochachah,* firstly because they are negating an early *takanah* (regulation) that dates back to Moshe *Rabbeinu's* time; and secondly, he writes, "These people make a fundamental blunder! Do they think that just because they don't read the Torah or look at the *Tochachah* that it won't befall them? To the contrary, that's the exact reason, Heaven forbid, that it could befall them!"

Then, in a rare deviation from the halachic content usually found in the *Biur Halachah,* the Chofetz Chaim expounds, "It is like the man whose friends warn him not to walk in a thoroughfare where there are pits and craters and he arrogantly responds, 'I'm not afraid, I have a thick covering over my eyes, so I can't even see any of those crevices in the street. If perchance I do fall in any of them, no one will blame me because they'll realize I didn't even see them.'"

The Chofetz Chaim asks, "Is there anything more moronic than this? To the contrary, the more his eyes are shut the more he will be hurt! The parable is obvious." [Not reading the Torah, even the *Tochachah,* is a prelude for trouble, not a shield from calamity.]

As he listened to the Torah reading, Reb Yisrael Salanter noticed that the *gabbaim* (those disseminating the *aliyos*) were pointing to an unsuspecting downtrodden beggar, indicating that they were going to call him to the Torah for the *Tochachah.*

As soon as the *aliyah* before the *Tochachah* was completed, before anyone could even be called to the Torah, Rav Yisrael Salanter went up to the *bimah* where the Torah was being read and recited the blessing for the next *aliyah* — the *Tochachah.*

Everyone in the shul was stunned — Reb Yisrael was taking the *aliyah* of the *Tochachah* for himself! The *baal korei* refused to read any further. How could he read the *Tochachah* with Reb Yisrael standing there, as if the *Tochachah* was directed towards him "*... these curses will come on you and overtake you* (*Devarim* 28:17)*... Accursed will you be when you come in and accursed will you be when you go out* (ibid. 19)*... Hashem will attach the plague to you ...* (ibid. 21)."

Left with no choice, Rav Yisrael proceeded to read the *Tochachah* himself!

Afterward he chastised the congregants and said, "Your priorities are mixed up. If you are afraid to have the *Tochachah* read in your immediate presence, how much more should you be afraid of humiliating a destitute man by calling him for the *aliyah*? That has much more severe consequences by far!"

Shame Withheld

Great people are sensitive to the feelings of others in exceptional ways. We all recognize that it is wrong to cause others shame or humiliation, but in the following two episodes, told by two prominent *talmidei chachamim* in Jerusalem, we come to appreciate the foresight and insight of *gedolei Torah* (great Torah sages) in these matters.

The Rav of the Old City of Jerusalem, Rabbi Avigdor Nebenzahl, was a dear friend and *chavrusa* (study partner) of Rabbi Shlomo Zalman Auerbach (1910-1995) for close to 40 years.

Every day, for years, Reb Shlomo Zalman and Rabbi Nebenzahl would go for a few hours to a private apartment where no one had permission to enter, so that they could study together uninterruptedly. When Rav Shlomo Zalman passed away, Rabbi Nebenzahl was one of the *maspidim* (eulogizers). He told me that he told the following story because, to him, it depicted Rav Shlomo Zalman's classic sensitivity.

There was a girl in Jerusalem who had suffered a broken engagement. She was very despondent and asked her father if he could take her to Reb Shlomo Zalman for a blessing. Her father promised her he would do so, but because of his busy schedule the visit was delayed.

Finally on *Purim*, the father told his daughter he would take her to Reb Shlomo Zalman that afternoon. By the time they came to Reb Shlomo Zalman's home in the Shaarei Chessed section of Jerusalem, Rav Shlomo Zalman had already washed [his hands for *Hamotzei*] and sat down to begin the *Purim seudah* (meal).

The father apologized for disturbing the meal, but explained to Rabbi Shlomo Zalman that his daughter had been waiting for quite a while to get a *brachah* from him because she was so depressed and pessimistic about her future.

"If the Rav will allow me," said the father, "I will bring in my daughter from the other room, for just a moment."

"No, no," protested Rav Shlomo Zalman as he made an effort to stand up, "I will go out to her. She needn't come in here."

"Please, Rebbe," the father said, "don't trouble yourself. She will be happy to come in. The Rebbe has already started the meal. Please don't get up."

Reb Shlomo Zalman disregarded the man's protests and got up to walk towards the anteroom where the young woman was waiting. When she saw Rav Shlomo Zalman coming towards her, she was overcome with reverence.

The father explained the situation of the broken engagement as Reb Shlomo Zalman listened carefully. When the father finished, Reb Shlomo Zalman began giving the girl encouragement and reassurance. He told her that he had every confidence that she would find her right *shidduch* (partner in marriage) in the near future and that Hashem would find the means to bring *simchah* (happiness) to her life.

The girl was so moved by Reb Shlomo Zalman's kindness and genuine concern that she burst into tears. She buried her face in her cupped hands and tried to thank him, but she could hardly speak.

Reb Shlomo Zalman waited for her to compose herself and wished her *"ah freilichen* (happy) *Purim."* As Reb Shlomo Zalman walked back to the dining room he turned to the young woman's father and said softly, "That is why I didn't want her to come in."

Reb Shlomo Zalman understood the emotion of the moment and anticipated that the young woman might cry. To spare her embarrassment, he went out to her — rather than have her cry in front of total strangers in the dining room.

❁ ❁ ❁

When I told this story to Reb Asher Arieli, the renowned Rosh Yeshivah in Yeshivas Mir of Jerusalem, he countered with the following moving story.

When the aged Rabbi Meir Chodosh (1898-1989), the late *Mashgiach* of Yeshivas Chevron, was in Hadassah Hospital in Jerusalem with his final illness, he was visited every day by his family and some close *talmidim.*

One day a young intern came to Rabbi Chodosh's room to draw blood from his arm. Before he could begin the procedure, Rabbi Chodosh sent everyone out of the room. This was surprising for he usually appreciated it when family members or close friends were there during the doctors' visits and procedures, so that they were up to date on his medical status.

The visitors tried to dissuade Rabbi Chodosh from being alone during the procedure, but he emphatically insisted that they leave. A while later, after a small vial of blood was drawn and the intern left the room, Rabbi Chodosh explained to his returning visitors, "It is very hard for any doctor drawing blood to find the veins in the arm of an older person. Usually the doctor must stick his needle in a few times until he finds the appropriate vein. It can't be a good feeling for the doctor. For a young doctor, however, the problem is compounded; first there is his inexperience in drawing blood from any patient regardless how old he is, and secondly my being an 'old man' makes it harder for him to even locate the proper vein.

"It would have been very embarrassing for him to have to pierce me numerous times in front of you until he found the vein. That is why I had to ask you to leave — to spare him shame."

❁ ❁ ❁

"Imagine," said Rabbi Arieli in amazement. "Rabbi Chodosh is being poked and stuck numerous times and each time it is painful. But *his* pain is not what disturbs him. It is the pain of the young doctor's humiliation that disturbs him. That's his concern! Where do you find such people? And how does one become such a person?" he sighed.

Rav Sholom Schwadron (1912-1997), the venerable Maggid of Yerushalayim, would have given a one-word answer to that question — "[the study of] *Mussar!*"

Part B:

Divine Design

A Song With a Life Of Its Own

Music is the language of the soul. Melodies penetrate our physical makeup and reach into the depths of our spirit. No wonder that a sad and melancholy ballad evokes tears or that a joyous ecstatic tune generates excitement and enthusiasm.

Perhaps the word זְמִירוֹת, *melodies,* comes from the root word זמר, *to prune,* signifying that a song shears away physical impediments, leaving only the emotion and passion emanating from the melody to connect ethereally with those who hear it.

The following is a heartrending story about a song that touched young people with a spirit and resilience of its own.

In October 1992 Rabbi Yonah Lazar left the comfortable surroundings of the Lakewood Kollel and traveled with his wife and child 10,000 miles away to head a yeshivah in Kishinev, the capital of Moldova, formerly of the Soviet Union.

After World War I, Kishinev became part of Romania and flourished as a vibrant Jewish community, in which there were more than 70 *shuls*! During World War II, Kishinev was taken over by the Germans who decimated its Jews. After the war, Moldova became part of the Soviet Union, and now it is an independent country.

One of the goals of Agudath Israel's Vaad Lehatzolas Nidchei Yisroel and its director Mr. Mordechai Neustadt was to reestablish the Yeshivas Kishinev that existed for more than 60 years until World War II. The project began in 1990. As boys and girls became inspired in the yeshivah, they were sent to mainstream yeshivos in Israel and America. By the time Rabbi Lazar arrived, 60 children from Yeshivas Kishinev had already graduated and gone on to study overseas.

Rabbi Lazar and his partner Rabbi Velvel Tabak gave daily *shiurim* (Torah lectures) to the boys, and Mrs. Shira Lazar and Mrs. Aviva Tabak gave *shiurim* to the girls. The children were eager to learn and the Lazars and Tabaks were equally eager to teach them, but at times 10,000 miles from family and friends felt like a very awful distance and life was lonely.

All in all, however, the accomplishments far outweighed the sacrifices. A highlight each week came Friday night during *davening*. Rabbis Lazar and Tabak taught the boys *niggunim* for the various sections of the Friday night *Maariv.* They would sing different tunes for *Lechah Dodi* and the children would join in enthusiastically. There was a whole array of songs that the children were taught, ranging from traditional *niggunim* of yesteryear to the modern-day music of JEP, London Boys' Choir, and others.

One Friday night as the boys were davening and completing the paragraph that begins ה׳ מָלָךְ, *Hashem will have reigned,* and were about to recite the last two verses starting from מִקֹּלוֹת מַיִם רַבִּים, *More than the roars of many waters* (*Tehillim* 93:4), Rabbis Lazar and Tabak taught them an old, slow, haunting tune for those words.

The children grasped the tune quickly so Rabbis Lazar and Tabak decided they would teach them the Yiddish words that are sung to the same tune. וָואלְט אִיךְ גֶעוֶוען בְּכֹחַ, וָואלְט אִיךְ אִין דִי גַאסְען גֶעלָאפֶען, אִיךְ וָועלְט גֶעשְׁרִיגֶען הוֹיךְ, שַׁבָּת הֵיילִיגֶער שַׁבָּת, *If I would have the strength, I would run out in the streets and I would proclaim aloud, Shabbos, oh holy Shabbos.*

To the boys, that song was electric. As though charged with vibrations from their inner soul, they responded to the words they could hardly pronounce and at first didn't understand. They sang the song with vigor and each time they repeated it they put more feeling into it, as the words *Shabbos, hailiger Shabbos* (Sabbath, holy Sabbath) became a rallying cry for their commitment to Torah-true Judaism.

The boys eventually translated the song into Russian, and Rabbis Lazar and Tabak sang it with them fluently with the proper Russian accent and emphasis. "Yeslee eemel yah seeloo..." There were Friday nights when Rabbi Lazar would watch his boys sway in unison with an exhilarating camaraderie. The intense emotion gave Rabbi Lazar the feeling of *kedushas Shabbos* (the holiness of Shabbos) as he had never experienced it before. It was the reason for his coming to Kishinev, the justification for all his sacrifice. Financial problems, local political problems, and loneliness dissipated every Friday night shortly after *Lechah Dodi.*

In December 1993, Rabbi Lazar and his wife left Yeshivas Kishinev and returned to America. He eventually assumed a position as the seventh-grade rebbe in Yeshiva Toras Emes in Los Angeles where every *Rosh Chodesh* he would tell Kishinev stories to his class.

The seventh graders of Toras Emes soon became familiar with their counterparts in Kishinev and looked forward to hearing about their "friends" in Moldova.

One day a student announced that his grandfather, Rabbi Aaron Twerski, was going to Kishinev. He had prominent ancestors who were buried there when Kishinev was part of Romania, and now that travel restrictions had eased he wanted to visit their gravesites.

Rabbi Twerski offered to give regards or take anything that Rabbi Lazar wished to send along, and promised he would return with a detailed report of events in the city — particularly in the yeshivah.

One Friday night while Rabbi Twerski was away, Rabbi Lazar was reading a *sefer* of recollections written by prewar *talmidim* of Yeshivas Kishinev, who survived the Holocaust and were now living in Rishon L'Tzion, Israel. Rabbi Lazar looked for references to Rabbi Twerski's ancestors.

What he read, he will never forget.

In one of the essays, Aaron Wasserman recalls with longing fondness the warm Torah atmosphere in Kishinev, as the community was led by the *gaon,* Rabbi Yehuda Leib Tzirelsohn (1871-1941), author of *Atzei HaLevanon* and cofounder of Agudas Israel in Romania with the Skulener Rebbe, Rabbi Eliezer Zusia Portugal (1896-1982).

He describes Shabbos in Kishinev, as Sadigerer, Boyaner, Tchortkover, and Chernobeler *chassidim* walked down the streets to their respective *shtieblach* (*shuls*). "But more significant than anything else were the *bachurim* in Yeshivas Kishinev who were so beloved for their sincerity and total dedication to Torah and *yiras Shamayim.*

"The *baalebatim* (lay people) in town would make their way down to the dining room of the yeshivah on Friday night, ostensibly to help serve the meal and make sure that each of the *talmidim* were fed sufficiently. But in reality we came to hear the boys singing their stirring *zemiros* (melodies) and provide that holy spirit of Shabbos.

"Who can forget that modest pious Jew, the Slonimer *chassid,* Reb Zechariah the watchmaker, who would lead everyone with his rapturous rendition of the well-known *niggun* of Rav Levi Yitzchak of Berditchev (1740-1810), וָואלְט אִיךְ גֶעוֶוען בְּכֹחַ, וָואלְט אִיךְ אִין דִי גַאסְען גֶעלָאפֶּען, אִיךְ וָועלְט גֶעשְׁרִיגֶען הוֹיךְ, שַׁבָּת הֵיילִיגֶער שַׁבָּת *If I would have the strength, I would run out in the streets and I would exclaim with power, Shabbos, oh holy Shabbos.'*

"It was then that we felt the holiness of Shabbos — a world that was filled with Shabbos. I can only reiterate that anyone who did not witness that sight [of everyone singing that song in unison] has never tasted the savoring flavor of Shabbos."

Reading this in Los Angeles, Rabbi Lazar sat stunned! More than 50 years had gone by since those original days of Yeshivas Kishinev. There had been spiritual desolation, destruction, and devastation. And yet the proverbial אָזְנַיִם לַכּוֹתֶל (*ears of the walls*) (see *Vayikra Rabbah* 32:2 and *Rashi, Berachos* 8b) in Yeshivas Kishinev were stirred by the very same song so many years later by a new generation of yeshivah students.

The Sages (*Yoma* 69b) teach that the אַנְשֵׁי כְּנֶסֶת הַגְּדוֹלָה, *Men of the Great Assembly,* were given that title, שֶׁהֶחֱזִירוּ עֲטָרָה לְיוֹשְׁנָהּ, *because they reinstated the crown [of Torah] to its original standing.* It refers to the study of Torah, but who would have thought it could refer to a melody?

Check Mate

It has been said that the word, *mazal* מַזָּל *(good fortune)* is actually an abbreviation for three words, מָקוֹם, זְמַן, לָשׁוֹן, *Place, time and speech,* symbolizing the fact that if one is fortunate to say the right thing at the right time in the right place, that's מַזָּל, *mazal.*

The following story, told to me by the participants, is a case in point. The combination of just the right discussion occurring at the appropriate moment at a fitting location makes this story exceptional. Names have been changed by personal request.

He had been Kenneth Lachman* for most of his life, but now that he had become a *baal teshuvah* he wanted to be known only by his Hebrew name of Akiva. He would be going to Ohr Somayach in Jerusalem, and he was committed to becoming a *ben Torah* and a Jew who would make a difference in the lives of others.

Akiva was a chess enthusiast and viewed life in terms of moves, countermoves, pawns, and kings. He and those who had influenced him to become observant were merely pawns in the hand of the Divine Grandmaster. By their positive influence his position was that Orthodoxy and a commitment to Torah was the only viable lifestyle for a dedicated Jew.

In Ohr Somayach, Akiva absorbed all he was taught from his teachers and study partners, and basked in the holiness of *Eretz*

* Name has been changed.

Yisrael. It seemed that every day he was reaching new spiritual heights.

In the summer of 1984, Akiva traveled with a group of friends through the northern region of Israel. Teveriah, Meron, and the holy city of Tzefas were on their itinerary.

Staying overnight in a youth hostel in Tzefas, Akiva met Bernie Yadler* from Hollis Hills, New York, a neighboring village to his own hometown of Clearview. Akiva tried to engage Bernie in religious conversation, but he soon realized that the yarmulke on his head was a barrier between them. To Bernie, Akiva was already "on the other side."

Determined to influence every nonreligious fellow he met, Akiva understood that he would need another topic of conversation to create a friendship with Bernie. The topic became chess.

Bernie had professed to be a chess authority who had participated in tournaments. Akiva seized the opportunity and challenged him. It wasn't even close. Before Akiva could say the words "Samuel Reshevsky" (the late Orthodox grandmaster from Spring Valley, New York), his bishops were trapped, his queen isolated, his knights captured, and his pawns sacrificed. But it was all trivial to Akiva's gambit.

By withdrawing the obstacles to open conversation, Akiva was able to get to the exchange he was planning all along. "Why did you come to Israel in the first place?" he said to Bernie, who had been traveling around the world.

"I guess I wanted to see if I feel any connection to the land of my people," Bernie said. "It's a heritage thing. Roots, nationality, ancestry. I guess I yearn to know if there is really something to all of that in relation to my own personal life."

"There is only one place to find out about all of that," said Akiva convincingly, "and that is in a yeshivah."

Akiva went on to explain about his own secular background and how he too sought answers and explanations. He extolled the virtues of Yeshivah Ohr Somayach in Jerusalem, and detailed his own progress there.

---

* Name has been changed.

The next morning the two parted company, each continuing his travels. As the new *zman* (semester) started at Ohr Somayach, Akiva decided that he would switch to Ohr Somayach's branch in Zichron Yaakov, 15 miles south of Haifa. He began making plans for his departure, spending a few days getting his things together, and saying his farewells to friends and mentors.

There were many new faces in Ohr Somayach, but as he walked in the hallway someone rushed up to him. It was Bernie. "Hi," Bernie called out. "Do you remember me from a few weeks ago?"

"Sure," replied a surprised and delighted Akiva. "What are you doing here?"

"Heritage, roots, nationality. Remember our talk in Tzefas? I thought a lot about what you said that night, and I came across others with your view on life. So I decided I would try Ohr Somayach for a few weeks. Do you think we could study together sometimes?"

Akiva was astounded. Had his words really had such effect? Was this exhilarating feeling he was experiencing what *kiruv* was all about? Bernie's anticipation of shared studying made Akiva feel awkward and uncomfortable.

"Bernie, I am actually on my way to Zichron Yaakov, which is up north near Haifa. It's another branch of Ohr Somayach."

Bernie looked crushed. "I came here because of you. I don't know anyone around here. I was hoping that you could show me the ropes and introduce me to what you were talking about that night. I made sacrifices to get here. You can't desert me."

Akiva's response was clumsy and difficult. He tried to explain that he had accomplished all he could in the Jerusalem branch, and that Zichron Yaakov was a step up. "It's like going from a tournament to a championship event," he said weakly. Akiva tried to assure Bernie that there were wonderful people at Ohr Somayach. They would help and guide him as they had guided hundreds, if not thousands, before him. Akiva offered to talk to certain *rebbeim* on Bernie's behalf but Bernie declined the offer.

The two parted company.

As Akiva traveled to Zichron Yaakov he couldn't help but feel guilty for having let Bernie down. After all, he had influenced Bernie to come to Ohr Somayach, but he was confident that he had to move on. "I can't impede my own personal progress," he convinced himself over and over again, "not at this stage of my life."

❁ ❁ ❁

Akiva stayed in Zichron Yaakov for two years and then decided that it was time to look for a *shidduch* (a marriage partner). He contacted friends in Jerusalem and let it be known that he was "available and looking." He had built a fine reputation, and people went out of their way to help him.

After a while he met Leah, originally from Boston, who was attending Nevei Yerushalayim. Her background was similar to Akiva's and after a short courtship they became engaged. After their engagement, Leah began talking about people who had influenced her to become religious. "There was a Shabbaton in Boston where Rabbi Dovid Gottleib spoke," Leah said one afternoon. "He was incredibly inspirational. That's when my odyssey to Orthodoxy began."

"But who even convinced you to go to a Shabbaton?" asked Akiva. "Most kids can't be induced to attend."

"There was this fellow Boaz, who was studying in Ohr Somayach. He came to Boston and rounded up a whole bunch of us. If not for him, we never would have gotten started."

"I studied in Ohr Somayach," said Akiva. "Who is Boaz? When was he there? What's his last name?"

Akiva nearly fainted when he heard the name, "Boaz Yadler."

Bernie was Boaz — but it took that chess game in Tzefas to begin his awareness of it. Akiva hadn't even known that Bernie had stayed on in Ohr Somayach. Obviously the *rebbeim* and *chavrusas* there were still doing their wonderful job.

Over the last two years Boaz had transferred the energy in his creative mind to the pursuit of Torah. He became a force in *kiruv* and grew in his dedication to inspire others.

Akiva and Boaz renewed their acquaintance and became good friends. Thrilled at the remarkable turn of events, Boaz attended the wedding. He was proud to have been brought to Torah through Akiva and equally proud to have been an influence on Leah.

Boaz became a steady Shabbos guest at Akiva and Leah's home. One Shabbos Leah suggested that Boaz meet a friend of hers, Devorah, from Nevei Yerushalayim. The two met.

Match!

Mate!

> We wish every *chassan* and *kallah* that they merit to build a בַּיִת נֶאֱמָן בְּיִשְׂרָאֵל (a faithful home in Israel). It is said that a man's home is his castle. In every castle there live a king and a queen. Who could have known that two castles would be built by a game that started on a "knight" in Tzefas?

Of Majesty and Royalty

This enchanting story contains elements of *Kiddush Hashem, Hashgachah Pratis, Hakaras Hatov* and *Emunas Chachamim.* Consequently, it is fascinating and inspirational.

I first heard this story in Golders Greens, London, from Mr. Amos Wittenberg. On a subsequent trip to Holland, Rabbi Yehuda Leib Lewis, the *Av Beis Din* of Amsterdam, and Rabbi Zev Van Dijk, the Jewish chaplain of the Dutch army, shared with me additional pertinent facts. Mr. Dov Aaronson, president of the *Nidchei Yisroel Yechaneis shul* in Amsterdam, and his son Reb Mottel added splendid color, flavor, and more vital details to this memorable narrative. I am grateful to them all.

Finally, I express my appreciation to Rabbi Dovid Cohen of Brooklyn for showing me references to this incident in one of the *sefarim* in his vast library, *Leket Kemach*

HaChadash. This story will be part of a documentary called "Yiddishkeit" being produced in Holland.

In 1908, Queen Wilhelmina of Holland went for a brief vacation to the popular resort area of Marienbad, Austria, near the German border.

Since it was not an official state visit, she had but a small entourage of people with her, and there was no welcoming ceremony on her arrival at the train station in Marienbad.

As she disembarked from the train, she noticed a huge crowd on the platform. Obviously, a prominent personality had just arrived and everyone was trying to get a glimpse of the celebrated individual. Upon inquiry, Queen Wilhelmina was told that a great Jewish personality, the Munkaczer Rebbe, Rabbi Tzvi Hirsch Spira (1845-1914, author of *Darkei Teshuvah* and *Be'er L'Chai Ro'ee* on *Tikunei Zohar*), had just arrived, and many disciples had come to greet him.

Upon inquiring as to what a rebbe is, she was told that a rebbe is a very pious man of great wisdom who bestows blessings and gives advice to his many followers. Thousands seek his counsel and beseech him to pray on their behalf. Often his prayers are answered and those who seek his blessings live to see their wishes fulfilled. The queen was fascinated; she had never heard about such people.

She and her husband, Prince Hendrik, were childless, and her sad plight was never far from her mind. Both she and her husband were duly concerned about the continuation of the monarchy in their family, and the thought that she was the last of her family's royal lineage gave them great anguish. An only daughter, the queen had three half-brothers who had died, and she was her family's only surviving heir to the throne.

She watched with more than curiosity as the huge crowd shuffled and pushed to get a look at the Munkaczer Rebbe, who was hidden from view.

The queen and her entourage left the train station but later that day she asked one of her attendants to try and arrange for her to meet the great sage privately. The attendant sought out the

Rebbe's *gabbai* (assistant), and word came back to the queen that night that the Rebbe would see her.

The next evening, without public knowledge of his whereabouts, the Munkaczer Rebbe was brought to a secluded area of a beautiful park just outside the city that had been designated as the meeting place. Queen Wilhelmina was accompanied by two attendants, and the Rebbe came with two *bachurim.* Seated on two park benches, in the cool breeze of a quiet summer evening, the majestic Rebbe and the cultured queen began their conversation.

She sensed immediately that the man sitting opposite her was a personality of great stature. She spoke candidly to the Rebbe and explained her torment and anxiety about not having a child to carry on the monarchy. The Rebbe listened attentively. Finally, he told her that she need not worry. Her monarchy would continue. He used the Hebrew expression כָּעֵת חַיָּה , *at this time next year,* the same words that Hashem used to inform Avraham *Avinu* that in a year, his wife Sarah would have a child (*Bereishis* 18:10). The clear implication was that within the year she would bear a child.

As Queen Wilhelmina was about to depart, the Rebbe said, מַלְכוּתָהּ לֹא יִנָּתֵק עַד כִּי יָבֹא שִׁילֹה, *"[Her] kingdom will not be severed until Mashiach comes"* (see *Bereishis* 49:10).

The next year, 1909, the queen had a little girl and named her Juliana. It was the only child she ever had. Thirty-nine years later, in 1948, Juliana became queen of the Netherlands. Her daughter, Beatrix, is the present queen.

> Hashem's orchestration of events in His universe are, more often than not, beyond our comprehension. Concealed in His mysterious ways are occurrences that we tend to overlook that eventually become significant. Read on for such a phenomenon.

Rabbi Yaakov Zvi Katz was a prominent *talmid chacham* who, like his father Reb Shlomo before him, served as rav, before the outbreak of World War II, in the Hungarian town of Hajduszoboszlo, just south of Debrecen, near the Romanian border.

During the war he was brought to the Bergen-Belsen concentration camp, where he suffered terribly. Twelve volumes of his writings on halachah were burned and his beloved 18-year old son Shmuel was deported from the ghetto and never heard from again. Rabbi Katz, though, was among those who survived the ordeal of the camps, and after the war he sought to rebuild his life.

He went back to Hungary, but saw immediately that there was little future there for the Jews. He tried to emigrate to Holland, but his visa application, like thousands of others, was rejected as the Netherlands government established a quota to immigration.

Rabbi Katz applied a second time and was told that Holland was accepting only those whose presence would benefit the country, but those who had professions that were already plentiful in the Netherlands would be rejected. There were already many rabbis in Holland, and more were not needed. Rabbi Katz's application was again declined.

One day Rabbi Katz decided to write directly to Queen Wilhelmina. He explained in detail the hardships he had gone through during the war and his longing to live in Holland. Then he wrote, "Surely Your Highness remembers the very momentous meeting that preserved the course of royalty in Holland."

He detailed the queen's encounter in Marienbad with "the great sage and scholar from Munkacz." He wrote that the Rebbe had insisted that two boys come along with him, for he would need an interpreter since the queen would be speaking in German. Rabbi Katz wrote, "I was that 18-year-old boy who accompanied the great sage, and it was I who transmitted to the queen the wonderful news from the saintly rabbi that she would bear a child within the year.

"I therefore plead with Your Highness," he wrote, "in recognition of my humble service to you in the past, to kindly grant me the favor of permission to emigrate to your wonderful country. I would be forever indebted to you."

The letter, written in Yiddish, was sent to government ministers for translation. An old Russian *chazzan* named Rabinowitz was summoned from his *shul* in The Hague and asked to translate the letter. The *chazzan* read the letter and, realizing its significance, translated it with all the gusto and fervor he could muster.

Rabbi Katz's son, Reb Moshe, of Stamford Hill, England, explained that his father did not write the letter in German for he feared that the Queen's secretary or others who understood German might read it and discard it. Written in a language no one could understand, the letter provoked their curiosity and thus they had it translated.

The translated text was brought to Queen Wilhelmina in her palace. When she read and reread what Rav Katz had written, she made it her personal agenda to see to it that he be granted immigration papers swiftly.

Shortly afterwards Rabbi Katz arrived in Amsterdam. He was there but a short time when the rav of the *Nidchei Yisroel Yechaneis shul*, Rabbi Aaron Neuwirth (father of Rav Yehoshua Neuwirth, author of *Shemiras Shabbos K'hilchasah*), decided to leave his position and move to Israel. Rabbi Katz was immediately appointed his successor and served the *shul* nobly for the rest of his life.

Rabbi Katz never forgot the graciousness of the royal family, and in his foreword to his *Leket Kemach HaChadash* Vol. 3 (the first of his *sefarim* to be printed after the war), he writes, "Hashem guided my footsteps to Amsterdam through the personal intervention of the magnanimous Queen Wilhelmina, may Hashem exalt her glory, before she abdicated in favor of her daughter, Queen Juliana. May her monarchy continue עַד כִּי יָבֹא שִׁילֹה (until Moshiach comes)."

Overcome by the incredible *Hashgachah Pratis* (Divine Providence) of his being in the right place at the right time, Rabbi Katz used the same words regarding the queen that the Munkaczer Rebbe had expressed years before: עַד כִּי יָבֹא שִׁילֹה, the words that depict the hopes and aspirations of all of *Klal Yisrael*. May all of us live עַד כִּי יָבֹא שִׁילֹה, speedily in our days, and become cognizant in our everyday lives of Hashem's extraordinary *Hashgachah Pratis*.

Deliverance Outside Detroit

The home of Mrs. Ilse Roberg in Oak Park, Michigan, is like a Jewish art gallery. Beautiful paintings, exquisite needlepoints, and graceful works of calligraphy bedeck the walls of the modest home, all done by Oma (German for grandmother) Roberg herself. The works reflect the appreciation and sensitivity that she and her late husband of more than 55 years, Reb Alexander, always had for *pesukim* (verses) in *Tanach* and the teachings of *Chazal*.

Alex and Ilse Roberg were teachers in the Jewish schools of Niderstetten and Stuttgart, Germany, before the war and narrowly escaped with their lives. Throughout their travails under the Nazis, the newlywed Robergs encouraged each other by the exhortation of David *HaMelech*, לא אָמוּת כִּי אֶחְיֶה וַאֲסַפֵּר מַעֲשֵׂי יָ–ה, *"I shall not die, I shall live and relate the deeds of Hashem"* (*Tehillim* 118:17). That *pasuk* became their personal source of strength.

Thanks to an uncle in Detroit, the Robergs were able to get an affidavit and came to America in 1940. They settled in Detroit where Alex was a principal and Ilse was a teacher in the United Hebrew Schools for more than 35 years. Over the decades, this dignified regal couple raised children and grandchildren with emphasis on Torah *chinuch*, integrity, exemplary behavior, and family devotion.

❁ ❁ ❁

In July 1996, Oma and Opa Roberg went with their son Ezra and his wife Naomi to visit their grandchildren in Camp Agudah Mid-West, in South Haven, Michigan. Ezra, who drove the family van, sat in front with his father discussing the week's *parashah* as the women sat in the back conversing and listening to the insights coming from the front.

The three-hour journey began uneventfully but by midtrip the weather changed abruptly as unanticipated dark clouds suddenly erupted in a fierce thunderstorm. Route 196, a two-lane highway in Coloma, Michigan, became slick and hazardous as sheets of rain sliced the air. Ezra had considered stopping until the rain let up, but the weather forecast was for rain to continue for the rest of the day.

Through the driving rain, Ezra could see that the road ahead veered sharply to the left. He turned the wheel, but instead of veering to the left, the van skidded in a circle, while simultaneously hurtling forward. There was no barrier along the right side of the road and, as the van spun for the second time, it bolted off the road down into a steep embankment!

It rumbled over rocks, crashed through bushes, and caromed off tree after tree. Suddenly a massive tree branch crashed through the left side window into Oma Roberg. Badly bloodied and bruised, she was pinned against her seat. The van smashed into a thick row of trees and abruptly came to a stunning halt. The impact of the collision immobilized Ezra, as he suffered excruciating pain from a dislocated shoulder.

Naomi was able to get her door open and realizing that she could not handle this situation herself, she rushed outside in the driving rain and began climbing the hill towards the highway to try and get help.

Frantically she waved for oncoming cars to stop, but in the rain, few if any drivers noticed her. Discouraged, she went back down to the van to tend to her injured mother-in-law and husband. Her father-in-law Alex was miraculously unscathed. As she neared the van, a man who had witnessed the accident was already there with his cell phone, summoning ambulances and medical assistance.

Medics arrived within minutes and the injured were transferred to the South Haven Community Hospital, where Ezra and his mother were attended to without delay.

Two days after the accident, police officers came to the trauma unit in Kalamazoo, Michigan where Oma Roberg had been transferred. They gave her a bag containing what they had found in the car. Slowly she took out the needlepoint she was embroidering at the time of the accident. She had intended it to be light-green Hebrew lettering on a dark-green background. Now it was bloodstained red, but the words were still legible. Remarkably the verse she was stitching at the time of the accident was: לֹא אָמוּת כִּי אֶחְיֶה וַאֲסַפֵּר מַעֲשֵׂי יָ–ה, *"I shall not die, I shall live and relate the deeds of Hashem."*

Oma Roberg held the needlepoint gently in her hands and read and reread the verse on the unfinished needlepoint. It was the verse that had given her courage and hope through the darkest moments of her life in another era. Now she perceived how the inherent strength in the verse was timeless.

Through subsequent operations and therapy, David *HaMelech's* expression of determination was a source of courage and resilience to the Robergs as it had accompanied them to the abyss and back.

Today the completed needlepoint hangs in Oma's living room. The bloodstains have been washed away, but the memory of the reassurance and motivation those words gave her in the hospital is eternally etched in her family's collective memory.

A Chance of a Lifetime

Dissension is devastating. Prolonged arguments and bitter controversy cause broken hearts, broken lives, and broken homes. Disputes are the tragic root of splintered communities and divided factions in *Klal Yisrael.*

To avoid such pain and heartache, David *HaMelech* exhorts: בַּקֵּשׁ שָׁלוֹם וְרָדְפֵהוּ, *Seek peace and pursue it* (*Tehillim* 34;15). He urges us to do everything possible in the pursuit of peace (see *Rashi*). The Sages instruct us, הֱוֵי מַקְדִּים בִּשְׁלוֹם, כָּל אָדָם, *Initiate a greeting to every person* (*Avos* 4:20). We are thus directed not to wait for someone else to make the first move; *we* should take the "first step" in our quest for harmony and compatibility.

The Midrash (*Bereishis Rabbah* 4:6) reveals an indication in the Torah's very first chapter of how much Hashem dislikes conflict and contention.

Numerous times in the Torah's description of the first week of Creation, Hashem inspected what He had wrought and saw כִּי טוֹב, *That it was good.* (See *Bereishis* 1:4,10,12,18,21,25,31.)

The Midrash (*Bereishis Rabbah* 4:6) notes that the creation of the second day was not called "good," because on that day נִבְרֵאת מַחְלוֹקֶת, *conflict was created,* as Hashem separated the waters that were beneath the firmament from the waters above the firmament (*Bereishis* 1:7). Although Hashem's act of separation was a necessity, the Torah does not say כִּי טוֹב, *that it was good,* on this day, because separation generally connotes conflict, and that is bad.

It thus becomes imperative that we pursue peace and harmony in all venues of life. The benefits can be extraordinary as they are in this remarkable story.

Dov Hager* is an exceptionally busy person. Aside from being a devoted husband and father to his six children, he is involved with local community affairs (yeshivah, Bais Yaakov, and the *eiruv*) and with national and international *tzedakah* organizations. Dov runs a successful curtain and window treatment business with offices in his home and in downtown Boston. At times his phones seem like a blaring out-of-sync orchestra, as his house seems like a raucous whirlwind of activity.

One night he had an appointment with a Mrs. Silver* in the neighboring town of Lowell, to show her swatches of fabric for curtains and to discuss various options of draperies, valances, Chinese shades, blinds, and screens.

Much to Mrs. Silver's dismay, Dov did not keep the appointment; he simply forgot about it. His many responsibilities had become chaotic and he had neglected to enter the appointment in

* Name and locale has been changed.

his calendar. At 10 o'clock in the evening, Mrs. Silver called his office and left a blistering message on his answering machine. The next morning when Dov retrieved his messages, the wrath of the woman's voice on the phone was almost tangible.

Immediately, Dov called Mrs. Silver to apologize. "I have no excuses," he said honestly. "I am simply overworked. I must have lost the note where I had penciled in our appointment. Please forgive me."

Mrs. Silver was not in a forgiving mood. "You're a businessman," she said. "It's your job to have a better system of recording things. My time is just as valuable as yours."

"I am truly sorry," said Dov in embarrassed humility, "Please — give me another appointment and let me make amends." He paused a moment and added, "And this time I promise I will be there on time."

Mrs. Silver was not a religious Jew and Dov was concerned that his failure to show up at her home, aside from being poor business practice, was a *chillul Hashem.*

There was a long pause on the phone. For a moment Dov thought Mrs. Silver had disconnected him, but then he heard her sigh and say reluctantly, "One Jew should always give another Jew a chance. You can come Monday morning at 10 o'clock and I expect you to be on time."

"You can count on it," Dov said confidently.

On Monday morning, at five to 10, Dov arrived at Mrs. Silver's beautiful home on Spring Lane in Lowell. He rang the doorbell and waited. Suddenly the door opened in a flash and a teenaged girl started screaming hysterically, "What are you doing here? I didn't call you. You don't belong here!"

Dov was shocked. "I have a 10 o'clock appointment with Mrs. Silver. Is this her home?"

"My mother just collapsed in the kitchen," the girl cried. "We're waiting for an ambulance. I think she had a stroke!"

"I'm a medic," Dov said as he ran back to his car. Dov was a mainstay of Hatzolah (volunteer medical squad) of Boston. He was the most experienced of the crew. He grabbed his medical kit, and ran back into the house. He saw at once that Mrs. Silver was barely breathing. Her neck muscles had become paralyzed and her tongue, which had fallen back, was not allowing her to breathe. Dov quickly opened up an air passage and got her to resume breathing. He saved her life!

A few days later when Dov visited Mrs. Silver in the hospital she said to him, "I thought I was the one giving you one more chance, but I realize now, that it was you who gave me one more chance — at life."

And it happened because Mrs. Silver understood that in the interest of harmony, a Jew should always give another Jew — one more chance.

Wheels of Fortune

Throughout history, Jews who endured hatred and persecution only because they were Jews, were tormented regardless of whether or not they were religious. Anti-Semitism did not recognize particular religious stripes. Those who shed their exterior Jewishness usually realized that it made no difference. The bitter malice was spewed at their identity — which for the most part they could not conceal.

Thus, in 1966, Sam Zeitlin of Brooklyn, a member of the American National Cycling Team, was grieved but not surprised when he became the target of a constant barrage of anti-Semitic jibes. He was sure that his teammates' comments were tinged with jealousy, for he was one of the fastest and most capable cyclists in America. After all, he had won the New York State Sprint Championship in 1965 and "The Jewish Boy" was heralded everywhere in the cycling world.

Cycling had been a passion for Sam since his early childhood, and he had won race after race, both locally and nationally. One afternoon as Sam was cycling in Kissena Park in Queens, in training for a national race, slanderous remarks were aimed at him by some beer-drinking hoodlums sitting in the stands that rimmed the track. He tried to put them out of his mind, for clearly they were trying to intimidate him. That night, however, as he was cycling home on his road bike, a car behind him swerved from its lane and lurched towards him. With the swift reflexes of a gifted athlete, Sam turned sharply onto the sidewalk. He looked back at the car and saw that it was his chief rival on the cycling team driving with one of the hoodlums from the stands. "You'll never stay on top, you dirty Jew," the driver roared as he sped by.

Sam had to admit that he was unnerved by the bigotry and the resentment.

A few months later in 1967, in the Grand Prix of The Americas, in Northbrook, Illinois, Sam finished first — only to be disqualified. Citing a rule that had never been enforced either before or since, the officials claimed that Sam had raised his hands in victory prior to crossing the finish line, and by taking his hands off the handlebars had endangered the safety of nearby spectators. Sam was convinced that the decision was tainted with anti-Semitism, and he decided to leave the United States and pursue his goals in another country.

He rejected Canada because the winters were too cold and he rejected Mexico because, with its high altitude, the air was too thin. If he was going to travel overseas, then Israel, where sports were popular, seemed a logical choice. And even though he was a secular Jew, Israel was the country of his people.

He came to Israel later that year and immediately contacted the authorities of the cycling division of the Hapoel Tel-Aviv Sports Club. His reputation had preceded him, since he had won the 1965 Maccabiah Games Cycling Sprint competition. Nati, the team's general manager, realized that if Sam became the team's trainer, as well as a member, he could bring the Israeli cycling team to world-class standards. Nati took a liking to him as Sam confidently proclaimed that he could enable Israeli cycling to compete for medals in the upcoming World Olympics.

One night, after strenuous training, Sam went to the *Kosel HaMaaravi.* He had never been there, but he knew that it was a place where people prayed. As he made his way across the plaza, he recalled the *Shema Yisrael* prayer he had learned in a Hebrew school in Brooklyn. He walked up to the huge sacred stones of the golden Wall, gently kissed them and recited the *Shema.* He said a few prayers in English and then began scanning the crowd for a familiar face. He was curious at how others at the *Kosel* seemed to be praying endlessly. What were they saying, what do they know that I don't know, he wondered.

He walked over to two religious-looking young men and began asking questions of a religious nature. The two brothers, R' Chaim and R' Dovid Goldberg of Chicago, were former *talmidim* of the Telshe Yeshiva in Cleveland. At the time, Chaim was a student of Rav Dovid Soloveitchik, and Dovid was a student of Rav Berel Soloveitchik.

After a lengthy conversation, the brothers recognized that Sam was sincerely searching for guidance and inspiration. They directed him to their native Chicago friend, Rabbi Gershon Weinberger, who was known for his warm personality and incredible hospitality. An architect who lived with his wife and family in the Kiryat Sanz section of Jerusalem, R' Gershon had a home that was a "home away from home" for dozens of young men and young women who had come to study in Israel. Their apartment was always accessible. Meals and Torah discussions were always available.

Rabbi Weinberger and Sam became very close friends, as the rabbi took an active interest in Sam's road back to Torah Judaism. They studied together during the week and every Shabbos. Sam, now known as Shimon, was regularly at the Weinberger home, participating with family and guests in the lively *zemiros* (Shabbos melodies), and stimulating *divrei Torah.*

After a few months, Rabbi Weinberger suggested that Shimon enroll in a yeshivah. "I have a very close friend, Rabbi Noach Weinberg, who is opening a yeshivah in Bnei Brak," said Rabbi

Weinberger. "You will get individualized attention. You should consider it."

Shimon Pesach Zeitlin thus became the fifth *talmid* in Yeshivah Magen Avrohom, which was the forerunner for the world-renowned Yeshivah Aish Hatorah, of which Rabbi Weinberg is the founder and Dean.

For Shimon, moving from the hills of Jerusalem to the flatter terrain of Bnei Brak was a tremendous asset for his cycling practice. Shimon would attend morning *seder* (session) and then, with the encouragement of Rabbi Weinberg, he would cycle for three hours in the afternoon with his custom-made English Holdsworth bicycle along the coast roads towards Caesarea or on the Tel-Aviv Haifa highway, tucking behind huge Israeli army trucks hauling tanks, so that he could pedal in the highest gear with no wind resistance. Shimon would practice his aerodynamically correct racing tactics, using his innovative techniques to gain power and speed, all the while singing to himself the quickly paced *niggun, Shabbos Hayom LaShem,* that he learned from his mentor, Rabbi Gershon Weinberger. His swift pedal cadence would parallel the tempo of the song.

As Shimon progressed in his observance of Torah and *mitzvos,* he tried to influence some of his cycling teammates to become Shabbos observant. His pleas fell on deaf ears. The cyclists and their coaches were fueled by their goal of an Olympic medal and international fame.

As the Olympics drew near, trials were to be held to determine which cyclists would represent Israel's team. The Israeli Sports Federation announced that the trials were to be held on Shabbos! Shimon was appalled. As much as he appealed to them, they were totally unsympathetic. Shimon knew the level of cycling talent of other countries. "You don't have world-class cyclists that can compete at Olympic levels unless I represent you," Shimon said.

"We don't change policies for anyone," he was told firmly, "even for you."

An internal conflict raged within Shimon. He had struggled for thousands of lonely hours, training, lifting weights, doing calisthenics, jumping rope, riding hills and valleys through rain, cold, sleet, and heat, all so that he could participate in the Olympics. If he could win an Olympic gold medal he would carve his name in sports history. His name would become a household word in millions of homes throughout the globe. Yet, Shabbos had taken on new meaning in his life. Shabbos defined his being — a subservience to a Higher Power that governed his life — and the chant of *Shabbos Hayom LaShem* had become the anthem of his identity. In the end, Shimon's decision was clear. Life as a religious Jew meant more than that one blazing moment of possible glory.

In the summer of 1972, Israel did not send a cycling team to the 20th Summer Olympic Games in Munich, Germany. The Israelis realized that their cycling team was not up to par. But they did send officials and athletes to compete in weight lifting, wrestling, fencing, and rifle shooting. During the games, Palestinian guerrillas attacked the Olympic Village and killed two Israeli athletes and took another nine hostage by helicopter to a nearby airfield in Munich. As the world looked on in shock, a shootout took place between German police and the Palestinians. The helicopters were blown up and the Israeli athletes were shot to death.

❁ ❁ ❁

Back in Bnei Brak, Shimon heard the tragic news on the radio. It was all anyone in Israel talked about. There was shock and outrage, sadness and mourning.

As he reflected on the tragedy, Shimon shuddered when he thought of a phrase of another Shabbos song, כִּי אֶשְׁמְרָה שַׁבָּת אֵ-ל יִשְׁמְרֵנִי, *If I safeguard the Sabbath, Hashem will safeguard me.*

Today, more than a quarter of a century later, when Shimon and his family sing around their Shabbos table, כִּי אֶשְׁמְרָה שַׁבָּת, he often utters a silent prayer of thanks to Hashem for his being led to become a *shomer Shabbos* and Torah-observant Jew.

By the Book

Joanne Ness was a nutritionist in California whose clients were mostly professional athletes. She was renowned in her field and was a popular lecturer on health and nutrition throughout the United States.

In her personal life, Joanne had become a *baalas teshuvah* and was becoming increasingly more observant. She drew much inspiration and guidance from the books and tapes given to her by her new friends in the Pacific Jewish Center in Venice, California, a small Jewish community just north of Los Angeles.

In May 1986 Joanne was invited to a nutritionists' conference in Philadelphia. As she checked her calendar, she realized the conference was scheduled the night before *Shavuos*. However, with the three-hour time difference between the East and West Coasts, she knew there would be no problem taking an *erev Yom Tov* 10 a.m. flight out of Philadelphia, which would get her into Los Angles by 2 o'clock in the afternoon. *Yom Tov* didn't start until about 8 o'clock in the evening.

As she packed her bags in Venice for the trip to the conference, she took along a book she had received from a friend, *From Generation to Generation*, by the renowned psychiatrist Rabbi Dr. Abraham Twerski.

The trip to Philadelphia was uneventful, the conference was informative and now, Thursday morning, it was time to go back home. But there was a terrible fog in Philadelphia and the airport was closed! Every minute of delay seemed like an hour, and then it was announced that it would be another 90 minutes before the airport would open.

Joanne's itinerary was to fly to Pittsburgh where she would change planes and continue to Los Angeles. With the fog delay, she realized her connecting flight in Pittsburgh would leave without her. She inquired and found there was a later Pittsburgh - Los Angeles flight leaving at 2 o'clock. It would still get her home in time for *Yom Tov*, but by the time she got to Pittsburgh, it was announced that the flight to Los Angeles was delayed for mechanical reasons.

She began to panic. She knew no one in Pittsburgh, and if the plane didn't leave soon, she would not be home in time for *Yom Tov.* She called her Rabbi in Venice who told her she could not risk the flight. She trembled as she realized she would have to stay in Pittsburgh for *Shavuos* — and she did not know a soul!

Then she remembered! The author of the book she was reading lived in Pittsburgh. He seemed like a kind and generous man, and it was clear from the book that his family had a history of concern for fellow Jews. Surely Rabbi Twerski would find her a place to stay for *Yom Tov*. She found Rabbi Twerski's address in the phonebook, ran downstairs to ground transportation, got into a taxi and set off.

A half an hour later, she was startled when the driver announced they had arrived at their destination. It was the pyschiatric office of St. Francis Hospital! She rushed in frantically and said she needed Rabbi Twerski immediately. Some of the nurses turned their heads and wondered if perhaps she had a psychiatric emergency.

She explained her situation to one of the secretaries, who called her superior, staff psychologist Dr. Ben-Zion Twerski, a son of Rabbi Twerski. Within 10 minutes he was in the hospital and assured Joanne that her worries were over.

Dr. Twerski drove Joanne to his home in Squirrel Hill, made a few calls and within a half-hour Joanne was settled with the Saks family for *Yom Tov*.

Over *Yom Tov* numerous people invited her for meals. When she finally met Rabbi Abraham Twerski on Shabbos, the second day of *Yom Tov*, she thanked him for his wonderful book, and he invited her for the noon *seudah* (meal). She gladly accepted.

In true tradition of the Twerskis, there were numerous guests at the table, and the lively conversation veered from Torah to medicine to Chassidus to events of the day.

One of the guests was a close friend of Rabbi Twerski, Mr. Brad Perelman. Brad had been looking for a *shidduch* for many years and as he sat at the table it occurred to him that maybe his *shidduch* had come to him. Surely the guest from California was worth considering.

He considered, she consented, they courted — and six weeks later they were engaged!

But there is more. Years earlier, Brad Perelman and Rabbi Twerski had a heart-to-heart talk. Brad said, "Rabbi, your family tradition is so rich and so inspirational, you simply must write and publish the stories of your parents and their remarkable way of life."

From that conversation, Rabbi Twerski began compiling the stories of his parents and eventually put them together in the book *From Generation to Generation.* In the introduction he thanks Brad (not mentioned by name), for encouraging him to write it.

Today Shlomo (Brad) and Chana (Joanne) Perelman thank Rabbi Twerski for publishing it.

A Leap of Faith

Steve Dubin was an outgoing, daring person. He enjoyed flying, writing, public relations, and photography, and the jobs he held usually reflected one of those interests. In the 1980s Steve was a free-lance aerial photographer selling his spectacular aerial photos to real-estate agents, advertisers, and photojournalism magazines.

Several times a week he would climb into a twin-engine, two-seater, high-wing Cessna, and instruct the pilot to fly over a specific location. As the pilot flew over the area, Steve would remove a side window from the Cessna, lean out the open space and, with his hand-held 35mm camera, photograph landscapes, seascapes, properties, and estates.

One day it occurred to Steve that it might be thrilling to learn how to jump from the plane and parachute down towards an open field. To accomplish that feat he would have to gingerly climb out onto the wing of the moving Cessna and then, when given the signal, jump out into the open airspace.

Steve did some research and found that there was a small airport in Lakewood, New Jersey, along the Garden State Parkway, which had a one-day learn-and-jump course. Though Steve had started on his path to become a *baal teshuvah* by then, he was not yet aware that, just a few miles from that airport, there existed one of the most prominent yeshivos in the world.

Steve's brother Gary (now Chaim) was already *shomer Shabbos,* and was teaching him the importance of that sacred day. Steve understood that it was improper to travel on Shabbos, so he consented not to commute to Lakewood for parachute training nor attempt his first jump on Shabbos. The only other time the parachute instructors were available was Sunday afternoon.

Conditions had to be perfect for instructors to allow their students to begin their training. Winds had to be less than 10 miles per hour, and the cloud ceiling had to be at least 3,000 feet high. Though one parachutes from a height of only 1,000 feet, when a chutist jumps off the wing, the wind force propels him upward; thus small planes and other parachutists need clear visibility to avoid him. Hence the necessity of the 3,000-foot cloud ceiling.

Every Sunday in the summer of 1985 that Steve was available, he would call the Lakewood airport and they would tell him conditions were fine, but whenever he drove down to the airfield, unfavorable conditions developed. One Sunday it suddenly became too cloudy, another Sunday it started raining, and on a third Sunday unanticipated winds were gusting.

There was only one Sunday left in the summer-training season; by autumn, wind conditions would already be too hazardous. Before the weekend, however, Chaim called his brother Steve and informed him about an Aish Hatorah Shabbaton that was to take place in the Homowack Hotel, in upstate New York. "The speakers are so inspirational," said Chaim. "You will learn so much about your roots, you will see wonders in the Torah as you never saw them before. Come spend Shabbos with us. You will never regret it."

Steve was hesitant to give up this final opportunity to become a parachutist but his brother's persistence was such that he eventually relented and decided to go. Parachuting would just have to wait.

The Shabbaton's organizers seemed to genuinely care for every individual in attendance, and Steve felt comfortable in his new surroundings. On Friday night the *davening* and the singing were uplifting. The speakers during and after the meals were entertaining and inspiring. By midnight, many clusters of guests that had been getting to know one another and were discussing the program began to dissipate, and almost everyone retired for the evening.

The leaders of the Shabbaton, however, would be hearing a special address from the Rosh Yeshivah of Yeshivas Ner Yisroel of Baltimore, Rabbi Yaakov Weinberg. He was a mentor and guide to many in the field of *kiruv,* and the Aish Hatorah teachers and leaders were anxious to hear his thoughts. (Rabbi Weinberg's brother, Reb Noach, is the founder of the Aish Hatorah program.)

Steve usually went to sleep very late at night and he thought it might be worthwhile to sit in on the Rosh Yeshivah's lecture. True, he had not been invited but he felt that if he sat unobtrusively in the back no one in the room would mind.

The leaders gathered around the Rosh Yeshivah, anxious for his guidance. "We all have a great opportunity and responsibility for *kiruv,*" he said. "There are more people today searching for authentic answers to the meaning of life. As Orthodox Jews we have those answers. We can provide them and it is our holy responsibility to furnish them."

Steve sat enraptured, for he could identify with the Rosh Yeshivah's words. He too, though successful in his business ventures, was searching for meaning in his life, which at times seemed empty. He listened further, "Young men are looking for excitement and they think that's where the answer is, but after the excitement wears off, they are back where they started from. Why there are young fellows who would even endanger their lives by seeking thrills, and even jump off planes ..."

Steve was stunned. Had the Rosh Yeshivah known he was in the room? Of all the hundreds of examples that he could have chosen, why did he choose that one? It was as though Rabbi Weinberg was talking directly to him.

Steve knew that he was not even supposed to be in the room, but then again, maybe he was. Suddenly Steve was soaring, gliding on a spiritual high, floating the rest of Shabbos and Sunday in an atmosphere of sanctity and piety.

On Monday morning he made his commitment as he enrolled in the Kol Yaakov Yeshivah in Monsey. From there he eventually transferred to Yeshivah Ohr Somayach where he studied for 13 years.

Today, down to earth, Simcha Dubin is a *shomer Torah u'mitzvos.*

The Swedish Connection

In 1946, Mr. David Turkel, a well-known activist in Agudath Israel affairs in Vienna, London, and, finally, New York, received a letter from Mrs. Rosa (Gertner) Backenroth from Orebro, Sweden. Mrs. Backenroth explained that her family had been wiped out in the Holocaust, but that she miraculously survived the death camps. She had been placed in a Displaced Persons camp and was eventually sent to Sweden.

She desperately wished to come to America to start a new life. She needed an affidavit, a declaration by a well-to-do American accepting financial responsibility for her, which would allow her to be admitted to the United States. She had already written numerous times to her relatives, the Riddlers* in San Francisco, asking them to file an affidavit on her behalf, but her pleas to them were unanswered.

Mrs. Backenroth had heard that Mr. Turkel was working diligently to get people affidavits, and so she pleaded with him to contact the Riddlers on her behalf, to explain the urgency of the matter. She explained that she had no one else to turn to and that her mental pain and anguish was becoming unbearable.

* Name has been changed.

She noted that she was maintaining her observance of *mitzvos* under the tutelage of Rabbi Zev Jacobson, a former rabbi in Hamburg, Germany, who had been sent to Sweden to serve the Jewish community there. She had heard that Mr. Turkel's mother's name was Backenroth-Heller, and she was quite certain that there was some family relationship.

Immediately Mr. Turkel wrote to the Riddlers in San Francisco, but he too received no reply. He wrote a second and third time, and like the pleas of Mrs. Backenroth, his were ignored. Mr. Turkel wrote Mrs. Backenroth assuring her that he would diligently pursue the matter, but inwardly he doubted that he would ever accomplish anything with the Riddlers. (Mr. Turkel himself had used all his personal privileges to issue affidavits to family members, and could not provide an additional one for Mrs. Backenroth.)

After making inquiries, Mr. Turkel found that the Riddlers were in the wholesale grocery business and were the sole northern California distributors for Manischewitz matzos and kosher-style meat products. He reasoned that if the Riddlers were in the kosher-food business, they surely had some affiliation with a rabbi in the area. Upon further investigation he found that Rabbi Gershon Katzman, a synagogue rabbi in San Francisco, knew the family well.

Mr. Turkel wrote a passionate letter to Rabbi Katzman, but received no reply. A few weeks went by, and one day Mr. Turkel received a call from Rabbi Katzman.

"Are you calling from California?" asked the surprised Mr. Turkel.

"No," came the reply. "I am here in New York for a few days for the wedding of a grandchild, and I would like to meet you."

The two men met and the questioning began immediately. Rabbi Katzman wanted to know about Mr. Turkel's background, his occupation, his birthplace in Europe, his lineage, his involvement with immigration problems, and so on. Finally, after what seemed like an endless interrogation, Rabbi Katzman said, "The Riddlers asked me to give you this for Mrs. Backenroth." And with that he gave Mr. Turkel a hundred dollars.

Mr. Turkel became enraged. "This is what you bring me?" he stormed. "Have you no shame? The woman needs a visa, not money. We here in New York have sent her money already but she has to get out of Sweden before the U.S. changes the immigration laws. The American consul in Stockholm is issuing visas liberally, but there is danger that it will stop almost any day now because of a Presidential directive that preferential treatment should go to displaced persons in the American zone of Germany. People in other countries may be stuck there for years. We need an affidavit now!"

Rabbi Katzman was crestfallen. He knew very well that Mr. Turkel was right. Indeed, he was a pawn in the hands of the Riddlers. He had tried to get the Riddlers to furnish an affidavit, but they refused. Now in the presence of the indignant Mr. Turkel, Rabbi Katzman, embarrassed, took back the hundred dollars. The two men shook hands and parted company.

A few days later, Rabbi Katzman boarded a train for his long trip back to California. As he sat on the train, a Jewish gentleman, Mr. Jack Heller, sat down next to him and soon they were engaged in conversation. Rabbi Katzman was a distinguished-looking *talmid chacham,* and Mr. Heller, though not very religious, thought he would be interesting to talk to.

Mr. Heller explained that he was on a business trip to Los Angeles and Rabbi Katzman told him about his grandson's wedding. As usual, when Jews meet for the first time, they exchanged information on family background and lineage. When Mr. Heller told Rabbi Katzman that he was from the small town of Schodnica in Galicia, Rabbi Katzman looked up surprised and said, "That's interesting. I just heard that town mentioned last week. A fellow I met told me his family had lived there."

"You met someone from Schodnica?" asked Mr. Heller. "Most of my family was from there. Whom did you meet?"

"I met a man named David Turkel, and I must tell you I was very impressed with him," said Rabbi Katzman.

"My cousin married a Turkel," exclaimed Mr. Heller. "You mean there are family members still alive? Do you know his telephone number?"

Rabbi Katzman gave Mr. Heller Mr. Turkel's telephone number, and from that moment on, Mr. Heller's demeanor changed.

He, too, had been born in Schodnica but when he was a young man he left his family and started a life of his own. Eventually he came to Canada, where he prospered in the watch and real-estate business. He was the only one of his family who left his home town. The elders of the family had forgotten him, and the younger generation hardly knew he existed.

When the train reached Chicago, Mr. Heller got off and made a telephone call. In New York, David Turkel picked up the phone. "Is this a member of the Turkel family?" came the long-distance question.

"Yes, I am David Turkel," came the reply. "Who is calling?"

"My name is Jack Heller."

"Jack Heller? I am sorry but I don't recognize that name."

Just then there was a shout from the other end of the room. A cousin of Mr. Turkel, Shmuel Yitzchok Heller, asked, "Did he say he was Jack Heller?"

The cousin grabbed the phone from David's hand and yelled into the phone, "You are Jack Heller? I am Shmuel Yitzchok Heller, your cousin. Where in the world are you calling from and how did you find us?"

The next day Mr. Heller was in New York in David Turkel's home, having canceled his trip to Los Angeles. The reunion with family members he hadn't seen in years was startling to everyone. There were tears, there was laughter, there was amazement, there was sorrow. Words tumbled forth as familial bonds that had been severed years ago began to converge.

However, David Turkel had one thing uppermost in mind. He saw Jack Heller as Hashem's messenger by whom many could be saved. And indeed, with his financial base Jack Heller became a savior, as he not only provided affidavits to many family members and friends of the Turkels, but also provided many of them with jobs and apartments.

Jack Heller even agreed to issue an affidavit for Mrs. Backenroth in Sweden, but shortly after Rabbi Katzman returned to San Francisco, the Riddlers relented and finally agreed to provide the required papers. In 1949, Mrs. Backenroth immigrated to America.

❁ ❁ ❁

Looking back, it is hard to understand today why a family would have been so obstinate as not to issue an affidavit for a close relative who had lost everyone and who was stranded in a DP camp. It is not for us to judge those people from a distance of 50 years and the advantage of hindsight. Speculation is unfair. However, this is definite: The initial refusal of the Riddler family to issue the affidavit was the catalyst for Mr. Turkel to meet Rabbi Katzman, who then met Mr. Jack Heller, who then contacted David Turkel, who began the proceedings for so many to be saved and supported and become reunited with their families.

And there was another reunion. By virtue of his reacquaintance with his family, Jack Heller became reunited with the *Yiddishkeit* of his youth.

In light of these events, we must ask ourselves: Who really knows what good can come from events that at first seem very bad? All that happens is part of Hashem's orchestration of human destiny. We are fortunate when we get a glimpse of even some pieces of the master puzzle fitting together.

Outside Chance

In the introduction to his recently published *sefer, Toras Hamelachos,* on the laws of Shabbos, Rabbi Moshe Shmuel Leitner of Jerusalem wrote a remarkable story about his grandmother and her diligence in Shabbos observance. I thank Rabbi Leitner and his father, Rabbi Dovid Leitner of Manchester, for sharing the details with me, and to Rabbi Moshe Grossman of Brooklyn for bringing the story to my attention.

In the 1920s, Reb Mordechai Kokish approached Austrian authorities for permission to build a kosher hotel in the beautiful holiday-resort area of Badgastein. His experience in the restaurant and hotel business convinced him that the locality was suitable and potentially profitable. However, his application was rejected; the anti-Semitic Austrian officials did not want a Jewish hotel in the center of town.

When he reapplied, the municipality told him that he could build his hotel on the outskirts of town. With no choice in the matter, Reb Mordechai built his small Hotel Bristol outside the city, along a picturesque waterfall. There was a *beis medrash* on the premises, and the food met the highest standards of *kashrus.*

Reb Mordechai and Sima Kokish had four daughters. Since there were no Jewish schools in Badgastein, the girls were enrolled in a local public school. R' Mordechai and his wife gave their children as thorough a Jewish education as they could in addition to their personal example of ardent commitment to *mitzvos* and steadfast honesty and integrity.

In 1930, R' Mordechai passed away, and the hotel fell to his widow. She was extremely efficient, and together with her four daughters ran a very smooth operation. As the 1930s wore on, anti-Semitism was intensified as restrictions and limitations were clamped on Jews and their businesses. Seeing the handwriting on the wall, many Austrian Jews tried desperately to secure entry visas to other countries.

Mrs. Kokish wrote to the family of a distant cousin who had left Austria in the 1890s and settled in Santiago, Chile. She explained her perilous situation and asked if they would be kind enough to sponsor her and her daughters so visas would be issued. Tragically, many of her relatives in Santiago had intermarried, but each of them, Jew and gentile alike, knew of the will that was written by their grandfather years ago, in which he wrote, "If my family members in Austria ever need help, you are to assist them in any way possible regardless of cost."

On *Kristalnacht* in November 1938, a night of looting, terror, and desecration of synagogues and Jewish businesses by vicious

Nazi sympathizers, Hotel Bristol was spared any damage for it was primarily a summer-resort hotel and therefore closed in November. Only Mrs. Kokish, her daughters, and two caretakers were in the hotel.

The following Shabbos morning as the Kokishes were eating their *seudah,* they were startled by a loud knock on the front door. The family froze in fright. Two Gestapo officers marched into the house and ordered Mrs. Kokish and their daughters to pack their belongings and prepare to come to Gestapo headquarters. "We will be back in an hour to pick you up and you had better be ready," one of the officers roared.

"Excuse me," exclaimed Mrs. Kokish as she stood up firmly. "Today is our Sabbath and we do not travel. Come back tomorrow. We are not going anyplace today!"

The soldiers were taken aback at the audacity of this woman. Very few Jews if any had dared question Gestapo orders until now. The soldiers turned and left the house in a fury. As soon as they left, Mrs. Kokish ordered the caretakers to take the *Sifrei Torah* from the *Aron Kodesh,* the *Chumashim,* the *Siddurim,* and the *Mezuzos* from the doorposts and wrap them in huge sheets, put them in laundry baskets and hide them in the warehouse, a mile from the hotel, so that they would be safe from the Gestapo.

Meanwhile the soldiers went directly to Gestapo headquarters and reported their encounter with the brazen woman. When their commander heard that the name of the woman was Mrs. Kokish, he closed his eyes for a moment as he tried to remember where he had heard that name.

Then it came to him. Years earlier in elementary school, he had been a classmate of one of the Kokish daughters, Raizel. She had noticed that he never seemed to have lunch like the other children. She learned that the boy's father was always drunk and spent any money he earned on liquor. There was hardly any food in the house, so his mother could not give him a lunch to take along to school. Raizel felt compassion for the boy and so every day she would have her mother pack an extra lunch for her to give the child. The Gestapo commander was that child.

The commander hesitated for a moment and said, "Leave them alone for today; you will pick them up tomorrow."

He knew the Kokish family was Jewish, so he allowed them that day for themselves. Remarkably, his gratitude was so minimal that he merely allowed them a grace period of 24 hours. To allow them total freedom was unthinkable even to him.

The next day the Gestapo soldiers came to pick up Mrs. Kokish and her daughters. They were ordered into a truck that took them to the train station in Vienna. The train would take them to a labor camp, most of whose prisoners were never heard from again.

The ride from the hotel at the secluded edge of town was so long that by the time they arrived at the train station, the train had already left. Every passenger on that train ultimately perished in concentration camps.

Frustrated at their inept timing, the Gestapo officers brought the Kokishes back to headquarters, where they were imprisoned for the rest of the week until the next train for Vienna. During that week, papers from their distant relatives in Santiago arrived, and the family was able to emigrate from Austria.

By incredible *Hashgachah Pratis* (Divine Providence), the remote location of Hotel Bristol, originally seen as a detriment to their religious and business life, actually saved the Kokish family.

❁ ❁ ❁

At the time of their escape, one of the daughters, Hinda, had been engaged to Yaakov Leitner. She waited eight years until after the war, when he was able to come to Santiago, where they married and raised a family. The Leitners ran a successful catering business and opened a machine-matzoh bakery for Chilean Jews. Eventually the Leitners moved to Manchester, England, where their children and grandchildren are *shomrei Torah u'mitzvos.*

Dovid *HaMelech* wrote, אָנָּה ה׳ כִּי אֲנִי עַבְדֶּךָ, אֲנִי עַבְדְּךָ בֶּן אֲמָתֶךָ פִּתַּחְתָּ לְמוֹסֵרָי, *Please Hashem, for I am Your servant, I am Your servant, son of your maidservant — You have released my bonds* (*Tehillim*

116:16). Rabbi Avigdor Miller explained, "Dovid *HaMelech* said to Hashem, The only reason that אֲנִי עַבְדְּךָ, I have merited becoming Your servant, is *because* בֶּן אֲמָתֶךָ, I had such a great mother who was Your maidservant."

The descendants of Mrs. Sima Kokish echo that sentiment.

Part C:

Prominence in Performance

Reaching Heights

Rabbi Simcha Barnett, director of the Aish Hatorah program in Philadelphia, has an identical twin, Michoel, who works for the Aish Hatorah office in Brooklyn. From infancy on, the two brothers, who grew up on Long Island, New York, were inseparable. They attended the same schools, had the same friends, played the same sports, attended the same colleges, shared the same hobbies, worked in the same professions, and then, in their 20's, became Torah-observant Jews — together.

As a result of the Barnetts becoming Torah observant when they were young adults, they are ideally suited for their work in Aish Hatorah, the world renowned organization for *baalei teshuvah.* Young professional, noncommitted Jews, searching for answers and meaning to life, identify with the Barnetts, who began their journey to Torah observant Judaism when they were promising Wall Street bankers.

On a recent *YomTov* morning, R' Simcha related an incident that happened to him and his brother years ago, before they became *baalei teshuvah.*

Among their many avocations, Simcha (Steve) and Michoel (Mitch) enjoyed bike riding. They had participated in bike tours in numerous countries and, in the 1980s, joined a group that was biking throughout New Zealand. New Zealand is comprised of two islands, North and South, separated by Cook Strait, a body of water that flows from the Pacific Ocean to the Tasman

Sea. The plan was to begin cycling at the tip of the North Island at the north cape, traverse the entire island from north to south, cross Cook Strait by ferry, and then cycle throughout the South Island to the tip of Invercargill, a distance of 1500 miles.

At the foot of the southern Alps in the South Island, they came to an eight-mile-long path with an incline so steep that it seemed as though they would be cycling up a straight wall! The cyclists struggled to pedal forward, their muscled calves strained to the limit. As Simcha rode slowly and excruciatingly onward, he saw something that he had never seen before. The bikers ahead of him were unzipping their backpacks and tossing away anything that was not absolutely necessary. One biker got rid of an extra wrench, another tossed away a heavy book, another discarded a broken helmet. Each was lightening his load, for every ounce he was carrying on his back was making the trek up the mountain more difficult. As Simcha watched what was transpiring ahead of him he thought to himself that indeed if he wished to reach the top of the mountain, he would have to rid himself of a lot of excess baggage.

Years later as he was becoming a *baal teshuvah,* he remembered this journey and realized that if he indeed wished to get to the top of the spiritual mountain, he would have to discard a considerable amount of secular baggage.

I was so taken by R' Simcha's insight that I shared it that afternoon with my children at a *Yom Tov seudah.* As I finished relating the incident, my son, Avrohom Zelig, exclaimed, "This concept is a *pasuk* (verse)."

"What *pasuk*?" I asked incredulously.

He replied, "It is the *pasuk,* מִי יַעֲלֶה בְהַר ה׳ וּמִי יָקוּם בִּמְקוֹם קָדְשׁוֹ? נְקִי כַפַּיִם וּבַר לֵבָב..., *Who may go up the mountain of Hashem, and who may stand in the place of His sanctity? One with clean hands and pure heart...* (*Tehillim* 24:3,4). *Clean hands* could be referring to one who has disposed of his 'extra secular' baggage."

Indeed, the *Olelos Ephraim,* cited by *Mikdash Me'at* on *Tehillim* (ibid.), writes that *David HaMelech is* comparing the ascent up the spiritual mountain to one's ascent up a physical mountain. Just as one will be unsuccessful in his mountain climbing if he is overburdened with a מַשָּׂא, *heavy load,* so too will one fail in his ascent up the *spiritual* mountain if he is hauling a heavy *secular* load.

The *Olelos Ephraim* then explains that the word מַשָּׂא, is an acronym for three words — מָמוֹן, *money,* שְׂמָלוֹת, *clothes,* אוֹכֶל *food.* If someone is totally preoccupied by his pursuit of the dollar, or overly obsessed by his clothes, or always insistent that he eat only the finest foods, that person is carrying a load that will ultimately prevent him from reaching the top of the spiritual mountain.

We all need money, clothes, and food to get along in this world. It is, however, the way we pursue these necessities that determines whether one is primarily a spiritual or a materialistic person.

Tunnel Vision

The Midrash (*Shir HaShirim Rabbah* 4:2) tells how Rabbeinu HaKadosh was giving a *shiur* (Torah discourse) when he noticed that some of his students were falling asleep. Wanting to startle them into paying attention, he said, "There was a woman in Egypt who gave birth to 600,000 in one pregnancy!"

Suddenly everyone awoke. "I was referring to Yocheved," said Rebbe. "She gave birth to Moshe *Rabbeinu* who was equal to all of *Klal Yisrael* (symbolized by the 600,000 men who left Egypt)."

Rabbi Nisson Wolpin suggests that Rebbe's statement can also mean that every Jewish child born is equal to 600,000. Many times, all Jews are judged by the actions of one Jew. Thus, when a Jew makes a *kiddush Hashem,* it reflects well on all of *Klal Yisrael* and if a Jew, tragically, makes a *chillul Hashem,* it reflects poorly on all of *Klal Yisrael.* Hence, being a Jew is not only a privilege but a responsibility.

The following story is a case in point.

A number of years ago, Mrs. Chaye Rifka Kleinbart of Boro Park was expecting her sixth child. When labor began one morning, she told her husband, Yidel, that they had to rush to Mt. Sinai Hospital in Manhattan to deliver their child.

"It's rush hour. How will we get there on time?" Yidel asked anxiously.

"Don't worry, we'll get there," his wife assured him, somewhat nervously.

Driving through the streets of Boro Park was manageable, but the Prospect and Gowanus Expressways toward Manhattan were frightening. The roads were clogged. Every passing minute increased Yidel's fear and trepidation that they would not get to the hospital in time.

The quickest way to Manhattan was through the Brooklyn Battery Tunnel, but the lines of cars bottlenecking toward the tunnel seemed endless. In desperation, Yidel turned illegally into the lane reserved for buses and taxis, and sped along, a lone car among yellow cabs and commuter buses. When he reached the tollbooth, Yidel sped into the tunnel, without paying the toll.

As they emerged from the other side, a policeman, notified of Yidel's "crime" by tunnel authorities, flagged down the car. "What's going on?" the officer demanded.

"My wife is in labor. We're rushing to the hospital to have a baby," shouted Yidel.

"Why didn't you call us?" the policeman called back. "We would have given you an escort. Go!"

The Kleinbarts resumed their rush and made it to Mount Sinai Hospital on time. The baby was born that morning.

That night Yidel returned to Boro Park from Manhattan via the Battery Tunnel, and when he reached the tollbooth, he handed two tokens to the toll collector. "What's this?" the toll collector asked.

"I was here this morning and I was rushing — "

Before he could finish the sentence, the toll collector said excitedly, "Oh, what did your wife have?"

Yidel was stunned. "How did you know?" he asked the toll collector in amazement.

"They told us that a guy like you would surely come back and pay," replied the toll collector.

❁ ❁ ❁

The officers in the tollbooth and the patrol car had seen Yidel for merely moments and yet were confident to make their evaluation. A remarkable *kiddush Hashem!*

However there are unsung and unknown heroes in this story — the wonderful Jews who at earlier occasions had acted nobly to give the officers such a lofty impression of Orthodox Jews. Mr. Yidel Kleinbart's admirable act merely reinforced what the officers had come to believe — that Orthodox Jews can be relied on to be honorable and trustworthy.

Delivering in Dallas

Every *Yom Kippur* we stand before Hashem with remorse as we recite 44 expressions of confession (two for each letter of the Hebrew alphabet), each one beginning with the words עַל חֵטְא, *For the sin.* The 20th one is עַל חֵטְא שֶׁחָטָאנוּ לְפָנֶיךָ בְּיוֹדְעִים וּבְלֹא יוֹדְעִים, *And for the sin that we have sinned before you knowingly or unknowingly.*

Since Hashem holds us accountable even if we unknowingly cause others to sin or unknowingly bring others pain, financial loss or embarrassment, surely we are rewarded when we unknowingly cause others to do good, bring them joy, financial gain, or honor. *Chazal* teach: מִדָּה טוֹבָה מְרוּבָּה מִמִּדַּת פּוּרְעָנוּת, *[Hashem's] measure of beneficence is greater than [His] measure of retribution* (*Sanhedrin* 100b).

In the following remarkable story, one Jew's deeds unknowingly influenced another Jew's deeds. The results were far reaching, both in terms of distance in this world and eternity in the next world.

In 1983, Rabbi Aryeh Rodin, a graduate of Yeshiva Chofetz Chaim in Forest Hills, New York, assumed the spiritual leadership of the newly formed Young Israel of Dallas, Texas. As a dedicated rav he gave *shiurim* (lectures) to the community at large, and with his painstaking *kiruv* (outreach) work, more families than ever before became committed to authentic Judaism.

One day Rabbi Rodin was sitting in his small office when a gentleman he had never seen before walked in. "Rabbi," he said in a deep Texan drawl, "Can I have a word with you?"

"Sure," said Rabbi Rodin. "Please sit down."

"My name is Leonard Fruhman," the man began, extending Rabbi Rodin a very firm handshake. Leonard and the rabbi became involved in a friendly nonconfrontational conversation about Judaism and after a while Leonard said, "I would like to make a contribution to your synagogue."

Rabbi Rodin was surprised. People do not usually walk into a *shul* off the street and give money without being asked, pressured, or honored. He expected to receive a check for $100.00 Instead, he was astounded when Mr. Fruhman told him the check would be for $2,000.00!

"I don't have any checks with me," said Leonard with an easy smile, "but I will be back next week. You can count on that, Rabbi."

Rabbi Rodin returned the smile and wished Leonard well. In his heart, though, Rabbi Rodin was convinced that Leonard would not be back. He had no synagogue affiliation or commitment to Orthodox Judaism, and $2,000.00 was a substantial amount of money for a first-time donation. Rabbi Rodin thought that Leonard would probably rethink his pledge and decide he had been too generous. No one gives that amount to a *shul* with which he is unfamiliar.

To Rabbi Rodin's surprise, Leonard returned, but the check was not for $2,00.00. It was for *three* thousand dollars! "I thought about our conversation throughout the week, Rabbi, and I liked what you told me," Leonard said with enthusiasm, "so I increased the amount I am giving."

Rabbi Rodin was speechless. When he regained his composure, he asked Leonard jokingly, "Perhaps you'd like to come back next week?"

That first donation began a long relationship between the Fruhmans and Rabbi Rodin. When the rabbi moved to Far North Dallas in 1986 to establish Congregation Ohev Shalom, Leonard came along.

Leonard passed away tragically at the untimely age of 49, and shortly afterwards his mother and family made substantial donations to rebuild and renovate the Ohev Sholom synagogue in his memory.

At Leonard's *shloshim*, a memorial held 30 days after his passing, Rabbi Rodin, in a moving eulogy, told the following remarkable story.

In 1986 Leonard made his first trip ever to Israel. He was determined to "see all the sights." One morning he went to the *Kosel Hamaaravi,* where Jews the world over come to pray, and where many write "messages to G-d" on small pieces of paper and insert them in the crevices of the holy wall.

Unfamiliar with the conventional text of prayers, Leonard walked up to the stately massive wall, respectfully put his right hand on the gnarled stones and slowly caressed the cool bulges. Leonard closed his eyes and in silent prayer expressed to G-d his innermost yearnings.

After a while Leonard became aware of a Yerushalmi Jew standing to his right totally immersed in prayer. Wrapped in his *tallis,* the fellow was swaying gently to and fro, his eyes glued to the worn pages of his *Tehillim* (Psalms). Every once in a while, the Yerushalmi Jew would close his eyes, raise his hands to Heaven and sigh.

As Leonard observed him, he noticed the rhapsody on his face, the peaceful bliss of a man connecting with his Maker. Leonard was overcome by a sense of spirituality he had never experienced before. He wished he could sense that bond between man and his Creator. If only he could touch it, feel it, or bottle it.

Leonard wished he could give the man some money but he would not even consider interrupting those moments of holiness. Besides, it would only taint the aura and would almost be profane.

Leonard left the *Kosel* uplifted and strengthened, but, in a sense, empty. Suddenly the Judaism he hadn't been close to meant more to him now than ever before. The noble experience stayed with him for the remainder of his trip in the Holy Land.

When he returned to Dallas, Leonard went to the Jewish bakery to meet his friend, the owner, Mr. Abe Preizler. He told Mr. Preizler about his trip to Israel and then he described his emotional experience at the *Kosel Hamaaravi.* "Tell me," Leonard said earnestly, "what synagogue in town do you think that man at the wall would feel comfortable praying in?"

The reply came quickly, "In Rabbi Rodin's synagogue."

"And that is how Leonard's friendship with the Orthodox community began," said Rabbi Rodin. "And from then on, Leonard and his family grew in their commitment to Judaism."

Rabbi Rodin paused and then said with emphasis. "Imagine, for a moment, the scene when that Yerushalmi gentleman who was davening at the *Kosel Hamaaravi* comes to Heaven after his prescribed years in this world are complete. Hashem will tell him that he is about to be rewarded for being instrumental in maintaining and refurbishing a *shul* in Dallas. The fellow probably never heard of Dallas, and if he did he certainly wouldn't know where to find it. Yet, because he *davened* the way he did, where he did, it turns out that we in this community owe him so much. And his reward in the *Olam HaEmes* (World of Truth) will be immense."

Rabbi Rodin directed everyone to reflect on this thought. "Consider the responsibility we have for each of our actions. Could the Yerushalmi at the *Kosel* ever imagine that donations to charity would be made only because of him?

"We should all be careful with anything and everything we do, for there are always people watching us, even if we are not aware of it. Our actions may influence their actions, for the good or, Heaven forbid, otherwise. It is one of our greatest obligations."

Broken to a Point

Sometimes an appropriate remark at an opportune moment can change the life of the listener, forever. We can never be sure of the effect of our words, however casually they may have been spoken.

This touching story, told by the famous *maggid* of Jerusalem, Rabbi Shabsi Binyamin Yudelevitz (1924-1996), illustrates how one sentence changed a life. The story was published in *Drashos LeMoadim* by Rabbi Aharon Zakkai, a prolific author in Jerusalem, who heard it from Reb Shabsi many years ago.

More than a hundred years ago, a poverty-stricken rabbi from Jerusalem, Rabbi Lipa Kalashefsky,* had to travel abroad to raise money for his family. His first stop was Italy. His boat docked in Milan on a Friday morning and, having no specific addresses to go to, Rabbi Kalashefsky began walking through the town trying to find where the Jewish neighborhood might be. As he walked along, he saw a horse-drawn carriage coming toward him. As the carriage drew alongside him, the owner ordered his driver to stop. He looked out of the window and called to Reb Lipa, "*Shalom aleichem*! What is a Jew like you doing in Milan?"

The rabbi looked up at the carriage, surprised that a man of such wealth would stop to talk to him. "I'm here from Jerusalem," Reb Lipa said, "and I am looking for the Jewish neighborhood."

"You are in luck," said the wealthy man as he climbed down the steps of his coach and greeted Reb Lipa warmly with a firm

*The name has been changed

We don't get to meet many people like you in this part of the world."

Mr. Hilvicht helped Reb Lipa into his carriage and together they traveled to the family mansion. On the way, the two Jews from different parts of the world engaged in friendly conversation. They exchanged information about their respective families and cities, and then Mr. Hilvicht said again, "Please, Reb Lipa, stay with us for Shabbos. We would be honored to have you."

Reb Lipa had no other place to stay and he was happy to accept this gracious invitation. When the carriage arrived at the mansion, Reb Lipa was shown to the guest quarters and he immediately began to prepare for Shabbos.

That evening Mr. Hilvicht and Reb Lipa went to *shul* where Reb Lipa was seated next to the rabbi. After *davening,* Mr. Hilvicht and his sons proudly escorted their guest to their beautiful home.

As the meal progressed, Reb Lipa was impressed by the crystal bowls, flasks, and silverware in the ornate cabinet in the dining room. He had never seen so much gold and silver before in a single home. Suddenly Reb Lipa noticed something strange on the middle shelf.

It was a broken glass flask. Sharp points of jagged glass jutted out grotesquely — hardly an appropriate showpiece for such a mansion.

As Reb Lipa sat staring at the grotesque broken flask, Mr. Hilvicht noticed that Reb Lipa's mind had wandered from their conversation. "Is everything all right?" he asked.

"If you don't mind my curiosity," said Reb Lipa softly, "that broken flask seems out of place in this beautiful cabinet. Is there a reason why it's there?"

Mr. Hilvicht smiled and looked at his children sitting around the table. They had heard the story many times before, but few visitors even noticed the broken flask. Usually Mr. Hilvicht would have to initiate conversation about it, but Reb Lipa was perceptive. "How wonderful it is to have a Jew from Jerusalem in my home," thought Mr. Hilvicht.

"It's a long story," he said. "If you like, I will be happy to tell it to you," he said, hoping Reb Lipa would be interested.

*The name has been changed

"If you don't mind telling it, I would like to hear it."

And then Mr. Hilvicht began:

"I was born in Amsterdam and always thought I would live there all my life. When I was 18 years old, my grandfather, who lived here in Italy, wrote my parents that his health was failing and he needed someone from the family to come for a while to help in his store. He asked if I would be kind enough to come for a short time.

"My parents thought it would be a good idea for me to get some business experience, and they encouraged me to go. I had been with my grandfather for a few months when he took a turn for the worse. He could no longer come to the store so, unexpectedly, I began tending to the business myself, reporting to my grandfather every night. That went on for only a few more weeks. Then he died.

"My parents wanted me to liquidate the business and return to Amsterdam, but I loved the atmosphere in the business world. I was getting a feel for money that I had earned on my own, and I asked my parents for permission to keep the store open for a while.

"To everyone's surprise, I began doing very well. Customers liked me very much and the business began doing better than ever. I was selling more merchandise than my grandfather ever did. I wrote my parents that I would remain in Italy.

"The business grew to the point that I opened a branch store. I was busy day and night. One afternoon, I was so involved with my work that I didn't *daven Minchah.* That was the beginning of my slide away from Judaism. Soon I missed *Shacharis* too, with the excuse that it was only today that I was negligent — but tomorrow I would be sure to *daven.* Tomorrow never came. One by one, my observance of *mitzvos* fell by the wayside.

"Eventually I was married and had children, but I had left the ways of my fathers and forefathers. I became very wealthy, and although I remembered that I was Jewish, my practice of *mitzvos* was almost nil.

"One afternoon, I was walking in the street where some Jewish children were playing. They all seemed to be very happy, as children usually are, but then I heard someone scream. A boy was crying bitterly, and none of his friends could console him. I watched for a few moments as the boys huddled around the child, who was repeating the same thing over and over between his bitter sobs.

" 'What will I tell my father?' he wailed. 'What will I tell my father?'

"I walked up to the boys and asked, 'Just what is going on here?'

"They all turned to look at the forlorn little boy who now looked up at me and said, 'I am in such trouble. What will I tell my father?'

" 'What happened?' I asked, 'Maybe I can help you.' The boys explained that their little friend came from a very poor family. His father had saved his precious few coins throughout the winter so that he would be able to buy a flask of oil for *Chanukah* lighting. This afternoon he had sent his son to buy the oil, and warned him to come home right away and not to play with his friends, because the flask of oil might break. The boy bought the oil — but when he saw his friends playing, he joined in. Sure enough the flask broke and the oil spilled.

"I looked at the boy who was still whimpering and saying worriedly to himself, 'What will I tell my father?'

"I felt bad for the boy and told him that I would help him. I walked him back to the store and bought him a much larger flask of oil than he had originally bought. I told him to be careful, and then, to the delight of all the boys who had followed us to the store, I sent him on his way home, overjoyed.

"As I walked home that evening, the little boy's words rang in my ears. 'What will I tell my father? What will I tell my father?' And I thought to myself, indeed, what will I tell *my* Father? My Father in Heaven — after a hundred and twenty years?I had-drifted so far from Judaism that I had forgotten it was almost *Chanukah*. What excuse would I have when I stood before my Father in Heaven on that final Judgment Day?

"I walked back to where the children had been playing before and gathered up the broken flask and the shards from the street and took it home with me. That night, to the surprise of my wife and children, I lit a *Chanukah* candle.

"The next night, I lit two and with each passing night, I increased the amount of candles I lit. I stared at the candles as they flickered and sparkled, remembering my parents' home back in Amsterdam. I had gone far away — maybe too far.

"That *Chanukah* was the beginning of my return to the observance of *mitzvos.* Eventually, with the understanding of my wife, we began training our children the way we had been brought up.

"Our road back had started with that broken flask and the words of that boy, 'What will I tell my father?' That is why I keep that flask as a treasured memento of what changed my life."

Reb Lipa smiled, his face aglow from the story he had just heard. He thought to himself that it was almost worth the trip just to hear this story first hand. Mr. Hilvicht's face was radiant as well, for even though he had told the story numerous times before, it hadn't lost its luster.

Spontaneously, both stood up and walked to the cabinet to inspect the precious pieces of jagged glass.

Mr. Hilvicht's thoughts correspond to an interpretation the great chassidic master Reb Meir of Premishlan [d. 1773], a *talmid* of the Baal Shem Tov (1698-1760), gave to a similar phrase uttered by Yehudah when he was standing in front of the viceroy in Egypt, whom he did not yet realize was his brother Yosef.

The viceroy, having accused Binyamin of stealing his silver goblet, was insisting to the sons of Yaakov that they return to their father and leave Binyamin behind. Yehudah opposed this idea vehemently, because he had undertaken responsibility to bring Binyamin back to his elderly father Jacob.

Yehudah exclaimed to Yosef, כִּי אֵיךְ אֶעֱלֶה אֶל אָבִי וְהַנַּעַר אֵינֶנּוּ אִתִּי, *"For how can I go up to my father if the youth is not with me?"* (*Bereishis* 44:34).

Reb Meir of Premishlan explains that this question is also an allusion to the question that we must ask ourselves, "How can we go up to our Father in Heaven on Judgment Day if our youth (our children) are not with us, i.e., if we have not educated our children to live according to the Torah?"

Interestingly, the first Rebbe of Ger, the *Chiddushei HaRim,* R' Yitzchak Meir Alter (1789-1866), also sees Yehudah's expression as a query we must ask ourselves, "How can I go to my Father in Heaven if I have not recaptured my youth by repenting the sins of my early years?"

These were the lessons that Aryeh Leib Hilvicht finally understood, thanks to a broken jar of oil.

True to Life

Living a life of honesty and integrity not only spares one from Hashem's wrath, it merits bountiful blessings. David *HaMelech* teaches:,מִי הָאִישׁ הֶחָפֵץ חַיִּים אֹהֵב יָמִים לִרְאוֹת טוֹב?, *"Which man desires life, and loves days of seeing good?* נְצֹר לְשׁוֹנְךָ מֵרָע וּשְׂפָתֶיךָ מִדַּבֵּר מִרְמָה, *Guard your tongue from [speaking] evil, and your lips from speaking deceitfully* (*Tehillim* 34:13,14). The following story illustrates this promise in an astounding way.

A number of years ago, while vacationing with her family in a bungalow colony in Monticello, New York, Mrs. Basya Rothberg* gave birth to a premature baby boy, who weighed a little more than two pounds. The child was rushed from Monticello by Medivac helicopter to a medical center in Valhalla, New York, where he was immediately placed in the neonatal intensive care unit.

The little boy's life was hanging in the balance as doctors and nurses tried valiantly to sustain him in every way possible. His heart was weak, his lungs were frail and he needed blood transfusions. Rabbi Rothberg, who came to visit his wife and baby every day, consulted with the doctors regularly as he continuously thanked them profusely for all they were doing.

"We are so grateful for all your efforts," Rabbi Rothberg said. "I know my son has had numerous transfusions. Is there any way that I can donate blood directly for him?"

*The name has been changed

"We have a blood bank here at the hospital," replied one of the doctors, "and if your blood type is the same as your son, it could be designated for him."

His type was indeed the same, so an appointment was made for Rabbi Rothberg to give blood. On the designated day Rabbi Rothberg came with his eldest son, Shimon, who also wished to donate blood. Shimon, too, had been born prematurely and identified with his new baby brother.

When they entered the room where they were to donate blood, Rabbi Rothberg saw a sign that read, "Only those between 17 and 65 can donate blood." He turned to Shimon and said, "I'm sorry but you won't be able to give blood. You are not 17."

"I'll be 17 in two weeks," Shimon protested.

"But right now, you are not 17 and the sign says only someone who is 17," said Rabbi Rothberg.

"But I am in my 17th year," Shimon complained.

"I'm sorry," answered Rabbi Rothberg, "it's *sheker* (falsehood) to say that you are 17."

"I'll ask a *sh'eilah* (a question of Torah law). I'm sure any rav will *paskin* (rule) that I can give blood for my brother," Shimon said.

"First of all," replied Rabbi Rothberg, "no rav can make you 17. Besides I don't even allow you to ask this *sh'eilah,* because if you do get a *heter* (rabbinical permission), you will be looking for loopholes all your life!"

Reluctantly, Shimon agreed that his father was right. It was not *pikuach nefesh* (a life-threatening situation), because there were others who could donate blood.

A few days later, Shimon was a passenger in a car that was involved in a serious accident. He lost so much blood that when the medics were finally able to extricate him from the crash, he had to be given 'concentrated blood' to keep him alive until he could be brought to the hospital.

When the doctor heard that Shimon had nearly given blood just days before, he said, "Had he given blood that day he would be dead now, because there would not have been enough time from then till now for his body to replenish the blood that he needed to remain alive."

Mrs. Rothberg, who told me the story, says today, "If not for my husband's *ehrlichkeit* and honesty, my son would not be alive today."

When David*HaMelech* wrote that those who refrain from speaking deceitfully will merit life, it was not a figure of speech. It was the literal truth.

Rabbeinu Bachya (*Kad Hakemach,* sec. *Emunah*) notes an interesting phenomenon regarding the first verse in the Torah, which, he says, is the foundation of the entire Torah. In בְּרֵאשִׁית בָּרָא אֱלֹקִים אֵת הַשָּׁמַיִם וְאֵת הָאָרֶץ *In the beginning of G-d's creating the heavens and the earth,* (*Bereishis* 1:1), Every vowel sound is present except one. There is the *kamatz,* the *patach*, the *segal*, the *tzeirei,* the *cholem,* the *shevah* and the *chirik*. The only missing vowel is *shuruk* (the *ooh* sound). This is because in Hebrew, the word *shuruk* שֻׁרֻק is compossed of the letters שֶׁקֶר, *falsehood,* and falsehood or deceit in any form, cannot exist in the foundation of Torah!

Perhaps, then, if we wish to structure a lifestyle that will bring us close to Hashem so that He brings us His bountiful blessings of life and good days, we must build it on a foundation of truth, honesty, and integrity.

Sole Nourishment

Rabbi Yaakov Yosef Moskowitz, a rebbi in the Belzer Yeshiva in Monsey, New York, is one of two directors of Tomchei Shabbos of Rockland County. Every Thursday night, Rabbi Moskowitz and his dedicated partner, Mr. Alan Rosenstock, coordinate the distribution of more than 150 boxes of Shabbos food to families in financial distress. The *chessed* and dedication of these two men is extraordinary.

For a recent fund-raising dinner, Rabbi Moskowitz published a short narrative about his grandfather that inspires him to this day.

When Rav Sholom Moskowitz (1878-1958) of Shutz, Romania, author of *Daas Sholom* on *Shulchan Aruch* and *Perek Shirah,* was a child, his family was extremely poor. Food was scarce and there were days when there was barely anything in the house to eat.

One evening little Sholom's mother, Faiga, measured out portions of hot broth for her children. Just as she brought the last bowl to the table, there was a knock on the front door. A poor man entered the house and asked if he could have something to eat.

At once Sholom picked up his bowl of broth and brought it to the gaunt, shabbily dressed man. "This is for you," he said gently.

The poor man sat down and ate it. Shortly afterward, he thanked the family for their kindness and left. When the pauper was out the door, Mrs. Moskowitz turned to Sholom and said sympathetically, "Don't you realize that I have no other food? Why did you give him your soup?"

"I thought to myself," said the child, "if I eat the soup myself, in two days there won't be a remnant or memory left of it. But if I give it to the poor man, the *mitzvah* will remain for eternity!"

> David *HaMelech* writes, טוֹב אִישׁ חוֹנֵן ... לְזֵכֶר עוֹלָם יִהְיֶה צַדִּיק, *Good is the man who is compassionate...an everlasting remembrance will the righteous man remain* (*Tehillim* 112:5,6).
>
> Is it a wonder that this story inspires Rav Sholom Moskowitz's descendants to be sensitive to others?

Confrontation on the Waterfront

As World War II raged in 1942, American forces and their allies battled the Axis on three continents. At home, every American male between the ages of 18 and 45 had to register with his local draft board. Policemen had the right to stop men in the street and demand to see their registration cards.

Married men with children were not sent to the front, but they could be assigned to war-related jobs, at which they had to work seven days a week, if necessary, for the war effort. Sam Brand, who lived with his wife Bernice and their children in Washington Heights, New York, was notified by his local board that he had been assigned to the War Plant at the Brooklyn Navy Yard, on the Williamsburgh waterfront. He was to report Sunday morning.

From the moment he read the notice, Sam worried about what to do if he was assigned to work on Shabbos. He consulted rabbis and friends and received different ideas on how he should handle the situation. Adding to his concern was the fact that his father Hyman Brand was known throughout New York City as a vigorous campaigner for *shmiras Shabbos.*

Hyman Brand had a truck with a loudspeaker from which he would appeal to Jewish shopkeepers to close their stores on Shabbos. He denounced families that drove their cars on Shabbos and he disseminated pamphlets, printed at his own expense, explaining the importance of Shabbos. He persuaded synagogues and advertisers not to advertise in the Sunday *Morgen Journal,* one of the foremost Yiddish newspapers, because it was widely believed that the Sunday paper was printed on Shabbos, since it was already on the newsstands on *Motzaei Shabbos.* In 1945 he was given a citation in City Hall by Mayor Vincent Impelitari for his campaign for Sabbath observance.

Thus when Sam appeared on Sunday at the navy yard where towering battleships were being built, he felt a mixture of trepidation and determination.

He was commissioned to do electrical and gas welding of battleships parts, and he was told that he would be paid time-an-a-half for working Saturdays and double for working on Sundays. The hourly wage at the time was 75 cents an hour. Sam decided that he would wait a day or two before he told his supervisor that he would not report for work on Shabbos. The supervisor was a nonobservant Jew, and Sam expected him not to take the news lightly.

There was tension throughout the plant from the stress of manufacturing the battleship parts on hectic deadlines. The war was going badly for the Allies in 1942, and the lives of American sailors depended on getting those parts in time. On Tuesday, Sam courageously told his high-strung supervisor that he could not come in on Saturday because he was a Sabbath observer.

The supervisor flew into a rage and shouted sarcastically, "In case you didn't notice, there is a war going on, Brand. Everyone has to show up every day, even you!"

Sam stood held his ground and explained softly that he could not violate his Sabbath. "If you find any extra hours for me to work during the week," said Sam, "I will be happy to do so, but I will not come in on my Sabbath."

"If you get fired from this job, you'll be sent overseas to the front lines," the supervisor threatened.

Sam tried to reason with him but to no avail. The supervisor walked away defiantly, when suddenly he whirled around. He pointed an accusing finger at Sam and said between clenched teeth, "If you say you're so religious, prove it! Show me your *tzitzis*!"

Sam was startled. This supervisor knew about *tzitzis*?

He waited for a moment before he responded. He wanted to dramatize the moment for those who stood watching and listening. Without saying a word, he lifted his shirt and picked up his *tallis kattan*. He gathered up his *tzitzis* and held them tenderly in his hands.

The supervisor was stunned. "Okay," he muttered, "but you'll only get time-and-a-half for Sunday."

Later that afternoon Sam quietly made the calculation that time - and-a-half meant he would get only $1.13 an hour on Sunday, instead of $1.50. What a bargain to remain a *shomer Shabbos.*

Dead Right

Rabbi David Stavsky is the senior Orthodox Rabbi in Columbus, Ohio, where he has served for over forty 40 years. He has participated in a myriad of life-cycle events ranging from the joyous festivities of birth and marriage to the sad times of illness and bereavement. His warmth and wisdom have guided and comforted countless people for two generations.

In the summer of 1994, Rabbi Stavsky received a telephone call that led to events that were as remarkable and moving as any he had witnessed and participated in all his years in the rabbinate. The caller spoke in Yiddish and said, *"Rebbe, ich ruf eich mitt ah tzubrochin hartz* (Rabbi, I am calling you with a broken heart.)" The man explained that he had come to Ohio a year ago from Kiev, Ukraine. He had a painful personal problem and he wished to discuss it privately. Rabbi Stavsky invited him to come over at once.

When Michel Darshevsky* came to Rabbi Stavsky's office, he broke down as he explained the events of the past year. When he had first come to the Columbus area, he became a member of a local Reform temple. "Why would a Jew from the Ukraine join a Reform temple?" asked Rabbi Stavsky with surprise. "There are no Reform Jews in the Ukraine."

Michel explained that he and his family had been waiting for years to come to America. They had been placed on a long waiting list and were told that they would have to wait until someone in America sponsored them. After years of waiting they were told that a temple in Ohio had agreed to sponsor their family. Thrilled with the news, they hastily made their plans to leave Kiev and soon afterwards, Michel, his wife, and their two children, who were in their early 20's, arrived in Columbus.

Upon their arrival, the temple provided them with an apartment, gave them money to establish themselves and helped the two children find jobs. "I had to join their temple," said Michel. "They were very kind to us and besides, as a newcomer I didn't know of any other synagogue around here."

"How can I help you?" asked Rabbi Stavsky.

Michel's demeanor changed as he went on with his story. In 1941, Ukraine's German conquerors, with their Ukrainian henchmen, forced hundreds of Jews — including Michel's parents — and gentiles considered enemies of the ruling government to march to a field outside the city. They forced the helpless people to dig a huge mass grave and then lined them up and murdered

*The name has been changed

them all. Michel had been able to run away from the group, and thus his life was spared.

Knowing where his parents were buried, Michel went there regularly and recited the few Hebrew prayers he remembered. He was constantly plagued, though, that his parents were eternally buried together with gentiles. When Michel realized that he would be coming to America, he went to the field where his parents were buried and dug up some of the earth and put it in a jar. To him, this earth represented the remains of his beloved parents, and his dream was to honor their memory by burying it in a Jewish cemetery.

One day, after having settled in the Columbus area, he went to see the rabbi of his temple. Michel told him how his parents had been murdered, and that he now wanted to bury their symbolic remains in a Jewish cemetery.

The rabbi assured him that it would be done and made arrangements to bury the earth-filled jar in the temple's cemetery. A few weeks after the burial, Michel came to the rabbi and told him that the time had come to put up the monument for his parents. Proudly, he told the rabbi that he had saved up money and had purchased a small monument with his parents' names engraved in Hebrew and in English.

The rabbi looked at Michel with astonishment. "You can't have that monument put up in our cemetery," he said. "That's not the way we do things here. Our cemetery allows only for a flat slab of marble, engraved with the name of the deceased, to be placed on top of the grave. Nothing more. We don't consider monuments aesthetic."

Michel protested, saying that monuments were traditional and that was the way graves had been identified for generations. The rabbi explained that the expansive rolling hills of the cemetery were beautiful and that the monument would interrupt the gracious panorama of the terrain. He tried to make Michel understand that things were done differently in America; Ohio was not the Ukraine.

Michel became angry and told the rabbi that if he couldn't put up the monument, he would dig up the jar and bury it somewhere else. The rabbi was not intimidated and told Michel that he could do so if he pleased but that the temple could not change its policy for one person, no matter how much he liked Michel.

❁ ❁ ❁

Michel's eyes now swelled with tears as he looked worriedly at Rabbi Stavsky. "Please, Rebbe," he said, "do you have a Jewish cemetery where I could bury my jar with the earth of my parents and then put up the *matzeivah* (monument)?"

Rabbi Stavsky was overwhelmed. Tenderly he assured Michel that the burial and the placement of the monument would be arranged with dignity and respect.

A few days later, Rabbi Stavsky and a *minyan* of 10 men went to his synagogue's cemetery. A small grave had been opened for Michel's jar.

Before they placed the jar in the earth, Michel sat down and wrote on a piece of paper, טייערע טאטע און מאמע, איך וועל אייך קיינמאל נישט פארגעסן. אייער ליבער זון מיכל, *Dearest Father and Mother, I will never forget you. Your loving son, Michel.*

Michel put the slip of paper in the jar and the people gently buried the jar of earth. Rabbi Stavsky led everyone in the recitation of some chapters of *Tehillim* and he helped Michel say *Kaddish.*

As they were driving home from the cemetery, Michel turned to Rabbi Stavsky and said with palpable relief, הַיינט בַּיי נַאכְט קֶען אִיך שְׁלָאפֶּען , *Tonight, I can sleep.* For all these years, I was so concerned and troubled that my parents were not in *kever Yisrael,* a Jewish grave. But tonight I know they rest in peace."

Esrogim Before Sukkos

Rabbi Aharon Kotler writes, "The world exists only by virtue of those who feel a responsibility to the public, and not by those who smugly tell themselves, 'Things are fine with me,' and disconnect themselves from the community" (*Mishnas Rav Aharon* Vol. 3, P. 176).

In this remarkable episode we witness a Rabbi whose regard for his townspeople is an everlasting testimony to his eminence.

Rabbi Elazar Meir Preil, (1878-1933), a renowned *talmid chacham* and author of *Sefer Hameor,* was the rabbi of Elizabeth, New Jersey for 14 years. American Jewish communities in the 1920s and 1930s were not as observant as they are today, and the rabbi's role in guiding his community in Torah and *mitzvah* observance was crucial. Quite often communal observance and understanding of Torah dictates and principles was totally dependent on the rabbi's commitment to these ideals.

Few Jews during those years brought their own *lulavim* and *esrogim*. They took it for granted that their rabbi would purchase sets of the *arbaah minnim* (four species) and allow the members of the congregation to use them.

In 1933, a few weeks before Succos, Rabbi Preil became very ill. A few hours before *Yom Tov,* Rabbi Preil called his friend and colleague, Rabbi Nosson Nota Zuber of nearby Roselle, New Jersey. "I need you to come in a hurry," Rabbi Preil said anxiously, "and I need you in person. What I need you to do for me cannot be done by telephone."

Although he was busy before *Yom Tov,* Rabbi Zuber came rushing to Rabbi Preil's home. Upon entering he found his friend in bed, weak and deathly ill.

"I have only one son, my Yehoshua Yosef who is nine years old," Rabbi Preil said to Rabbi Zuber. "If Heaven forbid I die before or during *Succos,* my sets of the *arbaah minnim* would automatically become his [by virtue of Jewish inheritance laws]. If the esrogim are his, no one in *shul* will be permitted to use them."

In order to fulfill the *mitzvah* of "taking" the *arbaah minnim* on the first day of *Succos* they must be owned by the user, (see *Succah* 29b). A minor cannot halachically transfer an item from his possession. Thus, the townspeople would not have *lulavim* or *esrogim* to use on succos because Rabbi Preil's nine-year-old son could not transfer ownership.

"I need you to take ownership of my *arbaah minnim* on behalf of my community," said Rabbi Preil. "Then regardless of what happens to me, the *arbaah minnim* would belong to the *kehillah* and everyone will be able to perform the *mitzvah* on *Yom Tov."*

The *kinyan* (the transaction) was performed.

Rabbi Preil passed away six hours later. Even in the face of death, with remarkable foresight and responsibility to his community, he prevented a potential spiritual disaster.

In his will, Rabbi Preil asked his community to delay appointing a successor until his daughter, Basya, married. He stipulated that if she married someone suitable for the rabbinate, he be appointed as rabbi of Elizabeth. In 1935, Basya married a young man, who was to become world renowned: Rabbi Pinchas Teitz (1908-1995), who served the Elizabeth Jewish Community for 60 years and became one of the most outstanding rabbis in America.

His son, Rabbi Elazar Meir Teitz, the present rabbi of Elizabeth, was named after his grandfather. I am grateful for his help with this story

Taking A Stand

There is a custom to stand during the recitation of the וַיְבָרֶךְ דָּוִיד prayer, which is part of the daily *Shacharis* service (see *Orach Chaim* 51:7, *Mishneh Berurah* note 19). Rabbi Yaakov Kamenetsky (1892-1986) once suggested that perhaps we stand because of a Mishnah in *Bikkurim* (3:3).

The Mishnah states that all craftsmen [would stop their work and] stand in honor of those bringing *Bikkurim* (the first fruits of one's crop) to Jerusalem. The *Bartenura* explains that the craftsmen stood because חֲבִיבָה מִצְוָה בְּשַׁעְתָּהּ, *A mitzvah [performed] in its appropriate time is beloved.* (See also *Kiddushin* 33a.)

["For this reason," says the *Bartenura,* "one must stand when seeing people carrying a coffin at a funeral, or bringing a baby to his *bris."*]

Based on the above, Reb Yaakov suggested that because it is proper for people to give charity when reciting the words וְהָעֹשֶׁר וְהַכָּבוֹד מִלְּפָנֶיךָ וְאַתָּה מוֹשֵׁל בַּכֹּל, *wealth and honor come from You, and You rule everything,* in the וַיְבָרֶךְ דָּוִיד prayer (see *O.C.* and *M.B.* ibid., and *Be'er Hativ* n.7), it is proper to stand in honor of those doing the *mitzvah.*

When I heard Reb Yaakov's insight, it brought to mind an incident Rabbi Dovid Weinberger, rav of Congregation Shaarei Tefillah in Lawrence, New York had with Rav Yaakov many years ago, when Rav Dovid was a *bachur.*

Once, while driving Reb Yaakov from Monsey to Brooklyn to attend a wedding, Rabbi Weinberger began to "talk in learning" with the great Rosh Yeshivah. However, Reb Yaakov refused to discuss detailed Torah matters. "Our Sages (*Taanis* 10b) teach that the phrase אַל תִּרְגְּזוּ בַּדָּרֶךְ, *Do not get agitated on the road* (*Bereishis* 45:24), cautions people not to study while traveling because they may lose their concentration on the road.

"Aside from being dangerous," laughed Red Yaakov, "the last driver who took me was talking in learning and got hopelessly lost!"

However, Reb Yaakov assured Rabbi Weinberger, "When we get to the wedding, we will have time to talk."

Throughout the wedding Reb Yaakov was besieged by questioners, but finally Rabbi Weinberger saw that he could get the Rosh Yeshivah's undivided attention. When he approached Reb Yaakov's table, the Rosh Yeshivah was standing. After asking a few questions, Rabbi Weinberger, asked Reb Yaakov if he wanted to sit. "We may not sit now," exclaimed Rav Yaakov.

"Why is that?" asked the surprised Reb Dovid.

"Because we are in close proximity to those doing the *mitzvah* of dancing in front of the *chassan* and *kallah.* When one is near those doing a *mitzvah,* one is obligated to stand out of respect, similar to the well-known Mishnah in *Bikkurim.*"

[Rav Yaakov also said that for this reason it is proper to stand for the *chassan* and *kallah* when they march to the *chuppah.*]

Chazal teach: גְּדוֹלָה שִׁמּוּשָׁהּ שֶׁל תּוֹרָה יוֹתֵר מִלִּמּוּדָהּ, *Attending to [those who study] Torah is greater than studying [Torah under them]* (*Berachos* 7b). If one is fortunate to observe a *talmid chacham's* practical application of his theoretical teachings, one is more apt to remember and follow the *talmid chacham's* ways.

Crash Site Concepts

In Israel there is a radio call-in show, *Radio Esser,* heard every Thursday night throughout the country. It is hosted by a young *talmid chacham,* Rabbi Mordechai Neugroschel, who has become famous for his spontaneous answers on any Judaic-related topic.

Rabbi Neugroschel, a former *talmid* of Yeshivas Chevron, teaches and gives public lectures throughout Israel, at yeshivos, seminars, and business offices. More than 700 hundred Hebrew tapes of his lectures are available, on topics ranging from in-depth study of *Tanach,* halachic issues and *hashkafah* (Jewish thought).

On a recent trip to Israel, I met this extraordinary man and his family and he told me the following story.

In May 1996 Rabbi Neugroschel's father-in-law became quite ill. He was taken to the Tel Hashomer hospital in Ramat Gan, where, despite the doctors' efforts, his condition deteriorated. Family members never left his bedside.

One night Rabbi Neugroschel stayed at his father-in-law's bedside, prepared to assist and give comfort in any way he could. After midnight, the nurses encouraged Rabbi Neugroschel to get some rest. "We will keep a vigil on him," they assured him. "You have a day of lectures tomorrow. Try to get some sleep."

Rabbi Neugroschel respectfully rejected the advice and remained at the bedside throughout the night. He was tired, but he felt that a family member should be awake, alert, and available should any need arise.

At 7 o'clock in the morning, another family member relieved Rabbi Neugroschel. He collected his belongings, went to a local *shul* to *daven Shacharis*, and then got into his family van to return home to Jerusalem.

As he drove onto the Tel Aviv - Jerusalem highway, he could feel his eyelids beginning to droop. The ride would take about an hour, but he was convinced that he could stay awake until he arrived home in Sanhedria Murchevet. He listened to *shiurim* (lectures) on tape as he drove alongside the cultivated fields, settlements, and small villages that dotted the panoramic Israeli landscape. After 40 minutes, however, even the taped lectures could not counteract his exhaustion. Traffic into Jerusalem was getting heavy and the long slow climb up the final leg of the highway, near Givat Shaul, only added to Rabbi Neugroschel's fatigue. The plodding row of buses, cabs and cars, jammed tightly in a seemingly hopeless web of gridlock, made his head sag, as his eyes closed for a moment. He snapped awake when he realized that his van was coasting close to the embankment on the shoulder of the road.

He was only 10 minutes from home. Surely, he hoped, he could force himself to remain awake until then. But suddenly the van was rolling down the side of the hill, plunging into a valley, ripping a tree from its roots, rolling over again and again until, finally, it landed on its side against a boulder. Rav Neugroschel was pinned against his seat, held fast by his seat belt, which was jammed.

Dozens of people saw the van going off the road, and within moments people had jumped from their cars and made their way gingerly down the hill to where the car lay on its side. Numerous people used their cell phones to call police, and soon police and ambulances converged on the roadside above bringing traffic to a complete halt.

Rabbi Neugroschel knew he had just been in an accident and he was aware of his surroundings. He didn't remember his car leaving the road, but he was awake now as people clamored around the van to upright it. He called to them to pry him loose from the van before they moved it. He was anxious to get onto solid ground.

Someone pried open a door and climbed into the van. He unlocked the rabbi's seat belt and helped him out. He was dazed and bleeding slightly from minor cuts and bruises, but once outside the van he was able to walk unassisted.

Within moments the van was set upright. Everybody seemed to be talking at once. However, one man took Rav Neugroschel aside and said, "The police will be here shortly. Whatever you do, don't tell them you fell asleep."

"Why not?" asked the surprised Rabbi Neugroschel.

"Because they will suspend your license, give you a big fine, and the insurance company won't pay your claim."

Within minutes an Israeli policeman was on the scene. When he was told who the driver of the van was, he approached Rabbi Neugroschel and asked, "What happened?"

The man who had just given Rabbi Neugroschel the advice was not within earshot. He was examining the dents and scratches on the van. Rav Neugroschel began, "Officer, I have been driving for 19 years. I never had an accident and never fell asleep at the wheel. However, last night I was at the Tel Hashomer Hospital in Ramat Gan with my father-in-law who is very sick. I was up with him all night, until 7 o'clock this morning, when a relative relieved me. I guess I was just so exhausted that by the time I came back to Jerusalem I must have fallen asleep at the wheel."

The officer looked at him, at the van, and at the roadside above. "The *mitzvah* saved your life," he said. "I won't issue you a summons. *Refuah shelaimah* to your father-in-law."

Rabbi Neugroschel thanked the officer, who went on to write his report.

❁ ❁ ❁

When he discusses the episode today, Rabbi Neugroschel says, "I'll tell you why I said what I did to the officer. Imagine that someone does you a great favor and right afterwards asks something of you in return. Wouldn't you comply wholeheartedly?

"The *Ribono Shel Olam* clearly saved my life. I walked away from the accident with barely a scratch. He asks us to tell the truth. Could I do otherwise? It was a matter of *hakaras hatov* (gratitude) — not even a question of the *mitzvah* of telling the truth or the sin of lying. Purely *hakaras hatov*."

Isn't there so much that we in our own lives have to be grateful for? And if so, are we showing Hashem gratitude by doing what He asks of us?

At a Threshold of Greatness

Chazal teach, וֶהֱוֵי שׁוֹתֶה בַצָּמָא אֶת דִּבְרֵיהֶם, *You shall drink thirstily from the words [of Torah scholars]* (*Avos* 1:4). We are encouraged to always be in close proximity to Torah scholars for we are bound to glean from them nuggets of wisdom and insight. A case in point is the following story, related in *Tiferes Banim II* by Rav Bunim Yoel Toisig of Jerusalem.

Rav Avrohom, the Maggid of Trisk (1806-1889), a scion of the Chernobeler (Twerski) dynasty of chassidic masters, had many disciples who sought his counsel and flocked to hear his words of wisdom. One year, on the first night of Succos, he offered a classic insight.

After *Maariv,* a number of *chassidim* escorted the Rebbe as he went to enter his *succah* and be engulfed by its rarefied atmosphere for the first time that holiday.

Yet as Rav Avrohom'eleh came towards the door of the *succah,* he stopped. Some feared that he had suddenly taken ill. Others thought that he had seen something to invalidate the *succah* or its *s'chach.* No one dared enter the *succah* before the Rebbe. After a short while, one of the puzzled *chassidim* asked the Rebbe why he was waiting.

The Rebbe smiled and said, "Just a few days ago we said, during the *Yom Kippur* service, that man is similar to an earthen vessel.

כִּי הִנֵּה כַחֹמֶר בְּיַד הַיּוֹצֵר, *Like the clay in the hand of the potter,* כֵּן אֲנַחְנוּ בְּיָדְךָ, *so are we in Your hand.* Out of respect to the sanctity of the *succah,* it is forbidden to bring pots or earthenware into it (*Orach Chaim* 639:1). If so, how dare we enter — for we too are like earthenware?

"The answer is that the only way to remove the spiritual impurity from an earthen vessel is to shatter it (see *Keilim* 2:1). Thus, if we undertake to be humble and shatter the impurity of haughtiness from our hearts, then we merit to enter the *succah,* for as David *HaMelech* wrote, לֵב נִשְׁבָּר וְנִדְכֶּה אֱלֹקִים לֹא תִבְזֶה, *A heart broken and humbled, O G-d, You will not despise* (*Tehillim* 51:19)."

The Rebbe and his *chassidim* then entered the *succah* with awe and reverence.

A Gift of Atonement

Shortly after the *chupah* at Asher Leitner's* wedding, Rabbi Peretz Steinberg, rabbi of the Young Israel of Queens Valley, New York, noticed that Asher's father, Mr. Max Leitner, was crying and visibly shaken. Rabbi Steinberg put his hand on Mr. Leitner's shoulder to calm him. Shortly afterwards, when Mr. Leitner composed himself, he told Rabbi Steinberg the following remarkable story.

Two years earlier, Asher needed capital to start a business, but his total savings, together with what his parents could provide him, were not enough.

Asher decided to approach an elderly family friend, Mr. Jack Stern,* who had just sold his business for more than $150 million dollars. Asher knew that Mr. Stern liked him, and, sure enough, without much coaxing, Mr. Stern lent Asher the $15,000 dollars he asked for.

For the next year and a half, Asher struggled to make his new business a success. Unfortunately, it failed. Embarrassed and upset, Asher went back to Mr. Stern and told him what had

*The name has been changed

happened. "I will pay you every penny I owe you," Asher said, red-facedly, "but I don't have it right now. I will always remember your kindness, so rest assured — I will repay you."

"Asher, I didn't *lend* you the money," said Mr. Stern. "I'm a businessman. I *invested* it with you. Some investments are successful and some are unsuccessful. This one didn't work out. It's okay, you don't owe me anything."

❁ ❁ ❁

A few months later, Asher became engaged. When he composed his list of guests for the wedding he made sure to include Mr. Stern. At the wedding, just 10 minutes before the *Badekken* (when the *chassan* covers the *kallah's* face with a veil), Asher went to speak to Mr. Stern privately. The elderly gentleman and the young *chassan* went off to a side, out of earshot of anyone else.

Knowing that Mr. Stern was not observant and possessed only limited knowledge of traditional Jewish law and custom, Asher began, "Mr. Stern, the day before a *chassan* and *kallah* get married has very special significance. For them it is like *Yom Kippur.* They fast and recite part of the *Yom Kippur* service. It is also a time when their sins can be forgiven.

"For my *kallah* and me, today was *Yom Kippur*. I feel as though I am about to start married life with a clean slate. But that is only with regard to my dealings with Hashem. With regard to my relationship with people, I still have one black mark on my record — the $15,000 dollars that I owe you. Please, Mr. Stern, I cannot go to my *chupah* knowing that I owe you this money. Please," Asher repeated as he took an envelope out of his pocket, "accept this check. It is for the entire sum that I owe you."

Asher would not allow Mr. Stern to protest. "Only if you accept this check can I go to the *chupah* and start my marriage with a fresh beginning."

Mr. Stern was flabbergasted. He wasn't sure what Asher meant about today being *Yom Kippur,* but he knew that his own religious knowledge was limited and now was not the time for philosophical debate. Besides, 10 minutes before a *chupah* was not the time to upset and aggravate a *chassan.* So, reluctantly, Mr. Stern took the check from Asher.

After the *chupah,* Mr. Stern went to Asher's father and said, "Your son was telling me something about a clean slate and today being his *Yom Kippur*. He told me he must return the money he feels he owes me. Max, I don't want to violate your religion, but would it be wrong if I gave him the $15,000 dollars here at the wedding as a gift?"

Now it was Max Leitner who was left speechless. He stumbled for appropriate words. He tried to thank Mr. Stern for his magnanimous act, but Mr. Stern interrupted him.

"Your son is a fine young man Max. May he and his bride use the money in good health."

With that he gave the check of $15,000 dollars to Asher's father.

A few moments later an overwhelmed Mr. Leitner began crying. It was then that he met Rabbi Steinberg and told him the story.

❁ ❁ ❁

Today, years later, Asher says that his mistake was to assume that he should pay back the loan in one large sum, and not piecemeal. "If only I had started paying Mr. Stern as little as a hundred dollars at a time, it never would have come to the point where I had to embarrass myself and tell him that I had nothing to pay back with."

"But where did you get the money to give him the check at the wedding?" I wondered. "Fifteen thousand dollars is a lot of money."

"Believe it or not," Asher said, "my *kallah* gave me most of it from her savings, because she believed so strongly that we should start with a clean slate."

He was right: I could hardly believe it.

Sanctity in the Woodlands

It was late Thursday night in May 1994 when Mrs. Lisa Lederer of Kew Gardens, New York received a call from Mr. Richard

Flanagan in Hartford, Connecticut. "Was that your husband Mike that I saw on local television just a few moments ago?"

Mr. Flanagan was the Hartford representative of the Phillips Electronics Company, and he dealt with the New York-based Lederers on a weekly basis, as they shipped him transistors and integrated circuits for his company. "I'm not sure, perhaps it was Mike," Mrs. Lederer replied. "I know that he is in northern Connecticut tonight with hundreds of people."

"What's the story with the little girl?" Mr. Flanagan asked. "And how did your husband get involved?"

Mrs. Lederer explained that a high-school girl from Brooklyn had become lost in the Bigelow Hollow Park, on the Connecticut-Massachusetts state border, where she had gone on a class trip. She had been walking with a sister and some classmates and inadvertently became separated from them. She was now missing for more than 30 hours. Her family, teachers, and friends were all frightened and frantic. Volunteers had joined to search for her.

"Are you or Mike related to the girl?" Mr. Flanagan asked.

"No, we're not," replied Mrs. Lederer.

"Do you even know who she is?" asked the incredulous Mr. Flanagan.

"No, we don't know who the girl is, but she is Jewish and the Jewish community feels a responsibility to get involved."

Mr. Flanagan could not believe that Moshe Lederer, or anyone for that matter, would travel more than a hundred miles from New York to look for a lost child they did not know, in a huge state park when the state and local police were already alerted and searching.

Over a thousand people had come to join police efforts in finding the girl. In yeshivos, synagogues, and homes in America and Israel, tens of thousands of men, women, and children were reciting *Tehillim* for her and many were setting aside specific times of learning as a *zechus* that she be found alive and well. Her disappearance was news on every station and in every newspaper.

"It's very cold out there in the park at night. Can I bring Mike blankets or sweaters?" Mr. Flanagan asked.

"They have so many people there; it's a well-organized search party. I am sure they took enough clothes and heaters to keep warm," said Mrs. Lederer.

"And food?" asked Mr. Flanagan, "I know Mike eats only kosher food, but I could pick up some fruit or get some food you tell me I can buy at some of the markets up here."

"That's very kind of you, Richard," Mrs. Lederer said, "but I believe they have enough food up there as well."

"Well then," said Mr. Flanagan, "I'm going to Bigelow Park and join the search for the girl. If it means that much to Mike, then it means that much to me. I have a little girl at home and I can just imagine what her worried parents are going through."

❁ ❁ ❁

Friday morning as Moshe Lederer was taking off his *tallis* and *tefillin,* having *davened* in one of the many *minyanim* that had been formed in Bigelow Park, he was startled to see Richard Flanagan coming towards him with an outstretched hand and warm smile.

"How did you ever find me here among a thousand people, and how did you even know I was here?" Moshe laughed.

Mr. Flanagan told Moshe what he had heard on the evening news and the conversation he had afterwards with Mrs. Lederer. "Mike," Mr. Flanagan said, "I'm here to give a helping hand. Just tell me what I can do. As I told Lisa, if it means that much to you, then it means that much to me."

Later that morning as the search resumed and thousands of people joined hands combing the marshes, swamps, and thickly wooded forest area, Richard Flanagan walked between two Jews participating in the search, surveying carefully the area of the park apportioned to his group, as they tried to find the girl.

Later that morning she was found.

❁ ❁ ❁

There is no doubt that the Torah that was learned and the *tefillos* that were said on the girl's behalf were a major factor in her being found. But perhaps too there was an additional factor that played a small but significant role in the fortunate conclusion of this story— the *kiddush Hashem* that was made by Moshe Lederer.

Not merely the *kiddush Hashem* of his participation with a thousand Jews united in the search for one Jew, but the *kiddush Hashem* that he and his wife had made constantly in the workplace, which caused a gentile to come in the cold, late night and join the search operation.

It is the essence of *kiddush Hashem,* as *Chazal* teach that the Name of Heaven is made beloved by someone who makes sure that מַשָׂאוֹ וּמַתָּנוֹ בֶּאֱמוּנָה וְדִבּוּרוֹ בְּנַחַת עִם הַבְּרִיּוֹת, *His business affairs are [conducted] faithfully and his manner of speaking with people is pleasant* (*Yoma* 86a).

❁ ❁ ❁

This episode has one other extraordinary element. When Moshe Lederer volunteered to travel to Bigelow Park, he had no idea about the identity of the girl other than she was from Borough Park. When he got there he found out it was Suri Feldman, his second cousin.

Relatively remarkable.

If the Truth be Told

The Gemara (*Yevamos* 63a) relates that Rav had a wife who went out of her way to provoke him. When he asked for lentil soup, she served him pea soup. When he asked for pea soup, she served lentil soup.

One day Rav asked for pea soup and actually received the soup he requested. He turned to his son Chiya who was at the table and said, "It seems that your mother is changing."

"Not really," said Chiya, "I told her you wanted lentil soup!"

Rav was not amused. He scolded his son and sternly told him that dishonesty incurs Hashem's wrath. Rav declared, "The prophet Yirmiyahu exclaims of those who speak falsehood, *'Shall I not punish them for these [things]...from a nation such as this, shall My soul not exact vengeance?'* (*Yirmiyahu* 9:8)."

❁ ❁ ❁

In *Kad Hakemach* (sec. *Emunah*), *Rabbeinu Bachya* offers hope and encouragement. He writes, "All those who maintain lives of honesty and integrity will have their prayers answered."He deduces this from the verse קָרוֹב ה׳ לְכָל קֹרְאָיו לְכֹל אֲשֶׁר יִקְרָאֻהוּ בֶאֱמֶת, which he interprets: *Hashem is close to all who call upon Him, to all who call upon Him [and can rightfully claim they are people who live] with truth* (*Tehillim* 145:18).

The following anecdotes reveal the scope and extent of honesty and integrity practiced by some outstanding Torah personalities.

❁ ❁ ❁

The *Chazon Ish,* Rabbi Avraham Yeshaya Karelitz (1878-1953), had a *minyan* for *Minchah* in his home in Bnei Brak every day, at 12:30 p.m. Once, there were only nine men present, and everyone waited for a tenth man to appear, so that they could begin *Minchah.*

At 12:45 p.m., a tenth man finally walked in. As they were getting ready to begin *Ashrei,* Rabbi Shmuel Greineman, said to his brother-in-law, the *Chazon Ish,* "I have a 1 o'clock appointment with someone. If I *daven* now, I will be late and will keep that person waiting. Should I stay here or leave?"

"An honest man must be on time for his appointments," said the *Chazon Ish.* "Coming late is deceitful. It is better that this *minyan* be dissolved today than you be involved in שֶׁקֶר, *falsehood.*"

Does it occur to us that when we are late for an appointment, we are not only transgressing principles בֵּין אָדָם לַחֲבֵירוֹ,

man to man, but also transgressing principles בֵּין אָדָם לַמָּקוֹם, *man to Hashem,* as well? This applies to everyone, professionals and laymen alike.

❁ ❁ ❁

When Rabbi Eliezer Gordon (1840-1910), the rav and Rosh Yeshivah of Telshe, Lithuania, passed away suddenly in England (see page 52), there was great sadness in Telshe. His 17-year-old grandson, Elya Meir Bloch (1894-1955), cried uncontrollably at the loss of his revered grandfather. Rabbi Yosef Leib Bloch (1860-1930), the father of Elya Meir and the son-in-law of Rabbi Gordon, said to him, "It would seem to me that your crying is a bit exaggerated. Are you crying so much so that people should see how sad you are about your grandfather's passing?"

Years later, Reb Elya Meir would say, "My father was right. I was overzealous in my emotional display."

When Reb Elya Meir was in the United States, he was often very critical of secular Zionism. A prominent rabbi who knew Rav Elya Meir from Telshe said to him, "If you don't soften your views, you will lose your financial base, and then the Yeshiva will close."

Reb Elya Meir peered at the rabbi and said, "My father told me that I don't have to be a *rosh yeshivah* but I do have to be an *ehrlicher Yid* (an honest Jew)."

❁ ❁ ❁

The Manchester Rosh Yeshivah, Rabbi Yehuda Zev Segal (1910-1993), would often quote the chassidic master R' Mendel of Rimanov (d. 1815), who said that many times sweet and innocent children stray from the way of the Torah when they are older. "It is because of הַלֵּב טִמְטוּם, *numbness of the heart,* which results from being given food that was purchased by their parents with money earned dishonestly."

Rabbi Segal's honesty was impeccable, as shown by the following incident. He was once on an intercity train on which the conductor passes through the cars to collect the fares. Rabbi Segal started his trip in the economy second-class section and paid his fare, but when rowdy fellow passengers made it difficult for him to concentrate on his learning, he moved to the first-class section.

Rabbi Segal was sure that the conductor would come through again and he would pay the difference for the upgraded seat. When he reached his destination, the conductor had not come through the first-class section, so Rabbi Segal went directly to the station agent to pay the difference. The agent told Rabbi Segal that it was not necessary to pay. Not satisfied, Rabbi Segal went to the stationmaster and paid the extra fare. As the Rosh Yeshivah left the booth, the stationmaster said, "That man is one in a million!"

✿ ✿ ✿

A gentleman wished to take *Purim* as a vacation day, so that he could celebrate with his family, but his employer refused permission, because things were very busy. The gentleman asked Rabbi Yaakov Kamenetsky (1891-1986) if he could call in sick. "This way I can spend more time with my children, and have the *Purim seudah* at the proper time." Reb Yaakov answered unequivocally that one may not call in sick if he is not sick. "Besides," said Reb Yaakov, "the Vilna Gaon had his Purim *seudah* in the morning so that he performed the *mitzvah* with alacrity and you can do the same." (See *Ma'seh Rav* no. 248.)

Reb Yaakov had the private unlisted telephone number of Rabbi Moshe Feinstein (1895-1986). When Reb Yaakov's wife was to have heart surgery, he wanted Reb Moshe to pray for her. He called Reb Moshe numerous times but the line was busy. When a family member asked Reb Yaakov why he didn't use Reb Moshe's unlisted number, he replied, "That was given to me to reach him on matters regarding *Klal Yisrael.* This is a personal matter, so I have no right to use Reb Moshe's private number."

✿ ✿ ✿

If these episodes seem to present a lofty standard of truth, it is most likely because for no other transgression in the Torah is there the warning — distance yourself! The Torah declares מִדְּבַר שֶׁקֶר תִּרְחָק, *Distance yourself from a false word* (*Shemos* 23:7).

Reb Zisha of Hanipoli (d. 1800) once explained this phrase homiletically "From a word of falseness, one becomes distanced [from Hashem]."

The words we write or speak, the appointments we make, the business deals we devise, the emotions we display, are all opportunities for honesty and integrity (and very often showcases for *Kiddush Shem Shamayim*, Sanctifying Hashem's Name). We must be careful not to overlook these opportunities.

Bar-Mitzvah Bonding

They thought it would be meaningful; they never realized it would be memorable. They were hoping it would be special; they never though it would be so unforgettable.

Rabbi Yaakov Salomon of Brooklyn and his son Avi were looking forward to their upcoming visit with Rabbi Avrohom Pam, the Rosh Yeshivah of Yeshivah Torah Vodaath, where Yaakov had studied for many years. In a little more than a month, Avi would celebrate his *Bar Mitzvah*, and within a few days he would be putting on *tefillin* for the very first time. Yaakov decided that the day before Avi put on *tefillin* would be an opportune time to get a *brachah* (blessing) from the Rosh Yeshivah. He had previously taken his older two boys to Rav Pam before their *Bar Mitzvahs*, and the visits had been inspirational.

On the morning of the meeting, Avi put on his finest suit, his new black hat, his best tie, and his freshly poslished shoes. With youthful innocence, he made sure to take his *tefillin* and *siddur* in the event that the Rosh Yeshivah asked to see them.

When they came to his home in Flatbush, Rav Pam greeted Reb Yaakov and Avi in his inimitable soft demeanor, sweet smile and velvet handshake. The Rosh Yeshivah asked Avi where and what he was learning and spoke to Reb Yaakov as well. He gave Avi a *brachah* and wished Reb Yaakov that he and his wife have *nachas* and *mazal* from Avi and from all their children. The Salomons then began making their way towards the front door.

Suddenly Rav Pam noticed Avi's *tefillin* bag. "I see that your name is actually Avrohom Tzvi," Rav Pam said.

The boy smiled and nodded approvingly, "Do you know what the name צְבִי stands for?" asked the Rosh Yeshivah.

Somewhat surprised by the question, Avi shook his head, indicating that he was not aware of what it stood for. "It stands for צַדִּיק בֶּאֱמוּנָתוֹ יִחְיֶה, *The righteous person shall live by his faith,*" said Rav Pam (see *Chabakkuk* 2:4).

Then Rav Pam said, "Let me tell you a little story. There was once a great *gaon* known as the *Chacham Tzvi* (Rav Zvi Hirsh Ashkenazi, 1660-1718). He wrote many *teshuvos* (responsa) and signed his name to each one of them as צְבִי. Someone once asked the *Chacham Tzvi,* "Why don't you sign your *teshuvos* by including your father's name as well? Sign them צְבִי בֶּן יַעֲקֹב (*Tzvi son of Yaakov*).

"Actually, I *am* including my father's name in my signature," the *Chacham Tzvi* replied. "The letters in the word צבי stand for צבי בן יעקב."

Reb Yaakov and his son were intrigued. Then Rav Pam added something that will stay with them forever.

He gently put his hand on the *bar-mitzvah* boy and said, "You too are צבי בן יעקב."

Rav Pam paused for a moment and said gently, "Every morning when you take your *tefillin* from this bag, look at the word צבי and remember your father — and all he has done for you. Let it be a daily opportunity for you to have *hakaras hatov* (gratitude) for all that your father has done for you."

A warm glow of intimate connection enveloped Reb Yaakov and Avi as the Rosh Yeshivah had created a precious moment of bonding between a father and son.

How fortunate we are to have *gedolim* in our midst, and how wise are parents who teach their children to relate to them.

Family Ties

A number of years ago I had the special opportunity to visit Rabbi Yitzchok Kalidetsky in Bnei Brak, author of the popular series *L'shichno Sidreshu,* a compilation of essays and stories about Torah scholars throughout the generations. Rabbi Kalidetsky shared with me a very warm family incident regarding his great father-in-law, Rabbi Chaim Kanievsky.

For years, every morning after *Shacharis,* Reb Chaim would visit his mother Rebbetzin Pesha Miriam who lived nearby. Often she would insist on making him a small breakfast and whenever his father, the Steipler Gaon, Reb Yaakov Yisrael (1899-1985), was there, they would share Torah thoughts.

When the Rebbetzin passed away two weeks after *Purim* in 1973, her daughter Rebbetzin Yuspeh Barzam, who had been widowed at a young age, moved in with her father to tend to his daily needs. Reb Chaim then stopped making his daily morning visit.

A few weeks later, the Steipler commented to Reb Chaim, "I, too, appreciated your daily visit."

It was an "off-the-cuff" remark but Reb Chaim immediately perceived the twinge of pain his father must have felt when he realized that his son had chosen to curtail his daily visits. Reb Chaim understood that a person bereft of a close family member needs other family members for strength and assurance. Every person, even one carrying the burdens of thousands, yearns for a bond with close ones.

From the next morning after the Steipler's comment, Reb Chaim visited his father every single day, for more than 12 years, until the great *gaon* passed away.

When the Steipler died in the summer of 1985, Reb Chaim did not forget his father's words. Until this very day, Reb Chaim visits his widowed sister, Rebbetzin Barzam, every single morning, without fail!

A Thought for the Ages

On a recent trip to Baltimore I had the opportunity to meet Rabbi Avrohom Bayarsky who learned in Radin, while the Chofetz Chaim (1838-1933) was still alive. Rav Bayarsky remembers the Chofetz Chaim vividly, and he recounted numerous incidents and insights from the great Torah sage. One of his most striking recollections is of the Chofetz Chaim's funeral and the moving *hesped* (eulogy) given by his seventy-year-old son, Reb Leib.

Rav Leib quoted the Gerrer Rebbe who asked the following question. "The Torah writes regarding Yosef, בֶּן שְׁבַע עֶשְׂרֵה שָׁנָה הָיָה...וְהוּא נַעַר, *[He] was seventeen years old...and he was a youth* (*Bereishis* 37:2). Since we are told that he was 17, what does the Torah add by saying that he was a youth?

"Rashi explains that he is called a youth to describe his behavior: שֶׁהָיָה עוֹשֶׂה מַעֲשֵׂה נַעֲרוּת, *Yosef would do things associated with youth,* he would fix his hair and groom his eyes so that he would look attractive."

"Yet", asked the Gerrer Rebbe, "when the Torah describes the journey of Avraham and Yitzchak to the *Akeidah,* the Torah writes, וַיֹּאמֶר אַבְרָהָם אֶל נְעָרָיו שְׁבוּ לָכֶם פֹּה עִם הַחֲמוֹר וַאֲנִי וְהַנַּעַר נֵלְכָה עַד כֹּה, *And Avraham said to his young men, 'Stay here by yourselves with the donkey, while I and the lad will go up to here'*(*Bereishis* 22:50). The Torah uses the word נַּעַר concerning Yitzchak and at the time he was 37 years old, and he surely did not behave like a youngster. But no commentary questions the use of the word נַּעַר!"

The Gerrer Rebbe explained that in a relationship between a father and son, age is insignificant. The son, in this context, is always his father's "child." Thus when Avraham was walking with Yitzchak, he referred to him as נַּעַר, my youthful son.

"My father," said Rav Leib in his eulogy for the Chofetz Chaim, "always called me *mein kind* (my child). But today," he added sadly, "I have grown old!"

Golden Opportunities

One Friday morning in December 1996, Sheppy Borgen was driving from Williamsburg to Borough Park. The corner of Bedford Avenue and Keap Street is an unofficial meeting place for religious Jews seeking rides to Borough Park. Dozens of people get their rides there every day. As Sheppy came to the light at Bedford and Keap, just two blocks before entering the Brooklyn Queens Expressway, he noticed a *chassidishe* fellow waiting on the corner, peering into each passing car hoping for a ride.

Sheppy slowed to a halt, opened the passenger-side window, and called out in Yiddish, "Do you need a ride?"

The *chassid* said yes, and Sheppy motioned for him to get into the back seat of his Town Car and told him to make himself comfortable.

Sheppy, who lives in Forest Hills, Queens, is a tall and imposing fellow with a heart to match. He is admired and liked by everyone. He was president of his *shul* for many years, has been honored by numerous organizations, and is an easy conversationalist. He and the *chassid* made small talk as traffic, in a rare departure from the usual, moved swiftly through downtown Brooklyn under the Brooklyn and Manhattan bridges past Atlantic Avenue onto the Prospect Expressway. Since it was Friday, the *chassid* spoke of the upcoming *parashah.* Sheppy countered with a relevant story from his repertoire of favorite stories.

The *chassid* spoke of his children and grandchildren and Sheppy spoke of the upcoming wedding of his daughter in three days. When they arrived in Boro Park the two wished each other *"Gut Shabbos"* and *"mazel* and *simchas"* in each other's families.

Within minutes of leaving the car, the *chassid* realized that he had left a bag with very valuable contents in Sheppy's car. He became frantic because he didn't know the driver's name, only that he lived in Queens and was about to marry off his daughter.

Later that morning when Sheppy came to his office in Long Island City, he emptied the contents of his car and he, too, realized that the *chassid* had left a bag in the back seat. He looked into the bag and saw that there were numerous brass pipes and tubes that seemed to be of little value. He put the bag in his office and figured he would deal with it when he got back on Monday. He, too, had no idea of the identity of the *chassid* except that he lived in Boro Park and had nice things to say about the *parashah.*

That afternoon, the chassid went to the Skulener Rebbe, Rabbi Yisrael Portugal, and worriedly told his Rebbe of his loss. "Much of my *parnassah* (livelihood) for the next year is in that bag," he cried. "How can I get it back?"

The Rebbe thought for a moment and then called in his *gabbai* (attendant) and gave him instructions.

Rabbi Peretz Steinberg, Rav of the Young Israel of Queens Valley and former president of the Vaad Harabbonim of Queens, was surprised to get a call from the Skulener *gabbai* that *erev Shabbos.* "The Skulener Rebbe wants to know if you know anyone in Queens that is making a wedding for a daughter in the next few days."

The *gabbai* explained that the contents in the missing bag were valued at close to $40,000. It was actually unprocessed gold that would be used for bracelets, earrings, and necklaces. "Queens is a big place," chuckled Rabbi Steinberg, "there is Kew Garden Hills, Kew Gardens, Rego Park, Forest Hills, Hillcrest, Jamaica Estates — a *Yid* from any of those places could have given the *chassid* a ride."

"The owner thinks that the driver said he was in the chemical soap business. Does that help?"

"That helps," said Rabbi Steinberg. "I'll see what I can find out."

"Please," the *gabbai* pleaded, "the man is desperate and he stands to lose a fortune."

Friday night as Rabbi Steinberg peered at the *balabatim* in his *shul,* he noticed Mr. Jerry Meyer. "Jerry is a photographer," thought Rabbi Steinberg. "He might know."

After *davening,* Rabbi Steinberg approached Mr. Meyer and said, "Jerry, I'm trying to help a *Yid* in Boro Park. Are you by any chance doing a wedding for a Queens family next week?"

Jerry thought for a moment and said, "Yes, I'm doing a wedding for Sheppy Borgen, Tuesday night in Westchester."

"Do you know what he does for a living?" Rabbi Steinberg asked anxiously.

"Isn't he in the industrial cleaning business or something like that?" asked Jerry.

Rabbi Steinberg was elated at the possibility of having solved the mystery so quickly. He couldn't wait to call Sheppy Borgen, who lives a few miles away in Forest Hills.

After Shabbos, Rabbi Steinberg called Sheppy and, in his usual upbeat cheery voice, wished him *mazel* on the upcoming wedding. Then, laughing, he asked, "Did you by any chance pick up a *chassid* yesterday in Williamsburgh?"

Sheppy laughed, "Rabbi Steinberg, are you a *navi?* How do you know? I actually did and he left a bag in my car."

"That's exactly why I'm calling. It's not some bag. It's got close to $40,000 dollars worth of unprocessed gold in it!"

"What?" exclaimed Sheppy. "It looked like cheap pieces of piping. But okay, if you say it's expensive, I'll bring it back on Monday when I go into the office."

"No," said Rabbi Steinberg. "I'm sorry to bother you, but it's too valuable to leave unattended for that long. Could I trouble you to get it to me soon as you can, tonight?"

When Sheppy readily agreed, Rabbi Steinberg called the Skulener *gabbai* and told him the good news. By Sunday morning the material was in the hand of its rightful owner.

> Often in life you don't need to know the answers; you just need to know who knows the answers. The Skulener Rebbe knew to call Rabbi Steinberg and he knew to ask Jerry Meyer.

A Lesson up in Flames

In 1906 Reb Hillel Berkowsky set out to America from the little town of Varanova, near Vilna, in Lithuania, promising his wife Hinda and their six children that he would send for them to join him as soon as he possibly could. Reb Hillel came to New York and shortly thereafter heard about a position available in the Landfield Avenue Shul in Monticello. He applied and was accepted as the local *mohel, shochet,* and *shammas.*

After two long years of frozen winters and lonely summers, Reb Hillel managed to put some money together, and in 1908 he finally had the proper documentation and financial backing to bring his family across the Atlantic. Their joy was boundless.

Five of the Berkowsky children stayed with their parents in Monticello and attended public school. Their oldest daughter Chaya Elka, who was 16 and became known as Ida, moved in with her uncle and aunt, Mr. and Mrs. Simon Schultz, in Manhattan, so she could find a job and attend night school. Reb Hillel understood that there were more job opportunities in the big city and more chances that she would eventually meet and marry a Jewish boy.

As the immigrant children became accustomed to their new surroundings, Reverend Berkowsky, as he was then known, tried to imbue his children with as much authentic Torah observance as he could, in the uphill battle against apathy and disregard for Orthodoxy that was prevalent throughout America at the time.

Reb Hillel and Hinda understood the perils of "free" America. Every day they heard tragic stories of their friends' children who no longer wished to be observant. For too many, freedom meant assimilation, choice meant forsaking their heritage.

In 1911, Ida went from shop to shop and factory to factory, trying to find a job that would pay decent wages for the amount of hours she would be required to work.

One day she came to the Triangle Shirtwaist Company and was told of a job opening. She was informed that many young Jewish women worked at Triangle and, because of a strike at the plant a few months earlier, people could now work overtime to fill the orders that had piled up during the walkout.

When she inquired about her required days and hours, she was informed that she would have to come in on Shabbos. No one would be hired without agreeing to work on Shabbos. Ida needed the money and knew many girls her age who succumbed to violating the Shabbos. She wondered if she knew any of the Jewish girls at Triangle.

She was already 19, and on her own. A fleeting thought crossed her mind. In the last three years, she had come to know many Jews who were convinced they were "good Jews" even if they were not observant. Perhaps they wouldn't be good Jews in the old country, but this was the New World. America had different standards.

But she was the daughter of Reb Hillel and Hinda Berkowsky. She had been told that the Torah was not given in any city or any particular country, rather in a desert, to signify that it must be heeded anywhere. Countries changed and cultures changed, but the Torah was constant. Accepting the job would be a rejection of the sacrifices Reb Hillel and Hinda made for *shemiras Shabbos* up in Monticello. Tempting as it was, she declined the job.

The next week, on Shabbos afternoon, March 25, 1911, a disastrous fire raged through the three floors that the company owned in a ten-story loft building. Narrow congested aisles and locked doors trapped many workers. A hundred forty-six people died, most of them young women.

The fire became a defining moment in business history, as an investigation led to the enactment of a strict industrial safety code and set the pattern for remedial factory legislation throughout the United States.

That Shabbos of the fire was *Parashas Vayakhel* and in *shuls* throughout New York and all over the world the following verse was read, לֹא תְבַעֲרוּ אֵשׁ בְּכֹל מֹשְׁבֹתֵיכֶם בְּיוֹם הַשַּׁבָּת, *You shall not kindle fire in any of your dwellings on the Sabbath day* (*Shemos* 35:3).

Today, Ida's daughter in West Haven, Connecticut, Mrs. Hannah Markowitz, and Ida's granddaughter and great-granddaughter in Baltimore shudder when they remember the allusion in the *parashah* to the events of that day. They talk with awe, gratitude, and pride of Ida's commitment to *shemiras Shabbos.* Referring to the Triangle Shirtwaist Company and the events of that calamitous day, one of them said, "Had she been there, none of us would be here."

Part D:

Eternal Heroes

For Bread in a Basket

Wisdom, erudition, and steadfast integrity have always been the hallmarks of the Munk family. For the last four generations, in Germany, England, France, America, or Israel, the Munks, as rabbis and community leaders, have served the Jewish people nobly.

I first heard this fascinating story about the Munks from Rabbi Yehuda Leib Lewis, the *Av Beis Din* (Head of the Rabbinical Court) of Amsterdam. Rabbi Lewis, who considers Rabbi Eli Munk (1900-1978) his mentor and guide, delights in telling this story, because it portrays the family's aforementioned traits so vividly. I am also grateful to the late Mrs. Martha Munk, the wife of Rabbi Yechiel Aryeh (Michael L.) Munk (1905-1984), who provided many of the details in this episode.

In 1929, the revered rabbi of the Adath Yisroel congregation in North London, Rabbi Dr. Avigdor Schonfeld, passed away. In his will, he asked that his young son Solomon, then studying in the Nitra Yeshiva in Slovakia, eventually assume his position. Indeed, Rabbi Dr. Solomon Schonfeld (1912-1982) succeeded his father at the age of 22, and became a legend for his work in saving Jewish children before and during World War II.

In the interim, the community conducted a search for a rabbi to lead them for the next three to four years, until Solomon was ready to succeed his father. After interviewing many candidates, Adath Yisroel selected Rabbi Eli Munk, of Berlin, Germany, to assume the temporary rabbinical responsibilities. Rabbi Munk expected to stay in England for three or four years, and then return to Berlin. During his tenure in England, however, the fierce winds of Nazi anti-Semitism raged throughout Germany, and Rabbi Munk realized it was best not to return there. Instead, he remained in England and became a British citizen.

During the 1930s, as the tumultuous passions of hatred and incitement grew under Nazi rule, life for Jews in Germany became increasingly perilous. In 1938, when Rabbi Munk's parents, Rabbi Ezra and Selma, went to Palestine to attend the *bris* of a grandson, the German consulate in Palestine refused to renew their expired passports. "We have orders from Berlin not to renew passports for Jews," he was told. It was thus impossible for the elderly rabbi to return to his congregation. The German refusal was a blessing in disguise for Rabbi and Mrs. Ezra Munk. They remained in Israel and were spared the horrors of the Holocaust.

When the elderly rabbi could not return to Berlin, his son Rabbi Yechiel Aryeh (Michael) became the rabbi. His public stand on the virtues of Jewish life, his defense against the rabid anti-Semitic propaganda printed in the weekly newspaper *Der Stuermer,* and his tireless community work such as procuring certificates and permits for Jews to emigrate to Palestine and England, was brought under close Nazi scrutiny. When Rabbi Munk tried to get passports for himself and his family to leave Germany, he was refused.

One Friday in December 1938, just a few weeks after the terrible onslaught of Kristallnacht, a night of synagogue burnings, beatings and arrests of Jews, and looting of their stores throughout Germany, Gestapo headquarters called Rabbi Munk. When his wife said that he wasn't in, the officer on the phone barked, "He had better be there to answer the phone tomorrow, even on your Sabbath!"

The hatred in the blunt order was unmistakable. Rabbi Munk had been summoned to Gestapo headquarters numerous times before, and each time he brought a small pair of *tefillin,* in case they might detain him more than a day. This time, however, he and his wife Martha believed that if he were to be summoned again, he would be imprisoned and perhaps not come out alive. Rabbi and Mrs. Munk decided that he must go into hiding.

They realized that his only hope to escape Germany was with the assistance of his brother Eli in England. Rabbi Munk would not be able to call Eli from his hiding place, because the lines were tapped and his whereabouts could become known, but his wife could call.

There was no direct dialing to foreign countries at the time, and though it was already Friday night, Mrs. Munk, fearing for her husband's life, placed a "trunk call" — an international call — to Rav Eli, in London.

Rabbi Eli Munk heard the phone ring, but it was Shabbos, and not being aware of any impending emergency he didn't answer it. The phone rang incessantly, but no one picked it up.

Mrs. Munk tried another means of communication. She sent a telegram to her brother-in-law saying, "Please pick up the phone, even on Shabbos. Martha."

Shabbos morning, as Rabbi Munk was about to go to *shul*, he was met by a messenger boy rushing towards him with a telegram. He read it and decided not to go to *shul*. He realized her call could be a matter of life and death.

Within half an hour, the phone rang. Rav Eli rushed nervously to answer it. He recognized his sister-in-law's voice immediately. Realizing that German authorities were listening to all international calls, they chose their words carefully.

"How is everything?" Mrs. Munk asked.

"We are just fine," he replied. "How is everything with you?"

"I am fine," she said as calmly as she could. And then she said the words she had planned so meticulously, "But your brother has no bread in his basket."

Rav Eli sensed immediately that those words were a cryptic message, but for the moment he couldn't grasp it. He was alarmed. He knew something was very wrong, but he was frustrated that he couldn't understand the message.

He paused for a moment to contemplate her words. He knew

that with German authorities listening, she could not elaborate. "We are fine," she assured him again, "except that Michael needs bread in his basket."

It was to no avail. It was not safe to say more. "I'm in a rush now," Rabbi Munk said, "I will have to call you back. Thanks for calling."

Troubled and concerned, Rabbi Munk went to *shul*. As he arrived, he saw his friend Arthur Rau who, with his cousin Fred Rau, were working tirelessly to get Jews out of Germany.

Rav Munk told Mr. Rau about the puzzling phone call and his distress at not understanding the intended message. Mr. Rau thought for a few moments and then smiled confidently, "Rabbi," he said, "the message has to be understood in Hebrew!"

Rabbi Munk was bewildered. "Your sister-in-law was alluding to the Talmudic teaching אֵינוֹ דוֹמֶה מִי שֶׁיֵּשׁ לוֹ פַּת בְּסַלּוֹ לְמִי שֶׁאֵין לוֹ פַּת בְּסַלּוֹ, *There is no comparison between one who has bread in his basket to one who doesn't have bread in his basket* (*Yoma* 74b). She used the word bread hoping you would translate it into the Hebrew word פַּת (*pas*), which in German means passport. Your brother has no passport, so he can't get out of Germany. That's what your sister-in-law meant when she said he had no פַּת — passport — in his basket."

Rabbi Munk was impressed at the cleverness of the message. "But how do we get my brother a passport?"

"Just look in the mirror, Rabbi," said Mr. Rau. Rav Eli Munk understood at once. Eli and Michael looked startlingly alike. Though Michael was five years older, they were always being mistaken for each other. Mr. Rau was sure that Michael could get out of Germany by using Eli's British passport.

"We must get your passport, even on Shabbos," said Mr. Rau, "and once we have it, I will contact my cousin Fred to make travel arrangements."

Fred would have no problem traveling to and from Germany because he was a British subject and had a United Kingdom passport. He would welcome the opportunity to save another Jew.

Half an hour later, the Raus met Rav Munk, who handed Fred

his passport. Rav Munk wished Fred success in this risky rescue effort, as they all knew that if something went wrong, both Fred and Rabbi Michael Munk could face drastic consequences.

Fred wanted to find out how imminent the danger was, so he called Mrs. Munk in Berlin and asked if he could visit her in a few days. When Mrs. Munk replied that his visit could not wait, "or it might be too late," Fred knew he must act at once.

Fred and Mrs. Munk devised a plan that called for her husband to travel from Berlin to the German city of Aachen, near the Dutch border. At a designated time, Michael would wait in the private home of a mutual friend near the train station for his rendezvous with Fred. There he would be given his brother's passport.

Mr. Rau went by train from London south to the port city of Dover. There he purchased a ticket for the journey from Dover across the North Sea to the Hook of Holland, a port on the Dutch coast.

Early next morning, he took the train for the four-hour ride across Holland to the last major station in the country — Maastricht. There he changed trains for the ride into Germany, and went directly to Aachen.

Late in the afternoon when Mr. Rau met Rabbi Munk, he was startled once again at the resemblance to his brother Eli. Mr. Rau explained the plan. They would travel by train from Germany to Holland and get past the border police by using his brother's passport.

"But how can I use this passport?" asked Rav Michael. "I don't speak a word of English."

Mr. Rau smiled confidently and with mock dignity exclaimed, "English gentlemen travel first class! They don't discuss anything with petty border police. You will just nod if they ask you anything. I will take care of the rest. And remember, you don't know a word of German, only English."

The next morning they bought two first-class tickets and nervously boarded the train in Aachen for the trip across the border to Holland. As they rode in the first-class cabins, Nazi passport officials at the border entered the train and checked everyone's documents. They looked through Rabbi Munk's passport and checked the picture on the passport to verify that it matched his face. Rav Michael avoided eye contact with the officer. That moment seemed to take forever. All Rav Michael could think was אָנָּא ה' הוֹשִׁיעָה נָּא, *Please Hashem, save now!* (*Tehillim* 118:25).

The officers didn't say a word. And as they proceeded to the next passenger, Rabbi Munk realized that his primary hurdle had been surmounted. Freedom and new life suddenly became a distinct possibility. He knew he could never thank the Rau cousins enough. Once the train was in Holland, Fred and Rav Michael exchanged quiet smiles of relief. Rav Munk's wife and three sons — Eli, Yecheskel, and Yehuda — were still in Berlin (their daughter Chana would be born years later in Boston), but women and children were not being taken to concentration camps yet, so there was still time to work for their freedom.

As soon as they arrived in Amsterdam, Rav Michael called his brother in England with the joyous news that he was free. Rav Eli was ecstatic to hear his brother's voice. "The plan worked to perfection. I hope to see you soon in England."

Rav Eli's response startled Rav Michael. "How will you get from Holland into England? You don't have a legal passport." Rav Michael hadn't thought at all about remaining in Holland. But his older brother continued, "Michael, you can't use my passport to enter England. That would be illegal. I could rationalize sending you my passport against דִּינָא דְּמַלְכוּתָא, *the law of the government*, because your life was at stake. But now that you are in Holland you are no longer in danger. I cannot violate the laws of England and allow you to use my passport to enter the country illegally."

Rav Michael agreed with his brother. Rav Eli reassured his younger brother, "The Dutch *fluchtling* (refugee) committee will help you get a Nansen Passport (named after the Norwegian statesman Fridtjof Nansen who devised an international identity certificate for stateless persons). It won't take you long to get one, and with that document you will be able to get into

England."

In three days Rav Michael was able to procure the appropriate documents for his emigration to England. Rav Michael eventually established the Hendon Adath Yisroel shul, which today, along with the Golders Green Beth Hamedrash, which his brother Rav Eli Munk established, are among the bastions of Orthodox Jewry in London.

❁ ❁ ❁

During the time her husband was in Holland, Mrs. Martha Munk and her three children left Berlin for the small town of Borken not far from the Dutch border. There she was sheltered by an extraordinary woman, Mrs. Haas, a widow who offered her home as a temporary sanctuary for those fleeing the Nazis.

Mrs. Munk's escape was another miracle. After what seemed like a harrowing betrayal by a German samaritan who had been paid to take the family across the border, a German border patrol officer allowed Mrs. Munk and her sons to leave the country only because she brought along her children's birth certificates, proof that her family owed no taxes, and proof that neither she nor any members of her family had a police record. With remarkable foresight, Rav Michael prepared these documents just two weeks earlier.

❁ ❁ ❁

The Munks' legacy of wisdom, integrity, precision, and erudition lives on to this day in the persons of their wonderful children and grandchildren, as the family continues to be a role model for all families in *Klal Yisrael*.

A Sense of Commitment

When Rabbi Aryeh Sokoloff became the rabbi of K'hal Adas Yeshurun of Kew Gardens, New York, he expounded on an event that took place during the reign of King Yoshiyahu. The event, which is detailed in *Yerushalmi* (*Sotah* 7:4) and is discussed by *Ramban* (*Devarim* 27:26), illustrates the power of a pledge and a promise.

Yoshiyahu was the last great king in the time of the First *Beis HaMikdash*. The *pasuk* says of him: וְכָמֹהוּ לֹא הָיָה לְפָנָיו מֶלֶךְ, אֲשֶׁר שָׁב אֶל ה׳ בְּכָל לְבָבוֹ וּבְכָל נַפְשׁוֹ וּבְכָל מְאֹדוֹ כְּכֹל תּוֹרַת מֹשֶׁה, וְאַחֲרָיו לֹא קָם כָּמֹהוּ *Before him there had never been a king like him who returned to Hashem with all his heart, with all his soul, and with all his resources, in accordance with the entire Torah of Moshe, and after him no one arose like him* (*II Melachim* 23:25).

During his reign, the *Beis HaMikdash* was in serious disrepair. Yoshiyahu sent his scribe Shafan to go to the *Kohen Gadol*, Chilkiyahu, who had stored money collected to repair the deteriorated Temple, and to make arrangements for the work to begin.

When Chilkiyahu and Shafan went to where the money was hidden, they found a *Sefer Torah* open to the verse, אָרוּר אֲשֶׁר לֹא יָקִים אֶת דִּבְרֵי הַתּוֹרָה הַזֹּאת לַעֲשׂוֹת אוֹתָם, *Cursed is the one who will not uphold the words of this Torah to perform them* (*Devarim* 27:26). This frightened Chilkiyahu and Shafan, for they considered this a rebuke from Hashem. Chilkiyahu ordered Shafan to tell Yoshiyahu what they had found.

Hurriedly, Yoshiyahu came. He examined the Torah and he too was unnerved by the message; Unnerved — but undaunted. Passionately he exclaimed, עָלַי לְהָקִים, *I undertake to uphold it!"*

Yoshiyahu's intent was not merely to uphold the Torah himself, but to become an inspiration to others as well. "It is not enough for an individual to learn Torah and observe *mitzvos*," says Rav Assi, "but if one has the opportunity to offer encouragement to others and fails to do so, then the verse of *Cursed is the one*...applies to him" (*Yerushalmi Sotah* ibid. and *Ramban* ibid.).

Yoshiyahu's fulfillment of his pledge is one of the reasons that he is considered extraordinary.

In conclusion, Rabbi Sokoloff promised his new congregation that he would do everything in his power to uphold the Torah and encouraged everyone do the same.

❁ ❁ ❁

This episode brought to mind a story I heard about a young girl named Esther Haas, who lived in the small town of Papa, Hungary, in 1944.

When Esther was 14 years old, she and her sisters, Eva and Gabriella, along with their father, Aryeh Leib (Leopold), were seized from their home by the Nazis. The family was forced into a cattle car and after days of weary travel, compounded by starvation and cramped conditions, they were transported to the concentration camp at Stutthof and then to Torun. At Torun, Mr. Haas was separated from his daughters. Tragically, the girls never saw him again.

The Haas sisters and the other girls in their barrack were ordered to dig trenches, often under a blazing hot sun. The work was backbreaking, torturous, and brutal. As the weeks wore on, many girls, gaunt from the lack of food, collapsed and died from the toil and horrid living conditions.

One morning Esther awoke feeling terribly sick. She could hardly walk. Her sisters told her that she must remain indoors. Eva pleaded, "If you try to work today it will be your end."

Their pleading was to no avail. "The Nazis are too precise," Esther protested. "They know exactly how many girls have to come to the line-up in the morning and if I am not there they will make everyone stand in the hot sun until they find me. They could even kill some of the girls in anger. I can't miss the line-up this morning."

Disregarding the pleas of her sisters, Esther hobbled to the early dawn line-up with the rest of her barrack mates. She struggled to remain on her feet as she walked to the forest and spent the day digging, loading, and carrying chunks of earth, all the while trying to avoid the probing eyes of the Nazi guards.

As the day wore on, she became increasingly weak. She tried desperately to conserve whatever energy she had left. Finally the strenuous day was over, and the girls began the long march back from the forest to the barracks.

Esther could hardly walk and after taking a few steps she fell to the ground. Many of the girls passed her, afraid to arouse Nazi anger by helping her. Two girls stopped and lifted her. Tenderly, they placed her arms over their shoulders and, with Esther between them, began to make their way back to the barracks.

After a few steps, however, Esther collapsed and her arms slipped from the girls' shoulders. She lay in a heap on the ground, moaning. The girls tried to lift her, but there was a shout from behind them. A Nazi guard, pointing his bayonet at them, ordered, "Go on and leave her here."

They had no choice but to leave Esther at the mercy of this cruel Nazi.

As Esther lay on the ground, the Nazi aimed his bayonet at her head and stormed, "Will you walk to the barracks?"

"I want to work for the Reich," she said softly, trying to save her life, which now hung by a thread.

"If you want to work, then get up and walk. Otherwise you are dead right here and now!" the Nazi yelled. "We have no use for weak people."

But she could not move. The strength had ebbed from her fragile body. The heartache, the physical pain, and the torment she had endured the last few months had taken its toll. In a moment she would be another victim, another name in the endless list of Jewish martyrs. In her last moments, she recalled how her father stood at the doorway of the cattle car, defying a Nazi soldier to dare touch his three daughters, who huddled in fear behind him. His defiance had saved them, but now he was gone. The name of Aryeh Leib Haas had already been permanently etched in the sacred book of those who gave their lives to sanctify Hashem's Name.

Suddenly, Esther was walking! From somewhere (and until this day she doesn't know from where) came a surge of strength she didn't know she had. As though carried by angels, she took step after energized step, plodding through the forest and eventually into the barracks, where the unbelieving girls welcomed her with tears and open arms.

❁ ❁ ❁

Now, as she told the story decades later, she reflected on her time at Torun. "The Germans convinced us that they had taken every Jewish girl in the world to a concentration camp. I met girls from Poland, Hungary, and Germany who had been apprehended and imprisoned. We had no reason to believe they were lying about the girls in England and America, who they claimed were in other concentration camps.

"Every night I recited the same prayer. I said, 'Hashem, help me get out alive and I promise you I will get married, have a family, and raise my children as *ehrlicher Yidden* (religious Jews). You will be able to start Judaism all over again with me. I will be your emissary. This is my promise, just give me the chance.'"

And then it occurred to me that her pledge was similar to King Yoshiyahu's pledge, עָלַי לְהָקִים, *I undertake to uphold it!* Young Esther wanted to live in order to build *Yiddishkeit.* It was her sincere promise, and perhaps for that alone Hashem gave her life.

It is the commitment that every Jew must make. As Rav Assi (*Yerushalmi* ibid.) counsels, we are obligated to encourage and influence people whenever or wherever we can. It could be at home, the workplace or in the community at large. Yoshiyahu pledged it to *Klal Yisrael,* Esther Haas pledged it to her future family, and Rabbi Sokoloff pledged it to his community.

Throughout the עֲשֶׂרֶת יְמֵי תְשׁוּבָה (*Ten Days of Repentance*) we recite in the *Shemoneh Esrei:* זָכְרֵנוּ לְחַיִּים ... וְכָתְבֵנוּ בְּסֵפֶר הַחַיִּים,

לְמַעַנְךָ אֱלֹקִים חַיִּים, *Remember us for life ... inscribe us in the book of life, for Your sake, O Living God.* We beseech Hashem to give us life so that we can live it for His sake — לְמַעַנְךָ. During Succos, we again appeal to Hashem, הוֹשַׁעְנָא לְמַעַנְךָ אֱלֹקֵינוּ ... הוֹשַׁעְנָא לְמַעַנְךָ בּוֹרְאֵנוּ ..., *Please save [us] for Your sake, our God ... Please save [us] for Your sake, our Creator...*

When one makes a genuine pledge to live for Hashem's sake and to uphold His Torah, one may well come to deserve the great accolades given King Yoshiyahu, who served Hashem בְּכָל לְבָבוֹ וּבְכָל נַפְשׁוֹ וּבְכָל מְאֹדוֹ, *with all his heart, with all his soul, and with all his resources.*

Bullet Proof Virtue

Sometimes a man's life is changed by a single decision. When he makes the decision, he may not be aware of the enormous effect it will have on his future, but because of it, his life takes a new turn and is never the same afterwards.

In the following story, a personal decision to perform a *mitzvah* under the most difficult circumstances set in motion a chain of events that eventually influenced the history of an entire Jewish community.

I am grateful to Rabbi Simcha Bamberger of Manchester for telling me this story about his remarkable father, Rabbi Yitzchok Dov, who from early youth overcame one adversity after another, confronting every challenge with zeal and persistence. I am additionally grateful to Rabbi Shmuel Bamberger of Antwerp for providing additional details.

Yitzchok Dov Bamberger of the small town of Schonlanke, Germany (near the German-Polish border) was only six years old in 1924 when his father died suddenly on the day of his daughter's wedding. (See *Along the Maggid's Journey*, p. 224.) Though his mother, Rachel Miriam was a *tzadeikes* and a woman of great fortitude, she realized she could no longer remain in Schonlanke with her four children, for it had only a tiny Orthodox community, and without a husband, she felt she could not raise her children properly there.

Mrs. Bamberger moved her family to Halberstadt, a German city, where the local rav, Rabbi Binyamin Auerbach, took a personal interest in her family's welfare. There, Yitzchok Dov and his siblings were imbued by his saintly mother with fervent *Yiras Shamayim* and strict adherence to *mitzvos*.

In 1937 she realized she had to send him to a major yeshivah. With tears in her eyes and determination in her heart, she sent him, her youngest child, to Yeshivas Eitz Chaim in the small village of Heide, in the Belgian countryside, where he heard *shiurim* from one of the most remarkable *talmidei chachamim* of that era, Rabbi Mordechai Pogramansky (1903-1949). (Rabbi Elchonon Wasserman used to visit the yeshivah for a few weeks every year.)

Yitzchok Dov's happy days in the yeshivah ended with the outbreak of World War II. As a German citizen, he was suspected of being a spy for the Nazis and was expelled from Belgium, along with thousands of other Jewish foreigners, to the southern part of France, where he was interned in a filthy, foul-smelling detention camp in St. Cyprien outside of Perpignan, near the Spanish border. Anyone who tried to escape from the camp was shot.

The French detention camps were part of France's collaboration with Nazi Germany. In May 1940, the Germans had invaded France, and within weeks immobilized the hapless French army. In June, Marshal Henri Philippe Petain, the French Chief of State, surrendered and signed an armistice with Germany. Petain was put at the head of a puppet regime in southern France, with its capital in Vichy.

France's traditional anti-Semitism reared its ugly head under the guise of loyalty to the ruling Nazis. Foreign Jews who had escaped or were transferred to France were subject to imprisonment and deportation to German death camps; more than 85,000 Jews were deported and barely 3,000 survived. In southern France, more than 5,000 Jews died as a result of French brutality.

Somehow, Yitzchok Dov was able to escape from St. Cyprien and make his way back north to Belgium.

Yitzchok Dov came to Nazi-occupied Antwerp, seeking a visa to any safe haven. He thought that as a German citizen he could still get proper travel documents. However, when he came to the municipal office and realized that the German authorities were snatching Jews who came for visas and locking them up immediately, he ran outside the office and hid down the block, warning any Jew he saw, not to dare go into the building.

For three days he stood down the block of the municipal office warning Jews to stay away. One afternoon, a car suddenly bolted towards him. Two Nazi soldiers jumped out of the car and pulled him back into their vehicle. They overpowered him and drove him out of the city to the torment of the detention camp called Breendonk.

> On an appropriately gray dreary day I visited Breendonk on a trip to Belgium. Even 50 years after Jews were imprisoned there, one is sickened by the dark, dingy, cold cinder-block cells framed by steel bars and locks, the torture chambers, the lone cattle car standing on isolated tracks that transferred Jews, the ghastly coils of barbed wire atop the fences, the watchtower from where guns were constantly aimed, and the repulsive drawings of former prisoners that depict the bestiality of the Germans and their vicious dogs biting the exposed legs of frail Jews crumbling under the weight of rocks they carried back and forth for no apparent reason.

In Breendonk Yitzchok Dov was forced into heavy-duty labor and slowly his body began to deteriorate. He lost weight and his strength. He lived by day merely to live another night. He survived the night just to see another day. Every day people were sent off to German concentration camps and never heard from again. Many collapsed and perished in Breendonk itself.

It was the end of September and *Yom Kippur* was soon approaching. If he survived until *Yom Kippur*, Yitzchok Dov wanted to fast. He found it hard to accept that he would not fast on *Yom Kippur* for the first time since his youth despite the horrendous conditions. But he understood the reality. If he was forced to work there was no way he could go without any food the entire day. He would surely die.

The only haven possible was the medical infirmary. If he could somehow feign illness and be exempt from work, he could manage to fast. The question that plagued him was: What could he possibly do to guarantee his being in the infirmary?

Yitzchok Dov decided on a plan. Three days before *Yom Kippur* he took a piece of metal and cut his gums. As they began to bleed he began coughing. Coughing blood is a sign of tuberculosis, a highly contagious disease. He figured if the Gestapo (Nazi police) at Breendonk could be convinced that he had tuberculosis then he would surely be quarantined. They wouldn't want to catch it either.

After hours of coughing and complaining of illness, he was brought to the infirmary. There he was told that he would be taken to the military hospital in Antwerp where X-rays would be taken to determine the nature of the illness. The next day he was taken to the military hospital in downtown Antwerp.

X-rays were taken, and Yitzchok Dov was told that the evaluation would be sent to Breendonk within a few days. Yitzchok Dov knew that the X-rays would show nothing, for though he may have been very frail, his lungs were fine. When he was alone with the radiologist, a Belgian gentile, Yitzchok Dov pleaded with him to send back the X-ray of a patient who indeed did have tuberculosis. "I want desperately to observe the holiest day of the Jewish year by fasting, I can only do it if I am in the infirmary and not out doing hard labor."

The radiologist, who likely was infuriated at what the Nazis were doing to his country, said he would try to help. It would be his small way of getting back at the hated Germans. But could a Jew like Yitzchok Dov be assured of anything in that era? Could he trust *any* gentile? He had no choice but to pray and take his chances.

Yitzchok Dov was driven under guard back to Breendonk and quarantined in the infirmary. By *Yom Kippur*, the X-rays had not yet been delivered to Breendonk, so he was in bed the entire day. He recited whatever *Yom Kippur tefillos* he knew by heart, and was able to fast the entire day. Though hungry, tired, and weak, a serenity enveloped him. He had won his battle; now he would be steadfast in his war for survival.

The next day the X-rays were delivered. Yitzchok Dov waited with bated breath to hear what they showed. A German doctor and policeman came in to deliver the news. "You Jewish swine! You are sick and can infect all of us," said the doctor.

"I should kill you now," said the sneering Nazi guard with a look of disgust of his face. "But I wouldn't waste a bullet on you! You're going to die in two days anyway. Get out of this place immediately. We caught you in Antwerp and if you are ever caught there again you will be killed on the spot." He would have to go to a different city.

Within an hour, Yitzchok Dov, frail, gaunt, and weighing less than 100 pounds, but blessed with perfect lungs, began his long trek to a new life.

It is 20 miles from Breendonk to Brussels. Once again, no one knows for sure how he made it there, but he came to Brussels and managed to revitalize himself in health and in spirit. News of his arrival in Brussels spread, and one day he received a message from his former Rosh Yeshivah in Heide, Rav Shraga Shapiro. "Undoubtedly you are upset that you are not in Antwerp, where most Jews in Belgium live, but rest assured, if the *Ribono Shel Olam* orchestrated that you be in Brussels, it is the place for you and you shall accomplish great things there."

The Rosh Yeshivah's message was prophetic. Immediately Yitzchok Dov began working with children in orphan homes, bringing them meals, saying *Krias Shema* with them and teaching them Torah, whenever the opportunity presented itself. He was not foiled when he was arrested numerous times for being out past curfew; each time he showed his identification papers that he was a physical education teacher for children. For the remainder of the war he was both the father and mother of children who had no parents.

After the war when refugees from Auschwitz and other concentration camps arrived at the Schaerbeek railroad station in Brussels, only the International Red Cross and various government officials were allowed to greet them. At the time, Yitzchok Dov was director of the O.I.B. (Orphanage Israelite of Belgium). He came to the train station with cards and identification badges that glaringly displayed the O.I.B. insignia. When asked who he was he said he represented the "Organization of Israelite Benefactors" (a fictitious organization), and thus was able to meet with each of the refugees, telling them where their Belgian relatives might be, which of their friends survived, and where they could be found. For the many who had no relatives left anywhere, Yitzchok Dov "found" relatives in Belgium so that they could be accepted into the country.

Shortly thereafter, when he was appointed director of the Tiefenbrunner Orphanage, he opened a school for the institution's 47 children. That ultimately became the Maimonides School, which eventually had more than 500 students. It functioned on the highest Torah standards of any Jewish school ever built in Brussels.

Aside from his remarkable *gemillas chessed* for Jewish patients in Brussels hospitals, he built the Maale *shul* in the Foret section of Brussels and headed the *Chevra Kadisha* (Jewish Burial Society) for more than 30 years. In 1993 the entire Belgian Jewish community mourned his passing.

As *Yom Kippur* begins to fade near the end of the day, Jews the world over cry out in the *Ne'ilah* service: פְּתַח לָנוּ שַׁעַר בְּעֵת נְעִילַת שַׁעַר, *Open the [Heavenly] gate for us, at this time when the gate closes.*

Yitzchok Dov Bamberger's determination to fast on *Yom Kippur* opened a gate when the gates for most other Jews were tragically closed. He emerged from this gateway to become the pivotal personality, along with his wife Rosa, for Orthodox causes in Brussels for close to 50 years. He leaves a legacy of children, grandchildren, and great-grandchildren who are all *shomrei Torah u'mitzvos.*

The German in Breendonk didn't want to waste a bullet. A Jewish community flourished in Brussels instead.

Reunited

The following story is among the most dramatic I have ever heard. The subject is unusual and heartrending. One can only imagine the intensity of emotion felt by the participants and how indelibly the story is etched in their minds.

I am grateful to Rabbi Pinchos Kornfeld of Antwerp for having told it to me and to Rabbi Yoel Reitzer of Antwerp for having added significant details.

The province of Limburg in Belgium is a sad footnote in the history of European Jews. From 1933 until 1940, German Jews, frightened by the cruel and savage Nazi regime, fled westward to Belgium and, for the most part, settled in Antwerp. By 1940 there were 55,000 Jews in the city. When the Nazis occupied Antwerp in 1941 and wished to make it *Judenrein* (clean of Jews), they forcibly transplanted 30,000 of the city's Jews who were not Belgian citizens (German, Polish, and Romanian Jews) 40 miles east to Limburg.

Shortly thereafter, these Jews were sent to a detention camp in Brussels and then brought to Auschwitz where they were put to death. After the war, there were no Jews in Limburg, and the survivors returned to the traditional Jewish neighborhoods in Antwerp and Brussels.

Trying to start their lives anew, many Belgian Jews found it difficult to make a living, so Rabbi Moshe Zev Reitzer and his family moved from Antwerp to the small town of Herk-de-Stad in Limburg. Because there were no Jews living in the vicinity, the Reitzer children stayed in Antwerp throughout the week where they attended yeshivos, and then went home for Shabbos.

Remarkably, the Reitzers, who still live in Herk-de-Stad, raised exceptional children. One of them is Rabbi Yoel, a noted *talmid chacham,* who studied in Jerusalem under the great Tshebiner Rav, Rabbi Dov Berish Weidenfeld (1879-1965), and for a while was his attendant.

The people of Herk-de-Stad recognized that the Reitzers were "different," but the family was very well respected as Moshe Reitzer became a successful and very charitable businessman.

When the Reitzer children were already adults, one of them, R' Yossel, was making small talk with the postman, who had just delivered the mail. The postman mentioned matter-of-factly that there was a Jewish gravestone in the town's cemetery. R' Yossel couldn't believe it. What Jew would be buried in a non-Jewish cemetery? He expressed his doubts about it.

"Come with me and I'll show it to you," the postman said.

That afternoon, R' Yossel and his brother R' Yoel went to the cemetery and, to their amazement, they saw that among the non-Jewish gravestones was a small monument engraved in Flemish topped with a *Magen David.* It was dated June 19, 1941 and it bore the name Ilsa Horowitz, who died when she was only 14 years old.

The Reitzer brothers were speechless! Who was this girl and how did she happen to be buried there? The postman remembered that when he was a teen-ager, Ilsa had drowned while swimming. He said that the tragedy frightened and unnerved the little town, and the Catholic nuns offered the church's horse and wagon to the family so that Ilsa's coffin would be carried with dignity to her final resting place. He remembered that, strangely enough, she had been buried just outside the cemetery, which since that time had expanded and now surrounded the lone Jewish grave.

Standing in the cemetery, the Reitzer brothers realized immediately that the family had intentionally buried their child outside the cemetery, for they hoped to move her to a Jewish cemetery after the war. Decades later, however, she was still there, now in the middle of a gentile cemetery. Undoubtedly her family had been killed by the Nazis.

When R' Yossel and R' Yoel came home they contacted Rabbi Boruch'l Kahane of Antwerp, who advised that they try to remove the remains and transfer them to a Jewish cemetery. Immediately they called Rabbi Pinchos Kornfeld who is the Vice President of the *Consistoire,* the officially recognized organization that represents the Belgian Jewish community.

R' Pinchos, a Gerrer *chassid,* is a human whirlwind of activity. An energetic *askan* (activist), involved in every project and endeavor for the needs of Belgian Jewry, he is one of Europe's most respected and admired Jews.

"Do you think that it is possible to move Ilsa's remains to a Jewish cemetery?" the Reitzers asked R' Pinchos.

"Most definitely," he replied in his usual enthusiastic voice. Politically astute, attentive to details, and mindful of the unexpected, R' Pinchos cautioned, "We must first sort out the historical background, get local governmental permission, have the proper documents signed, alert the *Chevra Kadisha* (Jewish Burial Society) in Antwerp, purchase a plot, and then plan a funeral."

Within days, R' Pinchos with the help of a Mrs. Barrett in the Brussels Ministry of Health, had assembled the chronology of events that led to the girl's burial in Herk-de-Stad.

Before the war, Ilsa's parents, Mendel and Regina Horowitz, had come from Vienna to the Jewish neighborhood in Antwerp, and lived on Lange Kievitsstraat. In 1941 they were among the tens of thousands rounded up by the Gestapo and transferred to Limburg. Mr. and Mrs. Horowitz were there when their only daughter drowned. Within a year, the Horowitzes were killed in Auschwitz.

R' Pinchos knew that he needed governmental permission to

disinter a body. However, if he did so without authorization of a family member he could face legal consequences in the future. He scrutinized Horowitz family records and was told unequivocally that both parents and their only child were dead and there were no immediate survivors.

R' Pinchos decided to call the *burgermeister* (mayor) of Herk-de-Stad. Mayor Henri Knuts, a member of the Socialist Party and the Belgian senate, told R' Pinchos that he remembered the funeral vividly. "My friends and I were sitting on the fence alongside the cemetery watching a procession we had never seen before. There were men in big black hats reading from books, all extremely solemn. It was a very sad day. For some reason," he added, "the girl was buried just outside the cemetery. We could never understand why. Today, though, her grave is among many others."

Speaking in Flemish, R' Pinchos said, "I have checked the records in Brussels, and there are no survivors. We of the Jewish community in Antwerp would like to transfer Ilsa's remains to a Jewish cemetery. Can we count on your authorization?"

"Yes, of course," said Mayor Knuts. "Write me a letter on official stationery and I will grant permission."

The letter was written and within a week permission was granted. R' Pinchos contacted his brother R' Moshe, a member of Antwerp's *Chevra Kadisha*, and plans were made for the *Chevra* to come to Herk-de-Stad and begin the difficult process of disinterment.

The work was scheduled to begin on a Wednesday morning at 10 o'clock and be over by noon. Local police would stand by to assure that only the correct grave was touched.

Later that Wednesday the reburial would take place in the Jewish cemetery of Putte, which is actually in Holland, a 20-minute ride from Antwerp.

No Jewish cemetery exists in Belgium because Belgian law permits graves to be destroyed or dug up after 49 years. Belgian Jews use the *beis olam* (cemetery) in Putte, Holland. The legendary *tzaddik* R' Itzik'l Gewirtzman (1882-1977) of Antwerp (see

Along the Maggid's Journey, p. 189) and his son-in-law R' Yankele Leiser (1906-1998) are also buried in Putte.

Posters were put up throughout Antwerp that the funeral procession for Ilsa would begin at 4 in the afternoon with the burial taking place at 4:30 in Putte. Announcements were made in every *shul,* and within the Belgian Jewish community the interment and memorial service began assuming immense significance. For those who had lost loved ones in the war, for those who knew children who had perished in the Holocaust, and for parents who could empathize with the late Mendel and Regina Horowitz, it was a day of redemption, prayer, and unity.

On Monday morning, R' Pinchos got a call from Mrs. Barrett in the Brussels Ministry of Health. She had opened the file on the Horowitz family once again and now noticed something she had overlooked the last time they spoke. She thought he should know about it. In pencil there was a notation along the margin that the Jewish Council of Vienna had inquired about the whereabouts of the Horowitz family.

R' Pinchos's heart sank. Such inquiries were usually made by a close family member. Did the Horowitz's have a surviving relative? Would he have to put the whole process on hold? He had been so meticulous until this point. How could this happen now, a mere 48 hours before the disinterment was to start? The Horowitz family had lived in Vienna; was that why the inquiry came from there?

"Who made the inquiry?" R' Pinchos asked anxiously. "Is there a name written?"

"It just says that the Jewish Council of Vienna made the inquiry for a woman in England."

With heightened urgency R' Pinchos immediately called the Jewish Council in Vienna and asked if they had made an inquiry years ago regarding the Horowitz family. "We may have," came the reply, "but we would have to check the archives."

"But I must know right away," R' Pinchos pleaded. "This is an urgent matter."

"There is no one here today who can search through the

archives, but call back tomorrow and we will try to help you," the secretary replied.

R' Pinchos was exasperated, but he had no choice but to wait. On Tuesday, R' Pinchos called, pleaded, beseeched, and implored the people at the Vienna Jewish Council, but there was no one who could check the files that day either. The disinterment and funeral were planned for the next day. Should he put everything on hold? Would there be a relative somewhere who would be opposed? Would the Jewish *Consistoire* someday be held liable for his actions? Instinctively, R' Pinchos decided to let things take their natural course. For now, he was not going to issue a hold order. He would call Vienna again on Wednesday.

On Wednesday morning, the council told him that they had located the records. A Miss or Mrs. Lipson from Southport, England had made the inquiry. His mind began to race quickly. Was she an aunt of Ilsa?

Meanwhile, it was already 10 o'clock and Antwerp's *Chevra Kadisha,* under the watchful eyes of the police and curious bystanders, had begun digging in Herk-de-Stad. R' Pinchos called the number of the Jewish Community Center in Southport, England, numerous times but there was no answer. He then called Southport's municipal office. "This is an urgent call from Antwerp," R' Pinchos said. "Can you please tell me, do you have a woman living in your area by the name of Mrs. Lipson or Miss Lipson?"

The answer was forthcoming quickly. "Yes, there is a Miss Lipson who lives at 27 Coventry."

"Is it Mrs. Lipson or Miss Lipson?" R' Pinchos wanted to be sure.

"It's Miss Lipson, that's what the records here say," came the reply. "Would you have a phone number for her?" R' Pinchas asked.

"Sorry," the clerk said, "she does not have a phone listed."

"But I must get in touch with her. This is an emergency and I'm calling from Belgium," R' Pinchos pleaded once again.

"There is nothing we can do," the clerk replied. "Someone would have to go down to her street and find her."

It was now 11:30. Most of the work in Herk-de-Stad would have been finished and they would soon be on the way to Antwerp. R' Pinchos asked the clerk for the number of the local police precinct.

Within minutes, R' Pinchos was talking to the Southport chief of police. He explained the urgency of the matter, making sure to stress words like funeral, Auschwitz, drowned, and reburial, that would convey the gravity of the situation.

"We'll try to help you. I'll send someone down to her house immediately," the police chief said. "Call us back in 25 minutes."

R' Pinchos could not sound exasperated — he had to sound thankful. "I'm very grateful to you sir for your help. I'll call in 25 minutes."

Exactly 25 minutes later the police chief picked up the phone and said, "We sent someone down there by bike and he just returned, but there was no one home. A neighbor didn't know where she was either. Sorry, we wish we could have been of more assistance."

Now, what? If he waited to contact her tomorrow it would be too late. Then he thought of it — the Jewish Community Center of Southport. He had called them earlier and they were not in. Perhaps now someone was there. He tried them once again and this time someone answered on the first ring.

R' Pinchos identified himself and quickly recounted his reason for the call. "Do you know a Miss Lipson of 27 Coventry?"

"Yes," came the reply. "She is a very nice person, a spinster who lives alone."

"The local police did not have a phone number for her. Do you know where or how I can reach her?" R' Pinchos asked.

"She works at the Jewish library and should be there now," came the reply.

However, when R' Pinchos called the library they told him that Miss Lipson had just gone out to lunch and would return in an hour. An hour that seemed like three hours later, R' Pinchos called the library and was put through to Miss Lipson.

R' Pinchos took a deep breath and began slowly. It was very

late already, close to 3 o'clock, but he could not rush the conversation, for every word would be significant.

"My name is Pinchos Kornfeld," he began slowly. "I am the Vice President of the Jewish Community Organization in Belgium. Are you Miss Lipson?"

She was. Did she have relatives in Belgium? She didn't.

"Did you by any chance know of a Mendel and Regina Horowitz who lived in Belgium before the war?" R' Pinchos asked.

There was a pause on the other end and then Miss Lipson said, "They were my parents."

"Your parents were named Horowitz?" R' Pinchos asked incredulously. His heart was beating rapidly. "But your name is Lipson?"

"When I was a very little girl, we lived in Vienna. In 1939 I was sent to England on one of the children's transports. At first I was cared for by a refugee society, but then an uncle of mine put an advert in the *Jewish Chronicle* and a Mrs. Louis Lipson of Liverpool responded to the advert and brought me to her home. Mr. and Mrs. Lipson treated me like their own daughter and eventually I adopted their family name. We moved to Southport during the war when the Germans were bombing Liverpool."

R' Pinchos's mouth was suddenly dry. "Did you have any siblings?" he asked.

"I had one sister."

R' Pinchos could hardly say the words, "Her name?"

"Ilsa." She paused and said, "Her Yiddish name was Perel."

R' Pinchos's mind was racing, but he struggled to remain calm. "Do you know what happened to her?" he asked softly.

"I was told that she drowned in a swimming accident, but that was long ago," she said.

R' Pinchos now understood why the records showed that the Horowitzes had only one daughter. Mendel Horowitz was afraid to say that he still had family in Vienna for he might be viewed as a spy. Thus once his daughter Gitel (Gertrude) was on the children's transport he did not report her existence to Belgian or German authorities.

"Was your father religious?" R' Pinchos asked.

"Oh yes, and my mother were very Orthodox."

"Part of the work of our organization here in Antwerp," said R' Pinchos, "is searching for those who perished during the war but never had the opportunity to be buried in a Jewish cemetery. What would you say about having Ilsa in a Jewish cemetery?"

"Mr. Kornfeld, that would be the ultimate grace for her soul," she said.

"Miss Lipson," R' Pinchos said in a soft hushed tone, "We found her and we are about to bring her to a Jewish resting place."

Gitel Lipson gasped and began crying uncontrollably. "I can't believe you are doing this," she said between sobs. "I am so grateful to you."

She cried softly as the anguish and agony of her sister's past welled up within her. She was overwhelmed by the concerned involvement of total strangers for her sister's benefit.

"I have been trying to reach you for the last 48 hours," said R' Pinchos. "But it was impossible. I wish so much that you could be here but the whole process is already in progress. The funeral is in less than half an hour and Perel will be reburied shortly afterward."

"Please call me and tell me how everything went," Miss Lipson said.

"I will, Miss Lipson, I surely will."

And so that afternoon in the presence of rabbis, community leaders, and close to a thousand men, women, and children of all ages, Perel (Ilsa) Horowitz was paid her final tribute, as she, the symbol of thousands of unknown children, was laid to rest among her people.

> When people comfort mourners, they say, הַמָּקוֹם יְנַחֵם אֶתְכֶם, *May the Omnipresent One comfort you.* Perhaps on that day

in Putte, the expression הַמָּקוֹם could have been given its other meaning, *place*: *may this place comfort you,* for surely there was consolation that day for the souls of that child and her martyred parents — and for her living sister — as she came to rest in a special place, reunited with her family — the Jewish nation.

A Number-One Gesture

The following incident took merely a moment but for those who witnessed it, it encompassed much of Jewish history — tragedy, dignity and generosity.

When the Gerrer Rebbe, Rav Yaakov Aryeh Alter, visited the United States in May 1998, thousands wished to see him and receive his advice and blessing. Though his schedule was extremely tight, an evening was designated for public access to the Rebbe at the Mesifta of Ger, in Borough Park, from 7 o'clock in the evening until midnight.

The exceedingly long lines wound around the staircases of the Mesifta, through the lobby, out the door and down the block, as young and old alike gathered to have a few precious private moments with the Rebbe.

When the *gabbaim* (attendants) saw the throngs of people, they decided to use a number system, whereby older people were given lower numbers and younger people were given higher numbers. The people with lower numbers would go in to see the Rebbe before the people with higher numbers, so that the elderly would not have to stand in line that long.

As the people in the long line inched slowly forward, an elderly bent-over gentleman entered the building and made his way to the *gabbaim*. As he walked towards the front, some people called out, "Excuse me, but there is a number system here. You will have to wait your turn."

The gentleman hadn't been aware of the system and, oblivious to all comments, he went to the *gabbaim* and asked when he could see the Rebbe.

"Do you have a number?" one of the *gabbaim* asked him.

The elderly man looked up silently and slowly rolled up his jacket sleeve revealing a number that had been tattooed on his arm in the Nazi concentration camps.

"Yes," he said softly, "this is my number."

The *gabbaim* and all those at the front of the line gasped! They let him go in next.

> A rule was broken for a man who had been shattered, but that was complete perfection.

Revelations in Jerusalem

The Iron Curtain, which for decades separated people under Soviet domination from the rest of the world, has disappeared. Travel to, and business with, Russia, is common. In our times, yeshivos, Bais Yaakovs, and synagogues are flourishing in Russia, Belorus, and the Ukraine, where not many years ago, Jews were terrified to openly display or even admit their Jewishness.

Actually, the revival of Torah learning and the practice of *Yahadus* in such places as Moscow, Kiev, and Kishinev began years earlier with heroes and heroines who clandestinely began a revolution by studying Torah and performing *mitzvos* in secret gatherings without the knowledge of Soviet authorities. Jews who came to learn about Judaism and teachers who came from abroad to teach them risked personal harm and imprisonment for their noble efforts.

Under the direction of Mr. Ernie Hirsch in England, a group of men and women from Manchester, Gateshead, Stamford Hill, Hendon, and Golders Green were chosen to travel to the Soviet Union to inspire, teach, and guide those who wanted to learn more about their religion. One of the heroines who came to Moscow during the 1980s to teach and to bring *sefarim, mezuzos, tefillin,* and *matzos* was Mrs. Yocheved Kahn of London.

❁ ❁ ❁

In the summer of 1996, my wife and I met Mrs. Kahn and her husband, R' Ezra, in Lugano, Switzerland. When I learned that she had lectured often in Russia and in England for the Ohr Somayach and the SEED programs, I asked if she had a favorite story. She replied that each time she returned to Russia, someone in a study group would ask her to repeat the story she told when she first arrived, for it gave them hope and faith. And so on this serene August night, as we waited with thousands of others along Lugano's magnificent waterfront to witness Switzerland's annual dazzling display of fireworks, Mrs. Kahn, who had told her story countless times to countless groups, told it once again.

As resplendent as the fireworks were, not one colorful burst of floral radiance that lit the sky that night would be remembered as much as her story.

❁ ❁ ❁

In 1940, Shloma and Rosa Leuvenberg, from Apeldoorn, Holland, had their third daughter, whom they named Yocheved. That year the Nazis were spreading terror against Jews all across Europe, and Jewish families sought ways to escape, or at least to save their children. But few opportunities were open to them.

When Yocheved was 2½ years old, a young gentile woman, Bertha Van Hof*, came to the Leuvenberg home and offered to protect and conceal her. She promised she would tend to the child and hide her from Nazi authorities. With heavy hearts, the Leuvenbergs reluctantly gave Yocheved to Bertha. Two weeks later, the Nazis swept across Holland and seized the Leuvenbergs and their two older daughters, Malka and Greetje,

The name has been changed.

and took them to the Dutch concentration camp in Westerbork. They were there only a few days, when on Shabbos, the 17th of Tamuz, they were herded onto train no. 19, headed for the extermination camp in Sobibor, Poland. Tragically, they were never heard from again. Meanwhile, Bertha found a family in a small fishing town, Enkhuizen, in northern Holland, who agreed to care for Yocheved. However, at no time was she told she was Jewish.

When the war ended five years later, Bertha traveled to the town of Utrecht, in the center of Holland, and went to see Aaron De Haas and his wife Margareta. Reb Aaron was chairman of the Agudath Israel organization in Holland and a member of Agudah's *Vaad Hapoel Olami* (World Executive Board). The woman told R' Aaron and his wife that their niece, Yocheved, had survived the war and that she was being cared for by a family in Enkhuizen, who had not told the child that she was Jewish.

The De Haases were flabbergasted. They had thought that the entire Leuvenberg family had perished in the war. They contacted the family tending to Yocheved and explained their relationship, and said they were willing to raise her as their daughter. Incredibly, the family agreed to release Yocheved, and they slowly broke the news to the little child that she was Jewish and that she would soon be moving in with relatives. Yocheved, who had no recollection of her Jewishness, was unwilling to leave her comfortable surroundings, but the family convinced her that she belonged with her relatives.

For the next 13 years, the De Haases raised Yocheved as their own child. She attended school and eventually received a teacher's diploma. In 1959 she traveled to Israel for seminary. One night, she went to a wedding of a friend in Jerusalem. Also attending that wedding was an elderly woman from Amsterdam, Mrs. Clara Asher Pinkhof. Someone asked Mrs. Pinkhof if she would like to meet a young woman from her home country.

"Why, of course," came the reply. When Mrs. Pinkhof saw Yocheved, she exclaimed. "You have got to be the daughter of

Rosa Leuvenberg! You look exactly as I remember her."

Yocheved and Mrs. Pinkhof had a heartrending talk as they each recounted searing parts of their lives and how they each came to be in Israel. As the conversation shifted from topic to topic, Mrs. Pinkhof took Yocheved's hand in hers and said tenderly, "My child, do you know how you got the name Yocheved?"

Yocheved was startled. It had always puzzled her. No cousins were named Yocheved, and as far as she knew, none of her ancestors or relatives who perished in the war had that name. She had often wondered why her parents chose that name.

"I have wondered myself," said Yocheved, nervously anxious to learn a secret from her past.

Mrs. Pinkhof felt she understood why Divine Providence ordained that she meet Yocheved at the wedding. She took a deep breath and began. "I used to write a weekly column for the NIW, the *Nieuw Israelitsch Weekblad* (New Israeli Week), the Dutch Jewish weekly newspaper," said Mrs. Pinkhof. "The Jews in Holland in the late '30s and early '40s were frightened and depressed. One week I wrote a column directed to families who, because of Nazi terror, were afraid to bring children into the world during those perilous times.

"I cited the Talmudic teaching (*Sotah* 12a) that tells of the reprimand that Miriam the prophetess gave her father Amram. When Pharaoh decreed that all newborn Jewish boys were to be thrown into the river (*Shemos* 1:22), Amram divorced his wife Yocheved. Miriam then said to her father, 'Your decree is worse than Pharaoh's. He issued a decree only against the boys, and you have issued a decree against the boys and girls.'

"I wrote, 'Jews of Holland, you must have faith and trust in Hashem. Surely the Jewish future looked bleak in Egypt, yet Amram, because of his daughter's reprimand, remarried Yocheved. Because of that, Moshe *Rabbeinu*, the redeemer of *Klal Yisrael*, was born.'

"The next week, your mother wrote a letter to the editor. She said that she was expecting a child and that indeed some of her friends had scorned her for having a child in those perilous times. 'I am uplifted by the writer's words,' she wrote. 'If I have a son I will name him Amram, and if I have a daughter I will name her Yocheved.' "

And then, as tears welled in her eyes, Mrs. Pinkhof said to the young woman standing before her, "That child was you. That's how you got your name."

In somber times of enslavement in Egypt, Yocheved was a source of inspiration and assistance (See *Shemos* 1:15,17 and *Rashi* ibid.). Is it any wonder that her namesake in our times still provides inspiration.

Holland— Moscow — Switzerland — England — Jerusalem— The roads of inspiration transverse the world. How fortunate we are to travel them.

Flawless Fulfillment

While it is true that every person needs to hear kind and encouraging words, there are some who need it more than others: the downtrodden because of tragedies, the distressed because of their past, and the frustrated because of their unfulfilled dreams.

How exhilarating and refreshing it is when one Jew inspires another with an innovative thought or concept. It is the ideal way to carry out the statement of Yeshaya: אִישׁ אֶת רֵעֵהוּ יַעְזֹרוּ וּלְאָחִיו יֹאמַר חֲזָק, *Each man would help his fellowman and to his brother he would say, "Be strong"* (*Yeshaya* 41:6).

In the following episode, first told to me by Rabbi Shimon Hirschler of Stamford Hill, England, a noted author of *sefarim* on Rabbi Akiva Eiger, we hear the thoughtful insight in the reassuring words of the Vizhnitzer Rebbe, Rabbi Chaim Meyer Hager (1888-1972). (See *Yamim*

M'Kedem Vol. 1, by Rav Yitzchok Dovid Resmovitz, page 144.)

In 1945, after World War II, the Vizhnitzer Rebbe came to Budapest, Hungary, to give solace and comfort to the countless people who were filled with hopelessness and melancholy after having lost their families, friends, and possessions because of Nazi atrocities. As the Rebbe made his way around the city, a group of young men, who had experienced the ghastly horrors of internment in labor and concentration camps, approached him.

With great sincerity and heartache, they told him that they were plagued by constant pangs of guilt for having eaten non-kosher food throughout their imprisonment.

"Perhaps we should have been stronger," said one of the young men with remorse. "Perhaps we could have survived without eating the food from their kitchens. What should we do to repent for our sins?"

The Rebbe was astonished at their sincerity. He was quiet for a few moments and then he began to cry. He took the hand of one of the young men and clasped it warmly in his own hands. "Isn't it true that the only reason you and your friends ate the *treifah* food was so that you should survive?"

The young man nodded yes.

"Surely the reason you felt you had to eat the food was because of the Torah's commandment וָחַי בָּהֶם, *And you shall live by them* [the commandments] (*Vayikra* 18:5)," said the Rebbe.

Again the young man nodded.

"The Nazis did not give anyone a morsel of food more than what they needed for survival," said the Rebbe. "Thus in fulfilling the commandment of וָחַי בָּהֶם, you fulfilled it to the exact specifications required in Halachah. In Heaven you will be rewarded in full measure for your observance of this sacred *mitzvah*."

"I only wish," cried the Rebbe, "that the eating and drinking that I do for the purpose of a *mitzvah* [such as the *k'zayis* matzah or *revi'is* of wine] should be as perfect and as holy as your eating was!"

Redemption and Rescue

In the late 1930s Mr. David Turkel was secretary of the Agudath Israel organization in Vienna, Austria, and editor and senior writer of its weekly newspaper. Mr. Turkel minced no words in his crisp and outspoken columns.

In the spring of 1938 he wrote an article against Adolph Hitler and the Third Reich. He warned Viennese Jews of the impending danger and implored them to pray and plan for their safety. Friday night, *Parashas Zachor,* Hitler and his Nazi army marched into an ecstatically cheering Vienna.

Mr. Turkel knew that he had to leave Austria immediately to save his life. He was high on the Nazi blacklist and arrest was imminent. Interrogation and imprisonment — or worse — were surely in store if he were caught.

Mr. Turkel began making plans for his escape. Compounding his problems was the fact that he had gotten engaged just a few weeks before. Now he would have to leave his *kallah,* Claire Zauderer, his widowed mother, Mrs. Gittel Turkel, and his two sisters, Henny and Sali, behind. He hoped that once he was safely out of Austria he could arrange for their escape as well.

Chaim Yisrael Neurath, a close friend who eventually married Sali, worked in the Vienna office of the international Japanese company Mitsui. He obtained a company letter stating that Mr. Turkel was an American agent for Mitsui. With that letter David Turkel was able to enter London as an American visitor and remain there for three months.

Once in London, his priority was to get visas for his immediate family members back in Vienna. Visas, however, were issued only for one of two reasons: either someone was sponsored by a wealthy individual who would guarantee the immigrant's full support, or the immigrant had to show that he was qualified for employment at a necessary job in the country. Many young women were able to enter England on the premise they would become housemaids. Indeed, in this manner, Mr. Turkel was able to get visas for his *kallah* and for his sisters. His mother, however, was already 50 years old, too old to be a domestic by British standards. Thus David found it almost impossible to get his mother to England.

He had no relatives or rich friends in England to help him, but he knew he had to do something. One night while lying awake trying desperately to figure out how he could possibly get his mother a visa, Mr. Turkel thought of an innovative idea. He spent the night refining his plan.

The next morning he took an ad in England's Jewish newspaper explaining that he needed a sponsor to get his mother a visa. He assured all readers that they would bear no financial responsibility for his mother. He could and would handle her support. He appealed to the compassion of his fellow Jews.

The advertisement ran for two weeks, but no one responded. During the third week Mr. Turkel received a letter from a Mr. Gabriel Fierstone. "Would you come to see me?" Mr. Fierstone wrote. "I would like to talk to you about your ad."

Mr. Turkel rushed to Mr. Fierstone's office and once there assured him that his mother would never be a financial burden on him. "As long as I have bread, she will have bread," said David Turkel.

Mr. Fierstone assured Mr. Turkel that he was not concerned about any financial liability; he merely wanted to know details about him and his family. After some conversation, Mr. Fierstone agreed to sign papers to enable Mr. Turkel's mother to enter England. The application was filed and after governmental verification that all papers were in order, Mrs. Gittel Turkel was able to come to England.

Mrs. Turkel landed on British shores a mere four days before her son's wedding. Though tempered by the crisis of the times, the joy at the wedding was extraordinary.

According to Mr. Turkel, it may have been the first *chupah* in London to be held outdoors under the sky, as the British custom was to have a *chupah* in the synagogue. Rabbi Solomon Schonfeld (see p. 177) and Moreinu Rabbi Yaakov Rosenheim officiated at the wedding.

After the *Sheva Berachos* week, Mr. Turkel said to his mother, "I think we should visit Mr. Fierstone and thank him for all that he did for us."

Mrs. Turkel agreed and they made an appointment to visit Mr. Fierstone in his office. On the day of the appointment Mrs. Turkel dressed in her finest clothes to meet the benefactor whom she had never known. After an exchange of introductions and greetings, Mrs. Turkel thanked Mr. Fierstone profusely and then asked, "In the town of Schodnica (Galicia) where I am from, there was a Feuerstein family. Did you have any relatives there?"

Mr. Fierstone was startled at the mention of Schodnica. He hadn't heard that little town mentioned in years. "What is your maiden name?" he asked Mrs. Turkel.

"My name was Backenroth," said Mrs. Turkel.

"Did you by any chance know Avrohomche Backenroth?" asked Mr. Fierstone.

Now it was Mrs. Turkel's turn to be startled. "Avrohomche Backenroth was my *father*!"

Mr. Fierstone turned pale. He was silent for a few moments as he tried to compose himself.

"My siblings and I were little children when my father died. We lived in Schodnica with my mother and we were poverty stricken. Your father was the one who supported us. We had food to eat only because of him.

"When he heard that we had family in England, he encouraged my mother to move here from Galicia, so that we could be close to family and be helped by them. We did move to London, and it was Avrohomche Backenroth who paid the fare for all of us."

Mr. Fierstone was silent as he wiped a tear from his eyes. Unknowingly he had rescued Avrohomche Backenroth's daughter! What an astounding orchestration of events.

And so in a London office, three people sat humbled, gratified, awed, and speechless at Hashem's majestic design.

Windows to the World

During *Chol HaMoed Succos* of 1998, my son-in-law R' Ephraim Perlstein and I visited his rebbi, Rabbi Rafael Shmulevitz, a Rosh Yeshivah in Yeshivas Mir, in his succah in Jerusalem. Reb Rafael, the son of the revered Mirrer Rosh Yeshivah Rabbi Chaim Shmulevitz (1902-1978), discussed a wide range of topics in *halachah, aggadah,* and *kochos hanefesh* (spiritual behavior).

The discussion turned to the days during World War II when the students of the Mir Yeshivah escaped from Vilna to Kobe, Japan, and from there to the Japanese-occupied international city of Shanghai. The Mirrer Yeshivah in Shanghai was the only yeshivah that had managed almost *in toto* to escape from Lithuania, where tens of thousands of Jews were trapped in the fangs of the Soviet Communists after the Baltic states had been occupied by Joseph Stalin.

Reb Rafael told us that although he still had family passports and visas from those days in Shanghai, he had no personal recollections of that era, since he was an infant then. He was aware of the historical events of that period however, and told us about an event held in 1995 in honor of one of the heroes of that time.

In 1995, the historian Dr. David Kranzler of Brooklyn, New York, arranged for a reception to take place in the home of the Rosh Yeshivah of Mir/Yerushalyim Rav Nosson Zvi Finkel, to honor the memory of Mr. Jan Zwartendyk, the wartime honorary consul of the Netherlands, who had helped provide thousands of necessary visas allowing the Mirrer *talmidim,* among others, to escape Lithuania for Japan.

The late Mr. Zwartendyk was represented by his children and grandchildren. At the reception, a former *talmid* of Mir in Shanghai, Rabbi Velvel Perkovsky, spoke with emotion and eloquence.

"The Torah tells us," began Rav Perkovsky, "that Hashem said to Noah, צֹהַר תַּעֲשֶׂה לַתֵּבָה, *A window shall you make for the ark* (*Bereishis* 6:16)."

Rabbi Perkovsky expounded, "Perhaps the purpose of the window was twofold. Not only for light, but for Noah to be able to look out at the desolation and devastation that was taking place outside his safe quarters and recognize how fortunate he was and how unfortunate others were. Hashem wanted Noah to be sensitive to the pain of others."

Turning to the Zwartendyk children, Rabbi Perkovsky said, "Your father of blessed memory had such a window. Though he was safe from harm, he realized that the Jews were not. He was not insensitive to our crisis. He therefore extended efforts on our behalf and brought light to many who were doomed to darkness."

In his succah in Jerusalem, Rabbi Rafael Shmulevitz marveled at that insight and said to all his guests, "It is a lesson in life that we should all remember. Those who are fortunate in life must never forget to look through that window and feel the plight of those who are less fortunate."

The story of how these visas to freedom were procured is fascinating and worth retelling, for it illustrates Hashem's orchestration of events. Additionally, those who played prominent roles in that successful *hatzalah* (rescue) are barely known to the children and grandchildren of the survivors and their contemporaries. They deserve to be remembered.

I am grateful to Dr. David Kranzler for his books and information on these historical events. I thank Mr. Nathan Gutwirth of Antwerp, Rav Binyamin Zeilberger and Rabbi Moshe Zupnick of Brooklyn, and Rabbi Yaakov Ederman of Forest Hills for sharing their very personal accounts of the miraculous rescue.

On September 1, 1939, the German Reich invaded Poland, and within three weeks, had conquered the western two thirds of the country, leaving the rest for the Soviet Union to occupy. Rabbi Chaim Ozer Grodzensky (1863-1940), the *gadol hador,* who lived in Vilna, Lithuania, sent telegrams to the yeshivos of Soviet-controlled Poland [including the yeshivos in Baranovich, Grodno, Kaminetz, Kletzk, Lomza, Lubavitch, Lublin, Mir, Novordok and Radin], directing them to come en masse to Vilna, where he felt every yeshivah could reestablish itself.

Lithuania at the time was neutral, and during the several weeks of flux before the Soviets had secured the border between Poland and Lithuania, escape to the still-free Lithuania was possible. (No Jews could leave Nazi-occupied Poland. Only people in the Soviet sector were free to go, and then only for a short while.)

On Reb Chaim Ozer's orders, a migration from 30 different yeshivos in Poland began, and by early 1940 close to 3,000 *talmidim* and their *rebbeim* had made their way to Vilna. Though most Polish Jews in Soviet-controlled Poland did not leave their hometowns, as many as 25,000 Jews, most of them impoverished, had come to Vilna, as well. The Jews in Vilna were magnanimous in their *hachnasas orchim,* but poverty became rampant and people waited on lines for hours to get a loaf of bread.

In response to Reb Chaim Ozer's plea, the Agudath Harabbonim of America organized the Vaad Hatzoloh, whose original mission was to help the refugee yeshivos.

At first, the *shuls* in Vilna and its suburbs opened their facilities to the various yeshivos, but the overcrowding was stifling. Many boys slept on the floors. Within a few months, however, the Lithuanian authorities dispersed the yeshivos, and they were quartered in *shuls* throughout the country. The atmosphere became relaxed and learning resumed almost with a sense of normalcy.

This tranquility lasted only a few months, for shortly after Shavuos, in June 1940, the Soviets marched into Lithuania and gained total control of the "liberated" country. They annexed it to the Soviet Union. Fear and terror now gripped every Jew in Lithuania, for they understood that they could not safely practice

Judaism, certainly not Orthodoxy, under Stalin's anti-Semitic, atheistic regime.

What should the Jews — especially the refugees — do?

Many thought they should try to leave Lithuania, and just as many thought that such a course would anger the Soviet authorities, who would have an excuse to brand the Jews as traitors, resulting in their imprisonment or expulsion to Siberia. That same year, the Soviets had banished tens of thousands to Siberia when they tried to leave areas ruled by the Communists, so they were prone to do it again. One thing was definite: to leave the country would be nearly impossible, because the Soviets hardly ever gave anyone an exit visa.

The Soviets began closing embassy after embassy in the Lithuanian capital of Kovno; the panic-stricken people lining up outside embassies that remained open began feeling the claws of entrapment closing around them. Simultaneously the Russians began closing yeshivah after yeshivah. Soon they closed the Lithuanian yeshivah of Telshe, along with its *mechinah* for younger boys, its school for girls and famous Yavne girls seminary for teachers.

In Telshe there was a *talmid* in his early 20s from the Netherlands, Nachum Zvi (Nathan) Gutwirth. (He recalls with melancholy today that his *shtender* in the *beis midrash* was next to that of Yankel Kahaneman *z"l*, who was tragically killed before he could reunite with his father, the Ponovezher Rav, Rav Yosef Kahaneman (1886-1969), in Israel. "He was as charismatic and as capable as his father," recalls Mr. Gutwirth sadly.)

Nachum Zvi, like thousands of others, wanted desperately to get out of Lithuania, but he needed help. He could not return to his homeland of Holland for it had already been conquered by the Germans. He knew, however, that there was an island, a Dutch colony, in the Caribbean Sea, 60 miles north of Venezuela, called Curacao (pronounced coor-ah-sow). He remembered from his elementary school days that Curacao had been captured by the Dutch in 1634, occupied by the British during the Napoleonic Wars, and returned to the Dutch in 1816.

Nachum Zvi reasoned that since Curacao was a Dutch colony and he was a Dutch citizen, the Dutch Ambassador to the Baltic countries of Lithuania, Latvia, and Estonia, Dr. B. de Dekker, could issue a visa allowing him to travel from Lithuania to Curacao. Once in Curacao he would try to make his way to America or Canada, but at least he would be out of the Soviet clutches.

Nachum Zvi wrote to Ambassador de Dekker who lived in Riga and requested a visa to Curacao. Ambassador de Dekker promptly replied that he did not need a visa to get to Curacao. All he needed was permission from the governor of Curacao. "Even the queen of the Netherlands can't give you a visa to Curacao. It is totally dependent on the wishes of the governor."

Nachum Zvi read and reread the letter from the ambassador. Fear and anxiety gripped him as he pondered his limited options. He understood well the geography of his planned escape and the necessity of the visas he would need to accomplish it. To get to Curacao, he would have to travel across the entire Soviet Union to the Siberian port city of Vladivostok. From there he would have to cross the Sea of Japan, and from Japan he would sail across the Pacific Ocean, through the Panama Canal to Curacao. To accomplish this he would need three visas: first an "exit visa" to get out of Russia, then a Japanese "transit visa," usually valid for only two weeks to journey through Japan en route to Curacao, and then an "end visa" indicating a territory of final destination. However, without an "end visa" in hand, no country would issue him a transit visa or exit visa. He feared that the Curacao governor would not allow immigrants from a Russian country, especially a Jew, to enter his colony.

Nachum Zvi's instinctive fears were correct. Years later the Curacao governor, Mr. Kastil, openly stated that he would not have permitted immigrants from Lithuania to dock. Curacao had oil refineries and processing plants, and Kastil would not take the chance that there could be spies among the refugees.

It was then, despite his tension and trepidation, that the 22-year old Nachum Zvi Gutwirth thought of the brilliant idea that would eventually save his life and the lives of thousands of Jews.

Nachum Zvi thought that if Ambassador de Dekker merely wrote on his passport, "No visa to Curacao required," and left out the second part about the permission needed from the governor, then conceivably that phrase could be interpreted by the Japanese and Russian embassies as a legitimate "end visa" because if no visa was required, then entry is permitted. On the basis of that "end visa," he hoped, the Japanese and Russian embassies would issue their respective visas.

He contacted Ambassador de Dekker again and requested that he write on his passport only, "No visa to Curacao required," and omit that one needed permission for entry from the Curacao governor. "You don't need me to do that for you," Ambassador de Dekker wrote Nachum Zvi. "There is a man in Kovno who was recently appointed as the Dutch honorary consul, Mr. Jan Zwartendyk, who can do it for you. I will authorize him to write what you wish on your passport and with that you can try to get your transit visa from the Japanese."

Ambassador de Dekker was convinced that the Soviet Union would never issue an exit visa to anyone, let alone a Jew; hence he had no hesitation to authorize anything being written on the Gutwirth passport. If it made his fellow countryman happy, let it be done.

Nachum Zvi was thrilled! He and Jan Zwartendyk were actually quite friendly. Far away from his family and being one of the only boys from the Netherlands who were studying in an Eastern European yeshivah, Nachum Zvi had longed for news from home and thus established a friendship with this Dutch businessman, who represented the Phillips Electronics Company. Nachum Zvi and Zwartendyk had corresponded periodically and Zwartendyk was able to provide his young friend with news and newspapers from his home city, The Hague.

Incredibly, Mr. Zwartendyk, who was a businessman with little if any diplomatic experience, had been appointed honorary consul of the Netherlands just a few months earlier. His predecessor in Kovno, a Dr. Tillmans, had been relieved of his post by the Dutch authorities because of his pro-Nazi sympathies. Thus the *Ribono Shel Olam* had placed His messenger, Jan Zwartendyk, right where He needed him, in a position to become a catalyst for a remarkable *hatzalah*.

Immediately, Nachum Zvi and two fellow Hollanders in Telshe, the brothers Chaim and Shmuel Nussbaum, went to their compatriot, consul Jan Zwartendyk, in Kovno. With permission from Ambassador de Dekker, Mr. Zwartendyk amicably wrote on their passports in French, "No visa to Curacao required." This endorsement was stamped to make it appear like a regular visa. In reality it was a sham.

With their documents in hand, Nachum Zvi and the Nussbaums ran to the Kovno office of the Japanese consul, Mr. Sempo Sugihara (pronounced Sue-gi-harah), to get a transit visa. Mr. Sugihara, also a recent appointee, pleasantly issued them a transit visa enabling them to travel through Japan on the way to Curacao.

> For the 21 years between World War I and World War II, Japan did not have a consular representative in Lithuania. By Divine Intervention, at the end of 1939, the Japanese government opened a consulate in Lithuania and appointed Mr. Sugihara, who would become a protector of Jews, as its General Consul.

When Nachum Zvi saw that it was indeed possible to accomplish this feat of getting "end" and "transit visas," he quickly got the passports of 17 other *bachurim* that he could locate and asked Zwartendyk to write on their passports, "No visa to Curacao required." He then went to Mr. Sugihara to get the transit visas. Thus in a matter of days 20 *bachurim* had a "legal" way out of Russia, if and when Russia would ever let anyone out.

Nachum Zvi and his friends were ecstatic, two pieces of the puzzle were in place. Now they prayed that one day the third piece, the exit visa from Russian authorities, would soon become a reality.

❁ ❁ ❁

Meanwhile in the city of Kaydan (Kedainiai), 40 miles north of Vilna where the Mir Yeshiva had settled, Rabbi Leib Mallin (1905-1962), a 35-year-old *bachur* in the yeshivah who was an exceptional *talmid chacham* (and who later became the Rosh Yeshivah of Beis Hatalmud in Brooklyn, New York), was also seeking desperately for ways to get himself and his colleagues out of Lithuania. Though some disagreed with him, claiming that Soviet authorities would react harshly and send Jews to Siberia if his plans were known, Reb Leib, true to his name, was lion hearted in his determination.

He and a fellow Mirrer *talmid,* Rabbi Lazer Portnoy, traveled to Kovno to visit the embassies that remained open, for any information that could lead to visas. At first their efforts were fruitless, but one day they heard about Nachum Zvi Gutwirth and the Curacao end visas. They became guardedly hopeful.

They knew that back in the Mirrer Yeshivah, R' Yaakov Ederman, a native of Lutzk, Poland, had accomplished a remarkable feat. Knowing that very few of the Mirrer *talmidim* had passports, Ederman realized that even if Rabbis Mallin and Portnoy could secure transit and end visas, they would be useless without passports. A visa had to be stamped on something.

Thus Yaakov and a friend, Yankel Gordon, went to Kovno to one of the only remaining Polish officials on Lithuanian soil, Ambassador Kowal, who represented the Polish government-in-exile. He had a small makeshift office in the British embassy. Ederman and Gordon discussed with Ambassador Kowal the possibility of issuing Polish passports. Standing alongside Ambassador Kowal's desk was his assistant. The assistant opposed the idea, for he claimed that all Jews were Communists.

"Tell me," said Yankel Ederman firmly, "how many Jews have come to Kovno for passports to leave and how many Polish people have come? Surely more Jews have come because we have no intention or desire to remain here with the Communists!"

The assistant relented and Ambassador Kowal issued passports to Yaakov and his friend. However, they refused to issue passports for anyone else in the yeshivah unless they had an authorized signature of each applicant.

Yaakov went back to Kaydan and introduced himself to the local chief of police. After establishing a friendly relationship, Yaakov asked if he would be willing to vouch for the signatures of the yeshivah *bachurim*. "The world will one day know of your kindness," Yankel assured him. "What you do for us will be remembered."

The police chief wanted to think about it overnight. That night Yaakov trembled as he fervently prayed that Hashem would prompt the police chief to assist the *bachurim*.

The next morning, Yankel went to police headquarters where he was told that a decision had been made. He waited with trepidation for the chief to emerge from his office. The chief came out smiling and shook Yankel's hand. He would indeed verify any signatures Yankel would bring him.

Yankel had everyone in Mir have his picture taken and sign the back of it. Many thought this whole scenario was foolish. "It's a waste of time and effort," they said, but Yankel persisted and they all complied. Yankel took the pictures to the chief of police who stamped the back of each of them with his seal, under the *bachur's* signature.

The police chief then called Mr. Kowal and urged him to cooperate by issuing passports to the young men in his district of Kaydan. Thus within days, 300 passports, one for each of the Mirrer *talmidim*, were issued.

The passports looked quite shoddy, a poor imitation of the genuine thing. Each passport was a plain sheet of paper that had a *talmid's* name, address, and birthdate in Polish and French. A photo of the *talmid* was stapled to the top of the paper. There was no expiration date. Incredibly, not one of the *talmidim* was required to show up at the police chief's office in Kaydan or at Ambassador Kowal's office in Kovno. In summing up this episode with the Polish consul and the Kaydan Chief of Police, Yankel Ederman says, "If the *Ribono Shel Olam* wills it, then *sheest ah bessim!* (a broom can shoot [bullets])"; that is, the impossible can happen.

Now that the Mirrer *talmidim* had passports, Rabbi Lazer Portnoy approached Nachum Zvi and asked if he would be willing to speak to Mr. Zwartendyk on behalf of the Mirrer *talmidim* and have their passports stamped, as well, "No visa to Curacao required."

Nachum Zvi was happy to help. He made the request and, although Zwartendyk did not believe that the Russians would ever let any Jews leave, he was willing to process their passports.

Nachum Zvi relayed the message and Rabbi Leib Mallin instructed Rabbi Portnoy to bring five *talmidim*, preferably those who spoke some German or English, to bring 60 passports each, and help process them in Zwartendyk's office. Rabbi Betzalel Tannenbaum (future Rosh Yeshivah of the Stoliner Yeshivah in Brooklyn) convinced R' Moshe Zupnick, R' Yisroel Kanarek, R' Moshe Korn, and two others to go to Mr. Zwartendyk's office. Within a day, all the passports were stamped. The Mirrer *talmidim* finally had their end visas, and the first piece of their puzzle had been successfully created.

R' Moshe Zupnick, a dignified young man who spoke German and a smattering of English, was chosen to go to the Japanese embassy to ask Mr. Sugihara for transit visas. He borrowed a pressed suit from another *talmid*, Rav Binyamin Zeilberger (currently Rosh Yeshivah of Bais Hatalmud in Brooklyn), and, carrying 300 Mir passports, went with Yaakov Ederman to the Japanese embassy in Kovno.

The lines in front of the embassy seemed endless as hundreds of people shouting in different languages were pushing and shoving to get in the front door. A guard stood firmly in front of the office door not allowing anyone in. He had little patience for the masses yelling in a cacophony of dialects and jargon that he couldn't understand. Realizing that the guard was Polish, Yankel Ederman engaged the guard in hometown conversation and softened the guard's demeanor with a gift of cash. R' Moshe and R' Yaakov were allowed in.

At the time, Mr. Sugihara had a German secretary named Herr Wolfgang (Walter) Gutsche. The German secretary asked Moshe what he wanted. "I am a delegate from a rabbinical school in Kaydan," Moshe replied in flawless German. "I have passports and end visas for students, for whom I need transit visas."

Moshe then froze in terror. Would this Nazi official reject his request and not even allow him to meet Mr. Sugihara? The whole project could be quashed right here and now. Herr Gutsche waited for a seemingly endless moment, peered at Moshe Zupnick, and then nodded slightly. He would take him in to Sugihara.

> Wolfgang Gutsche would later tell Moshe Zupnick that although he agreed with Hitler about most things, he disagreed with him about his hatred for Jews. Gutsche said that since his early childhood he respected Jews, especially Orthodox Jews.
>
> (One can only imagine the *zechus* of that Jew, whoever he or she was, who made such a lasting impression on Gutsche as a child, causing him years later to allow the Orthodox-looking Moshe Zupnick to see Sempo Sugihara.)

R' Moshe entered Sugihara's office and noticed how short he was. "Who are you and what do you want?" asked Sugihara in fractured English. He was obviously frazzled by the onslaught of thousands of people who were trying to get visas as quickly as possible.

"I am a representative of a school of 300 young men who merely wish to travel through Japan and then move on from there to Curacao," R' Moshe replied in English that equaled Mr. Sugihara's. "All we need are transit visas, and we would be forever grateful if you would grant them to us," he said.

"Three hundred of you wish to travel?" Mr. Sugihara asked incredulously. "Do you know that it is difficult to get ships today and the cost is prohibitive? Where will you get the ships and the money for the students to get out of Japan?"

"There is someone in America who has promised us that ships will be waiting and that the money will be available when we need it," said R' Moshe with confidence. "His name is Rabbi [Avrohom] Kalmanowitz (1891-1965). He assured us that we will all be taken care of."

Sugihara was trying to assess the young man's credibility. Lives and future generations hung in the balance. "How do I know that you are telling me the truth? What proof do you have?" asked Mr. Sugihara.

"We are Orthodox Jews and the Russian authorities despise us," R' Moshe replied in the finest English he knew. "All that we believe in and all that we practice is contrary to Russian law. Thus we have no choice but to practice our laws in secret and communicate with our sponsors abroad in codes. I therefore cannot show you anything tangible."

> To this day R' Moshe Zupnick can't believe he said that. "The words were Heaven sent and I just uttered them. I was too simple to have thought of them myself. The *Ribono Shel Olam* used me as His messenger," he says humbly.

Sugihara thought for a moment, and decided that this young man was sincere. He said, "I trust you. I'll help you, but on one condition. When you all come to Japan you will be able to enter only if you know exactly where you will travel to afterwards. I will have a special stamp made for your passports with the proviso that Curacao is the final destination."

R' Moshe nodded his approval. "Yes," he said, "we will not stay in Japan. We will move on."

For two weeks, hours every day, Moshe Zupnick and Wolfgang Gutsche stamped and processed the Mir passports and the passports of hundreds of others who came to Sugihara's office. Once again, by Divine orchestration, there was that rare Nazi Party member who disagreed with Hitler regarding Jews, positioned in the Japanese consul's office. Incredibly, he willingly assisted this young Orthodox Jew with the means that would eventually save hundreds of *talmidim* and thousands of others.

When the job was completed and R' Moshe was about to leave the Japanese office for the final time, he said to Herr Gutsche, "How can I ever thank you for all you have done for us? We will always be grateful to you."

Herr Gutsche replied, "The world is a circle. Today Hitler is on top. Who knows what tomorrow will bring? He could well be down under. Just remember what I did for you. Don't forget me."

Before R' Moshe left Lithuania he went to say goodbye to Wolfgang Gutsche, but he was already gone. He had been recalled to Germany.

❁ ❁ ❁

The Mirrer *bachurim* were not the only ones who received passports. There were thousands of others who tried in their own ways to get their end and transit visas. Dr. Zorach Warhaftig, formerly a prestigious Warsaw lawyer (who later became a National Religious Party cabinet minister in Israel) was extremely active in these matters. Dr. Warhaftig was connected with government officials in Palestine, and was urging people to get passports and visas. Dr. Warhaftig traveled from town to town throughout Lithuania, urging people to leave before it was too late. He, too, was in contact with Nachum Zvi Gutwirth, and through their joint efforts, Mr. Zwartendyk stamped thousands of passports, "No visa to Curacao required."

The Amshinover Rebbe, Rabbi Shimon Kalish (1883-1954), told his *chassidim* and anyone else that would listen that he was getting visas and they should do the same.

Those with passports went to the Japanese embassy while it was still open, and Sugihara continued to issue thousands of transit visas. However, Sugihara's benevolent actions came to an abrupt halt in August 1940 when the Japanese Foreign Office ordered him to stop issuing transit visas. Soon afterwards the Japanese consulate in Kovno was closed, and Sugihara was transferred to the Japanese consulate in Berlin, and then to Bucharest.

❁ ❁ ❁

The world was in turmoil, as battles raged in Europe and Asia. Then, in October 1940, the impossible happened. It caught everyone by surprise, but the Soviets were always unpredictable. They announced that anyone with a foreign passport should leave the country. The price was exorbitant, 170 to 240 American dollars. But at least the heretofore unthinkable was now a reality.

Many speculate that the Soviet Union changed its policy so that it could get American dollars to subsidize its war effort. Others contend that Russia tried to find favor in America's eyes by allowing Jews to leave. No one can be sure.

For the next three months an almost uncontrollable hysteria raged in the Russian consulates in Kovno and Vilna as people frantically tried to get exit visas to leave Lithuania. Lines formed from midnight the night before the offices would open. Now no one ridiculed those who had transit and end visas. Instead people without them tried to manufacture them.

One day two *bachurim* brought forged visas to an NKVD officer in Vilna, named Schlossberg. After intensive questioning, Schlossberg, obviously aware of the forgery, said to them, "Aren't you embarrassed to bring me these *shmattes* (rags)?"

The *bachurim* were frozen with fear. Schlossberg looked up at them and said with a half smile in Yiddish, *"Gei gezunterheit* (Go in good health)."

Another broom shooting bullets.

By now nearly all foreign embassies were closed and most of the officials had returned to their home countries. Panic prevailed, for who could know when the Soviets would once again seal their borders.

The Mirrer *talmidim* sent a cable to Rabbi Avrohom Kalmanowitz requesting funds for exit visas. As soon as he received the cable, Rabbi Kalmanowitz raced from *shul* to *shul* and community to community, even driving on Shabbos. Over one Shabbos he raised $40,000 (equivalent today to close to a million dollars)! He promptly wired the money to a bank in Kovno.

The Mirrer *bachurim* now had the necessary funds, and within a week they were on trains — 50 would travel every day — for the long 11-day trip on the Trans-Siberian Railroad, thousands of miles across the vast Russian landscape and the frozen Siberian tundra to the port city of Vladivostok.

Stormy seas and horrendous winds made the 36-hour trip across the Sea of Japan stretch into 60 hours! The small, frail 2,500-ton steamship the *Amakuza Maru,* overloaded with anxious refugees, swayed from side to side in the perilous seas. Week after week the fragile steamboat brought refugees from Vladivostok to a small fishing port on the Japanese island of Honshu. Finally, one day after all the refugees had crossed the sea, the decrepit boat collapsed and sank.

For the Mirrer *bachurim* and for thousands of others the escape was complete. Miraculously, the mission had been accomplished. From the thousands of Jews that were saved, tens of thousands would be born. From individual sparks of redemption would come a conflagration of Torah learning and *mitzvah* observance.

Rabbi Leib Mallin *z"l,* Rabbi Lazer Portnoy *z"l,* Rav Avrohom Kalmanowitz *z"l,* the Amshinover Rebbe *z"l, yibadel l'chaim* Nachum Tzvi Gutwirth, Dr. Zorach Warhaftig, R' Moshe Zupnick, R' Yaakov Ederman, the late Honorary Consul Mr. Jan Zwartendyk, the late Ambassador Dr. B. de Dekker, Mr. Wolfgang Gutsche, and the late General Consul Mr. Sempo Sugihara — each had a window from which they viewed and acted upon the perils of others.

Chazal teach, מְגַלְגְּלִין זְכוּת עַל יְדֵי זַכָּאי, *Benefit is imparted through one who is meritorious (Shabbos* 32a). These people must have been very eminent, for Hashem chose them to participate in *hatzalas nefashos* where they each acted nobly. May they and their families always be blessed.

As one sifts through the list of the more than 2,000 names of refugees who were issued transit visas, one is shaken and saddened at the thought of tens of thousands that were not on that list, the innumerable descendants that would not be born, the incalculable accomplishments that would not be brought to fruition.

In the recitation of *Kaddish,* the mourner does not mention the name of the individual for whom he is in mourning. Rather he proclaims, יִתְגַּדַּל וְיִתְקַדַּשׁ שְׁמֵיהּ רַבָּא, *May His great Name grow exalted and sanctified.* In essence the mourner declares that he will sanctify Hashem's Name by attempting to fill the empty chasm left by the deceased person.

May we who live today, together with those who were spared "yesterday," live to sanctify the Name of Hashem, so that we may fill, even if only in small measure, part of the gaping, prodigious void left by those who perished.[1]

1. In Japan there would be new surroundings, new problems, new heroes, and new villains. For detailed reading of that era, including the period of privation, emigration, and education in the Japanese-controlled segment of the Chinese city of Shanghai, see *Japanese, Nazis and Jews* by Dr. David Kranzler, and *Operation Torah Rescue* by Yecheskel Leitner.

Part E:

A Nation's Nobility — Torah and its Teachers

For a Bed in Ponevezh

The following story is one of the most beautiful I ever heard. Those who hear it are unfailingly amazed and enthralled by its tender and heartwarming lessons in priorities, parenting, and a sense of values.

I first heard this story from a son-in-law of Rabbi Shneur Kotler *z"tl*, Harav Uren Reich, Rosh Yeshivah in Perth Amboy, New Jersey. The details were provided by the child in the episode who is today a businessman in Bnei Brak who learns every morning in the Kollel Chazon Ish.

In 1955 Lazer Marilus, a 16-year-old boy from Zurich, Switzerland, came to Israel to learn in the great Ponevezh Yeshivah in Bnei Brak. To his chagrin, he was told the yeshivah already had an enrollment of 1,000, and new applicants were not being accepted for that *z'man.*

To Lazer it was clear that there was very little difference between 1,000 and 1,001 *talmidim* in the *beis midrash.* Surely the reason for his rejection was that his learning abilities were not up to par with those who had a stronger background. Understandably, Torah study in Swiss yeshivos was not as intense as in the Torah centers of Jerusalem and Bnei Brak.

Politely, Lazer asked if he could be taken to meet the Ponevezher Rebbetzin. The staff members smiled to themselves. The Rebbetzin had nothing to do with enrollment, but still they pitied the youngster, who had traveled thousands of miles only to be rejected. They complied with his wishes and took him to see Rebbetzin Hinda Kahaneman.

When he met her, Lazer took out a letter from his pocket and handed it to her. She read it intently and then looked up at the staff members and then at Lazer and said, "All of you come with me right away to the Rav (Rabbi Yosef Kahaneman, 1886-1969)."

Astounded, they all followed her to the Rav. He greeted them with his radiant smile and pleasant words. The Rebbetzin told him why Lazer had come to Israel and gave him the letter. The Rav read it, stood up, hurried over to Lazer, embraced and kissed him, and said warmly, "You will be accepted into the yeshivah."

The staff members were astounded. What could have been written in that letter?

Over the next few years the Ponevezher Rav told this story numerous times and that is how it became known.

When Lazer was a young child his parents used to vacation every summer and winter at the hotel Wengen, which was a popular Jewish resort. In the winter of 1955 the Ponevezher Rav underwent surgery in Israel. To recuperate away from the pressures of the yeshivah and the taxing stream of visitors, the Rav's doctors advised that he go to Switzerland.

When the Rav and Rebbetzin arrived, the hotel was filled nearly to capacity. There was one room available, but it was on the third floor, and the Rav was in no condition to walk the stairs to the first-floor *shul* and dining room. The hotel proprietor, Mr. Pugatsch, wondered if there might be a guest on the first floor who would exchange with the Kahanemans.

That winter, Mrs. Devorah Marilus was at the hotel alone with her son Lazer because her husband was away on business. As regular guests at the hotel, the Marilus family was always assigned an exclusive room on the first floor. Perhaps, the owner hoped, Mrs. Marilus would agree to move up to the third floor for the sake of the Ponevezher Rav.

Mr. Pugatsch walked to room 111 and knocked on the door. Mrs. Marilus opened it and he bowed courteously. "Mrs. Marilus, I am here to ask you for a very great favor. The Ponevezher Rav is here from *Eretz Yisrael* to recuperate from major surgery. It is hard for him to walk, but our only empty room is on the third floor. Would you mind giving up your room to the Rav and the Rebbetzin, and moving up to the third floor?"

"I certainly wouldn't mind," said Mrs. Marilus, "but" — turning to her six-year-old son, she said — "you have to ask the young cavalier (French for gentleman), as well. He, too, must be willing to give up his room."

The owner smiled, bent down to little Lazer and said, "Young man, the Rosh Yeshivah, the Ponevezher Rav, is here from *Eretz Yisrael.* He needs a room on the first floor because he just had an operation and it is hard for him to walk. Would you be willing to give him your room to make it easier for him? You and your mother would have a room on the third floor."

The little boy said, "Of course. I am happy to give my room to the Rav."

Mr. Pugatsch was overjoyed. Immediately, the hotel staff helped the Marilus family and the Kahanemans to their new accommodations.

About half an hour later, the Ponevezher Rebbetzin walked up to the third floor to visit Mrs. Marilus. "The Rav asked me to thank you for giving us your room," she said graciously. "We are very, very grateful. When you are on the first floor, the Rav wants to thank you in person."

"Don't thank me," said Mrs. Marilus, slightly embarrassed. Pointing to her son she said to the Rebbetzin, "You have to thank the young cavalier. He also gave up the room for the Rav."

The Rebbetzin smiled affectionately at Lazer. "We thank you, young man, for giving up your very comfortable and convenient room. Can I buy you a piece of chocolate? There is a very nice shop on the first floor."

"No, thank you," said Lazer, "It's not necessary."

"Well, I am going into town this afternoon. Can I get you a

special toy to show you how much we appreciate your kindness?" asked the Rebbetzin.

"No, thank you," said Lazer once again. "My parents have given me all the toys I need."

"But we would like to do *something*," insisted the Rebbetzin. "What can we do for you?"

The little boy thought for a moment and said, "I just gave my bed to the Ponevezher Rav. I would hope that if I ever come to the Ponevezher Yeshivah, the Rav would give me a bed in his yeshivah."

The Rebbetzin was stunned. What perception! What foresight! She took out a sheet of paper and wrote, "If this boy ever comes to Ponevezh, he will have a bed waiting for him in the yeshivah." She dated and signed it, and immediately went downstairs and had the Ponevezher Rav sign it as well.

A few minutes later the Rebbetzin returned to the Mariluses room and smiling broadly, handed the signed note to Lazer.

Mrs. Marilus took the paper from Lazer and, when they returned to their home, she put it in the family safe. There it remained for more than 10 years and when Lazer was ready to study in Israel, she gave him the letter and said, "Show this to the people in Ponevezh; you won't have a problem."

That was the piece of paper that Lazer gave the Rebbetzin after his disappointing rejection. Lazer Marilus went on to learn in Ponevezh for more than 10 years.

How does it happen that a six-year-old child wanted no prize other than a bed in the Ponevezher Yeshivah?

Chazal teach: שׁוּתָא דִּינוּקָא בְּשׁוּקָא אוֹ דַּאֲבוּהַ אוֹ דְּאִימֵּיהּ, *The conversation of a child on the avenue is [what he heard] from his father or mother* (*Succah* 56b). Children are a reflection of the *chinuch* they receive at home. Mr. and Mrs. Marilus were affluent, but their order of priorities was strong enough to be absorbed even by their six-year-old child. Thus, in his unrehearsed response Lazer Marilus manifested his parents' ideals.

An Unforgettable Love

At a recent *yahrzeit* observance for Rabbi Eliezer Yehuda Finkel (1965-1875), the founder and Rosh Yeshivah of Yeshivas Mir in Jerusalem, his grandson, Rabbi Aryeh Finkel, the current *Mashgiach,* cited a teaching from *Tanna D'vei Eliyahu* (10:8): אַשְׁרֵי מִי שֶׁמְּתַחֵדֵּשׁ דִּבְרֵי תוֹרָה עַל פִּיו ... וּבִשְׁבִילְךָ אֲנִי מַצִּיל אֶת יִשְׂרָאֵל, *Fortunate is the one who creates novel concepts in Torah ... [Hashem says to him,] "because of you I will rescue the Jewish people."*

This teaching is based on the homiletic understanding of the words Devorah the prophetess exclaimed, יִבְחַר אֱל-הִים חֲדָשִׁים, ... מָגֵן ... וָרֹמַח ... בְּיִשְׂרָאֵל, *Hashem selects innovations [in Torah thought, they serve as] shields and spears in [protecting] the Jewish nation* (*Shoftim* 5:8).

Rabbi Aryeh Finkel related that ever since his grandfather, Reb "Lazer Yudel," was a teenager studying in the Chofetz Chaim's yeshivah in Radin, he would give *bachurim* (young students) money if they told him a *chiddush* (new insight) in learning. There was nothing Reb Lazer Yudel cherished more than a new understanding of a *sugya* (topic) in *Shas* or an imaginative resolution of a difficult *Tosafos.* Shlomo *Hamelech's* words: יְקָרָה הִיא מִפְּנִינִים וְכָל חֲפָצֶיךָ לֹא יִשְׁווּ בָהּ, *It [the Torah] is more precious than pearls, and all your desires cannot compare to it* (*Mishlei* 3:15), aptly described Reb Lazer Yudel's sense of values.

It was said in the streets of the Holy City of Jerusalem that if a *kollel* member did not have enough money to buy food for Shabbos, he could come on Friday to Reb Lazer Yudel, say a *chiddush,* and walk out with the money he needed for Shabbos.

When Reb Lazer Yudel became the Rosh Yeshivah of Mir in Poland, succeeding his father-in-law Rabbi Elya Boruch Kamai (1840-1917), who was both town Rav and Rosh Yeshivah, he made it official yeshivah policy to offer payment to those who told him *chiddushim.*

One day, a *bachur,* Shmulik Shenkman,* informed Rav Lazer

* Name has been changed.

Yudel that he had received governmental notice that he was being inducted into the Lithuanian army. Dejectedly, Reb Lazer Yudel bid Shmulik farewell, but assured him that if he wrote a *chiddush* from wherever he was stationed, he would be sent the regular yeshivah stipend for a *chiddush.*

Shmulik left the walls of the *beis midrash* despondently, but felt that he could maintain a relationship, even from afar, with his Rosh Yeshivah. For the next few months Shmulik regularly sent the Rosh Yeshivah *chiddushim* on whatever he was able to study between army duties. Shmulik was thrilled to receive the stipend and soon looked forward to the letters containing his monthly check, and the accompanying kind words from the Rosh Yeshivah.

One month Shmulik sent a *chiddush* to Reb Lazer Yudel but did not get a response. He was surprised because Reb Lazer Yudel usually answered his letters promptly. Weeks went by and Shmulik heard nothing. He began to wonder if the Rosh Yeshivah ever got the *chiddush* in the mail.

The next time Shmulik received a furlough, he traveled back to Mir to visit Reb Lazer Yudel. When he met the Rosh Yeshivah he expressed his surprise that he had not received the stipend for his latest *chiddush.*

Reb Lazer Yudel peered at Shmulik sternly and said, "You know that I only give money for new *chiddushei Torah.* You told me this *chiddush* over a year ago while you were still in the yeshivah, before you left for the army."

Shmulik was astounded that Reb Lazer Yudel not only remembered the *chiddush,* but that he also remembered who told it to him! And surely the Rosh Yeshivah had heard hundreds if not thousands of *chiddushim* since then.

When Rabbi Aryeh Finkel told this story on his grandfather's *yahrzeit,* he added, "It should have come as no surprise to that *talmid.* Rav Lazer Yudel's love for Torah was so intense, his love for a *chiddush* so strong, that he retained and recalled *chiddushim* he heard years ago, long after the people who told it to him had forgotten them."

Another grandson of Reb Lazer Yudel, Rabbi Elya Boruch Finkel, a *maggid shiur* in Yeshivas Mir in Jerusalem, told me that his grandfather once said that he had heard and remembered 270 *chiddushim* on the *sugya* of יֵאוּשׁ שֶׁלֹּא מִדַּעַת (see *Bava Metzia* 21b) alone, and that he planned to repeat them to the Heavenly Court when he completed his life on this world.

Rav Lazer Yudel's concern for the success of others' learning was such that he would often fast so that a particular boy would merit gaining a love for learning.

Two days after I heard the above story I visited Rabbi Boruch Mordechai Ezrachi, Rosh Yeshivah of Ateret Yisrael in Bayit Vegan, and told it to him. He let me finish the entire episode and then laughed and said excitedly, "I have just the right story for you. It is a beautiful addendum to what you just told me."

When Reb Boruch Mordechai was 15 years old and studying in Yeshivas Chevron, he accompanied Rabbi Dovid Finkel (1917-1957) on *Succos* as he went to visit the great Torah luminary Rabbi Isser Zalman Meltzer (1870-1953). *Bachurim* from every yeshivah knew that if they came to Rabbi Isser Zalman, they had to have a *shtikel* (lit. a piece of) *Torah* prepared to repeat to him.

When Boruch Mordechai walked into the *succah,* Reb Isser Zalman greeted him warmly and asked him if he had anything to say. The young boy understood that "saying something" meant repeating a *shtikel Torah.* Boruch Mordechai was learning *Mesechta Menachos* at the time and began citing a teaching regarding the *sugya* of הוֹלָכָה שֶׁלֹּא בָרֶגֶל, *A Kohen who conveys blood to the Altar without stepping forward but by standing in place* (see *Menachos* 13b and *Zevachim* 13b). He had barely begun when Reb Isser Zalmen exclaimed, *"Du zugst duch azoi geshmak!* (You are saying [Torah] that is so pleasing)."

Young Boruch Mordechai was surprised and taken aback. He had not even gotten into the *sugya,* and already he was being complimented. Rav Isser Zalman let him finish what he prepared and praised him profusely for his *shtikel Torah.*

When Boruch Mordechai walked outside, he said to Reb Dovid Finkel, "I wonder if the Rosh Yeshivah even heard what I said. He was making comments even before I got into the *shtikel.*"

"You would be surprised," said Rav Dovid Finkel. "Reb Isser Zalman has tremendous perception and quickly grasps what one is about to tell him. Don't forget, he has heard thousands, if not tens of thousands, of *shtiklach Torah* in his life."

Still, the young boy had his doubts.

Nine years later, Reb Boruch Mordechai became engaged to Shulamis Chodosh, the only daughter of Rabbi Meir Chodosh (1898-1989), the *Mashgiach* of Yeshivas Chevron. Reb Meir was revered and beloved by the prominent *talmidei chachamim* in Jerusalem, and they all came to participate in his *simchah.*

Sitting at the head table were such Torah luminaries as Reb Isser Zalman, Reb Lazer Yudel, Rabbi Yecheskel Sarna (1895-1969), the Rosh Yeshivah of Chevron, Rabbi Eliyahu Eliezer Dessler (1892-1954), the *Mashgiach* of Ponevezh, and Rabbi Meir Chodosh. Dwarfed by such Torah giants, the young groom began saying a *shtikel Torah.* He had prepared very thoroughly, for he knew he would be delivering it in the presence of great *talmidei chachamim.*

He was barely into the first question when Rav Lazer Yudel interrupted with a question. An argument ensued as Reb Boruch Mordechai tried to defend himself, but Reb Lazer Yudel persisted. Finally Reb Lazer Yudel relented. The assembled were quiet once again as the *chassan* continued.

Soon, there was another interruption by Rav Lazer Yudel. He was not happy with a proof that Reb Boruch Mordechai was using to solidify a point. Reb Isser Zalman tried to stop Reb Lazer Yudel, exclaiming, "What he is saying is so good, one doesn't have to question his logic. And besides," added Reb Isser Zalman, "I know personally that he says Torah well. I remember when he came to me years ago and said a *shtikel* on הוֹלָכָה שֶׁלֹּא בָרֶגֶל."

Reb Boruch Mordechai was stunned! That visit had taken place nine years earlier! How could Reb Isser Zalman possibly remember the exact topic that was spoken about?

Reb Boruch Mordechai looked to the back of the room and saw his friend Reb Dovid Finkel. He wondered if Reb Dovid had heard Reb Isser Zalman's comment.

Already anticipating Reb Boruch Mordechai's amazement, Reb Dovid smiled and exclaimed loudly over the din of conversation that swirled around the table, "You see, I told you then, he was listening."

The impression of the love and retention of Torah by both Reb Lazer Yudel and Reb Isser Zalman stays with Reb Aryeh Finkel and Reb Boruch Mordechai Ezrachi until this day. It is the ideal they have tried to imbue in the thousands of *talmidim* they have had over the last three decades.

The current Rosh Yeshivah of Mir, Reb Nosson Tzvi Finkel, told me that when he was a youngster of 14 years old growing up in Chicago, he came to Jerusalem with his parents to visit his grandfather's brother, Reb Lazer Yudel.

Reb Lazer Yudel took a liking to young Nosson Tzvi and beseeched him to remain and study at the Yeshivah of Mir. Though his parents were at first hesitant to let him stay, eventually they consented.

(Mrs. Finkel, the Rosh Yeshivah's mother, told me that the Shabbos they were there was *Parashas Vayeira*. "I was reviewing the *parashah* with the daughter of Rav Chaim Shmulevitz [today, the wife of Rav Yitzchok Ezrachi] and we were discussing *Akeidas Yitzchak*. And then it occurred to me, if Avrohom *Avinu* could make such a sacrifice, I too should be able to make the sacrifice of letting my son stay in Jerusalem even though we would be returning to Chicago.")

At the insistence of Reb Lazer Yudel, young Nosson Tzvi moved into the Rosh Yeshivah's home where he was treated with a warmth and love that he treasures until this day. One incident, though, is indelibly etched in Rav Nosson Tzvi's memory.

Reb Lazer Yudel would get up between 2 and 3 o'clock every morning to learn uninterrupted for the next few hours until it was time to *daven*. [It was known that Reb Lazer Yudel learned seven *blatt* (folios of Talmud) a day!] One morning as Reb Lazer Yudel awoke, young Nosson Tzvi quietly came out of his room to observe, behind the narrow slit of an open door, how Reb Lazer Yudel would learn. Before Rav Lazer Yudel sat down at his table he walked over to his bookcase of *sefarim* and as though embracing his *Gemaras* he spread his hands across the entire *Shas* that spanned the width of his outstretched arms. Slowly he bent forward and gently kissed some of the *Gemaras* on the shelf.

The young Nosson Tzvi stood entranced at this personal private manifestation of love that Reb Lazer Yudel had for his *Shas*. Quietly he inched back to his room, affected by this scene forever.

The Philadelphia Inquirer

In the Har Hazeisim cemetery on the outskirts of Jerusalem, overlooking the site of the *Beis HaMikdash* and the Judean hills, there is a gravestone that has a curious one-line inscription on it: *Zevachim* 95.

It is the burial place of Rabbi Ephraim Eliezer Yolles (1890-1988), a chassidic rabbi from Galicia, who came to the United States in 1921 and became the rav of Congregation Kerem Yisrael in the Strawberry Mansion section of Philadelphia. He served as a rav in Philadelphia for more than 60 years. Rabbi Yolles' son-in-law, Rabbi Yosef Geldzahler of Monsey, New York, recently related the story behind the cryptic inscription.

Rabbi Yolles was a grandson of the Samborer Rebbe, Rabbi Uri Yolles. He did his best to bring warm and uncompromising Judaism to the parents and children of Strawberry Mansion, but it was a difficult task. There were six *shuls* in Strawberry Mansion, but Philadelphia had no yeshivos or Beis Yaakovs, and even the most religious families sent their children to public schools. Even families that struggled to remain *shomer Shabbos* were losing their children to the secular world.

Rabbi Yolles and his community were an island of Orthodoxy struggling to exist among the whirlwinds of apathy and ridicule. Philadelphia, like most American cities, was not conducive to Torah study or mitzvah observance. (For a heartwarming depiction of *Yahadus* in Philadelphia of that era, see ArtScroll's *The Way it Was* by my mother, Mrs. Hindy Krohn.)

One day in 1923, Rabbi Yolles received a letter from his father, Reb Sholom, who was the rav of Stri, Galicia. In glowing terms, Reb Sholom described his participation as a delegate to the magnificent first Knessia Gedolah of Agudath Israel in Vienna. He depicted the aura created by the presence of the Chofetz Chaim who was then nearly 85 years old, and he portrayed the excitement felt by the crowd at the presence of so many young dynamic individuals committed to the furtherance of *Yahadus* throughout the world.

"But one young rabbi captivated everyone with his eloquence and brilliance," he wrote. It was Rabbi Meir Shapiro (1887-1933), who made a strikingly original proposal. He suggested everyone learn the same *daf* (folio page) of *Gemara* every day. Thus Jews all over the world would establish a solidarity through the most vital unifying force in Jewish life — the Torah. The cycle of learning *Shas* would begin on *Rosh Hashanah* 5684 (1923) with the first *blatt* in *Berachos*, and end seven and a half years later on the 15th day of Shevat 5691 (1931).

Rabbi Shapiro cited the Talmudic teaching that Hashem took dust from Babylonia to create Adam *HaRishon's* body, dust from *Eretz Yisrael* to create his head, and dust from around the world to create his limbs (*Sanhedrin* 38b). "By uniting all parts of the world in His creation of Adam, Hashem guaranteed that man could feel at home wherever he was on the globe," he said.

"Let us examine the configuration of the *daf*," he continued. "The *Mishnah* was created by *Rabbeinu HaKadosh* from Israel, the *Gemara* was compiled in Babylonia by Rav Ashi, and explained by *Rashi* and *Tosafos* who lived primarily in France. The *Rosh* was from Germany, the *Rambam* from Spain and Egypt, and the *Maharshal, Maharsha,* and *Maharam* from Poland.

"The *daf* thus symbolizes unity," said Rav Meir Shapiro. "And by learning the same *daf* every day, Jews throughout the world now have an opportunity to be united through the bond of Torah."

Rav Sholom Yolles, excited about the idea, advised his son to start *Mesechta Berachos* on *Rosh Hashanah*, so that even from the tiny enclave of the Congregation Kerem Yisrael on the West Side of Philadelphia, he would be connected to Jews all over the world, wherever they studied Torah.

Rabbi Meir Shapiro, the young, 36-year-old *rav* of Sanoik, Poland, had ignited a flame of enthusiasm for learning the entire *Shas*, in cities, towns, and villages throughout the Jewish world. Thousands of individuals, including Rabbi Yolles of Philadelphia, seized that spark and ignited a blaze of their own on that *Rosh Hashanah*.

Rabbi Yolles struggled to maintain the rigorous *daf*-a-day schedule that moved inexorably forward every day. He had been accustomed to a slower and more profound type of study, and the change was taxing. His time for learning was limited because of his many rabbinical and communal responsibilities, and soon, he found himself reverting back to his old method of study. Thus after a few weeks, the flame for the *daf*, which glittered on *Rosh Hashanah*, flickered and began to fade. Soon it was extinguished.

A few weeks later, on a trip to America to raise money and promulgate the *Daf-Yomi* concept, Rabbi Meir Shapiro came to Philadelphia and visited Rabbi Yolles. After a pleasant conversation, Rabbi Meir Shapiro asked, "What is with *Daf-Yomi?*"

Rabbi Yolles admitted that although he had started *Berachos* on *Rosh Hashanah*, the *seder* fell by the wayside after a few weeks. "Start it again and stay with it," encouraged Rav Meir Shapiro. "Someday you will be very thankful to me for this. And besides, I will consider it a personal favor if you learn the *daf*."

Rabbi Yolles was moved by Rav Meir Shapiro's sincerity and commitment to the idea. He was inspired by the encouragement and the personal plea from the innovator himself. That evening he resumed his *Daf-Yomi* schedule, and it became an integral part of his life. The *daf* and Rabbi Yolles became inseparable. No obligation, no invitation, no communal responsibility deterred him. He completed the *Daf-Yomi* cycle eight times (1931, 1938, 1945, 1953, 1960, 1968, 1975 and 1982)!

❁ ❁ ❁

Rabbi Geldzahler recalls that shortly after he married Rabbi Yolles' daughter, he spent Pesach at his father-in-law's home. After the *Seder*, Rabbi Yolles asked for his *Gemara*. "But it's nearly 2 o'clock in the morning," protested Rabbi Geldzahler.

"I know that," said Rabbi Yolles, "but I haven't learned the *daf* yet."

❁ ❁ ❁

Four days before he passed away at age 97, Rabbi Yolles traveled from Philadelphia to Borough Park to be the *sandek* at the *bris* of a great-grandson. After the *bris*, he returned to Philadelphia and received a call from the baby's father, Dovid Geldzahler, thanking him for making the long trip. "Zaide," said R' Dovid, "I hope you will get some rest after such a strenuous trip."

"I'll get my rest, but first I have to learn the *daf*," answered Rabbi Yolles. It bears repeating, he was 97 years old!

In his will Rabbi Yolles instructed his family to engrave on his monument the *daf* he learned on the day he passed away. So there is a stone on *Har Hazeisim* with a two-word epitaph: *Zevachim* 95.

In the *Av HaRachamim* prayer we recite before *Mussaf* on Shabbos, we refer to, ... הַחֲסִידִים וְהַיְשָׁרִים, *the devout and the upright* ... ,הַנֶּאֱהָבִים וְהַנְּעִימִים בְּחַיֵּיהֶם, וּבְמוֹתָם לֹא נִפְרָדוּ, ... *who were beloved and pleasant in their lifetime, and not separated [from Hashem] in their death.*

Rabbi Yolles loved the *daf* with such everlasting intensity that even in death he wanted to be connected to it.

Life Spans

Every night, in the *Maariv* service, we recite the phrase כִּי הֵם חַיֵּינוּ וְאֹרֶךְ יָמֵינוּ, *For they [Torah and mitzvos] are our life and the length of our days.* Torah is the essence of Jewish life and the reason for our survival as a nation. In this poignant story told to me by Rav Nisson Wolpin, editor of *The Jewish Observer,* we witness a touching association of Torah and Israel's eternity.

Rabbi Yaakov Kamenetsky (1891-1986) was in his office at Congregation Bikur Cholim in Seattle, as he read a very harsh letter received from his brother-in-law Rabbi Avraham Grodzinski, the Mashgiach of the Slabodka Yeshivah in Lithuania.

"If you want to take your younger children and *shmad* (spiritually destroy) them with your own hands, then go ahead with your plan to bring them to America. I cannot stop you. But not Binyamin or Shmuel. They have experienced the taste of Torah and must remain here in Slabodka. In America they will have no future."

Reb Yaakov understood and sympathized with his brother-in-law's strong convictions. Many *frum* (religious) people in Europe referred to the United States as *"treifa America,"* yet Reb Yaakov felt he had reason enough to disagree with his brother-in-law.

Rabbi Kamenetsky had come to Seattle in 1937 to temporarily assume the rabbinical duties at Congregation Bikur Cholim, while its spiritual leader, Rabbi Sholom Pinchas Wohlgelerenter, accompanied his wife out of town for medical treatments. In Reb

Yaakov's brief tenure, he became acquainted with Rabbi Ephraim Ben-Zion Wolpin, a teacher in the community's afternoon Talmud Torah. Reb Ephraim spent a great deal of time learning *Gemara* and *Tanach* with his oldest son, Michoel, trying to make up for the yeshivah education that Seattle could not give him.

Reb Yaakov tested Michoel and was amazed at his perception, clarity, and love of learning. To him Michoel Wolpin was living proof that it was indeed possible to transmit a love of Torah even in America. Through Michoel, Rav Yaakov became convinced that even while surrounded by a hostile American culture, a youngster could acquire a yearning for spiritual growth; it was just a matter of diligence and perseverance by both father and son.

Thus, Reb Yaakov was not swayed by his brother-in-law's pleas and rebuke, and when Rabbi Wohlgelernter returned to Seattle, Reb Yaakov accepted a rabbinical position in Toronto in 1938, and brought his family from Europe to Canada.

For decades Rav Yaakov and his children were grateful to the Wolpins, for it was their example that convinced him to bring his family to this continent. Not only were the Kamenetskys spared the horrible fate of the many who remained in Europe, but they became *manhigim* (leaders) for the new generation of American *b'nei Torah.* Reb Yaakov remained in close contact with the Wolpin family, and made every effort to attend their family *simchas.*

At the *Bar Mitzvah* of Michoel's son Yonosan in 1980, Mrs. Kaila Wolpin, Reb Ephraim's wife, thanked the Rosh Yeshivah for coming. "The pleasure is mine," said Reb Yaakov. Then with his radiant smile he added, "In America when people say that, they don't really mean it, but you can be sure that I mean it sincerely."

Mrs. Wolpin then asked Reb Yaakov for a blessing. The Rosh Yeshivah smiled, "Hashem has already blessed you with *arichas yomim* (longevity). May you live for as long as I do."

On the 13th of Shvat 5758 (March 9, 1998), Mrs. Wolpin passed away. During the *shivah* her grandchildren figured out that Rav

Yaakov lived for 95 years and eight days. Incredibly, Mrs. Wolpin lived for 95 years and ten days!

> *Chazal* teach: אֵין נוֹתְנִין כּוֹס שֶׁל בְּרָכָה לְבָרֵךְ אֶלָּא לְטוֹב עַיִן שֶׁנֶּאֱמַר: טוֹב עַיִן הוּא יְבֹרָךְ, *One should only give the cup of blessing [to the leader of the Bircas Hamazon] if he possesses a good eye (i.e. is gracious and giving), as it says* (*Mishlei* 22:9), *"The one with the good eye shall bless"* (*Sotah* 38b).
>
> How special indeed to get a blessing for old age from a generous sage who possessed it himself.

Attention on Retention

Sometimes it is a smell, other times it is merely a few notes of a melody, but when we suddenly become aware of them we are unexpectedly brought back to an event or situation that we experienced years ago, one we thought we had forgotten. Our memory is triggered to recall something long stored in the recesses of our brain.

The brain's capacity to store information and details of incidents is mysterious. If memory begins to fade as we get older, does that mean that our brain no longer retains the facts it once held, or is it only that our capacity to recall those facts gets weaker with age, but nevertheless they are still in the brain, etched there indelibly?

Dr. Manny Kanal, a noted activist for Jewish causes in Pittsburgh, is a radiologist in some of the area's leading hospitals. He related a staggering incident he witnessed during a brain operation. It sheds light on our power of recollection and causes us to rethink the effect of experiences or scenes that we may at first consider "harmless" or "meaningless."

✿ ✿ ✿

In 1988, Dr. Kanal was assisting during an operation on a woman at The University Of Pittsburgh Hospital, to remove a brain tumor. The doctors wanted her to be kept awake during the operation, so that, as they touched parts of her brain, she could respond to the sensations. If she responded, they would leave that part of the brain; if she was not responding to contact, it meant the tissue was dead and the surgeons would remove it.

The operation had been going as planned, the doctors working meticulously and precisely. As each part of the brain was being touched they asked her to respond. Suddenly the woman screamed and the startled doctors jumped back from the operating table.

When they recovered from her unexpected shout, the chief surgeon asked the woman, "Are you all right?"

The woman said, "Yes, everything is fine. I know exactly where I am. It's just that I suddenly saw someone that I haven't seen in years."

The doctors waited in anticipation for her to continue. "I saw my aunt leaning over me, speaking words that I could not understand. My aunt died when I was 2 years old and I only recognize her from pictures. But I could see her standing over me as if she were right here."

When the doctor stimulated that part of her brain, the patient had actually visualized something that she had retained in her brain since she was two years old! Her aunt had been leaning over her crib, talking to her with sweet and endearing words. However, because she was so young, she could not understand those words. Now, however, the vision of her aunt became a reality the moment the brain was stirred.

The doctors were astounded, for it confirmed that all that we witness and experience makes an indelible impression. We may not be able to recall it at will but somewhere in the brain it is recorded for eternity.

✿ ✿ ✿

Dr. Kanal was so taken by this story that he told it to numerous people, including a *mechanech* in Baltimore, Rabbi Gershon

Langner.* Shortly afterwards Rabbi Langner told me that he undertook to stop reading secular newspapers and magazines.

"It had been my impression," said Rabbi Langner, "that when I read a secular newspaper or magazine and fleetingly see something inappropriate, I turn the page quickly and forget about it. Now though, I realize that one does not forget such things. One may not be able to recall something at a future date, but the image is implanted on the brain forever. If I can avoid it," said Rabbi Langner emphatically, "I don't want anything inappropriate implanted in my brain in any measure."

❁ ❁ ❁

Many summers ago I had the opportunity to spend time with the Telshe Rosh Yeshivah, Rabbi Mordechai Gifter, while he was vacationing in Camp Agudah, in Ferndale, New York.

One morning, after *davening,* Rabbi Gifter was talking to a group of *masmidim* that had gathered around him. "None of you should underestimate the blessing you have of being able to learn something in the morning and still remember it at night."

Rabbi Gifter explained that every day he suffers with anguish because, due to his illness and medications, he often has difficulty remembering his learning. Tears came to his eyes as he discussed his distress. "A while ago," he said, "I went to a young doctor in Cleveland and I said to him, 'I am in such misery. I came to this world primarily to learn and absorb as much Torah as I can. Now in my older years and with my illness I have forgotten so much of what I have studied! With what Torah will I come to the Next World? I will be tested but I will know so little.'"

Rabbi Gifter smiled through his tears and said, "The doctor said to me, 'Rabbi, you have nothing to worry about. The only reason that you are forgetting is because you are taking so much medication. In the Next World you will be off all medication and the Torah you studied here will be there when you want to recall it.' "

Holding back his sobs, Rabbi Gifter told us that he said to the doctor, "נִחַמְתָּנִי— You have consoled me!"

* Name has been changed.

Defining Life

The Torah leaders of a generation are referred to as עֵינֵי הָעֵדָה, *the eyes of the nation* (see *Vayikra* 4:13 and *Bamidbar* 15:24). With their perceptions and insights, they clarify events and situations through the prism of their vast Torah knowledge. Hence their recommended course of action warrants acceptance.

A close friend of mine was suffering from intestinal problems, and was facing major surgery. He asked me to seek counsel from Rabbi Yaakov Kamenetsky (1892-1986) regarding the illness, and to obtain his *blessing* for a *refuah sheleimah* (complete recovery).

When I met Reb Yaakov in his home in Monsey, New York, he wished the person well and then added, "Perhaps the individual should be more stringent with his standards of *kashrus*. Food is processed through the intestines, and lax standards of *kashrus* could be the reason for his ailment." After Reb Yaakov said it, it seemed obvious, but who would have thought of it?

Another story about the insight of a *gadol hador* (Torah giant of a generation) was told by Rav Yisroel Berl, a *mashgiach* in Yeshiva Torah Ore in Jerusalem. R' Leib Grossman* was a prosperous businessman who set aside two hours every day to learn with his 15-year-old son, Heshy,* in the Ponevezher Yeshivah, in Bnei Brak. One afternoon as R' Leib entered the yeshivah, there was a commotion. *Bachurim* were gesturing animatedly and everyone seemed to be talking at once, when two boys noticed R' Leib. Suddenly there was hushed whispering and everyone turned to him.

R' Leib was startled. Was something wrong? One of the boys broke the silence and said, "R' Leib, Heshy was just in an accident and he's been rushed to the hospital!"

R' Leib's face turned ashen. "How is he?" he screamed.

The boys didn't know. They told R' Leib what happened. "It was lunchtime and Heshy was crossing the street and was hit by a bus. He fell forward and was lying flat in front of the bus. The bus knocked him over and couldn't stop right away. Miraculously

* Name has been changed.

he was lying under the middle of the bus, so he was not even touched by the wheels."

"What hospital is he in?" asked R' Leib. "I must go there now."

Three boys accompanied R' Leib to the hospital. Upon inquiring at the front desk, R' Leib was ushered immediately to the emergency room, where doctors were attending Heshy.

"Your son was very badly bruised," said one of the doctors. "He is lucky to be alive."

It was a few hours before Heshy could be sent to a room to begin his recovery. Throughout the night, *bachurim* in the yeshivah recited *Tehillim* or learned on his behalf.

For the next three days, R' Leib and his wife did not leave Heshy's bedside. They realized that there had been so many miracles. Heshy did not fall on his head; he fell between the wheels so he was not crushed as the bus passed over him; he did not have internal bleeding; no bones were broken; and he was not permanently disabled. The doctors told the Grossmans that their son would be able to leave the hospital in about a week, and return to a normal schedule shortly thereafter.

The Grossmans had a lot to be grateful for. They wondered, though, how to express their gratitude to Hashem. R' Leib sent a friend to seek the counsel of Rabbi Chaim Kanievsky, who lives in Bnei Brak.

Reb Chaim said that Hashem had rewarded R' Leib and his family with life, and so now he had the obligation to give life to someone else, מִדָּה כְּנֶגֶד מִדָּה, *measure for measure.* "What is true life?" asked Reb Chaim. "We say every night in *Maariv,* כִּי הֵם חַיֵּינוּ וְאֹרֶךְ יָמֵינוּ, *For they [Torah and mitzvos] are our life and the length of our days.* In the blessing recited after the reading of the Torah we say, וְחַיֵּי עוֹלָם נָטַע בְּתוֹכֵנוּ, *[Hashem] implanted eternal life [the Torah] within us.* Torah is the genuine life of a Jew.

"In many yeshivos, especially the large ones," said Reb Chaim, "some boys fall by the wayside. The administration and faculty can't give enough attention to every student, and so there are boys who begin to lose their passion for learning. After a while they lose interest altogether. If this is not caught in time, such a *talmid* could be lost forever from learning. What such a student needs is an older *chavrusa* (study partner), maybe a *kollel* fellow, to give him individual attention, guidance, and encouragement.

"Therefore, R' Leib should inquire about a *bachur* in the *beis medrash* who needs this extra attention and then pay an older *chavrusa* to learn with him."

❁ ❁ ❁

When R' Leib was told what Rabbi Chaim Kanievsky had suggested, he almost fainted. Just a few weeks earlier, someone in the Ponevezher yeshivah had approached him with just such a proposal. A *bachur* from a broken home had shown early signs of indifference in his learning. Some of his friends, knowing that R' Leib was affluent and that he had a high regard for those who studied Torah, asked him if he would pay a *kollel* fellow to be an older *chavrusa* for this boy and give him the attention and inspiration he needed.

R' Leib had readily agreed, and issued six post-dated checks to the *kollel* fellow to cover tutorial payments for the next half year. The day the first check came due was the day the accident happened!

R' Leib had seen to it that a Jewish child would be "given life," and on that very day, R' Leib and his family were rewarded with life — the life of their beloved son, Heshy.

It was מִדָּה כְּנֶגֶד מִדָּה (*measure for measure*) just as Rabbi Chaim Kanievsky had said.

It was *obvious* — and astounding!

A Lasting Directive

Rabbi Avrohom Kellner (1909-1965) served as a rabbi for more than 30 years in many communities. In Albany, Baltimore, Miami, St. Louis, and Washington, D.C., his congregants were inspired by his eloquent sermons and moved by his dedication to *chinuch* (Torah education) for all Jewish children.

Two of his children are outstanding *mechanchim* today. Rabbi Yisroel Kellner is the founder and director of the Shalom Hebrew Day Schools in New Jersey and Mrs. Shana Kramer is the founder and administrator of Torah Umesorah's Creative Learning Pavilion.

On the last day of *Pesach* 1965, when many of his congregants in the Bais Avrohom shul in St. Louis had gathered to recite *Yizkor*, Rabbi Kellner delivered a dramatic talk. Unknown to him or his congregants, it would be the last *drashah* he would ever deliver as he passed away a few weeks later. In that sermon Rabbi Kellner told the following story.

❁ ❁ ❁

In 1648 and 1649 the Jews in Poland suffered horrible slaughter at the hands of the Ukrainian Cossacks led by their vile leader Bogdan Chmielnicki. In the course of their rebellion against the Russian Czar, they destroyed countless Jewish communities with unspeakable barbarism. These pogroms, which led to the deaths of close to 100,000 Jews, came to be known as *gezeiros Tach V'Tat*, the decrees of *Tach* and *Tat* (a reference to the corresponding Hebrew years of ת"ח and ת"ט, 5408 and 5409).

Jews tried to hide or escape, but most were caught and killed. One particular wealthy Jew, though, was able to elude the marauding Cossacks and remained secluded throughout the rampage. When the Cossacks finally left, he emerged from his hiding place and became painfully aware of the horrifying results of the onslaught.

He filled a container with gold coins and went directly to the town square. Soon a crowd gathered around him. "I will give one gold piece to anyone who brings me a dead Jew," he announced to the Polish gentiles that surrounded him. His intent was to be able to properly bury the victims whose bodies remained in the streets and fields.

The wealthy man continued his announcement, "And for those who bring me a live Jew, I will double the reward and give two gold pieces." His intention was to help any other surviving Jews resume a semblance of normal life.

❁ ❁ ❁

Rabbi Kellner peered at his congregants and exclaimed, "All who have come here today to recite *Yizkor* have made a financial commitment in honor of those who have died. Today it would be appropriate to double your commitment for those Jewish children who live — to assure that they get a Torah education!"

Scheduled for Arrival

At the *Sheva Berachos* of his youngest son, Rav Meir, at Wagshal's Hotel in Bnei Brak, the Brisker Rav, Rabbi Yitzchak Zev Soloveitchik (1887-1959), expounded on the words of each of the songs that were sung by the guests. With relish, the assembled would sing a *niggun*, and then delightedly wait to hear R' Velvel's spontaneous insights.

One of the guests was the renowned *tzaddik*, Rabbi Velvel Adelman. When asked to sing, he chose יָמִים עַל יְמֵי מֶלֶךְ תּוֹסִיף, *May You add days on to the days of the king* (*Tehillim* 61:7). Everyone joined in fervently to this implied prayer for the Brisker Rav.

When the singing ended, the Rav began, "There is a *machlokes* (difference of opinion) as to which king is meant by the word *melech* (see *Radak*, ibid.). If it refers to King David, then it is understandable that *Klal Yisrael* beseeches Hashem to add days to David's life, for as a mere mortal, David had been given a specific amount of years. If however, as some say, the verse refers to *Mashiach*, why pray for more days to his life? *Mashiach* will live on forever."

The Brisker Rav smiled knowingly and gave his answer: "We pray for *Mashiach* to come earlier! And if he comes before his scheduled arrival, there will be additional (תּוֹסִיף) days of *Mashiach's* reign."

May the words of the Brisker Rav come to fruition in our day.

Eviction Notice

Reb Asher Melitz* was a nineteenth-century European businessman who dealt with Jews and gentiles in his prosperous lumber business. R' Asher was a deeply religious person, who often spent long hours involved with his business dealings, oblivious to time and his personal obligations.

One afternoon, in a distant town, R' Asher concluded a huge financial deal with a gentile he often dealt with before. Both parties were happy with the terms of their contract, and, as was their custom, they went to a local tavern to celebrate with a beer.

As R' Asher left the tavern, he suddenly became pale and had a gnawing empty feeling. He remembered it was *Chol Hamoed Pesach,* and he had just violated a basic tenet of the holiday by drinking beer, which was *chametz!* He was devastated, embarrassed, angry at himself, and filled with remorse. He found it hard to believe that he had committed such a major sin.

Upon returning home, he went directly to his rabbi and cried about the terrible sin he had committed.

"How I can do *teshuvah* (repentance)?" R' Asher pleaded. "How could I have committed such a terrible sin?"

"You are a Belzer *chassid,*" the rav replied, "and the Belzer Rebbe (Rabbi Sholom Rokeach, 1779-1855) will be coming to town shortly after *Yom Tov*. Wait and ask him what to do. He will guide you properly."

R' Asher agreed to wait for the Rebbe, but for the remainder of *Yom Tov* he was a broken, inconsolable man.

When the Belzer Rebbe finally came a few weeks after *Pesach,* R' Asher, filled with regret, told him the story. After thinking for a few moments, the Rebbe said, "You have no choice but to go into *galus* (exile). You and your family must move from here and go elsewhere."

The Rebbe explained, "The *pasuk* (verse) in *Eichah* states (1:3) גָּלְתָה יְהוּדָה מֵעֹנִי, *'Judah has gone into exile because of suffering.'* The

* Name has been changed.

Midrash (Eichah Rabbah 1:28) interprets מֵעֹנִי to mean 'because of לֶחֶם עֹנִי, *bread of affliction (matzah),'* and translates this verse, *'Judah was exiled for their transgression of eating chametz on Pesach.'*

"Your sin can be forgiven only if you go into exile. You have to move," said the Rebbe, "but if you wish, you can move your family to *Eretz Yisrael.*"

R' Asher accepted the ruling and told his rav what the Belzer Rebbe had said. When the rav heard the Belzer Rebbe's edict he was astounded. "What he told you is remarkable," said the rav in awe. "I recall now that the Vilna Gaon (1720-1797) showed how this very edict is implied in the Torah.

"In the verse describing the severe punishment for anyone eating *chametz* on *Pesach,* the Torah writes, כִּי כָּל אֹכֵל מַחְמֶצֶת וְנִכְרְתָה הַנֶּפֶשׁ הַהִוא מֵעֲדַת יִשְׂרָאֵל, *For anyone who eats leavening — that soul shall be cut off from the assembly of Israel...(Shemos* 12:19). The phrase וְנִכְרְתָה הַנֶּפֶשׁ, *that soul shall be cut off,* appears many times in the Torah. However, only here, in the violation of eating *chametz* is the cantillation mark atop the word וְנִכְרְתָה a גֵּרְשַׁיִם, from the word גֵּרֵשׁ, meaning banishment or exile!"

Deciphering Direction

The following episodes engagingly evolve around two simple words, יָמִין וּשְׂמֹאל, *right and left,* whose meaning is known to anyone even vaguely familiar with the Hebrew language. These narratives impart the complexity and beauty of Torah study. One who studies Torah is said to navigate the יַם הַתַּלְמוּד, *the sea of scholarship.* These accounts demonstrate why someone who takes the plunge into this "sea" becomes totally absorbed and engrossed.

One Friday night, Rabbi Yonosan Sternberg was studying the laws of *Krias HaTorah* (the reading of the Torah) in preparation for a *shiur* to people in the Agudath Israel *shul* in Bayswater,

New York. The laws concerned the conditions under which it was necessary to correct a *baal korei,* Torah reader, who erred in his reading.

Rabbi Sternberg read words of caution to every *baal korei* that the *Mishnah Berurah* (142:6) cites from the *Maharam Mintz:* הַחַזָּן צָרִיךְ לַחֲזוֹר מִתְּחִלָּה הַסִּדְרָא שֶׁתְּהֵא שְׁגוּרָה בְּפִיו כָּל הַדִּקְדּוּקִים בַּמְּתָגִין לְעֵיל וּמִלְּרַע יָמִין וּשְׂמֹאל וְיִקְרָא בְּמָתוּן וְלֹא בִּמְהִירוּת וְאוּלַי יַבְלִיעַ שׁוּם אוֹת אוֹ תֵּיבָה , *The chazzan* [*baal korei*] *should review the sidra [in advance] so that he is fluent in the exactness of all accents, the upper accents and lower accents, the right and left, and he should read slowly, not quickly, for he may swallow a letter or word.*

Rabbi Sternberg was puzzled by the expression יָמִין וּשְׂמֹאל, *right and left.* What was it about "right and left" that the *Mishnah Berurah* wanted every reader to be careful about?

After Shabbos, Rabbi Sternberg called his friend Rabbi Herschel Welcher, Rav of Cong. Ahavas Yisrael in Kew Gardens Hills, and asked him if he knew an interpretation of the expression יָמִין וּשְׂמֹאל. Rabbi Welcher thought for a moment and replied, "Let me tell you a story I heard from Rabbi Lazer Pluchinsky of Jerusalem, about the Ohr Somayach, Rabbi Meir Simchah HaKohen (1843-1926) of Dvinsk.

The Ohr Somayach had a *chavrusa* (study partner) who, though a layman, was an exceptional *talmid chacham*. One afternoon, the Ohr Somayach and his *chavrusa* arranged to learn in a particular *shul*. When the Ohr Somayach arrived, the local rav was giving a *shiur* to a group of *balabatim.* As he was explaining a fine point, one of the listeners asked a question. The rav thought for a moment and gave an answer. However, as he was making his point, the Ohr Somayach's *chavrusa,* who had been sitting off to a side, suddenly spoke up and said, "Your answer is wrong. The fellow who asked the question is correct!" The *chavrusa* and the rav then got into a heated Talmudic discussion.

Everyone in attendance was surprised. What the rav had been

saying seemed logical, but now his words were being refuted categorically.

As this Talmudic confrontation was going on, the Ohr Somayach turned to his *chavrusa* and said firmly, so that everyone could hear, "I'm sorry, but you don't know your right from your left, and those who don't know their right from their left should not be offering their opinions!"

The Ohr Somayach's outspoken rebuke of his *chavrusa* sent the message to everyone that their rav was a competent authority, not the *chavrusa*. The Ohr Somayach's castigation closed the discussion at once, and the *shiur* resumed.

The Ohr Somayach and his *chavrusa* went off to another side of the shul to begin learning together. When they were out of earshot of everyone else, the Ohr Somayach said, "You certainly were right in your reasoning with the rav; however, you forgot a *Chazal* (Talmudic teaching) and that's why I said to you what I did.

"The *Gemara* (*Moed Kattan* 5a) teaches that Rav Yannai had a disciple who always posed difficult questions during his master's lectures. However, he raised these challenging queries only during private sessions. During public lectures, given before the holidays, the student would listen silently, for he might pose a question that Rav Yannai could not answer and that would be embarrassing.

"That is the proper way to behave," said the Ohr Somayach. "*Chazal* homiletically deduce this code of behavior from the verse וְשָׂם דֶּרֶךְ אַרְאֶנּוּ בְּיֵשַׁע אֱלֹקִים, *And if one sets his ways [to do good], I will show him the salvation of G-d* (*Tehillim* 50:23). The word וְשָׂם is spelled with a שׂ, *sin*. However, the word can also be read וְשָׁם with a שׁ, *shin*, meaning *and he who appraises*, i.e., a person who appraises every situation and evaluates the benefits or drawbacks of his actions [will be rewarded with Hashem's salvation].

"*Chazal* took the dot from the left side of the *sin* and placed it on the right side, to make it a *shin* and teach us that one must appraise his actions to make sure that he will not embarrass anyone, particularly one giving a public *shiur*. That is why," continued the Ohr Somayach, "I told you that you didn't know your right from your left. You didn't remember that the Sages took the dot from the left side of the *sin* and brought it to the right side."

❁ ❁ ❁

After telling the story, Rabbi Welcher added, "Based on this story, I believe that the *Mishnah Berurah* is cautioning the *baal korei* not to confuse a *shin* with a *sin* — thus the phrase 'right and left.' "

Rabbi Welcher then added, "There is another place where the commentaries term the difference between *shin* and *sin,* as the difference between right and left. In the commandment to be obedient to the Torah sages, the Torah writes, לֹא תָסוּר מִן הַדָּבָר אֲשֶׁר יַגִּידוּ לְךָ יָמִין וּשְׂמֹאל, *You shall not deviate from the word that they will tell you, right or left* (*Devarim* 17:11). *Rashi,* citing *Sifri* 154, writes: '[You shall heed the judge] even if he says to you about right that it is left, and about left that it is right!' Though we may see things differently, we are obligated to follow the judges' ruling.

"Some commentaries (see *Talelei Ohros,* ibid.) note that the *Sifri* is also alluding to a passage in *Taanis* 9a. From the verse, עַשֵּׂר תְּעַשֵּׂר, *You shall tithe* (*Devarim* 14:22), the Sages deduce עַשֵּׂר בִּשְׁבִיל שֶׁתִּתְעַשֵּׁר, *Tithe so that you shall become wealthy,* meaning that God rewards people with wealth for the funds that they give to charity. For the purpose of this teaching, the Sages took the dot from the left side of the *sin* in the word תְּעַשֵּׂר and placed it on the right side of the ש so it becomes a *shin,* which changes the word to תְּעַשֵּׁר, meaning *you shall become wealthy.* Thus, from 'left' they made 'right,' and we are obligated to believe and accept that teaching. Thus we must tithe even though rationally that reduces, rather than increases, our wealth.

"This is another case where 'right' and 'left' refer to the difference between the *shin* and the *sin,* and it is further proof to the *shin-sin* interpretation of the *Mishneh Berurah's* (ibid.) reference to 'right and left.' "

❁ ❁ ❁

I was so fascinated by all of the above that I repeated the story and insight to numerous people. One Friday night, a young *kollel* fellow from Borough Park, Rabbi Moshe Yehoshua Kramer, offered another novel interpretation of the *Mishnah Berurah's* reference to right and left:

The Talmud (*Yoma* 52a) states, חָמֵשׁ מִקְרָאוֹת בַּתּוֹרָה אֵין לָהֶם הֶכְרֵעַ, *There are five verses in the Torah whose punctuation is unclear,* i.e., each verse contains a phrase [or word] that can be linked to either an earlier clause or a latter clause of the verse.

> A case in point is the word מְשֻׁקָּדִים, *engraved like almonds* (*Shemos* 25:34). That verse, which describes the fashioning of the Menorah, reads in its entirety: וּבַמְּנֹרָה אַרְבָּעָה גְבִעִים מְשֻׁקָּדִים כַּפְתֹּרֶיהָ וּפְרָחֶיהָ, *And on the Menorah — four cups, engraved like almonds, its knobs and its flowers.* It is unclear whether the description *engraved like almonds* applies to the cups mentioned earlier, or the knobs and flowers mentioned later.
>
> See *Yoma* (ibid.) for the other four similar examples.

"It would seem," said R' Moshe Yehoshua, "that in these situations the *baal korei* cannot know יָמִין וּשְׂמֹאל — whether the word belongs to the 'right,' i.e. the previous clause, or the 'left,' i.e. the latter one. Regarding all other verses of the Torah, however, the *baal korei* has the obligation to know the meaning and grammatical structure of the verse, so that he can read it with its proper punctuation and attach the word to its appropriate clause."

When I told this second interpretation to an outstanding *baal korei*, Rabbi Laib Roberts of Kew Gardens, he commented that in the daily *Shemoneh Esrei*, we are faced with a similar dilemma of "right and left."

> In the section beginning with רְצֵה, *Be Favorable,* the phrase וְאִשֵּׁי יִשְׂרָאֵל, *the fire-offerings of Israel,* can refer to the previous

clause, וְהָשֵׁב אֶת הָעֲבוֹדָה לִדְבִיר בֵּיתֶךָ וְאִשֵּׁי יִשְׂרָאֵל, *Restore the service to the Holy of Holies of Your Temple and the fire-offerings of Israel.* Or it can begin a new sentence: וְאִשֵּׁי יִשְׂרָאֵל וּתְפִלָּתָם בְּאַהֲבָה תְקַבֵּל בְּרָצוֹן, *The fire-offerings of Israel and their prayers accept with love and favor.*

Reb Laib then proposed an ingenious third understanding of the words of the *Mishnah Berurah.* Perhaps the *Mishnah Berurah* is saying that in the five cases where the word in question can be explained as referring to either the previous or latter clause, the *baal korei* should have both meanings in mind, so that his reading will include both possible meanings.

"That is why," he said, "the *Mishnah Berurah* says יָמִין וּשְׂמֹאל, *right and left,* and not יָמִין אוֹ וּשְׂמֹאל, *right or left,* indicating that both meanings should be considered and not one instead of the other."

This is indeed the greatness of Torah: endless debate, endless discussion, and endless views. And as long as one does not present an opposing view merely for the sake of argument (see *Pesachim* 50b, *Tosafos* ד"ה וכאן), differing and even diametrically opposed views can be viewed as דִּבְרֵי אֱלֹקִים חַיִּים, *the words of [our] Living God.*

A Moving Message

Chazal (*Yevamos* 97a) teach that the lips of a deceased *talmid chacham* are [spiritually] stirred when someone quotes words of Torah that he spoke during his lifetime. This is homiletically deduced from the verse דּוֹבֵב שִׂפְתֵי יְשֵׁנִים, *The lips of the deceased quiver* (*Shir HaShirim* 7:11). [See *Maharsha, Yevamos,* ibid. and *Torah Temimah, Shir HaShirim* ibid.]

It is therefore reasonable to assume that not only are Torah scholars in the *Olam HaEmes,* the World of Truth, spiritually aware of people relaying their Torah, but that it affords them great joy, as well.

In this novel story we witness an affinity between *talmidei chachamim* from two worlds.

Rabbi Yochanan (he asked that his family name be omitted) is a *maggid shiur* in a well-known American yeshivah in Jerusalem. He grew up in New York where he attended local yeshivos. After his family immigrated to Israel, he continued his studies in the *beis medrash* and *kollel* of Mir Jerusalem where he studied with great *hasmadah* (diligence).

One winter while in the Mir Kollel, R' Yochanan became very ill with a severe case of viral pneumonia and was confined to bed. His head and body ached; he was coughing constantly and was on strong medication. Realizing he could not concentrate on the intricacies of *Gemara* and commentaries, Reb Yochanan decided to study some of the other *sefarim* from his bookshelf.

Among the *sefarim* he chose was the *Terumas HaDeshen* by Rav Yisroel Isserlein (1390-1460), an authoritative work of halachic essays presented in the form of responsa. (The decisions are frequently cited by later authorities, particularly the *Maharshal*.)

Late one afternoon R' Yochanan realized it was time to *daven Minchah* but he was so weak he could not get out of bed to stand for *Shemoneh Esrei*. He wondered whether a sick person may *daven* while lying down or is obligated to sit up in bed to *daven*.

As he thought about his dilemma his eye caught the responsum he was up to in the *Terumas HaDeshen* (2:57). He was so astounded by the words of that particular responsum that his body trembled and tears welled in his eyes.

These are the words of the *Terumas HaDeshen*: "The One Who dwells above should send a speedy recovery to my dear friend R' Yochanan. With regard to your query whether a sick person who cannot stand up should pray lying down or sit up in bed ..."

R' Yochanan was stunned. That was his name and his question, and the words had been written more than 500 years before! It was as though the *Terumas HaDeshen* was talking directly to him!

In a sense, perhaps he was!

Perhaps having become aware, through his spiritually stirring lips, that a young man, though bedridden with illness, was learning his Torah, the *Terumas HaDeshen,* through remarkable *Hashgachah Pratis,* was able to acknowledge R' Yochanan's presence, as it were, wish him well and, in a sense, say, "Thank you."

R' Yochanan recovered shortly afterwards, and today, 25 years later, still recalls the incident with awe and amazement.

The Wisdom of Extraction

At an Agudath Israel Convention, the well-known *askan* (community activist) and philanthropist Rabbi Yisroel Lefkowitz of Brooklyn, New York, told me a remarkable story about his late father, Dr. Yitzchok Dov Lefkowitz (1890-1970).

Dr. Lefkowitz, who was known as R' Berel, was a *talmid chacham* who knew the entire six sections of *Mishnayos* by heart! When he treated such Torah luminaries in Europe as Rabbi Yeruchem Levovitz (1874-1936), the *Mashgiach* of Mir, or later in America, the Satmar Rav, Rabbi Yoel Teitelbaum (1887-1979), he would delight them with his uncanny memory of any *mishnah* they would mention. The Chofetz Chaim's second wife, Faigeh, was also a patient of Dr. Lefkowitz.

As a youngster Berel had studied in some of the finest yeshivos in Europe. He was a talmid of the Unsdorfer Rov, Rabbi Shmuel Rosenberg, in Slovakia, studying in the same *beis midrash* as R' Shraga Feivel Mendlowitz (1886-1948). Later, he traveled to Galicia where he was a *talmid* of the world-renowned *posek,* the Brezhaner Rav, Rabbi Sholom Mordechai HaCohen Schwadron (1835-1911), and finally he studied in the Pressburgh Yeshiva under Rabbi Akiva Sofer (1878-1960), a great-grandson of the *Chasam Sofer,* Rav Moshe Schreiber (1763-1839).

In 1914 his learning was interrupted when, at age 24, he was drafted into the Austro-Hungarian army. Compelled to serve in the military for close to three years, he rose through the ranks to become an artillery officer, directing the shelling of the Russian army.

During a particularly perilous battle, R' Yitzchok Dov was trapped for nearly two weeks in a foxhole almost filled with water. Miraculously he survived and was eventually evacuated. In gratitude for his service to the military, the Austrian government granted him free schooling toward a career in either engineering, law or medicine. He chose medicine, for the reasoning that there were few religious doctors in Europe, and he could be a valuable asset to his community.

By the mid 1920s, Yitzchok Dov Lefkowitz became an internist and opened an office in Kosice (pronounced Kuh-zhitz-eh), Czechoslovakia. One day he was making his rounds in the local hospital, visiting patients, giving encouragement, and furnishing medical advice to those in need. At the end of the corridor he saw a gentleman nervously pacing back and forth. When the man saw Dr. Lefkowitz he ran towards him, his face white with fright, his eyes agape in anticipation of impending dread.

"Dr. Lefkowitz," he pleaded, "please help my daughter. She is a *kallah* (bride) and is supposed to get married in a week. Last Friday she swallowed a fish bone and it is stuck in her throat. The doctors want to operate on her tomorrow. The scar on her jaw and neck from the operation would be horrible. How can a *kallah* come to her wedding with a terrible scar? Please see what you can do. Perhaps you can get the bone out some other way."

In his soft voice Dr. Lefkowitz tried to calm the father, as he assured him that he would examine his daughter and see what he could do. Though the young woman was not his patient, he felt compelled to do whatever he could to reduce the family's stress.

As he entered the room, he saw the *kallah* lying still, a look of frozen terror etched on her face. Her moist pink eyes indicated she had been crying for a while. "*Mazel tov*," Dr. Lefkowitz said as he stood alongside her bed. "You should be *zocheh* (merit) to build a *bayis ne'eman b'Yisrael* (a faithful home in Israel)."

"Thank you," she replied softly.

Dr. Lefkowitz began a thorough examination of her neck and throat. The longer he explored the situation the more tense the father grew. Slowly it began to dawn on Dr. Lefkowitz that this was not a simple situation. He probed and reprobed, checked and rechecked, and finally he came to the same unfortunate conclusion — the young woman would need surgery and, unfortunately, the surgical scar would be visible.

Dr. Lefkowitz turned to the father and said softly, "The bone is lodged in a precarious position. Your surgeon is correct. Only by operating can the bone be removed."

The father was devastated. Dr. Lefkowitz tried to assure him that every *kallah* is radiant and that his daughter's appearance would be special regardless. They were kind words, but not the ones the father wished to hear.

Later that evening, Dr. Lefkowitz went to *daven Minchah* and *Maariv* with the Stropkover Rebbe, Rabbi Avrohom Sholom Halberstam (1854-1940). Dr. Lefkowitz *davened* there quite often, as he had the highest regard for the rebbe.

After *Minchah,* groups of people clustered together, some learning, others chatting, passing the time until *Maariv.* Suddenly the father of the *kallah* rushed into the *shul* waving his hands, beseeching people to show him where the rebbe was. The rebbe was sitting near the *aron kodesh* (the holy ark) surrounded by a group of men who were leaning towards him, straining to hear his every word.

The agitated father of the *kallah* began to cry uncontrollably when he came to the rebbe. Oblivious to the lack of privacy, disregarding the shame of his desperate need, the father explained the entire distressing situation to the rebbe. "Rebbe, help my *kallah,*" the father cried desperately.

With a wave of his hand the rebbe signaled everyone to step back and let him be alone with the father. The rebbe closed his eyes and with his brow ruffled he swept his hand back and forth across his forehead. Everyone, particularly Dr. Lefkowitz, who knew that this woman required surgery, waited anxiously for the rebbe's response.

The rebbe called the father closer to him. "Take a few people with you," he said in a hushed tone, "and go back to the hospital. All of you should then walk around the *kallah's* bed and say these words, נִנְעַצְתָּא כְּמַחַט נִגְעַלְתָּא כִּתְרִיס שֵׁייא שֵׁייא, *'You are embedded like a needle, you are locked [tightly] as a shutter. Go down, go down.'* "

Dr. Lefkowitz was incredulous! There was no way that bone could be dislodged except with surgery!

The Stropkover Rebbe motioned to Dr. Lefkowitz and called to him. "Berel," he said, "Bring me a *mesechta* (tractate) *Shabbos.*" When Dr. Lefkowitz returned with the *Gemara,* the rebbe turned to *daf* 67a and showed him the last few lines on the page, "For a fish bone [that is stuck in one's throat (see *Rashi*)], one must say, 'You are embedded like a needle, you are locked [tightly] as a shutter. Go down, go down.' "

Still Dr. Lefkowitz was skeptical. He didn't question the Stropkover Rebbe, but in his heart he was convinced that the *kallah* would need surgery.

Later that evening after *Maariv,* the father and a number of men went to the hospital and did exactly as the Rebbe instructed. By the next morning the bone had become dislodged! None of the medical staff at the hospital could believe it and Dr. Lefkowitz was left speechless and in awe.

Years later, when he was already in America, Dr. Lefkowitz was studying the laws of visiting the sick (*Yoreh Deah* 336). He noted Rabbi Akiva Eiger's first commentary on this section. He was astonished. For the rest of his life he would quote Rabbi Akiva Eiger's words verbatim to anyone who listened to this story.

Rabbi Akiva Eiger writes, "The *Maharil* tells us it is forbidden to experiment with any of the remedies mentioned throughout the Talmud because people are not able to ascertain the essence of the [Talmudic] remedy, and if people are unsuccessful in their efforts [with it], they will laugh and mock the words of the Talmudic Sages, except for the [advice] regarding the bone [that is stuck] (see *Shabbos* 67a) ... This utterance has been investigated and proven [successful], therefore only this [remedy] is permitted but no other!"

Close to the Heart

R' Leib Moskowitz* came to Monsey from his home in Detroit, to witness the moment when his grandson would put on *tefillin* for the first time. Though he would be returning to Monsey for the *Bar-Mitzvah* in a few weeks, this was an occasion he did not want to miss.

Three generations — a grandfather, son and grandson — rode together that morning to the daily students' *minyan* at the Yeshivah of Spring Valley. Slowly and carefully, the young boy took out his glistening new *tefillin* from its velvet pouch and, with help from his father, tightened and wrapped the *shel yad* on his left arm.

As R' Leib watched, he burst into tears. His muffled sobs were audible to a *rebbi* standing nearby. When R' Leib seemed settled, the *rebbi* wished him *mazel tov* and said, "I can understand this is a very emotional moment for you."

"It's not my grandson who brought me to tears," said R' Leib. "It's the hundreds of boys who are *davening* here. As I looked around, I remembered an incident that happened back in 1945, after the war. I was one of the only survivors of the Vilna ghetto and on *Simchas Torah* we had a *minyan*, but there were no children there.

"When we finished *davening* we wanted to make *Hakafos*, but we had no *Sifrei Torah*. They had all been looted or destroyed by the Nazis. We stood looking at each other, feeling anew the agony of what the Nazis had done.

"Suddenly, a young couple walked into the *shul* with a little boy and girl. The poor girl's vocal chords had not developed properly because she had been in hiding in an attic for over a year, where she was only allowed to whisper.

"We all looked at each other in amazement. No one had seen this couple before. But as they came into the *shul* we realized that those children would be the living *Sifrei Torah* of the future. Each of us took turns holding the children and that's how we danced, during the *Hakafos*, clutching the children to our hearts.

* Name has been changed.

"Today I look around here at your yeshivah," said R' Leib to the *rebbi* "and I see more than a hundred living *Sifrei Torah*. We weren't sure about the future then, but we are now. That's why I cried. I cried for joy!"

❁ ❁ ❁

Undoubtedly there were tens of thousands of Jews in the past like R' Leib who desperately worried that the Jewish nation would not — could not — be revived. And amidst the Holocaust, who could have blamed them for their distress. Yet, that morning in Monsey, R' Leib witnessed a prophesy fulfilled.

Moshe *Rabbeinu* reassurred *Klal Yisrael* כִּי לֹא תִשָּׁכַח מִפִּי זַרְעוֹ *It [the Torah] shall not be forgotten from the mouth of its [Israel's] offspring* (*Devarim* 31:21), and the prophet Yeshaya reiterated the prophesy when he stated, הִנֵּה אָנֹכִי וְהַיְלָדִים אֲשֶׁר נָתַן לִי ה׳ לְאֹתוֹת וּלְמוֹפְתִים בְּיִשְׂרָאֵל *Behold, I and the children whom Hashem has given me are signs and symbols for Israel [that Torah will not be forgotten]* (*Yeshaya* 8:17 and *Rashi* ibid.). The yeshivos and Bais Yaakovs in Jewish communities around the world are living proof of the fruition of these promises.

> *Tikunei Zohar* (*Parashas Nasso*) writes that even a *Sefer Torah* in the ark needs מַזָּל, *the blessing of good fortune.* It is said that the word מַזָּל stands for מָקוֹם, זְמַן, לָשׁוֹן, *place, time, and language.* Indeed, if children are similar to *Sifrei Torah* they need parents and teachers who will be there for them when they need them (i.e., מָקוֹם), spend time with them when they require it (i.e., זְמַן), and be wise enough to say the right things (i.e., לָשׁוֹן) to inspire them.

Smoke Screen

The Kotzker Rebbe, R' Menachem Mendel Morgenstern (1787-1859), was known for his terse, powerful comments that were lightning bolts of brilliance. The Chassidic dynasty of Ger had its origins in Kotzk and it is therefore no surprise that in this story about the third Gerrer Rebbe, the *Imrei Emes,* R' Avrohom Mordechai Alter (1866-1948), we witness a sharp Kotzker-style observation with penetrating insight.

The *Imrei Emes* once heard that one of his *chassidim* was going from Ger to Paris on business. The Rebbe called in the *chassid* and said, "I know they sell very good cigars in Paris. I would greatly appreciate if you would buy some for me there."

The *chassid* was surprised by the request but was only too happy to oblige. "Yes," he told the Rebbe, "It would be my honor to bring the Rebbe the best cigars in Paris."

The *chassid* conducted his business affairs in Paris and then began his trip home. On the way, through Belgium, he suddenly remembered about the cigars! He got off the train in the next big town, purchased the finest cigars he could find, and resumed his trip home.

Upon his arrival he went to the *Imrei Emes* and said apologetically, "Rebbe, I am so sorry but I didn't actually buy these cigars in Paris. However, I was told that these cigars which I bought on the way home are of the same fine quality."

"My child, do you think that I really needed cigars from Paris?" asked the *Imrei Emes.* "I wanted you to remember even in Paris that you have a Rebbe! And you forgot!"

A Symmetry of Balance

On a recent trip to Europe, a noted *talmid chacham,* a collector of rare *sefarim* and manuscripts, told me a remarkable story about his recently deceased father. May the inspiration of this story be a merit to his soul.

When R' Hillel Hochman * was in his 80s living in Jerusalem, he had a dream one night that puzzled and disturbed him. His distress at the dream was unusual because he had never given credence dreams, and had never told anyone about a dream.

* Name has been changed.

When he met his granddaughter the next afternoon in the streets of the Mattersdorf section of Jerusalem, he told her about his anxiety. "I dreamt that I had died and was being judged in the Heavenly Court," he said. "They put me on one side of a huge scale and I was weighing it down unfavorably. Suddenly they put a group of people on the other side of the scale and I asked the Heavenly Court, 'Who are these people and why did they come here?'

"I was told, 'You don't know them, but they came to help you.' I watched as the weight of the people tipped the scale in my favor. Then I woke up."

R' Hillel did not tell anyone else about the dream, nor did his granddaughter mention it to anyone. She was frightened, however, because the dream indicated that her grandfather was thinking about death and it was a reality she found difficult to face.

Up to then, the aging R' Hillel had become gradually frail, but he was basically in good health. His family was looking forward to gathering with him in America to attend the wedding of his granddaughter. Within three months, however, he became seriously ill and passed away.

His children from New York, England, Switzerland, and Israel gathered to sit *shivah* in Jerusalem. Many people came to the mourners, but on the fifth day a stranger walked in. He said his name was Hirsch Bachenstein* and he came from Straubing, Germany. He told the following story.

When R' Hillel was a young man, he was known as a quiet, brilliant, dignified scholar, who had a remarkable way with children. After World War II, he settled in Fuerth, in southeastern Germany, at the invitation of Rabbi Dovid Kahane Shapiro who started a community there. Eventually, R' Hillel married the rav's cousin and supported his family as a traveling tutor.

In outlying communities such as Straubing, Landshut, and Regensburg, there were no yeshivos or day schools, and local

* Name has been changed.

leaders would hire R' Hillel to come two or three times a week to teach children to read Hebrew, learn *Chumash* and *Tanach,* and, sometimes, *Mishnah* and *Gemara.*

R' Hillel traveled every day from Fuerth to one town or another and spent numerous hours with his students. He treated every student differently and taught by the motto חֲנֹךְ לַנַּעַר עַל פִּי דַרְכּוֹ, *Train a child according to his way* (*Mishlei* 22:6). Into the text, he interjected teachings of *yiras Shamayim, ahavas Hashem,* and a longing to perform *mitzvos.*

One day, after a session with a student soon to become *Bar-Mitzvah,* the boy's father complained to R' Hillel, "You are teaching my child too much! He wants to become more religious and we are against that!"

"I am only teaching what he wants to learn," protested R' Hillel.

"But I am the one paying you," the father said adamantly, "and it is up to me to decide what you teach!"

R' Hillel peered at the father firmly and said, "Do you want to have gentile grandchildren?"

The father was chagrined at this bold retort, but he understood at once what R' Hillel was implying. It was bad enough that his son was growing up without any formal Jewish education and a minimum of Jewish friends. It was bad enough that his father and mother were not setting an example of living an authentic Jewish life. And now that the child wanted some more meaning in his life, was that too going to be thwarted by his own parents?

The father relented; R' Hillel was permitted to teach the child as he saw fit. "I am that child," said the man who came to be *menachem avel* the Hochmans. "I am an observant Jew today only because of your father. My children follow in my ways and my wife and I are proud of them."

R' Hillel's granddaughter from Mattersdorf overheard the story and suddenly remembered the dream. In her mind's eye she could visualize this gentleman, his wife, his children, and perhaps dozens of others like them in the dream, tipping the scale in R' Hillel's favor.

She told everyone about the dream that only she knew about. It has now become a legend in the family.

> Let every *rebbi, morah,* or person involved in *kiruv* take note. Your accomplishments outweigh those of all other professions — because what you do is for generations — and no human scale can measure that.

A Class of Hatred?

At a gathering of principals and teachers at a Torah Umesorah convention, Rabbi Avrohom Pam, Rosh Yeshivah of Yeshivah Torah Vodaath in Brooklyn, recounted an incident that occurred when he was a *rebbi* many years before.

It was parents-teachers night and Rabbi Pam was discussing the performance of a student, with his parents. During the conversation, the child's mother said, "My son says you hate him!"

Rabbi Pam was taken aback. "I don't hate anyone," he said. "And certainly not my *talmidim* (students). I like every one of them."

Realizing her words may have been a bit harsh, the mother explained, "My son says you call on other boys more often than you call on him to say the *Gemara* or answer questions."

Rabbi Pam explained that although it may have seemed to her son that he wasn't being called on as often as others, it was really not the case. However, Rabbi Pam assured her he would be sensitive to her son's feelings from then on.

Now, years later, Rabbi Pam told the *mechanchim* (Torah educators) at the convention that the incident helped him understand a puzzling verse in the Torah.

"The Torah tells us, וַיַּרְא ה' כִּי שְׂנוּאָה לֵאָה, *'Hashem saw that Leah was hated [by Yaakov]'* (*Bereishis* 29:31). Could it be," asked Rabbi Pam, "that Yaakov would hate another Jew?

"What is even more difficult to understand," said Rabbi Pam, "is that the Torah tells us in the previous verse וַיֶּאֱהַב גַּם אֶת רָחֵל מִלֵּאָה,

[Yaakov] loved Rachel even more than Leah. That implies that Yaakov *did* love Leah, but he loved Rachel more. Why does the Torah then say Leah was hated?

"The answer," said Rabbi Pam, "is that Leah *felt* hated. That is why the Torah tells us that Hashem was the One Who saw Leah was hated. Only Hashem understood Leah's inner feelings. Yaakov himself didn't realize Leah felt that way.

"It is the same in a classroom," explained Rav Pam. "A child may feel disliked and even hated by the *rebbi,* not because of anything the *rebbi* did or said to *him,* but because the child thinks the *rebbi* likes another *talmid* more than he likes him. The *rebbi* — and the same applies to a parent — must be careful not to show more love for one child than another, because the other child's perception may be not that he is liked less, but that he is disliked altogether. That is what Leah felt, and that is what the boy in my class felt."

❁ ❁ ❁

Rabbi Pam's insight perhaps gives us a new understanding of the Talmudic teaching as to why the second *Beis HaMikdash* was destroyed. *Chazal* say that it happened מִפְּנֵי שֶׁהָיְתָה בּוֹ שִׂנְאַת חִנָּם, *because there was baseless hatred* (*Yoma* 9b).

It may well be that the word שִׂנְאָה does not necessarily mean only real hatred. Perhaps it also means causing one person to *feel* hated, by showing favoritism to a second person.

It behooves us therefore to reevaluate our relationships with others, for unbeknown to us, by acting in a manner that makes another Jew *feel* hated, we could be a cause of the *Beis HaMikdash* not beng rebuilt.

On a Stream of Tears

The Klausenberger Rebbe, Rabbi Yekusiel Yehudah Halberstam (1905-1994), was legendary for the encouragement he gave to the thousands of shattered Jews who came to the Displaced

Persons camps after their liberation from the horror of Nazi concentration camps. Families had been decimated, belongings confiscated, and spirits shattered — the people in the camps had lost everything but, perhaps, their will to live. Bereaved children walked aimlessly among the adults who were traumatized from their terrible experiences.

To each of the bereaved, the Rebbe had different words of comfort and consolation. Everyone knew that it was the Rebbe, more than anyone else, who could give people hope and strength to renew their lives.

At times, the Rebbe would refer to the unspeakable tragedies that he personally suffered. He lost his wife, Rebbetzin Pessel, and 11 children! Once, on Shabbos, *Parashas Vayishlach,* he said, "The Torah describes how Yaakov *Avinu* protected his wife and 11 children from the wickedness of Esav: וַיִּקָּחֵם וַיַּעֲבִרֵם אֶת הַנָּחַל, *And he took them and had them cross over the stream (Bereishis* 32:24*),* and then with uncontrollable crying he said, "I, too, took my wife and 11 children to the stream, but it was the stream of blood— to the sacred communities of קְדוֹשִׁים וּטְהוֹרִים (the holy and the pure)."

❁ ❁ ❁

The Klausenberger Rebbe had a keen interest in children. Even under dismal and sorrowful conditions he opened a yeshivah, *Sh'eiris Hapleita,* for 100 boys, and a Bais Yaakov school for 120 girls.

One day, two men told him about Meshulam Yalver.* When Meshulam was 16 he was known as an exceptional *masmid* (diligent scholar), punctilious in his *mitzvah* observance, a boy who had a bright future as an exemplary Jew. Now, having gone through privation, loss, and catastrophe, he rejected his Judaism and resisted any attempts to bring him back to the fold of observance.

The Rebbe asked the men to bring Meshulam to him.

When Meshulam entered the Rebbe's room, the Rebbe motioned for him to sit down next to him. "I'm told that you are the son of Reb Laibish, whom I knew," the Rebbe said.

*The name has been changed.

"Yes," Meshulam answered. He wasn't going to be lulled into much conversation where he would have to debate the Rebbe in topics of *emunah* (belief) and *bitachon* (faith). For him the world of religion ended in Auschwitz; there was nothing to discuss.

"They say that you were a great *masmid* back home. Is that so?" the Rebbe asked in a nonconfrontational tone.

Meshulam just nodded. He knew that to the Rebbe there was nothing as important as *limud haTorah* (Torah study), but he wouldn't give the Rebbe the satisfaction of saying that he had done something that the Rebbe deemed so meaningful.

"But now you are angry?" asked the Rebbe softly.

"Of course, I'm angry," Meshulam blurted out heatedly, not being able to contain himself any longer. "The best were taken away, the finest are lost forever."

The Rebbe extended his palm and touched the boy's face and said, "You are so right. Look at me. They left me alive while my wife and all 11 children were taken away. You're right," the Rebbe said again, "the best were taken away and look what's left..." And with that the Rebbe burst into tears and began sobbing. And then together the Rebbe and the boy cried without stop on each other's shoulders.

No more words were spoken — for no words *had* to be spoken — for no words *could* be spoken. Two tortured hearts melded in a stream of tears.

An hour later, Meshulam left the Rebbe's house.

That night when he was alone he recited *Krias Shema* for the first time in months. Within a few days he was wearing his yarmulka again.

Recently, Meshulam, now in his 70s, told me, "There was nothing anyone could say to me, and the Rebbe understood that. Everyone spoke to my head; the Rebbe touched my heart.

*The name has been changed.

Notice and Neglect

In a moving talk that the psychotherapist Dr. Meir Wikler gave on child-rearing and parenting, he told a poignant story that touched all who were present.

A young lady in her early 20s had been coming to his office for help with her personal problems. After numerous sessions Dr. Wikler recognized a pattern. She hardly spoke about her parents, despite Dr. Wikler's attempts to open the subject. One day when she made an oblique reference to her father, Dr. Wikler seized the opportunity and remarked, "You haven't said much about your father."

The woman lowered her head and stared at the floor. There was a long, heavy silence and then he noticed she was crying. Dr. Wikler realized that she was wrestling with herself as to whether or not she should express what was on her mind. He decided that the best encouragement he could offer was patient silence.

When she did look up with tear-filled reddened eyes, she wiped away tears from her face and said haltingly, "I just remembered a painful incident from my youth."

"Would you like to talk about it?" Dr. Wikler asked gently.

"I don't mind sharing it," she replied.

"It happened many years ago when I was a child. We were sitting at the *Seder* table on *Pesach* and I had taken the *afikoman.* My father knew that I had it, and after the meal he asked me what I wanted for it."

She waited for a moment before she continued. She took a deep breath and then she said, "I told him — I wanted a conversation."

❁ ❁ ❁

"It is what children want and need most," said Dr. Wikler to his audience. "We make a mistake if we think that expensive gifts or extravagant vacations are what will bond our children to us. But that is wrong. They need parental attention and quality time. And that, more than anything else, is what that little girl at the *Seder* table wanted."

When Dr. Wikler finished his lecture, people came to ask questions and comment on his talk. Numerous people commented at how moved they were by the *afikoman* story. However, nothing was as startling as the message he had waiting for him on his answering machine the next morning.

He recognized the voice at once. It was the young woman from the *afikoman* story. "You probably did not realize that I was in the large crowd that came to hear you last night."

Dr. Wikler was shaken. He immediately tried to appraise the woman's frame of mind. Was she angry? Upset? Disheartened? Hurt? Betrayed?

The message continued. "I am so happy you told that story."

Dr. Wikler thought to himself, "She is?"

She explained, "It showed that you were listening to me and meant that you remembered me."

Her comment merely underscored what he had said the night before. Children don't want to be ignored. Everyone needs attention, time, and recognition.

This story brought to mind an incident that happened with me at a *bris.*

As I was setting up my instruments to perform a *bris* one morning, I noticed a well-dressed handsome boy of about 10 watching me intently. "Are you related to the baby?" I asked just to make conversation.

"Yes," he said proudly. "I am the baby's brother. My name is Ezra."

I asked Ezra if he could take me to his mother and the newborn, so that I could examine the baby. He proudly told me that he would be happy to take me there.

When Ezra and I came into the room, the mother and infant were there as was another boy, much shorter than Ezra, also dressed beautifully. "And who are you?" I asked the boy.

"My name is Shlomo and I am the oldest," he said.

The room suddenly became very quiet. I had just asked him his name and nothing more, but I understood Shlomo's pain. He was shorter than Ezra, so almost everyone took him to be the younger brother. He was embittered at not being recognized for who he was — the oldest — and in his mind, the more significant one of the children.

We all need to recognized. We all need attention. It is the wise parent and teacher who provides it. The dividends are inestimable.

It Was Plane And Simple

Yaakov Budayov,* a seventh grader in Yeshivah Tomchei Torah* of Brooklyn, was an orphan who lived with his grandmother. His young mother had passed away two years before, while the whole family was still in Russia. In America his father married a woman who had no interest in raising the child, so Yaakov was sent to live with his aged grandmother, who spoke no English.

Yaakov was a brilliant student. Although he had received no Torah education in Russia, before long he was the top student in the seventh grade at Tomchei Torah. The *rebbi* merely had to say the *Chumash* or *Gemara* once, and Yaakov could repeat it almost verbatim. His comprehension was nothing short of astounding and often he would ask questions that had been raised by the *Rishonim* (early Talmudic commentaries).

However, there was a problem. Yaakov had a penchant for making intricate paper planes and flicking them across the classroom. His classmates thought he was hysterically clever, but the planes infuriated his *rebbis* and teachers. At times he would quietly build a squadron of tiny planes, set them up on his desk, and one by one propel them on missions all over the classroom.

Nothing that any teacher or principal said to Yaakov had an ef-

* Name has been changed.

fect. He knew the material, he achieved high grades — but planes were taking off and landing on a regular basis. One night in November, there was a parents-teacher conference. Since Yaakov's grandmother could not speak English, his aunt and uncle came from Manhattan to speak to the *rebbi* and teachers.

As they sat with the *rebbi,* he took out a few of the small planes from his desk. "Yaakov is a very bright boy," the *rebbi* began. "He knows the material very well and his mind is as sharp as any I have ever seen for a seventh grader. But he is always playing with these planes. He makes them and shoots them all around the class. I like him and he is a good boy — but he is very disruptive. He won't stop no matter what I say."

The aunt picked up one of the planes and held it up for closer inspection. As she turned the plane slowly examining its intricacy, she began to cry softly and tears rolled down her face.

The *rebbi* was shocked. "What's wrong?" he asked softly.

"My sister taught Yaakov to make these planes when he was a little boy," she said.

Now the *rebbi* understood his orphan student. In Yaakov's uncertain voyage of the future he was clinging to the security of his past.

Do we really know what is going on in another person's mind? It's therefore wise to choose all our words in all our conversations, carefully.

Fathers And Sons

Different Jews are moved at different moments during the yearly High Holidays. For Rabbi Nisson Wolpin, editor of *The Jewish Observer* an inspirational *drashah* (lecture) by a close friend left a memorable impression.

It was *Yom Kippur* eve and the *beis medrash* of Yeshiva Ohr Somayach in Jerusalem was filled to capacity. The institution's faculty and hundreds of young men from around the globe, most of whom had made their voyage from nonobservance to authentic Torah Judaism, had just completed the *Kol Nidrei* service. They settled in their closely crammed seats to listen to an address by one of their *roshei yeshivah*, Rabbi Nachman Bulman.

Rabbi Bulman is a brilliant Torah scholar, a profound thinker, and an emotional orator. He has been a teacher and rabbi in America and Israel for more than 40 years and has a very close relationship with his students. As their mentor and leader, he stepped to the podium in front of the *Aron Hakodesh* to address the assemblage. Wearing his *tallis* and white *kittel*, he looked majestic on this most solemn night of the Jewish calendar.

"There is a very touching scene that takes place in many Jewish homes just before everyone is ready to go to *shul* for the start of *Yom Kippur*," Rabbi Bulman said. "Fathers and mothers gather their children and fervently bless them. This prayer is known as the *Bircas Habonim*, the Blessing of the Children.

"Many of your fathers don't know about this *Yom Kippur* custom. Many of your fathers would not be able to bless you properly from a Torah prospective. Tonight, I will take their place. I will bless each of you, but first I wish to relate a bit of history."

Rabbi Bulman explained that when the Ponevezher Rav, Rabbi Yosef Kahaneman (1886-1969), first opened the Ponevezher Yeshiva in Bnei Brak, he also opened an orphanage, which he called *Battei Avos*. He was asked why he didn't call it *Beis Yesomim*, the standard name for an orphanage. He explained that he wanted both the children and their teachers to focus on the bright future ahead and not on the unfortunate past. "These little boys will eventually be fathers in *Klal Yisrael*," the Ponevezher said. "They will be part of our future. That's why it's called *Battei Avos*, Homes of Fathers, to emphasize their positive future."

"And so tonight," said Rabbi Bulman, "I will bless all of you, but I will not call it *Bircas Habanim,* Blessing of the Children; rather, I will call it *Bircas Ha'avos,* Blessing of the Fathers, for all of you are fathers, in the sense that from you will come new generations of Torah-committed Jews, who will be a pride to all of *Klal Yisrael."*

Part F:

Panoramic Vistas

A View From the Other Side

As one of the *gedolei hador* (Torah luminaries) of his time, the Brisker Rav, Rabbi Yitzchak Zev (Velvel) Soloveitchik (1887-1959), was visited by Jews from around the world seeking his Torah wisdom, advice, and counsel. One day an American gentleman came to Reb Velvel's home in Jerusalem. In the course of their conversation, Reb Velvel asked, "What are you? What is your occupation?"

"I'm a lawyer," he replied.

The conversation continued and a short time later, the Rav asked the gentleman again, "What are you?"

The man was surprised. Just a few moments earlier he had told the Rav that he was a lawyer. Perhaps the Rav wasn't paying attention, the gentleman thought, or maybe he hadn't made himself clear. He therefore repeated slowly and respectfully, "I am a lawyer. I work for a law firm in New York."

The Brisker Rav said sharply, "That is not how a Jew answers such a question! I will tell you how the prophet Yonah answered it.

"When Yonah was on the boat fleeing to Tarshish, and there was a sudden storm and the boat was about to break apart, the sailors cast lots and determined that he was the cause of the storm. They asked him, מַה מְּלַאכְתְּךָ, *'What is your trade?'*(*Yonah* 1:8).

"Yonah replied, עִבְרִי אָנֹכִי וְאֶת ה' אֱלֹקֵי הַשָּׁמַיִם אֲנִי יָרֵא, *'I am a Hebrew and I fear Hashem, the God of the Heavens*(*ibid.* 1:9).'

"That," said the Brisker Rav, "is how a Jew should answer the question. His profession is being a Jew and fearing Hashem is his vocation!"

Similarly, the *Radak* writes, "When Yonah replied, '*I fear Hashem, the God of the Heavens,*' he gave the proper reply to the query 'What is your trade?' (ibid.)"

A Jew is not defined by his job. A Jew is not a lawyer, doctor, graphic artist, diamond dealer, accountant, or real-estate agent. Those occupations are only the means to bring money to his family. The definition of a Jew is עִבְרִי אָנֹכִי וְאֶת ה׳ אֱלֹקֵי הַשָּׁמַיִם אֲנִי יָרֵא, *I am a Hebrew, and I fear Hashem, the God of the Heavens.*

Avraham *Avinu* was the first to be called עִבְרִי, a *Hebrew* (*Bereishis* 14:13). Literally the word means *the other side.* As the Sages teach, Avraham *Avinu* was on one side of a moral and spiritual divide and the rest of the world was on the other (see *Bereishis Rabbah* 42:8). This was Yonah's message to the sailors and the Brisker Rav's point to the New York lawyer, about the essence of Jews.

❁ ❁ ❁

Rav Yissachar Frand, the noted *Maggid Shiur* and lecturer, once told this story to a large audience in Baltimore. Weeks later, a businessman called him and said, "Your story about the Brisker Rav moved me so much that I had a paperweight made for my desk that has two words on it, עִבְרִי אָנֹכִי. I placed it strategically on my desk so that I can see it whenever I am on the phone making my business deals."

When a speaker gets such a response, it makes the hours, days (and sometimes weeks) of preparation well worth it.

Sounds, Smells, and Snakes

Rashi (*Bereishis* 37:25) teaches us that it was not mere coincidence that the Ishmaelites, who bought Yosef from his brothers, had their camels laden with sweet-smelling spices. Normally, Ishmaelite caravans were laden with foul-smelling cargo, such as naphtha and tar, but in order to spare the righteous Yosef from offensive odors, Hashem arranged that their caravan would carry fragrant merchandise.

Dr. Dovid Zalmen Rosenblum, a pediatrician in Monsey, New York, once thought of another reason why Hashem had the Ishmaelites carry incense. *Chazal* teach that the *ketores* (incense) offered on the Inner Altar was an atonement for those who spoke *lashon hara,* or gossip and slander. (See *Arachin* 16a with *Rashi,* and *Yoma* 44a.) Perhaps, Dr. Rosenblum reasoned, Hashem caused Yosef to smell the incense as a reminder of the sin that led to his being sold as a slave. He was guilty of slandering his brothers (see *Rashi, Bereishis* 37:2), thus the incense may have been a stimulus to encourage him to repent.

Dr. Rosenblum mentioned his insight to the Rosh Yeshivah of Ohr Somayach in Monsey, Rabbi Yisroel Simcha Schorr. Rabbi Schorr thought for a moment and then commented, "Perhaps that is why Yosef was thrown by his brothers into a pit where there were נְחָשִׁים (*snakes*) (see *Rashi* ibid. 37:24 and *Shabbos* 22a), for the original snake was guilty of speaking *lashon hara* against Hashem see *Medrash Rabbah, Bereishis* 20:1). Hence another reminder that repentance was in order."

Fascinated by two possible allusions to Yosef's sin of speaking *lashon hara,* the snake and the incense, Dr. Rosenblum shared these thoughts with his younger brother.

"There is a missing piece to the puzzle," said his brother. "Doesn't *Rashi* tell us that there were עַקְרַבִּים, *scorpions,* along with the snakes in the pit where Yosef was thrown? What do the scorpions represent?"

Dr. Rosenblum was perplexed. He was sure that if the incense and snakes symbolized Yosef's sin, then surely the scorpions had to be meaningful as well. But how?

Four days later, Dr. Rosenblum was in his office reading the medical journal, *Pediatric Neurology* (Vol. 17 No. 4). He was startled to read on page 304, that a thirteen-year-old boy suffered mutism (the inability to speak) for close to six months after having sustained a scorpion bite! This condition lasted for months!

Perhaps, then, the presence of the scorpions was another reminder to Yosef of his sin of *lashon hara.* Remarkably, then, there were three allusions to Yosef's sin of *lashon hara.*

❁ ❁ ❁

One *Purim,* I repeated these insights to a group of Yeshivah of Staten Island students, who were visiting homes in Kew Gardens to collect charity. One of them, Yitzchok Kaufman, suggested that perhaps the reason for three separate allusions to Yosef's sin was because he had brought three tales about his brothers to his father. He accused them of a) eating a [detached] limb of a living animal – אֵבֶר מִן הַחַי; b) belittling the sons of Yaakov's secondary wives; and of c) acts of immorality (see *Rashi, Bereishis* 37:2).

> When one studies the Torah, one is described as navigating the יַם הַתַּלְמוּד, *The Sea of The Talmud.* How wondrous it is when a joint expedition includes a wide array of people such as a doctor, a rosh yeshivah, a writer, and a yeshivah student. The results of these joint excursions are at times stirring and sensational.

Effective Prayer

We spend a significant amount of time beseeching Hashem with our prayers. (One who *davens* three times a day recites *Shemoneh Esrei* well over 1,000 times a year!) Many spend a considerable amount of time appealing to Hashem through the recitation of *Tehillim.* (Those who recite the entire *Tehillim* every month recite 1,800 chapters of *Tehillim* a year.) There are groups of people who divide the entire *Tehillim* into segments; each member recites the assigned chapters every day, and in this manner the full group recites the entire *Tehillim* daily!

We pray for health, financial security, peace in the world, peace within our families, and *nachas* from children. Yet we hear and witness degrees of pain and anguish that are staggering: young fathers passing away prematurely, leaving behind widows and orphans; children of religious families rejecting the lifestyle of their parents; unprecedented divorce rates; debilitating illnesses, oppressive financial hardship. The list of woes and tragedies seems endless.

Why does it seem at times that Hashem is not answering the *tefillos* of so many in *Klal Yisrael*? Is there anything wrong with the way we pray? Are our prayers insincere? Can we improve the chance of our prayers being answered?

A Talmudic episode regarding Rabbi Akiva and a parable by the Chofetz Chaim shed light on things we should and should not be doing, even before we open the *siddur* or *Tehillim,* so that we can hope for favorable and gratifying results.

❁ ❁ ❁

The Talmud (*Taanis* 25b) tells of a winter in Israel when there was no rain. If the drought continued, the crops would not grow, resulting in hunger and starvation. The leaders of the community asked Rabbi Eliezer to pray for rain. He did, but to no avail.

They then approached Rabbi Akiva and he formulated the אָבִינוּ מַלְכֵּנוּ, *Our Father, our King,* prayer. The rains came. When people saw how Rabbi Akiva's prayer was answered and Rabbi Eliezer's was not, they murmured that Rabbi Eliezer was not as righteous as they had thought. A בַּת קוֹל, *Heavenly voice,* came forth and declared: לֹא מִפְּנֵי שֶׁזֶּה גָּדוֹל מִזֶּה, אֶלָּא שֶׁזֶּה מַעֲבִיר עַל מִדּוֹתָיו וְזֶה אֵינוֹ מַעֲבִיר עַל מִדּוֹתָיו, *Not because this one [Rabbi Akiva] is greater than the other [Rabbi Eliezer], but because this one [Rabbi Akiva] is a forgiving person and this one is not a forgiving person*).

Rashi (*Rosh Hashanah* 17a) defines "a forgiving person" as one who does not retaliate against those who have wronged him. He is willing to "look away."

No one is perfect. We each want Hashem to "look away" from our sins, particularly when we beseech Him in prayer. If we are forgiving and are willing to "look away" when others are unkind to us, then Hashem, in turn, will overlook the inappropriate way we have acted towards Him. Then, our prayers, like Rabbi Akiva's, are more likely to be answered. (See *Rosh Hashana* 17a.)

The Chofetz Chaim (*Shemiras Halashon: Shaar Hazechirah,* Chap. 10) writes that when one prays or learns Torah, his words create Holy Angels that go to Heaven and appear before Hashem, on his behalf. The Chofetz Chaim compares the creation of these angels to building a piece of furniture. If one is equipped with inferior tools, such as a saw without teeth or a hammer without a handle, then it is nearly impossible to build a perfect table or chair.

The Chofetz Chaim writes that if one speaks *lashon hara,* lies, ridicules, speaks words that pain others or says things that cause arguments, then he has spiritually crippled his mouth and it becomes an inferior tool, with which it is nearly impossible to create perfect Heavenly angels to carry his words towards Heaven. His prayers, then, are imperfect and stand much less of a chance of being answered.

Thus there is much to be done before one even begins to pray. One must see to it that he becomes a forgiving person, able to overlook the personal slights of others. Additionally one must be sure, through all aspects of *shemiras halashon* that his mouth is a perfect instrument with which to pray.

If we can only learn the message inherent in the Talmudic episode and the parable, our words of prayer would undoubtedly be more effective.

Perhaps that is why immediately after we recite *Shemoneh Esrei,* we say, אֱלֹקַי, נְצוֹר לְשׁוֹנִי מֵרָע וּשְׂפָתַי מִדַּבֵּר מִרְמָה, *My God, guard my tongue from evil and my lips from speaking deceitfully.* We ask

Hashem for assistance in *shemiras halashon*, so that our mouths become perfect implements for *tefillah*. Then we say, וְלִמְקַלְלַי נַפְשִׁי תִדּוֹם, *And to those that curse me, let my soul be silent*, a prayer that we become forgiving people, of being מַעֲבִיר עַל מִדּוֹתָיו.

Suitable Reasoning

On the second day of *Chol Hamoed Succos* of 1996, eight-year-old Masha Miriam Silbergleit's soul returned to Heaven. She had been in the New York Hospital Cornell Medical Center Burn Unit for more than two months after having been trapped in a fire that consumed her Queens, New York home in midsummer. With her passing, Masha Miriam joined her youngest sister, Chana Bayla, and their grandmother, Mrs. Leona Rosen, who too lost their lives because of that raging summer inferno.

The tragedy was indescribable, the pain and the anguish unbearable. At Masha Miriam's funeral, since it was during *Succos*, eulogies were forbidden (see *O.C.* 547:1 and *Y.D.* 401); however, words of encouragement and inspiration to the assemblage were offered by numerous rabbanim.

It was in this vein that Rabbi Aryeh Ginzberg of Hillcrest, New York, whose daughter was a classmate of Masha Miriam, addressed the somber crowd.

Rabbi Ginzberg referred to the moving *piyut* (liturgical poem) *Eileh Ezkerah* (These I shall remember), recited during the *Yom Kippur Mussaf*, which details the horrifying martyrdom of the *Assarah Harugei Malchus*, the ten *Tannaim* who were tortured and murdered by the Romans. He recounted the unusual dialogue between Hashem and the angels, as Rabbi Yishmael the *Kohen Gadol* was tortured to death.

"Is this the Torah and this its reward?" the celestial angels cried out bitterly.

A voice from Heaven responded, "If I hear another sound [of complaint] I will transform the universe to water."

"The Heavenly reply to the angels' query seems puzzling,"

noted Rabbi Ginzberg. "The angels asked a legitimate question, but were not given an answer. Some explain the Heavenly reply with the following parable:

There was once a prominent anti-Semitic government official who wished to have an exquisite suit made for himself. He purchased the finest material for an exorbitant amount of money, and searched for the finest tailor in the area. To his dismay, all agreed that the best tailor was a Jew! It galled the official to award a Jew with the prestigious task of making a suit for him — especially such a special one — but reluctantly he commissioned him anyway, for he had been assured that no tailor could match the Jew's handiwork.

After a few weeks of measuring, cutting, sewing, fitting, and altering, the job was done. The tailor delivered the suit to the official. He put it on and admired himself in the mirror. Even he, despite his loathing of Jews, had to admit that the suit was a masterpiece. It fit perfectly and, indeed, it enhanced his image.

However, when the wife of the official, who despised Jews even more than her husband did, saw the suit, she laughed derisively and exclaimed to her startled husband,"That Jew made a fool of you. Don't you see what he did? He took your expensive material, cut off large sections of it for himself, and sold them for an enormous profit. Then, he made you your suit with the remnants!"

The official became enraged. The suit *did* appear to be smaller than the total amount of material he had given the tailor. The next morning he summoned the unsuspecting tailor to his office and roared, "You are a thief! You took all my expensive material and used only a small portion to make the suit. You took the rest and made a profit from it."

"That's not true!" retorted the incredulous tailor. "I used all the material you gave me for your suit."

The official insisted that the tailor was lying and nothing could convince him otherwise. Finally, the tailor took the suit from the official and began cutting it apart. "What are you doing?" shouted the shocked official.

"Wait, and you will see," said the tailor. The official tried to stop the tailor, but the tailor fought him off and said, "Be patient, and soon you will understand everything."

The tailor took apart the pockets and laid the flaps on a table. He undid the lining of the suit and laid it alongside the pockets. He separated the cuffs. He took apart the lapels. He opened every stitch he had sewn on the suit.

Finally when the suit was totally taken apart, the tailor turned to the official and said, "Now measure the pieces separately and you will see that all the material is there, just as I told you. Now you understand how a suit is put together from the start."

"And that was exactly the intention of the Heavenly reply to the angels who complained about Rabbi Yishmael's torture," explained Rabbi Ginzberg. "The Torah (*Bereishis* 1:2, see also *Chagigah* 12a) says that at the beginning of Creation, the world was filled with water. From that point on, Hashem created everything in the universe. Thus Hashem was saying to the angels, 'From your vantage point, you cannot possibly understand my design for the world. The only way you could comprehend my plan would be to view the world as it was in the beginning — when it was filled with water.' "

[In a similar vein, Hashem said to Iyov ,אֵיפֹה הָיִיתָ בְּיָסְדִי אָרֶץ, הַגֵּד אִם יָדַעְתָּ בִינָה, *"Where were you when I laid the foundations for the earth? Pray tell if you are so wise "(Iyov* 38:4).]

Rabbi Ginzberg looked out at the crowd that had gathered to bid farewell to little Masha Miriam and said, "We too cannot understand Hashem's plan and design for this world. It is beyond our comprehension. But as Jews of faith, we know that there is a Master Plan. One day, when Mashiach comes, we will be privileged to understand it."

A Sticky Issue

Chazal teach, מָקוֹם שֶׁבַּעֲלֵי תְשׁוּבָה עוֹמְדִין שָׁם צַדִּיקִים אֵינָן עוֹמְדִין שָׁם, *In the place where penitents stand, even the righteous cannot stand* (*Sanhedrin* 99a). The level of penitents is so exalted because it is harder for them to control their evil inclination than it is for the [perfectly] righteous who never became accustomed to sin (*Rambam, Hilchos Teshuvah* 7:4).

The word עוֹמְדִין in the aforementioned phrase is usually translated as *stand.* However, it can also mean *comprehend* or *realize,* as in the expression, אֵין אָדָם עוֹמֵד עַל סוֹף דַעְתּוֹ שֶׁל רַבּוֹ ... עַד אַרְבָּעִים שָׁנָה, *A person does not fully comprehend his teacher's ways of thinking...until 40 years later* (see *Rashi, Devarim* 29:6). In this context, the teaching regarding penitents and the righteous can be understood to mean that the ideas that a penitent comprehends, because he does things with a questing and probing mind, do not occur to the righteous, because they may at times perform *mitzvos* out of habit.

The following incident is a case in point.

Before *Yom Tov,* Reuvain Relnick* bought a number of pots and pans for his wife Brachah. Reuvain was told that before these utensils could be used, they had to be immersed in a *mikveh.*

He was cautioned to be careful to remove all labels from the pots and pans before immersion; otherwise they would constitute a חֲצִיצָה, *barrier,* not allowing the water of the *mikveh* to come in contact with every part of the utensil.

Reuvain went to the *mikveh* and diligently removed the various labels before the immersion. He immersed the pots and pans carefully and afterwards made a remarkable observation.

"The labels on the pots were not hard to remove," he said. "The glue under the labels remained stuck to the pot — that was difficult to remove. It occurred to me that in a sense, this is like man's relationship to Hashem regarding his sins. When a person sins, he creates a *barrier* between himself and Hashem. At times, however, it is the 'glue' of the sin — its long-term effect that remains with the individual — that can be worse than the sin itself. For when one sins, he has not only tainted his soul with impurity and embedded the memory of that transgressive act in his sub-

*The name has been changed.

conscious, but he has also lowered his level of resistance the next time the opportunity of this sin confronts him. עָבַר אָדָם עֲבֵירָה וְשָׁנָה בָּהּ ... נַעֲשֵׂית לוֹ כְּהֶיתֵּר, *Once a person commits a transgression and repeats his wrongdoing, the deed seems permissible to him* (see *Yoma* 86b).

There is the חִיצוֹנִיּוּת, *exterior* element of a transgression (the label), and the פְּנִימִיּוּת, *internal* element of a transgression (the glue). While it takes a determined effort to repent and refrain from committing a particular sinful deed, it is perhaps more difficult to rid oneself of the "glue" — the effect — of that sin.

> Perhaps that is why on *Yom Kippur,* we repeat the following verse numerous times, בַּיּוֹם הַזֶּה יְכַפֵּר עֲלֵיכֶם לְטַהֵר אֶתְכֶם מִכֹּל חַטֹּאתֵיכֶם לִפְנֵי ה׳ תִּטְהָרוּ, *For on this day he [the Kohen Gadol — High Priest] shall provide atonement for you to cleanse you; from all your sins before Hashem shall you be cleansed* (*Vayikra* 16:30).
>
> יְכַפֵּר עֲלֵיכֶם, *atonement for you,* refers to atonement for the sin itself, and לְטַהֵר אֶתְכֶם, *to cleanse you,* refers to the cleansing of the effect of the sin.

Visions From on High

The brilliance of Rabbi Yitzchok Hutner (1904-1980) was legendary. The original thoughts that emanated from his creative mind astounded even his closest *talmidim*. Among his many talents, Rabbi Hutner could take a phrase from *Tanach* or *Chazal* and ingeniously give it new interpretation. In a moving audiobiography on Rabbi Hutner, Rabbi Pinchas Stolper of the Orthodox Union cited three remarkable examples of this ability.

A few days before Rabbi Hutner passed away, he was in a hospital in Jerusalem. One afternoon, an attending nurse came into his room and inquired, כְּבוֹד הָרַב, אַתָּה בְּנֹחַ?, *Honored rabbi, are you comfortable?*

In a play on words on the order of the weekly Torah readings, Rabbi Hutner, who understood the seriousness of his illness, replied sadly but wisely, "אֲנִי כְּבָר בְּ״לֶךְ לְךָ״, *I am already on my trip [to the Eternal World]."*

❁ ❁ ❁

Rabbi Hutner remained close to his *talmidim* long after they left his yeshivah and corresponded with many of them, giving them guidance and offering encouragement. More than 200 of his letters were published in 1981, under the title *Pachad Yitchok, Igros U'ksavim*.

In letter 94, Rabbi Hutner addresses a *talmid* who was troubled by his own double standard of behavior. The *talmid* was concerned that in his private life he was behaving according to one set of rules, but in pursuit of his business career, he was acting in ways incongruous to his private life.

After complimenting the *talmid* for eloquently expressing the pain in his soul, Rabbi Hutner wrote emphatically that at no time would he ever acquiesce to anyone living a "double life." The Rosh Yeshivah explained that all aspects of a person's life, be it his personal activities or business activities, must be synchronized so that they are a fusion of the same outlook on life.

Rabbi Hutner added, "If a person rents a room in one house and at the same time rents a room in another house, that person is indeed leading a double life. However, if a person has two rooms in the same house, that is merely a broad life."

Rabbi Hutner described how the renowned Dr. Moshe Wallach (1866-1957), founder and director of the Shaare Zedek hospital in Jerusalem, visited a patient just before an operation. Dr. Wallach asked the man for his mother's Hebrew name so that he could pray for him during the surgery. (When praying for the sick, one uses the patient's Hebrew name and his mother's Hebrew name.)

"Is that a double life?" asked the Rosh Yeshivah. Dr. Wallach's blend of prayer with practical medicine was merely the conduct of a remarkable individual encompassing both fields in his own consistent person.

Cleverly employing a statement of the Sages (*Berachos* 13b), which discusses the virtue of extending the recitation of the word אֶחָד in the first verse of the *Shema*, Rabbi Hutner used the words of the Talmud to assure his student: כָּל הַמַּאֲרִיךְ בְּ״אֶחָד״ מַאֲרִיכִין לוֹ יָמָיו וּשְׁנוֹתָיו (*Whoever extends the oneness in his life* [acting similarly in personal and business matters] *will be blessed with length of days and years.*)

* * *

Chol HaMoed (the Intermediate Days of the festival *Succos*) gatherings in Rabbi Hutner's *succah* were unforgettable moments of spiritual ecstasy for those fortunate to attend. In a tender, touching letter (no. 101) to a former *talmid*, Rabbi Hutner reminisces about a *Simchas Beis HaShoeivah* gathering in a *succah* "atop a high building, distant and apart from the people below."

[The reference was to the building of Yeshivah Rabbi Chaim Berlin in Brownsville, where Rabbi Hutner made his home during *Pesach* and *Succos*.]

The Rosh Yeshivah recalled how lilting, majestic music flowed from a violin and from the cluster of voices of *talmidim* that fused in the singing of King David's impassioned appeal to Hashem, אַחַת שָׁאַלְתִּי מֵאֵת ה׳, אוֹתָהּ אֲבַקֵּשׁ — שִׁבְתִּי בְּבֵית ה׳ כָּל יְמֵי חַיַּי, *One thing I asked of Hashem, that shall I seek — that I dwell in the House of Hashem all the days of my life"* (*Tehillim* 27:4).

Rav Hutner recalled that as the singing continued, tears flowed freely down the face of this particular *talmid*. With loving kindness, the Rosh Yeshivah caressed the *talmid's* cheek. "I had seen tears on your face numerous times before that," wrote the Rosh Yeshivah, "but those times they were tears of remorse and sadness over your plight in life. That night in the *succah*, however, your tears were different. Just as the celebration of the *Simchas Beis HaShoeivah* was accomplished by drawing water from a spring, your tears that night were drawn from the river of your soul.

"And as those tears streamed down your cheeks, they transformed the עוֹר, *skin,* of your face to an אוֹר, *light,* of sanctity. Never before had I witnessed the concrete manifestation of the Talmudic teaching that א' וע' מִתְחַלְּפִים *the letters Aleph and Ayin are interchangeable."*(See *Berachos* 32a and *Rashi* in *Megillah* 24b, also *Bereishis Rabbah* 20:12.)

Poetic, lyrical, and regal. That was how Rabbi Hutner saw the world, and how he saw the words of *Tanach* and *Chazal.*

Future Song

On a plane trip from Switzerland to Israel I had the opportunity to meet Reb Mendel Yaakov, a professional *badchan* from Bnei Brak. The literal meaning of the word *badchan* is jester, but at Chassidic weddings the *badchan* is more than a mere comedian.

Before the *chupah,* the *badchan* performs at the *chassan's* reception and exhorts the *chassan* and assembled guests to appreciate the seriousness of marriage. Citing Talmudic and Chassidic teachings along with family history and parables, play on words, and *gematrias* (numerical formulations), the *badchan* sings his "sermon" in clever rhymes, creates a mood of reverence as the *chassan* is primed to be marched to the *chupah.*

At a wedding where the *chassan* and the *kallah* were orphans, Reb Mendel Yaakov sang and rhymed the following story.

❁ ❁ ❁

When the Belzer Rebbe, Rabbi Aaron Rokeach (1880-1957), came from Europe to Haifa, Israel, in 1944, he assembled a cluster of *chassidim* to join him Friday night for his first *seudas Shabbos* (Sabbath meal) in Israel.

The Torah reading of that Shabbos was *Beshalach,* and the day is known as *Shabbos Shirah* (the Shabbos of Song), because the *sidrah* contains the שִׁירַת הַיָּם, *The Song at the Sea,* in which Moshe led Israel in praise of God for the Splitting of the Sea.

At the meal, the Rebbe expounded on the *parashah* and said, "The words אָז יָשִׁיר מֹשֶׁה, literally mean *Then he, Moshe, will sing,*" in the future tense. When would this song be sung? It was *his* generation that was obligated to praise Hashem for redeeming them from Egypt and leading them safely through the Sea of Reeds.

"*Rashi* (*Shemos* 16:1) cites a Midrashic interpretation that Moshe *Rabbeinu* was referring to the era of תְּחִיַּת הַמֵּתִים, *the resurrection of the dead.* Then, all Jews will sing songs of praise. But, the Belzer Rebbe asked, "Why refer to a song of the future? The Jews who left Egypt had already seen enough miracles to evoke songs of praise.

"The answer is," said the Rebbe, "that so many Jews perished during the plague of חֹשֶׁךְ, *darkness* (see *Rashi, Shemos* 13:18). Surely the survivors had relatives and friends who perished. Moshe *Rabbeinu* understood their dilemma; how could they sing a song of gratitude when much sadness prevailed?

"Therefore Moshe told them, 'Don't worry, there will come a time when we will all be reunited with those who perished, and therefore we can sing praise today for our survival.'"

The Rebbe then addressed the assembled and said, "We have survived the onslaught of the Nazis, *yemach shemam* (may their name be erased), and have come to the holy land of *Eretz Yisrael.* Surely we remember our many family members who perished in the last few years under horrible conditions. However, someday in the future we shall be reunited with them at תְּחִיַּת הַמֵּתִים, *the resurrection of the dead.* Thus today we, like the people at the Sea of Reeds, can sing songs of praise to Hashem."

The guests at the wedding understood the *badchan's* sobering message. True, the *chassan* and *kallah* were orphans, but one day they would be reunited with their parents and thus, even now, their wedding day could be one of joy.

Advice on an Adversary

Great men hear and see the same things we do but their wisdom enables them to interpret events with innovative insight. A case in point is the interpretation of the Dubno Maggid, R' Yaakov Krantz (1740-1804), of the famous answer that the Talmudic sage Hillel gave to a gentile who came to convert to Judaism (*Shabbos* 31a).

The gentile said that he would convert if he could be taught all of Torah while standing on one leg. He wanted to hear a fundamental principle on which the Torah's ideals were based.

Hillel told him, דַּעֲלָךְ סְנֵי, לְחַבְרָךְ לֹא תַעֲבִיד *That which is hateful to you, do not do to your friend.* זוֹ הִיא כָּל הַתּוֹרָה כּוּלָּהּ, *This [summarizes] the entire Torah;* וְאִידָךְ פֵּירוּשָׁהּ הוּא, *the rest is an elaboration,* זִיל גְּמוֹר *go and learn it.*

The Dubno Maggid (*Sefer Ohel Yaakov, Parashas Kedoshim*) used a parable to give us a new understanding of Hillel's reply to the convert.

A young boy suddenly lost both parents and inherited a large sum of money. Realizing that he had no business training or experience, he asked his uncle for financial advice. "You have come to the right place," his uncle assured him. "I will invest the money for you and together we shall make a very big profit."

The trusting youngster readily agreed, and went home confident that he was in good hands. The uncle invested the money carelessly, however, and lost much of his nephew's wealth. But that was not all. When a venture went sour, he told his nephew that his losses were significant, and when there was a profit he kept the money for himself. Realizing that his money was dwindling, the nephew went to the town rabbi and apprised him of his unfortunate situation. "I don't know what to say to my uncle."

"At this point, it is useless for me to give you advice," said the rabbi. "Whatever I tell you will be refuted by your uncle. You, in your innocence, believe that he is your friend and that he has your best interests at heart. Nothing is further from the truth. He is your enemy! He saw an opportunity to get wealthy and took advantage of you. You must first acknowledge that he is your foe and not your friend. Then I can advise you."

The Dubno Maggid explains that this is the relationship between man and his *Yetzer Hara* (*Evil Inclination*). The *Yetzer Hara's* role is to convince man that by sinning he will achieve success and happiness. And even if man realizes that these acts are forbidden, the *Yetzer Hara* convinces him Hashem will surely forgive him. On the surface, it seems to be the advice of a friend. In reality, though, the *Yetzer Horah* is the enemy whose only goal is man's spiritual ruination. Nevertheless, man's twisted logic misguides him to mistaken perceptions.

This is what Hillel suggested to the convert, says the Dubno Maggid. "דַּעֲלָךְ סְנֵי (*The one who hates you,* i.e., your Evil Inclination), לְחַבְרָךְ לֹא תַעֲבִיד (*don't make your friend*). The rest of Torah is an elaboration on that central point."

No Change in the Custom

There is an expression מִנְהַג אֲבוֹתֵינוּ תּוֹרָה הִיא, *A custom of our forefathers is [recognized as] Torah* (*see Menachos* 20b, *Tosafos* ד"ה נפסל). Jewish customs that have continued for generations usually have a sound origin. The following is a good example of a little-known reason for a popular custom.

Rabbi Eliyahu Weisfish, author of the popular *sefarim Arbaah Minim* and *HaSuccah,* told me that when he was growing up in *Eretz Yisrael,* it was customary that children were given Chanukah *gelt* (money) specifically on the fifth day of *Chanukah.*

Rabbi Weisfish never knew why the fifth day was designated until he recently heard that when the Steipler Gaon, Rabbi Yaakov Yisrael Kanievsky (1899-1985), gave his son Rav Chaim *Chanukah gelt* for his children and grandchildren, Rav Chaim asked his father why everyone did this on the fifth day. The Steipler replied, "Because it's the only day of *Chanukah* that can never come out on Shabbos!"

Chanukah never starts on Monday night, thus by designating the fifth night for dispensing *Chanukah gelt* there would be no chance for *chilul* (violation of) Shabbos when money is *muktzah* and forbidden to be moved.

A Superficial Scope

As Yirmiyahu *Hanavi* described the saddened and forlorn city of Jerusalem following the destruction of the first *Beis Hamikdash,* he said, לוּא אֲלֵיכֶם כָּל עֹבְרֵי דֶרֶךְ, *May it not befall you — all who pass by this road* (*Eichah* 1:12).

The Sages understand from this verse that when one recounts his misfortune to another, one should add, "May my misfortune never befall you." (Since Yirmiyahu uses such an expression when speaking to the passerby, we learn that the custom is appropriate and not superstitious. See *Sanhedrin* 104b.) This is the origin of the expression לֹא אֲלֵיכֶם, *It should not happen to you,* and לֹא עָלֵינוּ *It shouldn't happen to us,* when discussing misfortunes.)

The Dubno Maggid, Rabbi Yaakov Krantz (1740-1804), gives additional meaning to Yirmiyahu's expression with the following parable. (See *Pardes Yosef, Parashas Acharei.)*

A very wealthy man had a spendthrift son. He had no regard for money and constantly squandered his father's funds. Concerned that his wayward son would deplete his assets, the father took all the money he had, and buried it in a secret place under his house, with the intent of recovering it when the son came to his senses.

A while later, a ghastly fire burned down the father's entire home. He was devastated because the fire had consumed the money as well. When people saw how forlorn the father was, they said to him, "Why are you so upset? You are so rich; with the money you have you can easily replace the house and all the furnishings."

"You don't understand," replied the father sadly. "You see only the house that burned, but you have no idea of the depth of the tragedy. My money is gone, for the fire consumed it all, because it was all buried beneath the house."

This, said the Dubno Maggid, is what Yirmiyahu *Hanavi* said to the passersby. לוֹא אֲלֵיכֶם, *It is not for you* to be able to comprehend the depth of our loss. "All of you view Jerusalem as a city like other cities, albeit a very beautiful city. But it is much more than a city of beautiful architecture with panoramic views of the surrounding mountains. It is a city from which Torah emanates, a city of inspirational holiness. This is something only we can mourn."

> We who understand the extent of the destruction of Jerusalem pray for its ultimate redemption and rebuilding. May it indeed speedily come in our day.

A Vintage Whine

> On the first day of *Selichos,* September 28, 1997, more than 70,000 Jews gathered in various arenas and auditoriums throughout the United States and Canada to commemorate the 10th Siyum HaShas of Daf Yomi.
>
> At the gathering in Toronto, Rabbi Aaron Dovid Dunner, of Kehillas Chareidim in London, set the tone for the upcoming days of *Rosh Hashanah* and the *Asseres Yemei Teshuvah* with a parable first told by Rav Yosef of Turtshin (1782-1818), son of the famous *Chozeh* of Lublin, Rav Yaakov Yitzchak Horowitz (1745-1815).

In Lublin there was a very wealthy magnate who had a lavish wine cellar. Vats, barrels, and bottles of vintage wines and liqueurs filled the shelves and floor space in his huge cellar under his mansion.

One day a prominent rabbi came to visit him. To honor his guest, the magnate sent his butler to bring some very fine wine from a barrel in the back of the cellar.

The butler dutifully went down to the cellar. When he did not return after five minutes, his master wondered what was taking so long. When he did not return after ten minutes, the master began to worry.

The master excused himself and went down to the wine cellar to investigate. When he opened the door he was shocked! Broken bottles were strewn all over. Barrels had been opened and wine was flowing onto the floor. Barrels of vintage wines were cracked and leaking. It was obviously the work of the deranged butler.

The master was horrified at the destruction he beheld. Frantically he began looking for the butler. He ran through the cellar but could not find him. He ran upstairs and searched the rooms of the house until he came to the parlor where, to his dismay, he saw the butler sitting in an armchair calmly reading a newspaper.

Before the rich man could say a word, the butler looked up nonchalantly and said, "I'm so glad you are here, sir. I would like to discuss an increase in salary for the new year."

The millionaire was enraged. Under such conditions the butler had the audacity to ask for a raise!

Rav Yosef Turtshiner asked: Aren't we all like that butler?

When *Rosh Hashanah* arrives, Hashem comes close to us and waits for us to speak to him. As the Sages teach, the verse דִּרְשׁוּ ה׳ בְּהִמָּצְאוֹ, קְרָאֻהוּ בִּהְיוֹתוֹ קָרוֹב, *Seek Hashem when He can be found, call upon Him when he is near"* (*Yeshayah* 55:6), refers to the ten days between *Rosh Hashanah* and *Yom Kippur* (see *Rosh Hashanah* 18a).

Hashem wants us to make a reckoning of the previous year, so that we repent. We ruined opportunities of giving charity, we squandered chances of performing *mitzvos*, we wasted time that should have been used for Torah study, we destroyed the reputations of others by slander and devious schemes — but instead of feeling remorse, we have the audacity to ask Hashem, אָבִינוּ מַלְכֵּנוּ כָּתְבֵנוּ בְּסֵפֶר פַּרְנָסָה וְכַלְכָּלָה, *Our Father, our King, inscribe us in the book of sustenance and support.*

Even more, says Rav Yosef Turtshiner, we ask to be inscribed בְּסֵפֶר חַיִּים בְּרָכָה וְשָׁלוֹם וּפַרְנָסָה טוֹבָה, *In the book of life, blessing, and peace and good livelihood....* We want a raise! We want פַּרְנָסָה טוֹבָה!

Are we not then like the butler?

❁ ❁ ❁

"However," added Rabbi Dunner, "if we have spent more time learning, if this year we increased our *chessed,* performed *mitzvos* with more alacrity, gave *tzedakah* with more enthusiasm, helped people more than we did in the year before, then indeed we have the right to ask for פַּרְנָסָה טוֹבָה, a bit more than we had the previous year."

Siberian Spat

Rav Shmuel Tyri, a *Maggid Shiur* in Yeshivas Rishon LeZion, Israel, recently recalled a delightful parable and powerful message he heard many years ago from his Rosh Yeshivah, Rabbi Chaim Meir Rovman of Yeshivas Tiferes Yisrael in Haifa.

One winter, a father and son living in the frozen tundras of Sibera got into an argument. There was only one warm coat available in their home, and the father felt that he was entitled to wear it. "I am an old man," he complained. "I am frail and freezing in this house. If I don't wear the coat I will die."

The son countered, "I am out working in the field where the wind is howling and I must be protected. I am the one supporting the family. It is only proper that I should have the coat to wear."

The father and son could not come to an amicable solution so they decided to let their rav rule on the situation. The rav listened with astonishment to their selfish arguments and said, "I have never seen or heard of such a quarrel about a coat between a father and son. I need two days to think about it. Please come back then."

On the way home the father began thinking, "My son is right. He is out in the cold where the winds are terrible. He is more susceptible to getting sick. I am living off the money he earns. He should have the coat."

At the same time the son was thinking, "My father is the one who deserves the coat. He raised me all these years. I owe him so much. I am younger and stronger. I'll figure out a way to stay warm. Maybe I can build a fire at the worksite."

Two days later when they returned to the rav, the father and son explained that they were now having a different argument, as each one was insisting that the other have the benefit of the coat.

When the rav heard their new dispute, he told them to wait a moment because he had to go into a back room. He returned with a heavy fur coat. "Here," he said. "One of you can use this coat; the other will have the coat you have at home. Now both of you will be warm."

The father and son thanked the rav profusely for his generosity. After a few minutes though, the son said to the rav, "I hope you don't mind my asking, but if you had this coat, why didn't you give it to us two days ago, when we first came to you?"

The rav smiled and said, "When you came here two days ago and each of you was claiming, 'I need the coat, I can't manage without it,' I thought about my own coat and said to myself, 'I too need my coat. I can't manage without it.'

"But now that you each say, 'I can do without the coat. Let the other person have it,' I, too, say to myself, 'I can manage without the coat. Let another person have it.' "

❁ ❁ ❁

David *HaMelech* teaches, ה׳ צִלְּךָ, *Hashem is your shadow* (*Tehillim* 121:15), meaning that Hashem acts toward people the way they act to others. Hashem uses a man's own behavior as a guideline for His actions toward that person.

Hashem proclaims, לִי הַכֶּסֶף וְלִי הַזָּהָב, *The silver is mine and the gold is mine* (*Chaggai* 2:8). Hashem can therefore choose to dispense money and material wealth to whomever He wishes (See *Rashi* ibid.). Thus if one is tight fisted and refrains from giving charity or sharing his bounty with others, Hashem, in turn, will eventually withhold His generosity from him. However if one is caring and good and shares his bounty with others, Hashem will bestow prosperity and good fortune upon him and his family. As the *Mishnah* teaches in (*Sotah* 8b), בְּמִדָּה שֶׁאָדָם מוֹדֵד בָּהּ מוֹדְדִין לוֹ, *With the measure that man measures [others], so he is measured.*

A Check on Money

Shlomo *HaMelech* warns us about an inescapable fact, הַכֶּסֶף יַעֲנֶה אֶת הַכֹּל, *Money is the resolution of everything (Koheles* 10:19). *Rashi* comments, "If there is no money, there is no meal, therefore a man should not be lazy, but [rather] work so that he can have [funds] for expenses." *Rashi* is counseling us not to be neglectfully idle, for if we have no money, we won't be able to provide food, clothing, and shelter for our families, and pay tuition or wedding expenses for our children.

Regrettably, even our greatest leaders had to humble themselves and raise money for their Torah and *chessed* institutions. Someone once gave the Satmar Rebbe, Rabbi Yoel Teitelbaum (1887-1979) $47 for the benefit of one of his many institutions. The Rebbe asked the gentleman, "Is there any significance to the figure 47?"

The man replied, "It is *b'gematria* (the numerical equivalent) of the Rebbe's name [י(10) + ו(6) + א(1) + ל(30) = 47)."

The Rebbe retorted in Yiddish, *"In der heim flegt mehn mich reefen Yoelish [יואליש] (In the old country they used to call me Yoelish)."* The extra two letters added $310 to the man's donation (י(10) + ש(300) = 310).

✿ ✿ ✿

It is said that the Ponevezher Rav, Rabbi Yosef Kahaneman (1886-1969), a master builder of Torah institutions, was once offered a large sum of money by a non-religious Jew to build a school where none of the students wear yarmulkes. The Rav immediately agreed to the condition and said he would build a religious girls school!

The gentleman was so impressed by the Rav's wit, warmth, and wisdom that he gave the money anyway.

❁ ❁ ❁

Though funds are essential, the *Kli Yakar,* with imaginative insight, provides us with the appropriate perspective towards money.

When Avraham sought a wife for his son Yitzchak, he summoned his servant, Eliezer, הַמֹּשֵׁל בְּכָל אֲשֶׁר לוֹ, *who controlled all that was his* (*Bereishis* 24:2). This is generally understood to mean that Eliezer was the administrator of Avraham's possessions.

The *Kli Yakar* (ibid.) suggests that the word לוֹ, *his,* is referring back to Eliezer. Eliezer ruled over all that was his, i.e., he controlled his money; his money didn't control him. He was not obsessed by money nor did he pursue riches relentlessly. The *Kli Yakar* writes, "This was why Avraham trusted Eliezer, for he knew that the lust for money would not cause him to act inappropriately."

❁ ❁ ❁

When Rav Avrohom Pam, the Rosh Yeshivah of Yeshivah Torah Vodaath in Brooklyn, gives his weekly talk on the *parashah* he often quotes this *Kli Yakar* during the week of *Parashas Chayei Sarah.* He stresses that people involved in *shidduchin* — the *shadchan,* the parents, and the young man and woman — must all have the proper perspective regarding money. Too often the issue of money is given undue priority and preference. Money does not guarantee happiness.

> In other words, a young man who marries a girl for her bank account will eventually lose interest!

The Man and the Mountain

One of the greatest *askanim* (communal leaders) of our time was Rabbi Moshe Sherer (1921-1998), who served as president of Agudath Israel of America for more than 30 years. Rabbi Sherer dutifully attended to *Klal Yisrael* and *Reb Yisrael*, representing the Jewish nation in the highest echelons of government while simultaneously benefiting the individual Jew who needed his intervention, encouragement, and warm smile.

Rabbi Sherer was a faithful servant to the *gedolei Torah* whose guidance he constantly sought. His scope was global, his integrity absolute, and his appearance impeccable and distinguished. In his presence, people felt more important about themselves. He was revered and admired by thousands.

In May 1998 as Rabbi Sherer lay in his hospital bed in New York with his final illness, he was struggling to stay alive long enough to attend Agudath Israel's 76th Annual Dinner. Two weeks before the dinner, his doctors assured him he was improving and there was a good chance that he would be able to attend.

Immediately he wrote notes for a speech he planned to deliver at the dinner. His speeches were always eloquent, emotional, and inspirational. This time would surely be no different. His failing health, obvious to all, would make his message even more memorable. Unquestionably he understood that.

Tragically, he passed away the morning of the dinner and the words he prepared seemed destined to remain unspoken and unknown, as they lay scrawled on a crumpled sheet of paper in a cabinet drawer next to his bed. After the week of *shivah*, however, when his son Rav Shimshon was going through his father's belongings, he found the sheet with his father's words written in a quivering and unsteady script.

In the first weeks after his father's passing, Rav Shimshon delivered eulogies for his father around the country. There was so much to say and so little time in which to say it. Rav Shimshon never had the opportunity to mention his father's prepared thoughts for the dinner.

As the *shloshim* (30-day) period approached, tributes and memorials were planned in many communities throughout America, and in every Agudath Israel *shul.* In an act of kindness and generosity that I will always remember, Rav Shimshon faxed me his father's notes so I could use them in a tribute to Rabbi Sherer, which I was to deliver in Rabbi Yisroel Reisman's *shul,* the Agudath Israel of Madison, in Brooklyn.

To me this would be more than an ordinary tribute. I had felt a modest personal connection to Rabbi Sherer, for he and my late father Rabbi Avrohom Zelig Krohn had been friends in Yeshivas Ner Israel in Baltimore, where they heard *shiurim* from Rabbi Yaakov Yitzchak Ruderman (1900-1987). In addition, in recent years Rabbi Sherer had shared with me some personal episodes, which he allowed me to use in lectures, and at Agudath Israel's 75th Annual Dinner, I participated in the dramatic presentation of a *sefer Torah* to Rabbi Sherer, that had been written exclusively for him.

In this tribute, I wanted to define his essence and describe his enthusiasm and emotional involvement in everything he did. Remarkably the following thought, with which he was going to end his address, penciled in Hebrew on that crumpled piece of paper, said it better than I could ever hope to say it.

The Torah recounts Hashem's warning to the Jewish nation as they encircled Mount Sinai, הִשָּׁמְרוּ לָכֶם עֲלוֹת בָּהָר וּנְגֹעַ בְּקָצֵהוּ כָּל הַנֹּגֵעַ בָּהָר מוֹת יוּמָת, *Beware of ascending the mountain or touching its edge; whoever touches the mountain shall surely die* (*Shemos* 19:12). The Kotzker Rebbe, Rabbi Menachem Mendel Morgenstern (1787-1859) interpreted the verse homiletically.

He declared that there are times when a man embarks on a project wishing to accomplish something important. After concerted effort, he realizes he has achieved only part of his intended goal, yet he is satisfied because he feels at least he has attained something. But that, exclaimed the Kotzker, is wrong. Citing the verse, he exclaimed, הִשָּׁמְרוּ לָכֶם עֲלוֹת בָּהָר, beware if you are trying to climb a mountain to accomplish something, וּנְגֹעַ בְּקָצֵהוּ, and you will touch only part of your goal. Don't be satisfied! כָּל הַנֹּגֵעַ בָּהָר, if you have merely touched the mountain and not conquered it, מוֹת יוּמָת, that is not life — that is a form of death!

Then Rabbi Sherer wrote the words that would have been his final oration and the phrase that would encapsulate his life, אִם זְכִיתֶם וַעֲלִיתֶם בָּהָר אַל תִּהְיוּ מִן אֵלּוּ הַמִּסְתַּפְּקִים בְּמוּעָט אֶלָּא הִשְׁתַּדְּלוּ לַעֲלוֹת מַעְלָה מַעְלָה, *"If you have merited to climb the mountain, don't be like those who are satisfied with a little, but instead endeavor to climb higher and higher!"*

That was how he lived, and how he accomplished all that he did in his incredibly productive life. It is his legacy to all he left behind, a legacy we should emulate in all aspects of our lives.

May we each merit to see *Mashiach* and serve *Hashem* בְּהַר הַקּוֹדֶשׁ בִּירוּשָׁלַיִם, on the holy mountain, Jerusalem, the place of the *Beis Hamikdash*.

Index of Personalities

Note: Included in this index are those historical personalities who played a role (or made a comment about) the stories which appear in this book. Excluded are most fictionalized names, minor characters, and narrators of the commentaries cited in the text. Page numbers indicate the first page of the story in which the person appears.

All titles have been omitted from this index to facilitate finding names.

Index of Topics

Note: Included in this index are topics from all five Maggid books. **MS** indicates *The Maggid Speaks;* **AMT** indicates *Around the Maggid's Table;* **FM** indicates *In the Footsteps of the Maggid;* **MJ** indicates *Along the Maggid's Journey;* and **EM** indicates *Echoes of the Maggid.*

Index of Sources

Scriptural and Talmudic Index for all five Maggid books.

Note: **MS** indicates *The Maggid Speaks*; **AMT** indicates *Around the Maggid's Table*; **FM** indicates *In the Footsteps of the Maggid;* **MJ** indicates *Along the Maggid's Journey;* and **EM** indicates *Echoes of the Maggid*.
Page numbers reflect the page on which stories begin.

Tanach

Medrashim

Mishnah and Talmud

Other Sources

Mesorah Publications, ltd
4401 Second Avenue
Brooklyn, New York 11232
(718) 921-9000